C000293104

The Grass Widow

The Grass Widow

Vanessa Edwards

Copyright © 2023 Vanessa Edwards

The moral right of the author has been asserted.

Apart from any fair dealing for the purposes of research or private study,
or criticism or review, as permitted under the Copyright, Designs and Patents
Act 1988, this publication may only be reproduced, stored or transmitted, in
any form or by any means, with the prior permission in writing of the
publishers, or in the case of reprographic reproduction in accordance with
the terms of licences issued by the Copyright Licensing Agency. Enquiries
concerning reproduction outside those terms should be sent to the publishers.

This is a work of fiction. Names, characters, businesses, places, events
and incidents are either the products of the author's imagination
or used in a fictitious manner. Any resemblance to actual persons,
living or dead, or actual events is purely coincidental.

Troubador Publishing Ltd
Unit E2 Airfield Business Park,
Harrison Road, Market Harborough,
Leicestershire. LE16 7UL
Tel: 0116 2792299
Email: books@troubador.co.uk
Web: www.troubador.co.uk/matador

ISBN 978 1805140 719

British Library Cataloguing in Publication Data.
A catalogue record for this book is available from the British Library.

Cover Photos © Nick Gregan

Typeset in 10.5pt Adobe Garamond Pro by Troubador Publishing Ltd, Leicester, UK

Matador is an imprint of Troubador Publishing Ltd

Epigraph

Definition of grass widow:

A woman whose husband is away often or
for a prolonged period.
> *'grass widows parted from their husbands by golf*
> *or similar obsessional activities'*

Lexico.com

Prologue

The clear, moonlit night had given way to fog, rolling in over the water. The sun struggled to make any headway at first but as it inched higher in the sky the vapour, hovering like smoke on the surface, slowly faded. The river flowed swiftly, dark and secretive between the banks and towards the old lock, now a weir. But in one corner where the structure met the bank the current slowed, choked by weeds. And by something else, something out of place. A hand, small and pale, could be glimpsed among the green. It moved fractionally with the faint rippling motion of the water, as if waving. Or drowning, or signalling for help. But it was too late for that.

One

February

It had ended badly. She supposed affairs with married men usually did. He'd been a good lover as lovers go, and as lovers go, he went. As — not entirely coincidentally — had her job. But now Leonie had a plan to deal with both problems. Stir up trouble at home for philandering Hugh while earning enough to tide her over until she found a new position as a lawyer.

Feeling self-conscious, she rang the bell of New Brooms Cleaning Services Ltd. Ridiculous to be nervous about an interview for a cleaning job — she'd had interviews for university, the College of Law, the European Parliament and several law firms, and always passed with flying colours. Or at least until the recent legal recruitment agencies. She reminded herself that she was Jane Toussaint not Leonie Holden — if she ever did end up cleaning the Standings' house, she didn't want her cover to be blown by Hugh's wife mentioning her new cleaner Leonie — tucked her hair behind her ears and smoothed her jacket.

The door opened. Cathy Henderson introduced herself as co-owner and manager of New Brooms, invited Leonie to take a seat in a small side office and offered her a coffee.

'So, Ms Toussaint,' said Cathy. 'As you may know, we are looking to take on extra cleaners at the moment. In fact we've just run an advert in a couple of local papers, though I know you contacted us directly. I've had a quick read of your CV. It does seem a bit, well, sparse. Can you tell me about yourself and why you think working for us will suit you?'

Leonie segued into interview mode while reminding herself to stick as close to the truth as she could. Which probably wouldn't be very much. 'Well,' she said smoothly. 'I've done various jobs, as you'll have seen. I did want to qualify as a solicitor for a while but —' she coughed, and took a sip of coffee '— I couldn't really afford the training. I worked for several law firms as a legal secretary and then I was made redundant. I decided I wanted to do something different for a while. I'd like a job with flexible hours. I enjoy cleaning. The idea came to me, actually, when I decided to stop hiring a cleaner and do it myself to save some money,' she added disingenuously.

'And why Winchester?'

'It would be a change from London. I may sell my flat there and move somewhere else, and I've always loved Winchester — perfectly placed for fast regular trains to London and easy access to the New Forest and the South coast.' Leonie realised that she was echoing Hugh in one of their early meetings, though she couldn't recall which. Perhaps she was already obsessing less about him.

She remembered that her non-existent marriage was supposed to have broken down. 'And also I've recently split up with a partner of many years —' she nearly added 'standing' and repressed the urge to giggle, though she thought her lips might have twitched in an un-grief-stricken way '— which adds to the desire for pastures new.' God, what a cliché; she hoped it wasn't over the top.

It seemed that it wasn't. Cathy said, 'Thank you Jane. Of course you realise it won't be cash in hand?'

'Oh of course not,' said Leonie primly. 'I wouldn't want that.'

'We'll need your national insurance number and bank details. We'll also need a reference from your last employer and you'll have to do a couple of trial sessions with me or Jenny as we can't get a reference for your cleaning.'

'That all sounds fine,' said Leonie. 'I'll give you the name of the personnel manager at my last job. I used my married name Holden at work, they know me as Leonie Jane Holden. My bank account and NI number are also still in that name — I haven't got round to changing all the formal stuff. But for everyday I've reverted back to my maiden name of Toussaint, which I'd prefer to use wherever possible for emotional reasons.' She tried to look a bit more grief-stricken and hoped that, if New Brooms did bother to ask for a reference from Mainwaring & Cox, HR would churn out a generic two-liner which wouldn't say too much about her.

*

It was one of Amanda Standing's book club friends who put her in touch with Simon Long. The book was Elizabeth Jane Howard's *Falling*, in which the main male character was a jobbing gardener. The conversation flowed easily over white wine in the drawing room and soon veered away from the novel when they moved to the breakfast room to eat.

'How's your wonderful garden, Amanda?' asked Stephanie. 'I'm hoping to do a makeover of mine but we're still only at the planning stage.'

Amanda puffed out something between a sigh and a snort. 'Somewhat less wonderful since I sacked the firm that helped me with the project. They got complacent once they'd more or less finished: missed the odd day and didn't work the hours they were supposed to and then put their prices up one time too many. I think they lost interest when it was humdrum maintenance rather than creative genius. I fired them a few weeks ago.

'But,' she continued, 'I'm so glad you brought it up, Stephanie. Nothing much to do outside now so finding a replacement had dropped to the bottom of my list. But I ordered some bare-root roses in the autumn for delivery in February, and here we are already. I got the despatch reminder today. And everything else will be starting to come to life. Can anyone recommend a gardener?'

'Yes,' said Barbara. 'He's called Simon Long. I got his name from a friend who contacted him after she found his flyer in her letterbox. I remember getting one too but I threw it out — too many cowboys around. But Hannah said he was brilliant — reliable, cheap, knows what he's doing. So I gave him a trial and she was right.' She took out her mobile and read out a number.

Amanda phoned Simon Long the next day and arranged to meet him the following week.

*

Amanda was upstairs when she heard the scrunch of gravel signalling the gardener's arrival. She looked out and saw him park his bike in the drive and gaze up at the house and around the front garden. She tried to view it with his eyes, relieved that he was seeing that aspect first — though untidy, it was in a better state than the back. A velvet-budded *Magnolia stellata* like a bull's-eye ringed by the gold and violet of early narcissus and dwarf irises and then by the circular lawn; mixed beds, still winter-naked, under the bay windows and the dry-stone wall fronting the street; an unusual white-flowered Japanese quince sprawling against the house to one side of the front door; the ribbed frame of a wisteria threatening to take over on the other side.

Amanda went downstairs as the doorbell rang. She came out, introduced herself and led the gardener through the gated driveway and the picket gate next to what had been the coach house. They walked across the terrace to the unkempt main lawn, fringed on the far wall by the leafless skeletons of false acacias; past the rose beds, some planted with black stumps, others empty; through the ivy arch sending out tendrils like an early Dr Who episode; past what Amanda called the tea lawn with a summerhouse; through a narrow gap in a tall hedge screening soft-fruit cages, herb beds and compost bins with a small overgrown orchard beyond a trio of sheds; and back across a square of chamomile, still velvet-green. Amanda came to a halt as they returned to the terrace.

'I had a firm doing it for years,' she said. 'They did most of the work to recreate it — it was a wilderness when we bought the house — but there were various problems and I got rid of them in December. I haven't had time since then to find someone else. Do you think you could fit it in, Mr Long? Starting in the next couple of weeks?'

'Simon is fine,' said the gardener. He had a pleasant voice, towards the deeper end of the spectrum and with the shadow of an accent — South African perhaps? 'It looks as if it hasn't had much attention for a while. Even though not a lot's growing now, it's a big garden. Once it's back on course I think a couple of sessions a week will be enough; maybe more in peak growing season and less in the winter.' He took his phone from a jacket pocket, pecked out a code and scrolled briefly. 'I could do Tuesday and Thursday mornings, and also Monday mornings for a few weeks to tidy it up again and get your roses in, and anything else you've ordered or want planted before it warms up. I'm sure we can work something out. I can start next week.'

Amanda smiled; it was a relief not to have to search any further, and Simon came with a personal recommendation. They agreed a price, then Simon said, 'I always ask for payment in cash. It saves you VAT. That's why I'm not registered for VAT; my turnover's not high enough.'

Amanda frowned, confused. Hugh always cautioned her against paying workmen cash. He said it would be defrauding the Revenue and could lead to professional problems for him as a tax lawyer. On the other hand, if the gardener wasn't registered for VAT then it must be all right. Hugh didn't need to know, after all. It wasn't as though he showed much interest in the garden unless it was warm enough for a gin and tonic on the terrace. Or in the day-to-day household finances, which she managed. The thought of deliberately hiding the detail from him sparked a fleeting pulse of something unfamiliar — excitement, daring, risk?

Simon left on his creaky bike. Amanda tried to recall whether she'd ever seen him before. She didn't think so, but there was a ghost of familiarity. Perhaps he looked like someone she'd met in passing.

That evening, Amanda put a portion of the cassoulet she'd made at the weekend into the oven, then poured herself a glass of wine which she sipped thoughtfully as she reflected on the day.

The garden as a major project had finished; it was a question of maintenance now. And the house as a major project had finished a while ago. And as a result, she was at something of a loose end for the first time in her long marriage.

Hugh didn't need to know any details about the gardener because he was only here at weekends and wouldn't think to ask. He commuted in and out of her life in a mirror image of his commute to and from London; the weekend with her, the week with — well, she sometimes wondered. She suspected he'd had an affair or two since they'd moved to Winchester and bought the pied-à-terre in the City. Even though he had his Monday-to-Thursday shirts laundered in London, she could sometimes smell perfume on his Friday shirt. They'd fallen out of the habit of chatting on the phone when he was away, but when she did call him because she needed to discuss something — normally a house or garden something — he often let it go to voicemail and then called her back shortly afterwards, obviously from the street.

But he was always his usual charming and affable self when he was home, and on the occasions she caught herself fretting she reasoned that even if he was having the odd fling, Hugh wouldn't want to get too involved, to disrupt his comfortable routine, tear her life in two again and dash his parents' expectations with the scandal of a divorce. And she couldn't imagine confronting him about it; after all, he'd given her this house that she'd made so perfect and the perfect life that went with it. If he wanted the odd surreptitious dalliance in London, that was a small price to pay. But if any of the affairs became serious, if he wanted to leave her … She shivered. Without her house and garden, the invisibility cloak of his wealth, she would be nothing, just another divorcee in a poky flat. She'd seen first-hand what happens when a wealthy and well-connected man divorces a naive and over-trusting wife. She loved Hugh, and she couldn't believe he'd do that to her. But then that's what her sister Jennifer had thought about her husband. She'd found out the hard way that she'd been wrong.

Amanda hadn't really noticed other men since meeting

Hugh all those years — decades — ago. But she had noticed Simon. There was something about him. He seemed slightly exotic, attractive in an edgy, almost dangerous way. Still, he was obviously an excellent gardener, and that was what she needed now. And maybe he'd be able to do the odd repair job — one of the steamer chairs, for example, had a broken hinge. Hugh was hopeless at anything practical, and she'd never liked to ask the agency gardeners.

She finished her wine and, before pouring a second, went to check that the burglar alarm was set, her heels on the parquet sending faint echoes through the empty house.

Two

March

The light was waning. An English winter evening, thought Simon. Not like an African dusk where day wheeled into night with a stunning but brief rainbow of colours, the sun falling to the horizon in a blaze of spilt crimson and gold. Here the sky was fading slowly to pewter with soft streaks of apricot stippling the clouds. Still time enough though to get the roses in.

His spade moved rhythmically, turning the soil and dimpling the virgin beds. Images of other types of bed drifted in his head. An attractive woman, Mrs Standing. Not that he'd seen much of her; she kept herself to herself.

Simon circled back and forth to the compost heaps, lining each small well, adding a sprinkle of blood-and-bone like a farmer feeding his chickens. He brushed aside the memories triggered by the stench, redolent of carrion, which evoked darker days dealing with poachers in Zimbabwe. He eased each rose into its nest, patted in fresh earth and unfurled the hose to give them all a round of drinks. He was thirsty himself and warmed at the prospect of a cool beer and a cool joint in his camper van. He'd need to go to the leisure centre in the morning. Simon was a strong and stylish swimmer, though he preferred the open water. But the pool was fine for his daily ritual of shower, lengths, shower. He'd spruce himself up while he was at it and then he'd be back to check the roses, sweep up more leaves, prune some of the shrubs and fruit trees. And perhaps he'd have — or make — time to scrub the terrace, make a good impression on Mrs Standing.

He'd seen her at an upstairs window when he arrived to discuss the job the previous week, before he swept his gaze round the front garden. No doubt she assumed he was assessing the state of the magnolia, the bulbs, the grass, the climbers. Which he was, but he was also appraising the house. Large, elegant, everything looking new and well-appointed. Simon had a good sense of smell, especially for money. And Whiteacre fairly reeked.

Simon had decided to turn his hand at gardening a year or so previously, over a couple of pints in the White Buck in Burley. He'd been lucky since returning to England for the second time, he'd thought, finding one temporary job after another. But he had an instinct that his run of luck was about to run out. And once his luck ran out, so would his money. His post as a seasonal New Forest ranger was due to finish in September. Beyond that, he wasn't sure. Even casual work was getting harder to find. He was in his forties — late forties, if he was honest — and suspected that it wouldn't get any easier. And it never paid much. Not that his expenses were high, given that he lived in his camper van and acquired a fair amount of his food for free. Whether you called it foraging or poaching was another matter. But still. He needed money. A lot of money.

Enough to set himself up somewhere and not worry about the next job. Enjoy life. Put his feet up. Or even do more travelling, but without having to count the pennies all the time. Or rather the rands and kwatchas and euros and whatever.

Ideally, he needed to find a rich woman. He'd always liked and got on well with women, but he'd been a drifter for most of his life and most of his relationships had drifted in parallel. And it wasn't obvious how someone in his position would meet rich women.

Maybe, Simon had thought, it would be better to focus on ways to identify and get access to property. Property with valuable contents. He had contacts for the contents.

He'd left the pub through the main entrance, past the painted arrow at the bottom of the stairs inscribed 'Stylish bedrooms' and the wall-mounted map of the Forest in its broader context: the Isle of Wight to the South and Winchester to the North. He paused in the carpark and glanced back at what had been a grand country house. Balanced on a long ladder, a man in overalls was pruning a vigorous climbing rose which framed a first-floor window.

Simon had headed across the cattle grid and into the Forest. He'd studied horticulture back in the day as part — admittedly a very small part — of the land management course he'd dropped out of, though he hadn't done much since. Perhaps it was time to start. Walking helped him think and he let the germ of his plan ripen. He was sure he could make a success of gardening; he'd have to bone up, but it was so easy these days to do that. It was a business he could carry on from his van, going from house to house, getting new clients by word of mouth. He'd need to choose a good location to make it worthwhile; somewhere full of wealthy people with big properties, and somewhere he could get to without difficulty over the next few months for research purposes. Winchester, for example.

And now, he reflected, as he coiled the hose back onto its stand, that research had been worth the investment of time and money. He'd paid a few visits to Winchester once he'd decided on his new career: driven up on his day off and given himself a guided tour of the residential areas. And walked round the city centre, looking in estate agents' windows. So easy to find where the priciest houses clustered. Nightjars Holt, in particular. Very upmarket enclave.

He'd also had some flyers printed. He wanted something that looked classy and arresting. Simon had a good eye and a bit of background in art — a bit of background in most things, really — and came up with a design that balanced references to his horticultural training (mostly fact) and experience (mostly fiction) with some stylish visuals and a few quotes from satisfied clients that he'd enjoyed writing. He bought a battered bike at a car-boot sale and fixed it up to an adequate standard. As the final act of preparation for his plan, he cycled round the wealthier residential areas, giving each house a rapid once-over as he slipped a flyer through the letterbox.

He just needed one job, however small, which he would do cheaply, efficiently, promptly, courteously and well. From that first seed, he was confident that word-of-mouth recommendations would sprout and he could build up his gardening business. And in due course, perhaps, it would lead to the other, more lucrative, business he had in mind.

As Simon lingered on that pleasing thought, he heard Mrs Standing's car turn into the drive. He sprinted into the yard in front of the old coach-house, now garage, and swung open the oak gates so she could drive straight in. He closed them behind her and slipped back through the little gate into the garden to make it obvious that he wanted only to help, not to intrude or impose. Not that he'd had any indication that she'd noticed him.

Over his next few visits Simon didn't see much of Mrs
Standing once she'd unbolted the door in the double
gates to let him in each morning. He was aware of her comings
and goings in her sporty red car and sometimes glimpsed her in
the house. She didn't offer him tea or coffee so he brought his
own in a thermos flask.

One day when he knew she was out he went round
the ground-floor windows at the back, peering into the
sitting room and breakfast room. Nice art. Some silver
candlesticks, looked as though they might be Georgian — he
must remember to bring his binoculars. He returned to his
weeding, thoughtful.

The following Thursday Mrs Standing didn't go out.
Halfway through his session, aware that she was pottering
about downstairs, Simon slipped through the picket gate into
the yard and knocked at the kitchen door.

'Yes?' she asked.

'Sorry to disturb you,' he said respectfully, resisting the
urge to doff the cap he wasn't wearing. 'I left my thermos
behind this morning — would it be possible to have a glass
of water?'

She hesitated, looking surprised, confused and reflective in
rapid succession.

'Would you prefer a hot drink?' she asked. 'I was about to
make myself a coffee.'

'Thank you very much,' said Simon. 'Black, please.'

She handed him a steaming mug with two upmarket
biscuits on a tray and closed the door on him. Still, he thought,
one foot in.

Leonie was back in the New Brooms office a few weeks later, having completed her supervised cleans without problem. Cathy had asked her to come in to finalise her paperwork and had suggested a Friday afternoon so she could meet some of the other cleaners over tea and cake. 'We do this every Friday,' she said, 'and coffee and croissants on Monday mornings. It's a good opportunity to catch up.'

A pretty, petite brunette was on her way out of Cathy's office when Leonie was called in.

'Jane, this is Tina,' said Cathy. 'She's also just started.'

'Hi Jane,' said Tina. 'See you in a few minutes if you're staying for tea?'

'Sure.'

The paperwork didn't take long and Leonie found Tina chatting to a tall, harried-looking woman. Both were younger than Leonie, maybe late thirties, but then everyone seemed to be younger than her these days.

'Hi Jane,' said Tina again. 'This is my friend Brenda. She also cleans here. In fact she showed me the advert.'

'Hello Jane.' Brenda was wrapping a slice of banana bread in a paper napkin. 'Nice to meet you. Got to run. I don't often make Friday tea and cake, too close to school gate time, but I had to pick up keys for a new job first thing Monday. Hope to see you again soon. Enjoy the cleaning!' She almost jogged out of the office.

'She's got two kids,' said Tina. 'Probably taking the cake for them. Her partner walked out on her.'

'What about you?' asked Leonie. 'Do you have family?'

'Like Brenda. Half a family. I'm divorced, with a teenage son. Lost my job before Christmas — I was a secretary — so the cleaning's a lifeline.'

For me also, thought Leonie. A friend had tipped her off the previous week that later in the year the European Court of

Justice would open one of its regular procedures for recruiting to its panel of freelance legal translators. She thought she had a good chance of getting through but knew the procedure would be slow and laborious. In the meantime she needed a lifeline to fund, and provide the cover for, her plan to get even with Hugh.

*

Amanda had been surprised when Simon knocked and asked for a glass of water. It hadn't occurred to her to offer a drink to the numerous men who'd worked on the house or their earlier properties over the years, or to her previous gardeners. She had a vague recollection that they usually brought sandwiches and a thermos for the lunch break, but now she wondered whether she should have provided refreshments. Is that what wealthy women did? She had tried so hard to recreate the world she'd lost when tragedy had struck her family, but she'd been thirteen then, too young to notice how her mother had treated all their workmen and gardeners. Though she suspected that the treatment hadn't been generous. Her mother had been too busy trying to slough off her own past as she took on the mantle of a rich man's wife, and hobnobbing with the staff she'd only recently been able to employ would perhaps have been too close to her former home. And of course there'd been no workmen or gardeners after her father died, at least until her marriage. She felt a spark of shame as she shook off the memories, and decided that she'd offer Simon coffee and biscuits in the future.

Two weeks later, Simon asked if it would be possible to move his Thursday morning slot to the afternoon. The following week he knocked on the kitchen door as he was leaving.

'Sorry to disturb you,' he said. 'I caught some trout in the Itchen this morning and wondered whether you could use a couple? I've got more than I can eat while they're fresh. Which they are, very.'

Amanda was surprised again. 'Thank you,' she said after a brief pause. 'Yes, I'd love them.'

She had one for her supper that night and froze the other. At first she'd intended to keep them both to eat with Hugh the following evening, but then decided not to risk it in case it somehow led to awkward questions about her cash payments to the gardener.

*

Tina let herself into her flat, weary after three cleaning jobs. Still, at least she had work. And since the previous evening she had the prospect of making some extra money, though she'd need to think that through carefully.

She called out to Peter as she shrugged off her coat, then put her head round his bedroom door. He was lying on his bed, messaging or something on his phone in that amazing way only teenagers could, thumbs flying. He glanced up briefly, then back to his screen. 'I'll get some supper sorted,' said Tina, and headed to the kitchen.

She'd bought some mince that was half-price as it had hit its use-by date and started going through the motions of making a basic spag bol. Thank goodness the spaghetti was cheap and would stretch out the meat enough for a growing boy's appetite. She'd give Peter most of the sauce, just have a dribble with hers.

Tina sat down while the pan simmered. She'd been cleaning for New Brooms for over a month now. It wasn't like being a secretary, nor was it as well paid. The not-like-being a secretary was OK; when Brenda had suggested Tina answer the New Brooms ad, she'd done so as an urgently needed stopgap and hadn't expected to enjoy the cleaning, but it was all right. The not-as-well-paid was more of a problem. She couldn't work longer hours than she already did; she wanted to be home when Peter was back from school. Not that he communicated much but she'd let that run its course. His father had been violent towards both of them and had finally left when Peter had suddenly shot up a few inches and started filling out. She'd divorced him but it had been unpleasant and expensive and she rarely received the maintenance payments he was supposed to make. Tina reckoned that with her cleaning income she could only just make ends meet.

Which is where her brother-in-law, Finn, came into it. She'd known he was a wide boy, dabbled in the odd bit of dodgy business — rehousing stuff that fell off the back of a lorry, as he called it. Fencing, others would say. Handling stolen goods, the police would say. She'd had a couple of glasses of wine too many the other evening when she was at her sister's. Daisy had asked how the new job was going and Tina had made a joke about how careless people were, leaving papers and valuables lying around their houses. Finn had looked up sharply from the phone he was fiddling with, almost like a dog pricking its ears at the sound of its food bowl.

'What sort of papers?'

Tina shrugged. 'All sorts. Even bank statements sometimes. Utility bills. Insurance documents. Not everywhere, some places are really tidy, they must do everything online or maybe the papers are locked away or shredded—'

'Do they have shredders then, these grand houses?'

'Some, yes. There's one where the papers to be shredded are just left in a pile on top of it. What a laugh. And there are some that don't have shredders, or at least not that I can see. I guess they put stuff in the recycling.'

Half an hour later Daisy left the room to go and check on the children and Finn poured Tina another glass of wine. 'You ever see bank cards or things lying around?'

Tina shook her head.

'Never mind,' said Finn. 'Keep your eyes peeled though. Meantime we could have ourselves a nice little earner with your phone and the papers. Tina the cleaner!' He laughed as if he'd made a hilarious joke and insisting on calling her that from then on.

Tina thought she might give it a go. She wasn't comfortable with dishonesty but needs must. It was mainly for Peter, so she could buy him the odd treat. She'd only try it in the big, wealthy houses, whose owners could surely afford to spare a little. Probably wouldn't even notice. And if she ever met someone … well, she'd need a couple of nice things to wear at least; maybe she could buy herself the odd treat also. Not that there was much chance of meeting anyone given that she didn't go out much, except for the odd coffee with Brenda. Brenda had suggested internet dating but Tina didn't feel ready for it. No, she'd wait for a while, keep an eye out for a Prince Charming who didn't turn into a frog — or was she mixing up two fairy tales? — and in the meantime, however reluctantly, try and make a bit on the side.

Three

April

Simon hadn't registered that the last Monday of his extra sessions to get the Whiteacre garden up and running was Easter Monday. Mrs Standing had said at the outset that if the gates to the drive were open, as they were when he arrived today, he should go straight through to the garden without ringing the doorbell, so he did. He collected a couple of pruning tools from one of the sheds and started working round the established roses.

A door slammed shut and Simon looked round. A tall, bespectacled man was striding towards him, shouting something that was whipped away by the unseasonably cold wind. Simon waved the secateurs and gestured at the bag full of trimmings at his feet and the man stopped.

'Sorry,' he called. 'You must be the new gardener. My wife said she'd found someone, but didn't mention you'd be coming today. She's out and I saw someone I didn't know so thought I should check.'

Simon took off his gloves and held out a hand. 'Yes,' he said. 'I'm the gardener. Simon Long. Lovely garden, it's a privilege. Nice to meet you, Mr Standing.'

Mr Standing, who didn't have a lot of natural padding, had obviously not paused to put on a jacket. He was wearing a green V-neck sweater over a white polo shirt — doubtless sporting a polo-player or alligator logo — and shivered as he shook Simon's hand. 'It's looking a lot better already, even I can see that. It's Amanda — my wife's baby really, I just admire it through a gin and tonic sometimes. Though not in this weather.'

'Aptly named, the Beast from the East,' agreed Simon, pulling his gloves back on. 'A hot toddy would be more appropriate. Well, I'll be getting on.' Mr Standing looked relieved and almost ran back to the house.

Simon watched as he let himself in through one of the French windows that opened onto the terrace, pulling his sweater tight around him. He was a good-looking man, with a spare, almost gangly frame and dark hair with a dusting of silver. The same sort of age as Mrs Standing — Amanda, Simon now knew — and himself. Mr Standing's hand, though cold, had felt soft against his, which was calloused by gardening; Simon had glimpsed long fingers and clean, square-clipped nails. And he tucked himself back into his deluxe house without a backward glance. Well, why should he look back? He'd briefly stepped out of his moneyed, comfortable bubble and had now stepped back in, waiting for his beautiful wife, doubtless savouring his beautiful life.

*

Engrossed in *Gone Girl*, Leonie tutted at the interruption of a ping signalling an incoming text from her bank.

The message notified her that a modest sum had been paid into her account from New Brooms. It was nothing like her former salary, of course, but a handy infusion even so. Leonie's only additional expense was her train fares, which she kept manageable by a combination of advance booking, cheap day returns and her Network Railcard. And she was surprised how much less she spent in Winchester than London, where every time she stepped out of the front door money seemed to evaporate from her wallet.

She was also surprised by how much she enjoyed the work. Because she was new to New Brooms, most of her jobs were flats and smaller houses. The young professional couples were more untidy than anything else, with the only signs of use in the kitchen often the coffee machine and the microwave. The young families were more untidy still, but Leonie took pleasure in reimposing order — however temporary — on the post-hurricane-like debris of the children she didn't have. And the homes of the occasional older couple, children flown the nest, needed little more than hoovering and dusting and an easy wipe round the kitchen and bathroom.

She made an effort to clean well and often overstayed her allotted hours in her determination to create a good impression. Between and after jobs she explored Winchester. Leonie remembered Hugh's address from the partners' emergency contacts list that Mainwaring & Cox circulated each year to all lawyers. Whiteacre was in Nightjars Holt, one of the most desirable areas in the city, and she found it without difficulty. Set back from the road, of course, it towered above her: three tall storeys, steeply pitched roof, porch with stained glass, huge gates into what was presumably an extension of the drive leading to the garden and garage.

Leonie gazed at the house to and from which Hugh shuttled every weekend and which was, from what he said, his wife's obsession. She thought back to the one time he'd come to her flat in Clapton, some time last year. He'd peered into the patio garden below as he opened the champagne he'd brought, easing the cork out with a controlled pop. 'Nice. We're working on ours, or Amanda is. Vicariously of course. House more or less finished a couple of years ago, seems to have taken forever. Years of workmen trooping in and out leaving a trail of builders' dust and rubble. And since then hordes of gardeners all over the place trying to tame the wilderness. At least it's mostly in the week. And we're into the home stretch at last.' Whiteacre certainly didn't suggest dust and rubble now, or a wilderness. It suggested wealth and taste. The taste doubtless Amanda's, but the wealth indubitably provided by the man who'd dumped Leonie.

Leonie couldn't see into the ground floor windows from the road and didn't dare go into the neat front garden and press her nose against the glass in case she was spotted. With a sigh she carried on to her next job, but when she was in the New Brooms office on Friday afternoon she told Cathy that her mother had been brought up in Nightjars Holt and often talked about her childhood. 'I don't have a record of the address,' she said, truthfully if unsurprisingly, 'but I've got a lot of second-hand memories and impressions. I'd love to get to know the area better. If you ever need someone to fill in for a regular cleaner there, do bear me in mind.' Must remember that snippet of newly minted family history if it came up again, she thought.

*

A couple of weeks later, Amanda was offered more trout. Simon handed her the cool, damp parcel. 'Please forgive me if this is forward. I see you've got a braai — I mean a barbecue — in the garage. If it would save you the trouble of cooking them, I could grill them for you before I leave. They're nice cold also, with salad.'

'Thank you,' said Amanda. 'That's very kind. I never cook on the barbecue — what did you call it?'

'A braai. I was born and bred in Zimbabwe. "Braai" is chilapalapa I expect, a sort of southern African pidgin. Or more likely Afrikaans.'

'Well, I'm not very good with it, whatever word you use. My husband barbecues sometimes at the weekend. Perhaps you can show me how to get it going — I can give him a surprise one evening.'

At about five o'clock Simon knocked again.

'I'm about to start the fire,' he said. 'I didn't like to disturb you while I was laying it, but I can tell you how to do it. And building it up is easy if you're patient.'

Amanda stepped out of the kitchen into the gated yard that linked the drive with the old coach house. Simon had set the Weber up in front of it. The lid was off and a delicate lattice of kindling cobwebbed a crumpled page or two of newspaper. He had a pile of sticks and bits of wood of different sizes on a small makeshift table.

'You have to start with little twigs and slivers and work up to bigger pieces.'

'But where's the charcoal?' she asked. 'And the lighter fluid? My husband says you can't get a barbecue going without it.'

Simon laughed. 'I'm used to starting with paper — or dried leaves — and kindling, and burning wood,' he said. 'It's more satisfying somehow. And anyway, there's no charcoal or lighter fuel in the bundu. Bush, I mean.' He struck a match and touched it to a corner of newspaper, which flared with an eye of green. Simon crouched down and began to feed the fire with splinters of tinder, gradually increasing the size and focusing intently on the flames as they licked and curled. The paper and wood crackled and a slender spiral of smoke floated up on a diagonal before fading away.

'It's glowing nicely now,' he said after a while. Amanda smiled with relief; even with the warmth from the Weber she was starting to shiver. 'You'd need to build it up more for anything heftier than a couple of trout, but I can put them on whenever you like. I'll wait to take them off for you to make sure they don't burn. If you're cooking anything fatty which makes the fire flare up, you can squirt beer onto the flames.' He mimed shaking a bottle with his thumb over the top, then directing it to the smouldering cavity. Amanda almost laughed. 'I'm afraid I don't have any beer in the house,' she said.

Later that evening Amanda was sitting on the terrace in the gloaming, wrapped in a soft poncho and sipping from a frosted glass of good New Zealand Sauvignon Blanc. Simon had cycled off when the trout were cooked; she'd put one in the fridge once it had cooled down and boiled some new potatoes and made a salad to partner the other. The fish was delicious. The skin was ribbed with charred black; when she eased it back, the exposed flesh was a contrasting, succulent cream. It tasted and smelled of fire and smoke.

The trout were the first things she'd been given by any of her workmen. Until Simon, as she'd mused the other day, she hadn't offered them anything either. She hadn't thought about him as a real person before he'd knocked on the door and asked for a drink; he'd just been one in a long line of people she'd employed to help her move the house, and then the garden, towards perfection.

But Simon seemed different. Not pushy, but ready to engage. He always thanked her for the coffee and biscuits, and it was kind of him to bring the trout and offer to show her how to barbecue it. Not that she was much the wiser about how to get the fire going. Maybe she'd ask him to show her again.

He was quite good-looking really. As, she remembered, she'd thought when she first met him. Not as tall as Hugh, but taller than her. Nor as dark as Hugh, but darker than her — at least she assumed so, she'd long ago lost track of her natural hair colour. Something more than stubble and less than a beard. Olive skin, perhaps from all those years in the — bundu, had he said?

The evening was getting cooler and darker, and she moved inside and topped up her glass.

*

Leonie had found out from the job schedule pinned to the New Brooms' corkboard that Amanda's cleaner was Judy Marsh. Since then she'd been hoping to run into her, and struck lucky one Friday afternoon.

Cathy made the introduction. 'Judy, come and meet Jane. Jane's mother grew up in Nightjars Holt and she's keen to get to know the area. You can tell her about Whiteacre.'

Judy was plump and smooth-faced. She grinned at Leonie and rolled her eyes. 'The house is unbelievable,' she said. 'Well, not by Nightjars Holt standards I suppose, it's on the small and simple side compared to some of the mansions around. But it's stunning. I've only been cleaning there for the last couple of years, since the refurb was finished. Frances cleaned for a while before me and saw a lot of the transformation before she moved away. I've seen pictures of how it looked when they bought it. Almost a shell. No expense spared. Must be super rich. He's something in the City, I think; I never see him. Probably commutes — there's never much to do when I clean on Friday.'

'What about the wife?' asked Leonie, having resolved that she wouldn't. Realising that she wasn't supposed to know the Standings, she added, 'At least, I assume there's a wife?'

'Don't see a lot of her either; she's usually out when I'm there. Not over-friendly. Not the sort to chat to the cleaner over coffee. Or even to offer the cleaner a coffee. I don't think it would even occur to her.'

Leonie resisted the urge to ask more but did say that if Judy was away she'd love to cover for her.

'I'm on holiday for a fortnight at the end of July,' said Judy. 'School holidays, more's the pity. Roll on the day when they've left school. I'll suggest that you cover, if you're around then. Several of us are away over the summer for the same reason, so Cathy'll be pleased if you are.'

'Oh, I'll definitely be around,' said Leonie, before wishing everyone a good weekend and heading off to the station. She made a small detour to the Wykeham Arms. She'd noticed the pub a week or two before and remembered Hugh mentioning it one evening. He'd suggested a drink in the Bunch of Grapes near Borough Market, and once they'd sat down with a bottle of wine, he'd looked around and said, 'We should come here more often. I like the decor. The pine tables and the walls covered in old pictures remind me of the Wykeham Arms. We usually go there for lunch on Saturday.' She'd snapped back, '"We" in two different senses.' It was the time when she was beginning to have difficulty with the two senses of 'we'. Towards the end of their affair. Which, she supposed, she'd hastened by wanting more. And not hiding it.

Curious, and feeling slightly voyeuristic, she'd ventured into the Winchester pub. She found it congenial and had taken to stopping for a glass of wine on her way to the station. Now, she treated herself to a better wine than usual to celebrate being one step nearer to getting into Hugh's house. And to puncturing his cosy marital bubble as payback for his puncturing their cosy non-marital bubble.

*

Hugh sank gratefully into the first-class seat, loosened his tie and pulled the *Financial Times* out of his briefcase. An uninterrupted hour to switch from urban playboy to home-coming husband. Which, he had to admit, felt an easier switch than it had with Leonie. More like with his lovers before her. Younger, more casual. Once or twice a week, a bit of fun in bed, a meal out. Not too close to the office. Or to his heart. A couple had wanted more — not in the sense of more commitment from him, though that might have come, but they'd suggested varying the routine, trying different, more cultural pastimes. Theatre, cinema, galleries, the Eye. The energy of youth. He remembered that drive, the reluctance to slow down, the urge to explore the new. He'd been like that when he was courting Amanda and in the early years of their marriage. But now, approaching his half-century, he wasn't sure he had the enthusiasm anymore. Not at the expense of other enjoyable activities anyway.

Hugh had had an easy and undemanding life. He sailed through school, through university, through the College of Law, through his training contract, through his years as a junior and then a senior associate, through his election to income partner and then equity partner. He coasted comfortably in the wake of his elder brother, secure in the knowledge that, while he would never match the career heights of Peregrine, who was tipped to be the next foreign secretary, he would always work fewer hours for more money. And even more comfortably ahead of his younger brother, who came out at school, dropped out of university and made a tenuous living playing bass guitar. Hugh knew that against the foil of Tristan, his parents rejoiced all the more in his choice of profession and success in its practice. And rejoiced also in his ostensibly stable and happy marriage. He wasn't sure they'd cope with the scandal of a divorce on top of Tristan's flagrant breach of convention.

Not that he ever contemplated divorce: his marriage was also easy and undemanding. He and Amanda got on well for the first decade or so, but were perhaps beginning to be bored and restless in each other's company when they moved to Winchester. The timing was perfect for both of them: he had his pocket of freedom during the week to wander from the marital bed and she had Whiteacre to absorb and fulfil her.

Hugh relished his succession of affairs, although he suspected the women didn't relish his inevitable ending of the relationship. Leonie was the first of his lovers whose company he liked out of bed as much as in it — well, almost as much. He hadn't known how to respond when she started to become more demanding, talking about time out and ultimatums. Why couldn't she accept what they had for what it was and enjoy it when there was so much enjoyment there? And he'd never promised, or even hinted at, anything more.

Margot was more of a challenge in some ways: younger again, professionally successful as a corporate partner, a stunner with her flaming hair, clever. Though Leonie was clever too. She was bright and quick and —

His work phone, on silent, vibrated with a breezy text from Margot, wishing him a good weekend. No chance that she'd become clingy; she, like him, just wanted some fun for a while. Hugh smiled and sent a jokey reply, clocking the time as he did so. Winchester was only ten minutes away. He'd been so caught up in his musings that he hadn't even noticed the lack of a drinks trolley. He tucked the unopened *FT* back into his briefcase, checked that there was no sign of rain and prepared himself for the pleasant walk home and a frosty gin and tonic with Amanda.

Four

May

The burglar alarm was on and the drive was empty. Almost certain that no one was in then, but Tina did a rapid check of the whole house as soon as she'd stepped inside and keyed in the code. Then she hung her coat and bag after taking out her phone and started her mix of cleaning and checking.

First, the huge basement kitchen where the home shredder was. Tina always found that odd, but Finn said it was probably because that was where they opened the post. As usual there was a helpful stack of papers piled on it, waiting to be shredded. Some people had no idea ... She leafed through the documents but the only new one since her last clean was a note about a neighbour's planning application. She went through the door that led to the garage and checked the recycling bin, but it was almost empty. According to the rubbish collection schedule stuck to the fridge, it would have been cleared the day before. Pity her cleaning slot wasn't earlier in the week.

She took the hoover and cleaning kit up to the top floor. How could one family need so much space? And it was so modern, all huge windows and straight lines and sharp corners. Tina preferred more traditional houses. Not that she could ever afford anything on the scale of this one anyway, even with the extra cash she sometimes earned from Finn. She wished she didn't need to rely on him but as she'd hoped, his infusions, erratic as they were, made her income stretch just enough to manage.

Maybe she'd start in the teenage boy's room. He was careless. No surprise there. She was always telling Peter to be careful with his phone and bank card. She tidied and cleaned as well as she could given that the boy complained if she moved too much stuff around and carried on, empty handed, to the girl's room. That was a quicker job as the girl was compulsively neat and never left anything interesting lying about.

In the master bedroom she checked that nothing had been left in any jacket or trouser pockets and reminded herself to do the same with the coats downstairs.

In the home office she tried the desk drawer and filing cabinet, but all were locked as usual and there were no papers on the desk or in the waste-paper basket.

Tina cleaned the rest of the house and left. Finn wouldn't be happy. It was a couple of weeks since she'd found anything useful. Perhaps tomorrow's clean would be more fruitful.

*

Once Amanda decided that Simon was reliable and trustworthy, she gave him a key to the door in the back wall of the garden. The door opened on to a small alley running from one of the side roads, and Amanda suggested he use that entrance. 'But remember always to lock it when you leave.

Oh, and this is the key to the coach house,' she added. 'It's also normally locked but it's where we keep ladders which you might need for pruning the climbers, and it might be handier than the garden sheds for the big tools.'

After that, she didn't see him for a fortnight or so. Then one Thursday when she was at home in the afternoon and was handing him the usual coffee and biscuits, he said he had more trout.

'They're sea trout this time, not brown. I got lucky. If you like, I'll braai them again,' he offered. 'I don't have to rush off at five, so I could show you how to start the fire if you want?'

'Thank you,' said Amanda. 'Yes, I'd like that. I even remembered to buy some beer.'

An hour or two later, Simon wheeled the Weber onto the terrace. 'I hope you don't mind,' he said. 'Even if it's not warm enough for you to eat out later, I thought it would be more comfortable for you if I cook the fish here rather than in the drive.'

He'd laid kindling in the base over a couple of crumpled pages from the free paper *Winchester Today*, which he must have found in the recycling pile in the coach house.

Simon demonstrated again how to feed the nascent flame, adding bigger and bigger pieces of wood until it was burning comfortably. 'At this point,' he said, 'you have to wait, but keep an eye on it. You need to put the food on as soon as it's ready. And then damp it down if it flares up.'

Amanda blinked, went into the house and returned with a chilled bottle in each hand. She held them out to Simon. 'I don't know much about beer. We don't drink it at home. I bought a lager and an ale, I hope that's all right.'

It was. Simon took a penknife from his pocket, opened the Peroni and had a thirsty swig.

'Sorry.' He wiped his five o'clock shadow of a moustache. 'I'm used to drinking from the bottle round the braai. Bad habits from Zim. I shouldn't be drinking anyway if you're not, it's not polite.'

'I'll join you then,' said Amanda, going back into the kitchen. She poured herself a glass of wine and came back out to the terrace.

She watched him flip the trout over, virgin quicksilver skin replaced in a shiny flicker of movement by black-striped gunmetal, and was thinking how the fish almost looked as though they were turning in the water when she realised where she'd seen Simon before. It was at the swimming pool. She usually swam at her gym but the pool had been closed in January for refurbishment and she'd gone to River Park Leisure Centre for a few sessions. One day she went earlier than usual after waking up before six. There was only one other swimmer. He executed a perfect dive from the edge — prohibited, but he waited until the lifeguard turned away before gliding into the water with only a whisper of sound — and then sliced up and down the pool in a powerful but elegant crawl. It was Simon.

She realised that she was staring at him. Did he recognise her, she wondered? Had he even seen her that day? She felt herself blush. She'd been wearing a bikini.

But Simon turned back to the fire, seemingly unaware of Amanda's discomfiture. Once the fish were cooked, he slid them onto a plate for her, finished his beer and said he'd see her next week. He headed off towards the door in the wall and she wondered whether she should have invited him to stay and share them with her.

*

Amanda didn't see Simon for the next couple of weeks. She realised that she missed the contact. Although she had a number of local friends, including through her book club, she wasn't close to any of them. They tended to meet around a meal or a drink and Amanda often found them overwhelming, the noise increasing in proportion to the amount of wine consumed. Wine made her more relaxed but not less quiet. She sometimes felt she got on better with her house than with people. Except Hugh in their early days, but they seemed to communicate less and less over the years. It was as if he was drifting away from her like smoke.

In the third week Amanda rearranged a Thursday appointment so that she was at home in the afternoon. It was raining heavily, and when she took Simon's coffee and biscuits out to the coach house she suggested that he might want to call it a day.

'It's OK,' he said. 'I thought I'd sort out the garden sheds if that's all right with you. I'll give them a good clear-out, and a good sweep too. Oh, and I've got two trout again. They're in the fridge in the van — too wet to cycle today. Too wet to braai also. I'll drop them in before I leave.'

Simon knocked at the kitchen door at about five. He wore a shabby waxed jacket with the hood up; the water ran off it in rivulets. He was holding the usual damp package.

Amanda had noticed the VW camper parked in the street. 'It must be difficult to dry a wet coat in your van,' she said. 'Why don't you hang it in the utility room and let it drip a little? You could wait in the kitchen.' She took the jacket and hung it above the drain by the washing machine.

'Would you like a beer?' she asked, pouring herself a glass of wine.

'Ah, thanks.' He took the proffered bottle — and the glass — with a grateful smile. The rain was now torrential, beating against the windows like a drum roll.

'African rain,' he said. 'Like an upturned bucket in the rainy season. I expect it won't last too long. But I could cook the trout on the grill while I wait if that would be helpful?'

He was an adept cook, neat and organised. He must have to make efficient use of the small space in a camper van.

Simon turned the trout. 'By the way,' he said, 'I cleared out a lot of old garden chemicals from the shed. Mostly poisonous and mostly illegal now I expect. I'll take them to Bar End, they'll dispose of them safely.'

'Thanks,' said Amanda, her attention on the trout's crisp, blackened skin and smoky fragrance. 'We might as well eat them while they're hot,' she added. 'Hugh and I are eating out tomorrow. And the rain shows no sign of easing.' She put together a green salad and turned cold new potatoes in olive oil, lemon juice and crushed garlic. And topped up her glass.

'Were you brought up in Zimbabwe?' she asked.

'Between there and South Africa. I studied land management and horticulture in Zim then trained as a game warden Down South, as we say. I worked in game reserves in both countries. Then travelled overland to Europe. I wrote a book about it, I'll bring you a copy. Self-published, but I've sold a few through Amazon.'

Amanda realised she'd run out of beer. She offered Simon a choice of red or white wine and gave him a bottle of Madiran to open. He was deft with the corkscrew.

A couple of glasses later, Simon said 'I don't think this rain will stop for ages. I'd better be on my way.'

He came closer and, without warning, kissed her on the cheek. 'I'm sorry,' he said. 'I didn't mean to do that. You're just so beautiful.'

Amanda stood still for a moment. Feeling heady and reckless, she leaned in to him. He put his arms round her. She felt warm and safe and briefly cherished. It had been a long time since she'd felt cherished.

Simon put his hands on either side of her face and gave her a long, lingering kiss. 'Shall we go upstairs?' he said.

It had also been a long time since she'd had good sex. Or much sex at all, come to think of it. Hugh had been enthusiastic, thoughtful and sometimes creative in bed in the early years of their relationship and had given Amanda unexpected pleasure, but over time — particularly since the move to Winchester — his enthusiasm, thoughtfulness and creativity had waned and she had never felt comfortable enough about her body or her needs to push him or even discuss it. Now he often used the second spare room. He said he slept better alone and needed a good night after a week at work and the Friday evening commute.

Simon was gentle and generous.

'Would you like another glass of wine?' asked Amanda, as they lay curled together afterwards. She remembered that Hugh used to ask this. Perhaps most men liked it. She didn't have experience of most men.

Simon offered to go down to the kitchen but Amanda jumped up. 'No, it's too risky now it's dark — neighbours might see you if you turn the lights on. I'll go.'

'I can find my way in the dark, like a leopard,' said Simon, but Amanda put on an emerald-green silk robe and padded out of the room.

'You know a bit about me now,' said Simon after she'd come back with the wine. 'What about you? Where did you grow up?'

Amanda was quiet for a minute or two. 'London,' she said eventually. 'Leyton, then Hampstead.' She didn't like to think about her childhood, or at least her teenage years. She took a long sip of her wine.

Simon didn't ask any more, for which Amanda was grateful. Instead he said, 'This evening has been lovely. All of it. But I'll understand if you don't want to see me again. I'll leave and let you find another gardener if so, but I do hope not. I want to see you again. A lot. And not just across a tray of coffee and biscuits.'

Amanda said nothing, but she gave him a warm smile and a warmer kiss.

'Do you mind if I take a quick shower?' he asked. 'I'm living in my camper van at the moment and don't have proper washing facilities. I swim every morning, so I shower then.'

'Why are you living in a camper van?'

'I didn't have much money when I came back from Africa the second time — I haven't told you about that, it's for the next instalment. Which I hope we'll have. Anyway, an uncle died and left me a small legacy, but not enough to buy a property. I'd always wanted a VW camper, so I bought one of those instead. It's perfect for now, as long as I can get to a decent pool every day. Which I can — I'm parked at Worthy Lane, near the leisure centre. Or sometimes if the weather's good I swim wild, at Compton Lock.'

After Simon had left through the kitchen and garden gate, Amanda locked up, set the burglar alarm and went back to bed. She was relaxed and — she realised with surprise — happy. *He was a veray parfit gentil knight*, she thought sleepily. She'd starred at English Literature and had a good memory for what she'd read; even now quotations that had been in hibernation for decades would sometimes bubble to the surface. In her last year at school, the harassed-looking careers adviser used the allotted ten minutes to try and persuade her to read the subject at university. But Amanda was adamant. What she wanted more than anything in the world was to recreate her home, her life, Before. She needed to learn how to make a beautiful house. And how to make — or better, find someone else to make — lots of money. She graduated with a first in Kingston University's BA in Interior Design.

Amanda woke to the scent of Simon lingering on the sheets. A masculine smell. Sweat and smoke and something burnt. Another quote bubbled up — *In the rank sweat of an enseamèd bed, Stewed in — what was it, seduction maybe? — honeying and making love.*

She got up and headed down to the kitchen. *Hamlet.* Not seduction, corruption. None of that here. Must remind the cleaner to change the bedding.

Five

June

Amanda didn't see Simon again until the following Tuesday morning.

She had no appetite for breakfast after a fitful night and was drifting round the house. The summer sun highlighted the sitting room in ruthless detail. She noticed with a flicker of irritation the dust motes fluttering and dancing in the beam, the eye-catching smear on the coffee table revealed when she straightened the latest copy of *Architectural Digest*, a small tumbleweed of cloudy fluff under a sofa. The cleaner was becoming either careless or complacent; must speak to —

A tentative knock interrupted her thoughts and she almost ran to the kitchen door. Simon was standing further back than usual, his fists clenched round a small packet, which for once didn't look like trout, and a posy of flowers which he held in front of him like a shield.

He cleared his throat. 'I hoped you'd be in. I wanted to see you.'

The roses were striped. Amanda buried her nose in the delicate, papery petals, splashed with crimson and white, and inhaled the scent. It was so intense as to be almost overwhelming. 'Lovely,' she said. 'Hugh used to bring me flowers often. A long time ago.' Now it was just on Valentine's Day and her birthday, and she was sure they were chosen by his secretary.

Simon's shoulders relaxed and he grinned. 'Stolen goods I'm afraid. I was working in a walled garden yesterday where the roses were so fantastic I couldn't resist. They're Rosa Mundi. And the other package is my book. Go on, open it!'

Amanda took the parcel and stepped back, holding the door for him. He accepted the implicit invitation and followed her in.

She unwrapped a paperback with the title *An African Odyssey* set against a photo of well-camouflaged leopard relaxing in a tree. Amanda couldn't remember the last time she'd been given an impromptu gift – well, apart from the trout of course – and warmed at the thought. She hesitated, then gave him a quick kiss on the cheek.

'Thank you. I can't wait to read it,' she said, and added, 'I was worried you might call me when Hugh was here. Then I realised you didn't have my number so I stopped worrying.'

'Oh but I do. Remember, you phoned me to ask about the garden? As soon as I'd left here that first time I saved it.'

'Oh. Well, please don't phone me at weekends. No, best not to phone me at all, I might be with friends.'

'You're not with friends now. Apart from me, of course.' Simon leaned towards her; she didn't turn away and he gave her a long, gentle kiss.

'I'll go and get on out there,' he said. 'There's lots to do and I should take advantage of the good weather. But can I cook you supper again one evening?'

Amanda had enjoyed being cooked for. Her mother had employed a superb cook before the family's comfortable existence had been ripped apart, and Amanda had yearned to be as skilled in the kitchen. When Hugh's parents asked what they wanted for a wedding present, she convinced him to suggest that they paid for a cookery course for her. They were surprised but saw the benefit. Hugh, like his elder brother Peregrine at least, was clearly destined to flourish in his career and would need a wife who could host. She felt that her request had cemented her relationship with her future in-laws, who had until then been somewhat cool and distant towards her. She did a Cordon Bleu course in Paris and loved it. But she couldn't remember anyone cooking for her, just for her, except occasionally her sister Jennifer when Amanda visited. Hugh barbecued now and again, but in the time-honoured way she shopped for and prepared all the food, made salads and dessert, poured drinks and cleared up.

'OK. Let me get something in for you to cook. You say what. I'm free tomorrow evening. But you'll have to come round the back again.'

'And if I need to contact you before then? If there's a change of plan?'

Amanda crossed her arms, hugging herself. 'You can text me. But … as if were about the gardening. And only if it's really important.'

Amanda was arranging the roses in a marbled blue glass vase which set off but didn't overwhelm the pink, white and green. Rosa Mundi. Rose of the world? She'd been good at Latin Before but never studied it again After. She checked on her iPad. The rose was named after Rosamund Clifford, the long-term mistress of the twelfth-century King Henry II. Henry was forced to marry Princess Eleanor who, jealous of her husband's relationship with the fair Rosamund, allegedly arranged her murder by poison.

Later, as Amanda was putting *An African Odyssey* on her bedside table underneath her current read, *Apple Tree Yard*, she remembered that the narrator and her lover in that novel had secret phones. Maybe she and Simon should do that. It seemed exciting, adventurous, a bit risky.

There hadn't been much excitement, adventure or risk in Amanda's life. And now that the house and garden were, well, so very *House & Garden*, she was conscious of more time to fill. She had had very few close friendships since the wholesale desertion of her childhood friends once she'd moved schools and house, although now she knew a number of local women through her book club and gym and was rarely short of invitations to lunch, coffee or the cinema. She was aware from this circle that many women of her age suffered from empty nest syndrome. Perhaps she had full nest syndrome now that she had so beautifully feathered hers.

Her friends, such as they were, would be salaciously horrified if they thought she'd bedded her gardener. Come to think of it, so was she. And she would have to be careful. She had a lot to lose. But she could be careful. And why shouldn't she have some fun? After all, she suspected that Hugh had been playing away since they'd moved, though she imagined he thought she had no idea. Maybe it was now her turn to play at home. And it wasn't as if anyone was going to get hurt.

She realised that Simon hadn't said what she should buy for him to cook that evening. Would he want to barbecue? She would get steak; that should work either way. He was most likely a carnivore. *A lean and hungry look* ... She'd intended to buy ribeye, but at the butcher's display counter the word 'sirloin' leapt at her. She bought two pieces. Sir Loin.

Simon looked good. Clean jeans, a Marlon Brando white T-shirt, leather flip-flops.

She poured them each a glass of wine and showed him the steaks. 'They won't take long to grill,' he said, starting the fire in the Weber. The weather was warm enough now to eat outside and, as she'd pointed out to Simon, the terrace — and indeed the whole garden — wasn't overlooked at all.

Amanda laid the teak table and watched as he smashed a bulb of garlic with the flat of one of her lethal knives and stirred it into olive oil. Once the fire was ready, he dribbled the infused oil over the steaks, rubbed it in with some coarse salt and pepper and dropped them onto the grill. Amanda brought out baked potatoes and a warm salad of grilled Mediterranean vegetables.

After the meal, accompanied by several more pourings of wine, they retired to bed, coming down later to enjoy a last glass on the terrace.

'Tell me the rest of your story,' said Amanda. 'You came back from Africa twice?'

'Yes. After I first arrived in England from Zimbabwe I did various casual jobs, mostly in garden centres, but hated being here. It's so different. So I went back, back to working as a game ranger. Then I got restless and headed north again. Overland, as I mentioned. Mostly on the move, though slowly, but I spent months in Spain, working the bars. And then I worked for a while in the New Forest, mostly in conservation, then decided I'd rather choose my own hours. So I started the gardening business.'

Simon lit a Gauloise.

'Hugh hates anyone smoking,' said Amanda. 'I must remember to get rid of the ash-tray.'

'I'll sort it tomorrow when I'm doing the garden. Would you like me to cook something for you again?'

'I'm going to the cinema. It'll have to be next week.'

Simon agreed with Amanda that he would move his Tuesday morning slot to the afternoon. He started to spend Tuesday and Thursday evenings with her at Whiteacre if she was home alone. He usually cooked. He was fastidiously tidy and always helped clear up. Amanda felt cosseted for the first time in her life since Before. Or at least since the heady months leading up to Hugh's proposal and their wedding. She realised that she'd been feeling lonely for a long time.

*

There was more heavy rainfall one Tuesday evening a couple of weeks later. When Simon rolled away from Amanda to get out of the brass bed, she said, 'Listen to that. It's your African rain again. You can't cycle to Worthy Lane, you'll be drenched. Or drowned! Do you want to stay the night?'

Simon rolled back towards Amanda. He did.

Later, Amanda said she was going down to set the burglar alarm. Simon was about to ask why she needed to since he'd be here to protect her from any intruder but stopped himself just in time. He followed her silently half-way down the stairs until they turned the corner and he could see the burglar alarm keypad. He watched her put it on the night setting and then key in the code.

Simon had noticed a small safe fixed to the wall of the coach house — as Amanda liked to call it; he thought of it as the garage — hidden behind a ladder draped in a folded burlap sack. The following Thursday, after Amanda had gone out saying she'd pick up something for him to cook, he unlocked the coach-house door — handy of Amanda to have given him the key — and tried the same code. The safe opened to reveal a key-ring with three keys and, by the look of it, the burglar alarm fob. Bingo. The system probably required the fob rather than the code on entry and now he wouldn't have to search the house for the spare set, which would have been trickier. Pity — though not surprising — that the two keys other than the Yale were security models that were virtually impossible to get copied. And doubtless the fob also.

*

Tina was covering the regular cleaner of another huge house. Or rather mansion. When she started working for New Brooms she'd asked to cover holiday and sickness absences, thinking she'd like the variety. Cathy had been pleased. It seemed most of the other cleaners preferred not to cover because of the extra time and effort getting to know a new house, what needed cleaning, where the kit was kept. But now Tina had, even if reluctantly, started her sideline with Finn, she was glad to be cleaning more houses.

The owners of this house, however, were annoyingly efficient with their shredding, and the ribbons of paper in the machine was too fine to even think of piecing together. She couldn't see a safe in the house, which was surprising for this area. Maybe it was just extra well disguised, or maybe they used a safe deposit or whatever they were called at a bank. Finn said some rich people did that. Unlikely though for passports if these owners travelled regularly, which Tina thought they probably did as there were loads of framed photos of sunny beaches and snowy mountains. So if there was no safe there was probably a hiding place.

Tina did a rapid but adequate clean before starting a thorough examination of the house. She hoped the owners would be out for long enough. If she overstayed her hours she'd say she arrived late because her train was delayed.

She found what she was looking for, tucked away at the back of the walk-in cupboard off the utility room, hidden behind the array of brooms and ironing boards, hoovers and steam cleaners, bin liners and bleach which was a bit of a laugh. Funny the hiding places people use. She opened the briefcase.

First, a neat bundle of papers. Tina took them out, careful to keep them in order. Most of them looked to be about a dead person's ... estate, was that what they called it? New Brooms said that even a cover cleaner should remember the owners' names so she could address them politely if they met, and the dead person had the same surname as these owners so was probably the husband's mother given that she was called Jemima. Tina didn't know anything about estates and things but she could recognise a will when she saw one, though it was only a copy. There were also bank statements and a birth certificate. She took photos of the papers and of the passports which — she'd been right — were with them.

But the real prize was the card case tucked into a zipped side pocket. She found several credit cards, took photos of both sides, then put everything back in the original order and returned the briefcase to its original hiding place. Job done, though she still didn't much like doing it.

*

Amanda had said she'd be away with Hugh for the following fortnight, for their early summer break on the Riviera.

Simon knew the cleaner came on Mondays and Fridays. On the Thursday of Amanda and Hugh's second week, two days before they were due back, he went from the garden through the drive gate to the front of the house. He'd weighed the risk that one of Amanda's friends or neighbours might see him from the road and decided that it was small. None the less, he carried a basket of flowers cut from the garden: if challenged, he would say he was going to leave it by the front door for their return. Once in the porch, which was well screened by the leafy magnolia, he felt almost invisible. He worked his fingers into disposable latex gloves and let himself in with the keys from the safe in the garage.

Simon waved the fob over the burglar alarm and passed a fruitful hour working his way round the house. He'd been itching to explore since he first stepped inside on that memorable evening, which had culminated so satisfyingly, just a few weeks before. He'd been in the house a few times since but mainly in the kitchen area or Amanda's bedroom. Amanda's bed. He'd been sidetracked from — or at least postponed — his original burglary plan when he'd so easily stage-managed that entrée, preferring to enjoy the heady summer evenings and, more recently, nights while they were on offer. But then the code, keys and fob were more or less handed to him on a plate shortly before the house was empty for a while.

He started at the top, where the two home offices gave little away. Simon made a mental note of the Mac in Amanda's office and the laptop and locked filing cabinet, which was extremely well secured — not a paperclip job, sadly — in Hugh's. He glanced quickly into Amanda's desk, which was mostly full of interior design catalogues, and Hugh's, which contained nothing except some neatly stacked blocks of paper, a small box of business cards, a bottle of black ink — good god, the man must use a fountain pen — and three elegant propelling pencils.

The first floor had some fine paintings and some jewellery in Amanda's bedside table which he'd already clocked, but not much more of obvious interest. He used his phone to take a few photos, then went downstairs.

In the sitting room, Simon studied the pictures on the walls and the silver candlesticks he'd previously spied through the French windows. There were a number of photos on the piano, all framed in silver. Curious, he picked a couple up and examined them more closely. Hugh and Amanda on their wedding day, looking irritatingly handsome and smug (him) and beautiful and radiant (her). They were on the steps of a church, being showered with confetti. He glimpsed the bonnet of what looked like a vintage Bentley in one corner of the shot. And a more recent photo of Hugh sitting on the Whiteacre terrace and raising a wine glass, no a champagne flute. Simon studied the man through narrowed eyes. Again, he looked irritatingly handsome and smug. As well he might; he had plenty to be smug about.

He took photos of the candlesticks and some of the art, including some fine prints in the dining room. And he noticed a collection of first editions in a glazed bureau bookcase that might have been yew. Not that there was much point coveting items of furniture; they were too big.

Talking of big ... Whiteacre was vast. Of course Simon had seen it from outside and been in a couple of rooms but somehow the scale of it, as he prowled around alone and at his leisure, was still a shock. And the air of wealth, of privilege, of entitlement was breathtaking.

Finally, he checked the drawers in the utility room which he hoped — correctly, it turned out — would contain keys. They all helpfully bore a neat label, and he thought with amusement that he must talk to Amanda about improving her home security. But not just yet. Unfortunately there was nothing that looked like the key, or more likely keys, to the filing cabinet.

Simon retraced his steps, spent another twenty minutes in the garden and set off on his bike. He stopped off at the Wykeham Arms for a pint and sat down at one of the cast-off Winchester College tables — a traditional school desk, with inkblots and names scratched into the surface. It reminded him of his schooldays in Zimbabwe. He dragged himself back to the present and the empty evening that stretched ahead of him. Killing time again. The woman at the next table looked up from her phone with a triumphant smile and his thoughts turned to Amanda. He had got used to their dinners and found he missed her easy company. And the aperitif or digestif, depending on how soon he enticed her into bed. Not that she needed much enticing. She'd been neglected for too long.

Simon picked up his phone and checked the programme at the Everyman. The usual mix of old and new, arty and blockbuster. *Free Willy*. He grinned. No such thing, he thought.

Six

June

Leonie turned into the Wykeham Arms, looking forward to a glass of wine before the reverse commute back to London. She enjoyed that aspect of the journey, watching weary passengers pour off the packed train at Winchester to allow those who'd been standing for an hour to collapse gratefully into a seat. She was always careful on a Friday in case she crossed paths with Hugh, though he travelled first class and almost certainly arrived later than her usual departure time. But today was Thursday anyway.

She ordered a glass of wine at the bar and sat down at one of the small, battered tables. After a reviving gulp, she picked up her phone to check Twitter. An email from Cathy Henderson flitted across the screen.

July provisional schedule to follow, just wanted to check you're happy to cover Whiteacre for Judy for two weeks beginning 22nd. Four hours on Monday and Friday afternoon. It's a big house but Judy says it's not hard to clean.

Leonie felt a pulse of triumph. She was almost tempted to punch the air but instead looked around with a smile. A good-looking man at the next table cast her an appraising glance then turned back to his phone with a wolfish grin. She sent a reply to Cathy and decided to celebrate with a glass of champagne. Or perhaps prosecco, given her new lifestyle.

*

Simon had no plans for the following weekend apart from a one-off gardening job on the Saturday morning. After he'd finished, he cycled back to his van, chained the bike to a rack by the car park and drove down to the New Forest. It was difficult to wild camp there in summer, at least in the more popular areas, but there were pubs and campsites where you could park overnight for a reasonable fee. He headed for the Filly Inn, just the other side of Brockenhurst.

He walked in Roydon Woods for a couple of hours, thinking. He could do a burglary now with a good chance of getting away with it. Make a killing. He knew where the spare front-door keys and burglar alarm fob were kept and how to get to them. He could go in one night next time Amanda and Hugh were on holiday; she'd said they'd be off to Sicily in September and then skiing in January. All right for some. Anyway, he could sweep up the smaller pictures of value: the Dufy, the John, the Feddens, all signed; maybe take the Feddens out of their bulky frames, and conversely take the silver frames off the photos. Pick up the candlesticks, maybe the laptop, a few first editions and the jewellery. And anything else he spotted between now and then. Go out by one of the French windows, leave the goods by the door in the garden wall, smash a window pane from outside — he'd need to get duct tape — go back in, locking the French windows behind him, set the alarm and get out again via the smashed window. He'd be halfway down the back alley, or in the woods behind, by the time the alarm went off, and who knows when anyone would notice? Even if it went straight to the police or a security firm — which of course it would, it was bound to be a state-of-the-art system — there'd be a time-lag before anyone arrived since, unlike most burglars, Simon would trip the alarm on his way out rather than in.

He could dispose of the pictures. Simon had been interested in art since a brief stint at the Delta Gallery in Harare. His interest was not wholly aesthetic. He'd acquired, not always honestly, several originals of well-known Zimbabwean and South African modern artists, both black and white — Robert Paul, Richard Witikani, Arthur Azevedo, Martin van der Spuy. He'd hung on to a few; they were stored at his step-brother's house in Bournemouth, an address Simon also used for the limited formal correspondence he couldn't avoid. The rest he'd sold; there was a good market for them among whites who'd moved to the UK from southern Africa — 'whenwes' as they were known. He had swum comfortably in the murky waters of selling art with dubious provenance and still had the contacts, who would themselves have contacts for the other valuables he had in mind.

He'd miss Amanda though. It was a comfortable routine. Bedded, fed and watered twice a week. And the pleasurable, undemanding company of a very attractive woman. He parked the thought and turned back towards the pub, where he sat at the polished wooden bar under the web of exposed beams and drank two unhurried pints accompanied by a steak and ale pie. He then headed out to the camper and rolled and lit a joint. With the first draw Simon felt body and — more importantly for present purposes — mind relaxing. He knew his thoughts would meld and clear over the life of the spliff.

Illumination followed. He could be burglar and lover if he was careful. And he could be very careful. He'd heard only the other day on the radio that the police were so overstretched and burglaries so common that, in the absence of exceptional value or violence, investigations were perfunctory and owners were advised to claim on their insurance rather than expect any follow-up. He could even be a source of support and solace for Amanda. To his surprise, he enjoyed that prospect. He liked the idea of having someone — especially a beautiful woman — rely on him. And his bed and board would continue and he would in due course have a healthy infusion of cash. He could have his cake and eat it.

But — he took another drag, frowning. There was a flaw with the burglary-plus-solace-plus-continuing-Amanda plan. Simon wasn't worried about the security cameras themselves: given what he and Amanda got up to in the master bedroom under their unblinking eyes, he knew that they didn't record all the time. And he'd have got in with the fob so wouldn't have triggered them. But with a high-end security system — though maybe even with bog-standard ones these days; technology had doubtless moved on since his last burglary, which was a while ago — there would surely be a running record of when the fob, and maybe even which particular fob, had been used to turn the alarm on and off in the previous 24 hours or two weeks or whatever, and after an incident the owners would, he imagined, automatically be given the details. That, plus the fact that he'd probably not have the opportunity to return the spare keys and fob to the key safe before it was checked, would point an all too accurate finger at him. Whichever way he looked at it, if he burgled, he'd have to disappear. Which wasn't a problem in itself; after all, he'd done it before. But he wouldn't make enough from the haul to set himself up for the rest of his life. And again, he'd miss Amanda and the comfortable routine. Back to the original flaw.

And this time he needed flawless. He should park both the burglary-plus-disappearance and the burglary-plus-solace plans in favour of an even better one. Strains of a Bob Dylan song that he couldn't quite place floated into his mind. Something about a big brass bed and you can have your cake and eat it too. He needed to play a longer game.

*

Brenda preferred to get her cleaning done first. That way she knew how much time she had left for her other business. Of course if anyone was at home she used the time virtuously and, where possible, visibly: polishing silver or dusting behind the radiators or cleaning the odd window. Window cleaning now, that could be a lucrative sideline. Though not with her vertigo. Even looking out of the top-floor windows in today's house made her feel a bit iffy, but she could put up with that. She looked forward to catching up with the goings-on in the rear neighbour's garden. Some episodes were even better than East Enders. Maybe she should write a soap for the telly. There, another sideline. Good thing she was so inventive. She wouldn't like to have to manage on her cleaner's wages alone. Which reminded her, she was going to need to supplement them again soon.

The cleaning here wasn't so difficult. Affluent couple — well, obviously affluent, who else could afford a huge pile in this part of Winchester? What they did with all that space she didn't know. She'd put a backstory together from the numerous photos, studying them as she buffed the frames. Three children judging from the different graduation photos. Dressed up like pillocks in those silly square black hats with tassels and black robes, one with some red on it and one with gold and another with some white fur. Buildings behind, a bit like the cathedral here. They were probably all successful high earners now. She'd occasionally overlapped with their visits home for a long weekend in their smart little cars.

The couple were probably retired, though they were rarely in when she came. But of course the woman might never have worked; a lot of the wives round here didn't, or maybe had some soft part-time job. All right for some. Brenda worked like a dog — where did that expression come from? Some of her owners had dogs and they clearly lived a life of luxury. She'd seen the eye-watering price labels on bags or tins of pet food; more than she could afford to spend to feed her kids. Anyway, few of the wives she came across worked like a dog, or at all.

That rear neighbour, for example. She thought it might be the same house Frances had cleaned before she left New Brooms. Brenda remembered her saying ages ago, when the couple had moved in but there was still work going on — it had been a wreck apparently — that he was something in the City and she had an interior design business. No children. Frances said there was never any sign of her working though, just the odd sample fabric or wallpaper in her 'office', and most of those ended up being used in the house. She'd been useful, Frances, in more ways than she could have expected when she'd suggested Brenda answer the New Brooms advert. Not the latest one, which Brenda had told Tina about. There was something pleasing about that, a sort of chain reaction.

Time to stop thinking about other things, or at least do some cleaning while she thought. Brenda liked to start at the top and work her way down the house, even though it meant climbing all those stairs back up again to dip into the soap opera. It was one of the ways she kept fit, going up and down the stairs in the houses she cleaned, sometimes while carrying heavy hoovers and stuff. Of course the soap opera might not be airing today. It was a big nippy for hanky-panky in the garden to be honest.

'**Y**ou look fantastic,' said Simon as Amanda brought coffee and biscuits onto the terrace for them both. His eyes feasted on her long legs, smooth and tanned in white shorts. 'Good weather?'

Amanda leaned back in the teak steamer chair and stretched her linked hands upwards. 'It was lovely. I missed you though. I've decided to get a second iPhone so we can send secret texts. WhatsApps — the reception's often patchy here.'

'Great idea. It's been frustrating not being able to contact you. And I missed you too. I've got some nyama for this evening by the way.'

'Some what?'

'Nyama. Meat. Sorry, another Zim word. I shot a couple of rabbits this morning. They'll braai well but need marinading first. I'll do that if you like before I get on with the garden — I'll have to gut and skin them. I've got my hunting knife with me — I'll do the messy stuff in the coach house then finish in the kitchen.'

Simon lounged in the matching steamer chair. He'd wheeled them both out onto the terrace earlier, having sanded and oiled them while Hugh and Amanda were away.

'That's Hugh's chair,' said Amanda. 'It suits you.'

'They're beautiful wood,' he said. 'This one had a broken hinge which I fixed.'

'Ah, thanks so much. I've been asking Hugh to mend it since last summer. He's not very good at things like that.'

They went to bed before eating, luxuriating in the pleasure of rediscovering each other's bodies after two weeks apart. Later, Simon spotted *An African Odyssey* on the bedside table.

'Have you started it?' he asked. 'Are you enjoying it?'

'It's interesting,' Amanda said cautiously. 'I don't know a lot about Africa. But so far it's about the various women you sleep with on your travels. I thought it would be about your adventures when you were a game ranger, and wild animals. Leopards and things.'

Simon grinned. The book was about his adventures, at least the more printable ones. Some of his other adventures were less so: the time he killed a poacher for example. As for leopards, he reckoned he'd seen more leopard skin in a fortnight's casual work in a Benidorm nightclub than he had in a year in Africa. It was clear, though, that Amanda was intrigued and impressed by what she saw as his exotic Africanness. He must remember to keep salting his conversation with the odd word of chilapalapa. Not that many people in Zim used it since independence, but a few words had become too entrenched to discard. And some were Shona anyway. Or Afrikaans. Which wasn't much better as Afrikaans was also seen as a language of oppression. Just as well he wasn't bothered about political correctness.

The rabbit tasted of fire and garlic. They came out on the terrace again later so Simon could smoke. Music played inside; the ghostly outline could be heard in the background. Simon made out *50 Ways to Leave Your Lover.* Catchy tune, though he preferred to improvise and improve. Fifty ways to join your lover. Fifty ways to leave your husband. Abandon the van, man. He needed to work on his plan some more. Work and wait and watch.

*

Amanda drifted round the bedroom the following morning after Simon had slipped out of the garden door to his next job. Slipping — sliding — gentle chords from the evening before echoed in her head. Paul Simon's honeyed voice. *Slip slidin' away.* Like Hugh and her marriage seemed to be doing.

She was pleased to be back at Whiteacre. Much more so than after previous holidays. She found it increasingly difficult to remember how it had been with Hugh in the early years — even the first decade or so — of their marriage.

Hugh was never bad company — well, only on the last weekend of the tax year, when he worked flat-out at home and refused to socialise or even come out of his office except to eat, wash and sleep. She usually went to a spa for that weekend, often treating her sister, and left a fridge full of meals for Hugh to reheat.

But increasingly they seemed to move and even converse in parallel lines, with little engagement. Amanda wondered whether Hugh had changed or she had. Was it simply the contrast with Simon, who gave her his whole attention when he was with her? He was thoughtful and generous, bringing food all the time. Even though she knew it was mostly poached. Like the stolen flowers he brought. But he gave her his time, taking the trouble to cook and to clear. And he was adept and passionate in bed.

Seven

July

It was almost eight o'clock when Amanda heard Hugh's key in the lock. He liked to walk from the station if the weather was fine, saying that the easy mile and a half cleared his head after a week in the office and an hour in a crowded train.

They exchanged automatic pecks on the cheek. Hugh went upstairs and came down in jeans and a polo shirt. Amanda knew she'd find his work clothes in a jumble on the chair in the spare bedroom he used as his dressing room — though normally tidy, he would be desperate for a drink after his journey. Later she would hang the suit and put the shirt in the laundry basket for the cleaner to deal with.

'Gin and tonic?' she asked. 'Or a vermouth? Or white wine?'

Amanda had already had two generous glasses of a cold, steely Chablis, taking advantage of not having to drive to the station. She mixed a G & T for Hugh, who sat down at the pale ash breakfast table so they could talk while she cooked.

She was making risotto with fresh peas and lemon. She peeled an onion with a samurai-sharp knife, halved it and triple-sliced each hemisphere so it collapsed with a flourish, like a magic trick, into a pile of neat, tiny dice. These she swept from the chopping board into melted butter in a copper sauté pan. Must remind the cleaner to polish the copper. She's really not very good, the current girl.

Amanda stirred the onion in a slow, gentle rhythm, leaning back against the unit next to the gleaming range cooker so that she faced Hugh. 'How was your week?'

'Usual,' said Hugh, the ice clinking in his glass as he took a mouthful. 'Too much work. Not enough play. A client actually paid a bill without complaining. Another one didn't. A couple of work dinners. Nothing new. And you?'

'Nothing new either. Cinema with Georgina. Lunch with the gym crowd.'

She turned back to the hob. Hugh had been fun when they first met. Outgoing, amusing and prone to flashes of mercurial banter, he was the antithesis of her. He took her out to wine bars where bright lights transformed their glasses to jewels, to clubs where the darkness was the perfect vector for rippling currents of jazz, to candlelit restaurants where he always asked the waiter to give her a menu without prices. He had just qualified as a solicitor and was working in a good City firm on what seemed to both of them an astronomical salary.

It seemed less astronomical after they married and moved into their first flat, which they bought with his parents' help. By then she had a job with an interior design company and went part time so she could direct their own refurbishment. Her alchemy transformed it from a cramped cluster of poky, dark rooms into an elegant, white-painted open space, the second bedroom swallowed by the big sitting-cum-dining room with a small but efficient kitchen in one corner. They sold it for a decent profit and began the scramble up the London property ladder.

Amanda picked up her glass. 'Would you like a top-up?' she asked. Hugh was fiddling with his work phone as usual.

*

Hugh took a long, lemony sip of his gin and tonic. 'Smells good,' he said. 'Risotto?'

He looked at Amanda, shapely in neat white trousers and a peacock-blue blouse, her golden head tilted over the hob, the wooden spoon in her hand gently revolving the onions. She was still arrestingly beautiful. That was what had attracted him when he first saw her at his older brother's wedding. He was stuck in a conversation with some friends of his parents, or possibly his brother's newly minted in-laws, he couldn't recall now. He'd heard a brittle crack, turned and noticed a slim girl in a demure waitress's uniform bending over the scattered fragments of a plate. Seizing the opportunity to escape the chit-chat, he went to help her pick up the pieces. Startling green eyes in a pale, fine-boned face, a rope of hair wound up in some sort of plait, a grateful, if anxious, smile; Hugh was smitten. He sought her out and chatted to her off and on throughout the reception in the brief periods when she wasn't waiting, serving or clearing tables.

She was the polar opposite of most other girls he'd met: the neighing horsy teenage daughters of family friends, the earnest, cerebral students at Cambridge and the College of Law, and the smart, flashy trainee solicitors the baby lawyers morphed into. Amanda was quiet, reflective, with a faint and alluring shimmer of vulnerability. His parents had been doubtful at first; even though he'd edited out the more brutal aspects of her family history, they were still concerned that she wasn't from the right background, wasn't as glossy and self-assured as his previous girlfriends, and seemed nonplussed that it was those traits that he found attractive. He liked to think she was a latter-day damsel in distress and that he was rescuing her, offering some sort of redemption, the chance of remaking her life. She loved listening to him, loved cooking for him, came to love him and to love looking after him, and his parents came round. Savouring the fragrance drifting from the hob, he thought that might have been when Amanda had asked for a French cookery course as a wedding present.

And she seemed to Hugh to become even more beautiful as she was able to spend more on herself. Not that she was spendthrift, but she bought impeccably elegant clothes, wore just the right amount of make-up, kept her hair well-cut and well-coloured. At least he assumed it was coloured, he couldn't remember exactly what shade it had been when he'd first seen her.

Amanda was still drop-dead gorgeous, as his brother Tristan always described her, but the chemistry between them had evaporated over time. Hugh supposed this often happened in a long marriage and, once they'd bought Whiteacre and the London flat and he'd started to commute weekly, he had drifted guiltlessly into a delicious succession of discreet and ephemeral affairs which he was sure that Amanda never suspected. He knew she was emotionally as well as financially dependent on him and he wouldn't want to hurt her. And their life suited him perfectly.

His thoughts turned to Margot. That part of his life suited him perfectly also. Though he did sometimes miss Leonie and her less conventional approach to things. Like her habit of sending indiscreet messages from her work phone when it was easier for her to look as though she was emailing. Once, in one of the monthly meetings for London legal staff, they had been sitting apart but texting about arrangements for breakfast sex the next day. He saw Leonie frown down at her device and stab irritably at the keys. When she'd finished, she put it on the empty chair beside her with apparent relief and glanced at the chairman, who was visiting from the international law firm's head office in Pittsburgh and for some reason that baffled the London lawyers was wearing a Steelers jersey. Or Pirates maybe? And which played what? Hugh, who'd known the rules of cricket since the age of nine, had never learned to differentiate between the alien US sporting rituals. Anyway, he saw Leonie catch the chairman's eye and, with a disarmingly simple moue and an apologetic shrug of her shoulders, neatly convey the impression that, however reluctantly, she'd had to interrupt the rapt attention she'd been giving him in order to deal with a fretful client. Margot in contrast, determined for the sake of her career that there should be no risk that their affair be discovered, only ever communicated with him from her personal phone.

And on another occasion Leonie texted him one afternoon in the office:

> Forgot it's group Xmas party this eve. All secs went to loo and came back in black, bling and blusher. Am v underdressed but bet I'm only one who had other type of secs at lunchtime :) xxx

He sighed. Margot was fine but not so much fun if he was honest with himself. He missed that side of Leonie. He wondered how she was doing. And what. She would almost certainly not have been able to walk into another legal job.

Feeling perversely that he'd been disloyal to Margot, Hugh took his work phone out of his pocket and typed a quick and cheery 'have a good weekend' message to her. 'Please,' he said, when Amanda offered a top-up. He put the phone away.

Leonie took a deep breath, squared her shoulders and stabbed the doorbell with an unsteady hand. She hadn't expected to be so shaken at the prospect of meeting Hugh's wife. Perhaps the Cleaning Plan wasn't such a good idea after all.

The door opened. Leonie knew that Amanda was attractive — she'd once invented a reason to leave something on Hugh's desk at Mainwaring & Cox so she could check the inevitable 'happy families' photo — but the camera hadn't done justice to the slim woman before her. She tried not to stare at the fine-boned face, the gold-blonde hair, the cat-like green eyes echoing the emerald silk blouse. Why had Hugh strayed from the marital bed, she couldn't help wondering? But he'd evidently found Leonie attractive enough. And he was a man.

She mentally shook herself. Don't think about Hugh; remember what he did. Don't be beguiled by Amanda; remember she was your rival. Or one of them.

'Good morning Mrs Standing,' she gabbled. 'I'm Jane Toussaint from New Brooms. I'll be cleaning for you this week and next.'

'Please come in.' Amanda stepped back and Leonie followed her into a balconied hall. 'You can hang your coat on the bannister for now. I'm going out after I've shown you round so you'll need to lock up when you leave. I assume New Brooms gave you the keys and the burglar alarm fob?'

Leonie nodded, not trusting herself to speak. She'd done it. She was in Hugh's house and his wife didn't know who she was.

Amanda gave Leonie a guided tour, radiating quiet pride as they glanced into each room. A dining room painted olive-green, a perfect foil for the monochrome prints of scenes from *Don Quixote*. Another touch of the unexpected in the open-plan breakfast room and state-of-the-art kitchen where one wall was a dramatic burnt orange, a vivid flame in the surrounding white. A gleaming utility room beyond. A bright and airy sitting room, a shimmer of écru and light wood. A cloakroom and loo with black gloss paintwork and bold fuchsia flowered wallpaper. A pastel room with a large flat-screen television and a cream leather corner couch. Leonie stopped absorbing the detail as she shadowed Amanda up the staircase; she could explore at a gentler pace in her own time.

Two floors later, they'd completed the circuit and headed back down. Amanda said she'd be leaving shortly and disappeared into the cloakroom. Leonie waited by the hall table for any last-minute instructions, resisting the urge to drum her fingers. Amanda must be fiddling with her hair or whatever Ladies Who Lunch do in front of the mirror for so long. She certainly looked beautifully coiffed and freshly lipsticked when she came out in a subtle cloud of orange blossom. Leonie suggested that she take Amanda's mobile number in case of any queries and they exchanged details. Amanda put on her coat, picked up her bag and closed the front door behind her, leaving a brief and distracted 'Goodbye' hanging in the air.

Leonie breathed a deep sigh of relief: meeting Hugh's wife hadn't been as bad as she'd feared and now she was in the house, unsupervised, for four hours. She set off on her own, more focused, tour. No point trying to plant any clues about Hugh's latest affair; it was too risky on this visit. But she could do some sniffing around before she gave Whiteacre what she intended to be the best clean of its life. She'd paid a series of less than competent cleaners for years and knew how to impress enough, she hoped, to be taken on as Amanda's regular cleaner.

First, of course, the main bedroom, via the wardrobe-lined dressing room opposite. Easy enough to slip a lingerie receipt into a pocket of one of Hugh's suits — though most of the clothes in these wardrobes were evidently Amanda's. Easy enough also to spray a squirt of scent. Lipstick on a collar might be trickier as his shirts were mostly laundered in London. But he came home every Friday in his work clothes so there was some leeway there. Her duties included the laundry so perhaps an indelible stain could be found. She remembered he'd once spotted a smear of her lipstick on one of his cuffs. He threw out the shirt so that Amanda wouldn't see it; Leonie had rescued it from the bin and taken it back to her flat to wear as a pyjama top. She blinked away the memory and moved on to the master bedroom.

A king-size brass bed; she swallowed, and tried not to imagine Hugh and Amanda together in it. But the room struck her as a woman's domain, with books and an Apple Watch charger on one bedside table only. She shook out the duvet and wondered whether she was supposed to change the bedlinen, but nothing had been mentioned and the sheet looked crisp and fresh.

Another bedroom, described by Amanda as the second spare room, also showed signs of regular use. Had Hugh been telling the truth after all when he told her that he and Amanda slept apart? She'd dismissed it at the time as a standard married man's line to his mistress, though it had hurt to think so.

Next was a bigger spare room, the bedcover unwrinkled, the coordinating curtains and carpet pristine. And the smaller room next to it — the third spare room? Who had three spare rooms? — must be Hugh's dressing room — who had a dressing room? Or in fact two. There was another wardrobe hung with an impressive array of suits and a few shirts, and an en-suite redolent of the mint body wash and tea-tree oil shampoo he used. Leonie realised with a start that, as it was a Monday, Hugh would have been standing in the shower only a few hours before. She shook the thought away.

The top floor, up a long staircase, was divided into two rooms with high, steeply pitched ceilings, the original attic beams exposed. Amanda had described the front one as her office for her former interior design practice. The small hand basin in the corner suggested it had once been a bedroom, but it was now dominated by a sleek, modern desk on which stood a sleek, modern Mac. Leonie nudged the mouse. The screen came to life but, as expected, was locked. In a detective story the password would be written on a scrap of paper under the blotter. Here there was no blotter, no scrap of paper and no clue to the password. A puzzle for another time. Leonie had a quick glance in the drawers, which were full of stationery and wallpaper and fabric catalogues, and moved on.

The other second-storey room, at the back, was evidently Hugh's home office, with a filing cabinet bristling with locks and a traditional partners' desk for his Mainwaring & Cox laptop. She checked the single drawer but it contained nothing more interesting than paper, ink, pencils and a box of his business cards. A printer and router squatted on a table in the corner and she keyed the WiFi code into her iPhone. The mansard window offered a vertiginous view over the garden, and Leonie took in the terrace overlooked by a vigorous climbing rose in full creamy flower, the two lawns, the ivy arch, the borders and hedges, all neat and elegant, fifty shades of green a perfect foil to a rainbow of harmonious colours. Amanda must have a good gardener.

Leonie went downstairs for her kit and started a meticulous clean. When she'd finished, she wrote a note using an impersonal large and neat script in case Hugh saw it (though come to think of it when had he ever seen her handwriting — who wrote billets doux on scented paper, or indeed anything much at all, these days?):

Dear Mrs Standing, you have a lovely house. I've done a
thorough spring-clean downstairs. I'll do the same upstairs
on Friday. There wasn't enough wax in the jar for me to
do your beautiful breakfast table. Please let New Brooms
know if you'd like me to buy some. Have a nice week.

She began to sign the first version 'Leonie' and had to tear it
up and write it again, remembering this time to sign 'Jane'.
It would be so much easier to be one of New Brooms' other
cleaners — just cleaning, not being a sort of undercover agent.

*

The weather was better than it had been when she'd last
checked, warm and sunny, and Brenda hoped there'd be
something worth watching in the rear neighbour's garden. The
house she was cleaning was on a small knoll — made it a bit
like a castle, and she called it the Castle House to herself; its
real name was the much blander Brambles. The top room was
almost like a turret. She imagined herself as Rapunzel in Lily's
favourite fairy tale. No long hair to let down, but long-distance
binocs to get out of the small backpack handbag she always
kept with her.

Had the house not been raised, it would have been
impossible to see into the soap-opera garden, as Brenda was
beginning to think of it, even from the turret room. She must
find out the name of the house. Almost certainly a name,
hardly any houses around here had a mere number. She should
be able to work it out and walk round and past it. It would
be easier if the Castle House backed directly onto it, but that
space was taken up with a copse and the soap-opera house was
beyond the copse, across a small alleyway and one house along.
The garden directly below the Castle House and the strip of

woodland was very boring. Huge of course, and stunning, but seemingly just for show, though she sometimes saw a woman doing sedate lengths of breaststroke in the pool.

The soap-opera garden was also huge and stunning, though without a pool, but a lot more happened in it. There was always a gardener there on Thursday afternoon, which was Brenda's slot at the Castle House. There he was now. Brenda fiddled with her binoculars and brought him into focus. He was hot. Probably in both senses: he was weeding and trimming in full sun. Wearing a hat though, he must have some sense.

The woman came out onto the terrace. She had a bottle of beer and a glass of white wine which she set on the wooden table. The man put down his tools and went to meet her. They kissed. Definitely a soap-opera kiss, not a peck on the cheek. After the kiss, he raised the bottle to his mouth and took a long draught; must have been thirsty work. The gardening, not the kiss. Though maybe that too. Then he went off to the side, out of Brenda's view. It was like when she'd taken the kids to a pantomime one Christmas and could only afford seats at the end of where the balcony wraps round and there was a slice of stage they couldn't see. Restricted view they called it.

The woman was blonde and beautiful. She went back in through the open French doors and came out with a plate of something, maybe olives, an empty dish and a newspaper. The man came back into view wheeling a barbecue. He disappeared again and returned with a wheelbarrow full of wood. He finished his beer, crumpled a few pages of the newspaper, put them in the barbecue, arranged some small bits of wood on top and then took something out of his pocket. Matches, she could just make out; he must be about to light the barbecue. But then he took out a packet of cigarettes and lit one of those instead. The woman went back in and brought out another wineglass and a bottle of wine in a chiller. Then he kissed her again, leaving his cigarette burning in the empty dish; ah, it must be an ash-tray. They walked down the garden, arm in arm, and into a shed. Probably called a summerhouse or something poncy. Brenda put her binoculars away, disappointed. Obviously not quite warm enough today. Once she'd seen an X-rated episode on a small lawn. They must assume the garden wasn't overlooked, and probably from where they were that's how it seemed. Her turret window would be a tiny speck to the naked eye, and its being off centre and beyond the copse would make it even less noticeable. She needed to find out who the woman was and whether she was married. Handled right, the soap opera could provide something more than lurid entertainment. And she'd waited a long time for this.

Eight

July

'You've got some good music here,' said Simon. Amanda had a mix of pop songs playing in the sitting room. The French windows were open and the strains of *Summer Nights* floated out, twining around them in the balmy evening air with the fragrant smoke from Simon's Gauloise. The sounds transported him back decades, to school perhaps? Or maybe later. One of his nomadic trips across a continent? A woman in a cabin on a lake steamer? The Victoria Falls Hotel, in better times?

'It's one of Hugh's playlists. He used to enjoy putting them together. We don't listen so much anymore.'

Amanda stood up and topped up their wine glasses. Simon took the bottle from her and put it on the table. '"This wine will evolve",' he read aloud from the label, '"from simple and enjoyable in its youth to more complex and demanding as it matures. Dark, smoky and long."

'Doesn't Hugh notice you're drinking more wine now?'

'I don't know. Maybe. He wouldn't mind, it's one of the

good things about him, he's very generous. If he did notice, he'd just assume it was my book club evenings, gifts when I'm invited out, friends to dinner.'

'Which it is,' said Simon. He caught her wrist and pulled her down to sit beside him on the bench. 'But more than friends. I think I may be falling in love with you.'

Amanda was silent for a few moments.

'Tell me about leopards,' she said eventually. 'I asked you once before, ages ago. It's what I picture when I imagine Africa. Which I do often, now.'

'Well,' said Simon. 'They can't change their spots, for a start. Because what you see aren't spots, but rosettes. They're predators. They're solitary, well-camouflaged, opportunistic. They have excellent binocular vision. They're nocturnal, though they're often drawn to water holes at dusk. They pluck the fur and feathers off their food before eating it. They're master stalkers, relying on the element of surprise.'

And — but he didn't say it aloud — the constant calling of a female in search of a mate is how the male detects her.

Later, in bed, he remembered to ask something he was curious about. 'Why didn't you and Hugh have children? Didn't you want any?'

'It wasn't a conscious decision. Hugh was always busy working when we got married, and I was focussed on doing up our first flat and then the later ones. It wasn't the right time. But then it carried on not being the right time. We moved here, the house was a far bigger project than anything I'd done before, Hugh spent the weeks in London. It's too late now; I'll be fifty next year. And anyway …'

She trailed off.

'And anyway what?'

'We stopped having sex a while ago. Hugh always got back

exhausted on a Friday. I didn't enjoy it anymore. I thought I must have lost interest. Until you came along.'

Simon rolled over and kissed her, unexpectedly pleased. 'You don't look as if you'll be fifty next year.'

*

After she'd finished her clean and her not-so-X-rated soap-opera viewing, Brenda parked down the street from the Castle House and walked round to where she thought the soap-opera house was. She didn't have a good sense of direction, but setting the map on her phone to satellite and seeing herself as a moving spot in a life-like landscape gave her a better feel for the geography and she thought it was probably the imposing house called, according to the elegant wooden notice at the entrance to the drive, Whiteacre.

At home that evening she was distracted and found it difficult to concentrate on helping Tommy and Lily with their homework. They grew impatient with her and then, when she apologised and sat down with them, asked her when they could have new phones. Brenda looked around at the worn furniture, the tired curtains, the battered saucepans; so different from the sumptuous reception rooms and vast, gleaming kitchens she cleaned. Best not even to think about the car with its MOT looming. It had been hard since her partner had walked out on her, leaving no money and no means of contacting him. She'd started cleaning for New Brooms because the job required no formal qualifications and most of the time she could work the hours she wanted. Getting school holidays off was difficult, but some of the cleaners without children at home were good about working extra hours to cover for her and the other school mums. She'd return the favour in term time when asked. That was how she'd stumbled onto her first opportunity to make some extra cash.

Not at the Castle House but also in Nightjars Holt, her second cover clean there. She'd assumed no one was home when the tastefully quiet doorbell wasn't answered, so let herself in and decided to start in the master bedroom at the back of the top floor. She walked right in on the wife in bed with a man. No sounds to warn her that anyone was there: the woman had a soft gag on her mouth and her wrists were bound to the bedposts with what looked like silk scarves. The man was down on her so wasn't saying much either. It took a few seconds for him to realise what had happened since the woman could neither speak nor remove the gag. He probably took her wild wriggling and writhing as encouragement. Afterwards Brenda wished she'd used those seconds to take a photo. Or even better, a video.

The man leapt up, looked round wildly, put his hands over his rapidly wilting cock, grabbed his boxers from the floor, and untied the woman. She ripped off the gag, seized the twisted sheet, pulled it up to her neck and sat up while the man snatched up a few more tumbled clothes and shot into the en-suite. The woman's first words were 'Who the fuck are you?'

'Er — sorry — I'm your cover cleaner,' mumbled Brenda. She'd been frozen in the doorway but now started to back out, embarrassed but also bewildered. OK so she hadn't met the owners, as cover cleaners often didn't, but surely they'd been expecting her?

'It's not your time for fuck's sake,' snapped the woman. Good choice of words, Brenda thought later. 'Get the fuck out of —' She broke off. 'Fuck,' she said, and Brenda wondered whether her vocabulary was normally so limited.

'Jesus.' Ah, a new word. 'Shit.' The woman got out of bed and wound the sheet round herself. She stomped over to the dressing table. 'Someone's fucked up …'

Brenda smirked. That was one way of putting it. She was about to back further out of the room, take the cleaning kit downstairs and leave, though she was worried about losing money as she'd barely started her four hours and wasn't sure of the protocol. She didn't think this situation had been covered in New Brooms' terms and conditions. But then she decided to stand her ground. She'd come to the house to work, to work hard to earn much needed money. She wasn't going to slink away just because she'd caught the owner with her knickers down. The woman clearly had the leisure for what Brenda assumed was an affair, but she, Brenda, had fuck all leisure for such pleasures, or indeed the time or the opportunity or, realistically these days, the energy.

The woman rooted around in the vast handbag on the dressing table and produced a handful of notes. Brenda gulped. They looked like fifties. 'Here,' said the woman. 'I don't want any trouble. Take these and don't come again. I'll tell the agency I prefer to wait till my normal cleaner's back. But if you breathe a word of what you've just seen I'll make sure you never clean for them again. I've been a customer for years and they'll believe whatever I tell them.'

Brenda wasn't sure about that but decided in a nanosecond that she'd rather take the cash than put it to the test. She couldn't risk losing the New Brooms job. Afterwards she realised how it had happened. Her phone had given up the ghost the previous week and she'd replaced it with her first smartphone. Although it was at the bottom end of the market and she'd bought it second-hand on eBay, it did the job. But when she'd entered her two cleaning jobs for that day on its calendar, she'd confused the times as she struggled with the unfamiliar process.

Brenda never went back for more money in case the woman's threat was genuine, but the episode gave her an idea for quietly making a bit on the side. As it were.

On the Friday after her first clean at Whiteacre there was no answer when Leonie rang the doorbell. She waited for a few minutes then let herself in, waved the fob over the burglar alarm and hung her coat and bag in the hall.

The ground floor looked much the same as when she'd left on Monday. Leonie tidied and straightened the reception rooms and wiped down the kitchen sink and counters. Under the wooden block which bristled like a crouching porcupine with a panoply of knives she found a note from Amanda (must remember not to call her that to her face) starting *Dear Ms Toussaint* (must remember that's me and not my grandmother):

> *Thank you for the thorough downstairs clean. I've left the*
> *kitchen clear of dishes today to give you time to do the*
> *same upstairs. On Fridays please could you change the bed*
> *linen in the main bedroom and put the laundry through*
> *the washer and dryer. Mrs Standing*

Leonie lugged the hoover, floor mop and bucket of cleaning stuff up the stairs. She decided to start in the master bedroom and was stripping the bed when she noticed that there was a roll of loo paper underneath one bedside table. She paused and shook out the sheet with a snap. It rippled then settled gently on the mattress. A couple of ghostly Rorschach blots mottled the fabric. Leonie stumbled back, the sour taste of bile catching her throat, then realised Hugh wouldn't have been home since she'd cleaned on Monday. Or not unless he'd changed his commuting pattern, but that was most unlikely given that he was in the early stages of a new affair.

She bundled the bedding into the laundry basket in the en-suite bathroom, found fresh linen in the airing cupboard in the second bathroom, took the basket down to the utility room and set the machine off, deep in thought. Perhaps it wasn't only Hugh who was in the early stages of a new affair. And if so, here was another, maybe even better, way to puncture his cosy marital bubble. Once she'd found out more. While she was still just the cover cleaner, she needed to concentrate on the cleaning. But if she were taken on as Amanda's regular cleaner, she could make time to do more than seeding the odd fake clue. Do some digging as well as planting.

*

When Simon had abandoned his burglary plans over his post-recce joint outside the Filly Inn, he had briefly wondered whether Amanda might decide, perhaps with some prompting, to divorce Hugh, leaving a neat husband-shaped gap in her life which he could gallantly fill. He had thought about raising the issue with her but feared that if he did so too soon she might think he was after her money. Which of course he was, but he didn't think she had any inkling. He tried to keep their conversations light and entertaining, to give her pleasure in bed, to cook for her and ply her with Hugh's excellent wine. He'd more or less given up on the prospect of sounding her out, and in any event he had doubts about divorce as a solution — wouldn't Hugh's family and all Amanda's doubtless equally wealthy friends smell a rat and persuade her not to get married again too quickly, especially to a jobbing southern African gardener who lived in a camper van? But to her surprise she raised it herself one evening, though from a different angle.

The cusp of midsummer had passed and the evenings, though still light, were cooler. They were on the terrace, relaxed after good sex, good food and good wine. Simon had taken to keeping the fire going in the Weber and the glowing ashes warmed them as the second bottle ebbed. He'd asked her idly whether she had any plans for the following week.

'I'm going to Folkestone on Wednesday, to see my sister,' she said, her voice flat. 'I'll be back on Thursday afternoon so it won't affect us.'

Simon had almost forgotten that Amanda had a sister, though now he vaguely recalled her mentioning — Jennifer, was it? Maybe he could score a brownie point, at least if he'd remembered the name right — one evening, something to do with treating her to a haircut.

'What does she do?' he asked. 'Jennifer, isn't it?'

Amanda smiled. 'Yes, well remembered. I don't see her often. We're not close, really.' She chewed her lip, her brow furrowed.

'How's that?' asked Simon.

'We were, when we were younger. Then Jennifer married — a property developer, lots of money. She lived the high life, loved it. They moved to France and during one of their parties she walked in on him in bed with his secretary. Anyway, they got divorced. He, her husband, started proceedings very quickly, in France. Hugh said it was because he'd come out of it much better there and by the time Jennifer told us it was too late.'

'What happened?'

'She did come out of it badly. She lives in a small flat in Folkestone now, works in a dead-end job in the Shuttle office in Dover. And she … she just really seems to resent the fact that I have so much more than her.' Amanda rubbed her eyes.

Simon frowned. 'That's hardly your fault.'

'I know. We give her money when she needs it, but it's hard for her to ask. But I always say that it's not my fault I married a nicer man. I don't think Hugh would try and shaft me if we divorced. Not that I've ever thought of doing so,' she added quickly. 'Apart from … I'd lose the house. And not have much money. And I couldn't face that. Not after …' She stopped.

Simon thought he might as well probe a bit. 'You'd get half of everything, surely?' Half of Hugh's everything would be a great deal. In both senses.

'Our main asset is this.' Amanda gestured widely to encompass the buildings and garden. 'We put all our money into buying it and doing it up. I stopped working years ago to do it; not that I ever earned much. Even though the house was a complete wreck and the garden a jungle, the price was sky high because of the area. We had to increase the mortgage. We've paid that off now, but there's not much cash left over. We don't save anymore.'

'But Hugh must earn quite a lot?' ventured Simon.

'I suppose he must. But he spends loads in London with all his work entertaining, though he says he gets it back in some deal to do with tax which I don't understand. He's very clever with that sort of thing. And anything left goes into his pension; again it's apparently very tax-efficient. But then it's locked in — Hugh says it's much better to leave the pension untouched until he dies, there'll be more for me that way. Anyway, so we'd have to sell the house and I'd only get half. I'd end up in some semi on the outskirts. I just couldn't.'

She was trembling, almost shaking. Simon stroked her arm as if gentling a nervous horse and topped up their wine.

*

When Leonie arrived on the following Monday for her third clean, Amanda let her in and said she'd be going out shortly. As Leonie was hanging her coat, Amanda put her handbag and her iPhone in its striking fuchsia, red and white Marimekko cover on the cherry table in the hall and went into the downstairs loo. Leonie decided to start on the first floor to keep out of the way and was heading up the stairs when she heard a muffled chirrup from the hall.

She began to polish the mirrors, windows and glazed pictures that she hadn't had time to do the previous week. It was pure chance that she was at one of the front windows when Amanda left the house a few minutes later and got into her car. Before setting off, Amanda rummaged in her handbag and pulled out her iPhone. Except it wasn't her iPhone, which Leonie had seen when they'd exchanged numbers the previous week and again on the hall table seconds earlier. The phone that Amanda was holding was in a green cover. Apple green, appropriately. Amanda's fingers did a quick tap-dance on the screen, then she glanced at the phone, appeared to turn it off, tucked it back in the bag and reversed out of the drive.

Another puzzle, thought Leonie. Or another piece in last week's puzzle. Why would a married woman have two phones? She could think of only two reasons. For work, like Hugh, who'd always preferred to keep a separate phone for office use — but hadn't Amanda described her interior design practice as 'former'? Or for a lover. Which of course also applied to Hugh. She gave the window a final, and somewhat savage, wipe, straightened the sheets in the main bedroom, noting that Amanda hadn't asked her to change them this time, then moved to the second spare room — or was it the third? The bed had been slept in since Friday, again confirming what Hugh had told her. Not that that made her feel much better at the moment. She tried not to think about what he might be up to in the bed in his flat. Which reminded her of the Agent Provocateur receipts in her handbag. A minute or two later and they were in the jacket pocket of one of Hugh's suits at the back of a wardrobe.

Buoyed by that small triumph, she finished upstairs and started in the kitchen, where Amanda had left the clutter of what Leonie assumed was yesterday's evening meal. A large glass with a wilted yellow half-moon slice and a transparent dribble at the bottom, presumably G&T — no surprises there. Two wine glasses with remnants of white and two with stains of red. A copper sauté pan with what looked like the remains of a mushroom risotto. A superb scoop of an olive-wood bowl with a smear of oil and avocado sludge.

Leonie ran hot water into the copper pan, admiring its heft and the solid shaft of its angled handle. A pity the metal was dulled and mottled … Her thoughts changed tack and after a swift Google search she restored the shine with lemon juice and salt, then did the same for the family tree of matching saucepans hanging against the wall. She hand-washed the glasses, dried and polished them with the linen cloth folded over the rail of the range cooker, wiped the salad bowl clean and cleared the rest into the dishwasher.

Nine

August

Amanda was hosting her book club again.

It was still warm and light enough to eat out on the terrace. The table was laid for a cold supper and wine had been poured. They were discussing Shari Lapena's *The Couple Next Door*.

'I found this quote interesting,' said Juliet. '"Maybe she's a complete fool. The wife is always the last to know, right?" Because in the end Marco hadn't been unfaithful so there was no infidelity for her to know about. But Alice, her mother, was cheated on. And Alice knew all along. Knew about and tolerated a whole string of affairs which didn't seem to mean much to her husband, and then realised that the last one was different and that he'd want to leave her and sting her for a few million first.'

Amanda took a sip of wine and said nothing. Had Jennifer's husband had a whole string of affairs before the one that Jennifer had discovered? She thought he probably had. Would he have wanted to leave Jennifer if she hadn't caught him *in flagrante delicto*? The phrase sounded seductive. Fragrant delight. In bed with Simon.

She offered round olives and cheese straws.

'Perhaps that's the point,' said Stephanie. 'That it's the husband who thinks the wife's always the last to know, but that in fact the wife always knows. And also knows whether an affair is serious or not.'

Amanda brought out cold chicken sofrito, green salad, tabbouleh, tomatoes in basil-scented olive oil. She set the dishes gently on the table, taking pleasure in the succulent appearance of each — the sofrito's creamy flesh in quivering, turmeric-golden jelly, the tomatoes glistening in their slick of dressing, the lettuce in fifty shades of green, the tabbouleh a soft mound of parsley-stippled ivory. She poured more wine.

The sun inched behind the false acacias, infusing the leaves so they flared lemon and lime in an echo of their spring blaze. The terrace was still warm, the stone releasing the heat absorbed earlier. Amanda brought out ripe peaches and a riper Brie. The conversation drifted back to the book.

'Well, I've had enough to drink to be indiscreet,' said Stephanie, scooping her hair from her face and lacing her hands behind her head. 'I'm sure John's had the odd fling. When I first suspected I felt hurt and angry of course. But I decided not to challenge him, but to wait and see. Like an experiment. I studied his behaviour. And guess what, he was less grumpy when he was home. More relaxed. Brought me flowers. Hardly ever wanted sex, which suited me.'

Amanda rested her knife on the oozing wedge of Brie. She felt the slight resistance as it sank through the creamy softness. She eased the knife sideways and lifted it, then ran her finger along the blade, gathering the sliver of cheese into a curl soft enough to lick from her hand. 'Sorry,' she said. 'It's runnier than I thought.'

'But would you know if he was getting serious with his — what would you say, girlfriend, lover, mistress?' Juliet asked Stephanie. 'It's one thing to turn a blind eye and enjoy the flowers. But you wouldn't want him to leave you for her, would you?'

'No, I suppose not,' said Stephanie. 'If only for the children's sake. Even though they're grown up now. But not just that. I guess we rub along OK. You get a kind of patina after decades of marriage, don't you? Like an omelette pan. Things don't stick. It's easier to look after.'

Juliet persisted. 'Still leaves the question how you'd know if it was serious. Why did you suspect anyway?'

Stephanie took a peach from the bowl and cupped it in her hand, rubbing her thumb over the velvet skin. 'Background noise. He came back late a few times and was a bit evasive. I noticed a trace of lipstick by his mouth, almost but not quite wiped off. One evening he smelt of Miss Dior, which I never wear. Men are pretty hopeless at this sort of thing. But it never got beyond that. No-one else with anything indiscreet to share? Confessions with a window-cleaner?'

'If I thought Ron was having an affair I'd tear him limb from limb,' said Juliet. 'I've kept to the straight and narrow so I expect him to have done the same. No sign that he hasn't. Barbara?'

Barbara shrugged. 'Not that I've noticed. Not sure how bothered I'd be, to be honest. Hard to predict. I'd take him to the cleaners if he wanted to divorce me though. Maybe it would turn out to be a good thing. What about you, Amanda?'

'Hugh and I seem to work as well as ever. Could be because he's in London all week. No sign of any affairs that I've seen. We always enjoy our weekends and holidays.'

'You're so inscrutable, Amanda,' said Stephanie. 'A dark horse. But you seem happy enough.'

No one else seemed inclined to be indiscreet and the discussion lapsed into a lazy silence. Amanda made coffee and lit a couple of candles.

'I meant to say,' Barbara said to her, 'the garden's looking lovely. Did you get that hunky gardener chap I mentioned?'

'He came for a few weeks to get it back on track,' said Amanda smoothly, 'then I found another agency. Hugh doesn't like me to pay cash.'

*

On the day of her fourth clean at Whiteacre, the house was empty when Leonie arrived at her scheduled time of noon. As she let herself in her phone chimed with an email from the European Court of Justice confirming that her application to tender as a freelance translator had been accepted and requesting evidence of her academic and professional qualifications by a somewhat distant deadline. If those were in order, she would be sent a French legal passage some weeks later to translate by an even more distant deadline. Good. The process was, as she'd been warned, clearly slow and ponderous, but it would chug along and hopefully give her a get-out if she needed one at any point, or when she'd had enough.

Leonie switched her thoughts back to her current job and remembered that she was supposed to change the bedding in the main bedroom on Fridays. She felt voyeuristic, even prurient, as she peeled back the double duvet. Again, the tell-tale quasi-watermarks stippling the sheet. She stripped everything off and took it down to the utility room, then started in the kitchen which, as on her previous clean, was cluttered with the residue of what looked to have been a good evening. Hadn't Amanda's regular cleaner said there was never much to do on a Friday? Maybe Amanda's life had only recently become this interesting.

Another piece of the puzzle. Perhaps she could reconstruct Amanda's evening by deconstructing the culinary flotsam.

There was nothing on the breakfast table or on the more formal claw-footed one in the dining room, but there was a Weber barbecue among the teak garden furniture on the terrace. And an ash-tray on the bench.

She knew how much Hugh hated smoking. Even if he hadn't, as usual, spent the week in London, Amanda clearly hadn't been cooking for her husband. Or perhaps her non-husband had been cooking for her? Leonie somehow couldn't see the elegant, perfectly coiffed Amanda wielding tongs over raw flames.

She brought the ash-tray in and threw out the stubs. Gauloises unfiltered. Then set about the kitchen. One beer glass. Two lager bottles in the recycling bag in the utility room. How would Amanda explain the bottles to Hugh, who as far as Leonie was aware never drank beer? Would she say she offered some to workmen if they'd done a good job? Hugh had made it sound as though the work on the house was largely finished, but a garden of this size must need a lot of upkeep; perhaps the lager was for the gardener after a hot afternoon's digging.

Leonie dragged her thoughts back to the cleaning. One large shallow glass dish with a tideline of oil and crushed garlic. The stunning salad bowl, with feathery shards of fennel caught in the dribble of dressing. The copper sauté pan soaking again, this time with a scum suggesting ratatouille. A stainless-steel pot with the faint rust of fine soil that new potatoes, however well scrubbed, always left in their wake. A plate scattered with cherry stones and stalks. Three wine glasses, one puddled with white and two with red lees. A half-empty bottle of Cloudy Bay in the fridge, a rather more empty bottle of St Julien with the recycling. Two espresso cups stained with dark powdery shadows, a bright smear of lipstick on one rim. Another good evening by the look of it. But who with?

After clearing up the kitchen, Leonie transferred the bedding to the tumble drier and ironed the clothes that she found in the utility room under a note from Amanda. Mainly Hugh's casual shirts and trousers. It was strange pressing the unfamiliar, non-London wear. How many polo shirts could one man have?

It was after five when Amanda let herself in. Leonie explained that she'd arrived late because of a delayed train and was making up the time. She'd used the extra hour to do additional jobs on top of her already thorough general blitzing: she polished the silver candlesticks, cleaned the ovens and waxed the breakfast table now that Amanda had replaced the jar. Leonie thought Amanda looked pleased and impressed, and crossed her fingers.

*

Amanda heard the front door open and went into the hall to greet Hugh. His crumpled jacket was draped over his arm, his shirt limp and sweaty.

'Hot and sticky train ride, and indeed walk from the station,' he explained, and headed upstairs. He came down ten minutes later, damp-haired and rosy from the shower, the waft of tea-tree oil and mint echoing the freshness of his crisply ironed polo shirt and jeans. Amanda mixed him a gin and tonic and he revived further. 'Thanks,' he said. 'Sorry. Tough week. With any luck, everyone will bugger off for August and I can catch up on some outstanding stuff. How's your week been?'

'OK,' she said. 'Nothing new. Oh, except a new cleaner, I hope. The girl who's just been covering is brilliant. She's even done my copper pans. I don't think the house has ever been so clean. I'm going to ask if she can replace Judy or whatever she's called.'

Hugh peered vaguely around the kitchen and breakfast room. 'It all looks great.' Amanda rolled her eyes behind his back. She was sure he hadn't noticed any difference, but then she hadn't expected him to. She looked around with a contented smile at the spotless hob, the glow of the recently waxed table, the gleaming coffee machine. She paused and bit her lip. Should she have offered the cleaner a cup of coffee? Or invited her to help herself? Probably she should have done; she must remember in future. She hadn't thought about that in her recent epiphany concerning workmen and gardeners. One gardener in particular.

Hugh's gaze moved to the picture window overlooking the terrace. As if reading her mind he said, 'Garden's looking lovely I must say. Is it still that gardener chappie I met at Easter?'

Amanda turned away to top up her glass of wine and flip over the chicken breasts she was marinading. 'Yes. He's very good.'

Hugh cut another slice of lemon to add to his drink. 'Lethal edge to this knife. Did the cleaner sharpen the knives too?'

Amanda opened her mouth to say no, Simon had done it, then closed it again. Must be careful — even to say the gardener had done it would seem odd. 'Yes, she seems to be able to turn her hand to everything.'

Hugh stifled a yawn and took another mouthful of gin and tonic. 'A true polymath,' he said and pulled his work phone out of his pocket.

*

Leonie's attention to detail and surreptitious overtime at Whiteacre paid off. She was covering for another cleaner on the Monday after her second week there when Cathy texted her to ask her to drop into the office when she'd finished.

'Mrs Standing called me this morning,' Cathy said. 'She's so impressed with the thoroughness of your cleaning that she's asked whether you could start as her regular cleaner. How do you feel about that?'

Hoping she was hiding her feelings of achievement and triumph, if not the snag of guilt about Judy, Leonie said 'Well, that's very gratifying. It's a beautiful house and a pleasure to clean. I'd be happy to become the regular cleaner. But what about Judy?'

'I've already spoken to her. To be honest, she's not bothered where we send her as long as she gets the hours she needs. There's plenty of work around, especially over the summer. And Nightjars Holt isn't ideal for her on days when her husband has the car.'

Leonie let out a deep breath of relief. 'OK, great. When would A — Mrs Standing like me to start?'

'I explained that we couldn't organise today but she said it didn't matter as you'd left the house so clean on Friday. I did say you might be able to fit it in tomorrow but it seems Tuesday and Thursday afternoons aren't convenient for her. You've got two jobs scheduled already for Wednesday, so we agreed that you'd start on Friday and do an extra hour. Noon to five, I hope that's OK?'

For the second time since the genesis of the Cleaning Plan, Leonie resisted the urge to punch the air. It was more than OK!

*

Amanda had tried to forget her conversation with Simon about leaving Hugh. Divorce was inextricably linked in her mind with a rapid descent from wealth to poverty — a horrible echo of her childhood.

But Simon raised the topic again a couple of weeks later, this time when they were in bed, relaxed and sated and with a glass of post-coital wine each.

'I was just thinking about what you said,' he started. 'My sister divorced her husband, and it was the same story — they had to sell the house and she got half and not much else, but she's fine now, no regrets. Got a new man, she's a lot happier.'

Amanda shivered. 'My sister got divorced also,' she said, her voice as brittle as tinder. 'As I said. Her husband was very rich but she didn't end up with much at all. She's had Before, After and Before again. I just couldn't.'

*

Tina was in luck: she had another cover clean. August was turning out to be a good month. Wicked even, as Peter would say. Though she supposed she was wicked in the old sense, stealing stuff for Finn. She chewed her lip. She didn't like doing it but she still needed the extra money. She tried to put her discomfort out of her mind for the moment. As usual.

The house, also in Nightjars Holt, looked promising. Not as vast as some of the mansions so the cleaning shouldn't take her the full four hours. But even better was the level of untidiness. Tina was used to children's and teenagers' bedrooms looking like TV pictures of scenes after a tornado or something, and often the owners left the kitchen in a state of chaos for the cleaner to sort, but the reception rooms and home office — there was usually a home office in these huge properties — were mostly better organised. With papers locked away in desk drawers or a filing cabinet. Or already shredded.

But here, delightfully, there was no tidiness, no organisation. Tina decided to search as she cleaned. She started at the top as usual and worked down from the home cinema in the converted loft through bedrooms and bathrooms and dressing rooms in various states of disarray, a living room, dining room, kitchen-cum-breakfast room, utility room. No home office though. And no recycling bins or boxes except for the food-waste caddy under the kitchen sink and a small paper bag on the counter stuffed with a few torn envelopes, crumpled till receipts and junk mail.

The recycling bin must be in the garage as Tina hadn't noticed it outside the house. Handier for searching if it was out of view. There were two garages. Both were locked but the neatly labelled keys were helpfully hanging in the utility room. The first garage housed a vintage car, shiny green with a soft top and spotless windows, and not much else. According to the disc on the front of the bonnet, the car was a Lotus. The house was called The Lotus Garden, which Tina had thought was as poncy as most of the names round here, but she'd assumed it was something to do with the flower.

She moved on to the other garage, which was larger and had been converted into what looked like a practice room for a band — a drum kit, keyboards, guitars, speakers, microphones and goodness knows what other bits of kit. And a door in the interior partition wall — heavily sound-proofed, she noticed — leading into a home office.

Tina opened the door and blinked at the unexpected brightness. The practice room had no natural light, but here a generous picture window, with bars on the outside, framed a view of a patio, striped lawn and lots of flowers. Funny how such untidy people could have such a neat garden. She supposed they just left it to the gardener. Everyone round here seemed to have a gardener as well as a cleaner. Luckily there was no sign of him or her or anyone else out there today. Tina took out her duster and cleaning spray in case the owners came home — her instructions had been vague and general and she could probably get away with cleaning the office since the keys were so visible, though she would prefer not to have to — and started a rapid search of the desk. As expected, it was littered with jumbled piles of papers. And the drawers were unlocked. The room dimmed as a cloud rolled over the sun and Tina turned on the convenient desk lamp and took out her phone.

Ten

August

Simon arrived at The Lotus Garden on his bike, having made his usual arrangement to use the garden tools kept at the property. He found the name surprising given that there wasn't a water lily to be seen; he assumed it must be historic, though there were no obvious traces of a former pond.

The owners had been ecstatic the first time he'd mown the lawn into neat stripes; in fact he thought that might have been why they'd kept him on after his trial session. Later, after he'd looked through the ground-floor windows on a day when he was reasonably confident there was no one home, he'd been surprised: he'd assumed they'd like neatness inside as well as out, but the rooms he could see were untidy and cluttered. Including what looked like the home office at the back of one of the garages.

He leaned his bike behind the smallest shed, fetched a trowel, small fork, secateurs and a bag for the waste and started at the back of the garden. He'd do the mowing at the end after the routine weeding and trimming.

Simon came round from behind the rhododendrons which screened the sheds and compost heaps from the house. He was pushing the silent mower. One of the benefits of gardening was that most of the time it was quiet work. He enjoyed the birdsong — so different from the African soundtrack — and the mental space to think and plan.

As he turned to face the patio and leaned forward to pull the starter cord, he noticed a flicker of light and movement behind the barred window in the garage office. One of the owners no doubt, though he'd barely seen them after his trial session. He tugged the cord and the motor whirred into life. The light in the garage went out immediately and a shadow moved rapidly out of his view. It seemed unlikely to be a burglar — Simon had some knowledge of their habits — but he supposed he should check. He killed the motor and jogged through the gate beside the garage and into the drive, where there was a small Peugeot which he hadn't noticed on previous occasions. The front door opened and a woman stepped out backwards, pulled it shut and triple-locked it with some fumbling as though she was unfamiliar with the keys. Or in a hurry. She turned towards the Peugeot and stopped, one foot on the doorstep and one on the gravel, when she saw Simon.

'Who are you?' they said in unison.

'I'm the gardener,' said Simon as the woman said 'I'm the cleaner'.

'I thought you might be a burglar,' said Simon. 'I haven't seen you here before.'

'I'm just covering for the regular cleaner,' said the woman. 'She's on holiday.'

She ducked into her Peugeot, twisted the key in the ignition and accelerated out of the drive.

Simon walked back to the garden and mowed the lawn, reflecting. It must have been her in the garage but she'd been very quick to get out of there when she heard the motor and equally quick to drive off after they'd spoken. He assumed the regular cleaner also came on Wednesdays. He'd never seen her in the garage but come to that he'd never noticed her elsewhere in the house. Maybe she cleaned the ground floor after he'd finished in the garden.

Depending on the length of the regular cleaner's holiday, the woman might be back on the following Wednesday. Perhaps he would stay hidden if so. If she went back into the garage office and he was careful, he might be able to see what she was doing. He had a hunch that it wasn't cleaning. But if it was what he thought it was, she could be very useful to him.

*

Leonie rang the bell and, after waiting a minute or two, let herself in. To her surprise the burglar alarm didn't bleep; instead, Amanda's heels clicked down the stairs.

'I'm sorry, Mrs Standing,' Leonie said. 'I did ring, but when there was no answer I assumed you were out. I would have waited if your car had been here.'

'That's all right. I was up in my office and don't always hear the bell, and even if I do it takes a while to get down. My car's still in the yard. I'm going out now, I won't be back till late afternoon. Oh, sorry, wait —'

Amanda paused, frowned and turned towards the kitchen, gesturing to Leonie to follow. 'Um, do feel free, if you want a tea. Or a coffee.' She waved vaguely towards a cupboard, then reached into the one next to it and pulled out a packet of Duchy Organic biscuits which she put on the counter. 'So … please, help yourself.' She gave Leonie a tense smile, trotted out of the room, put her handbag on the hall table and disappeared into the loo beyond the cloakroom.

Leonie was puzzling over Amanda's uncharacteristic hesitation, almost embarrassment, when she felt her phone, tucked into a back pocket of her jeans, vibrate, remembered Amanda's secret phone and took an instant decision. On the past couple of occasions when Amanda left the house after Leonie arrived, she'd spent a good few minutes behind the locked door before leaving, doubtless touching up her hair and make-up. And the table wouldn't be in her direct line of sight until she came right out into the hall. Moving swiftly and silently, Leonie opened the soft leather bag and saw the iPhone with the Marimekko cover. She thought for a moment, started a rapid search of the several zipped compartments and found the secret iPhone in the second one. She made a mental note of the model, closed the zip and almost ran into the utility room to pick up her kit.

Leonie decided to clean from the top of the house. She headed straight up to Amanda's office and looked longingly at the Mac. She had been pondering likely passwords and had a few obvious ones to try first — Whiteacre, Amanda, Hugh's birthdate. If none of those worked, she'd need to find out Amanda's birthdate, which should be possible though she wasn't sure how. And if that didn't work, she had no idea where to go next.

Although she'd resolved not to try to get into the computer until Amanda left, Leonie couldn't resist touching the mouse. And recoiled with a hastily stifled squawk of shock when the screen flared into life with no password request.

Thankful that she had a MacBook Air and so knew how to navigate, Leonie opened System Preferences / Security & Privacy. 'Require password for sleep and screen saver' was set for 'after 15 minutes'. She must have just squeaked in. She paused, tempted to sit down at the keyboard immediately. But Amanda, if she was still in the house, might wonder what

Leonie was cleaning so quietly, so, after jiggling the mouse again, she turned the water in the corner basin on full blast and gave the taps a noisy and unnecessary scrub. She then raced downstairs, checked that Amanda had gone, lugged the hoover up to the top as fast as she could and settled in a chair in front of the Mac. At last, the chance to find out more about her ex-lover's wife. And possibly even about her ex-lover's wife's lover.

Leonie opened the email app and skimmed the messages in the inbox. They fell into two categories: routine communications about pending orders, deliveries and the like, and correspondence with friends and family, or at least Hugh's family on the basis of the names, mainly about social arrangements. She searched for emails to or from Hugh but found nothing other than a couple of exchanges with someone called Gillian Hughes. She assumed that Hugh and Amanda communicated by texting; certainly he had preferred to do so with her. Leonie cancelled the search.

She then ran down the titles of Amanda's mailbox folders. Accounts and memberships, Banks and finance, Car, Council Tax, Family, Health, Insurance, Internet, Phones, Receipts and guarantees, Travel, Utilities, Whiteacre. Nothing financial apart from the banking folder — no doubt Hugh dealt with anything like investments, tax and wills, leaving Amanda to manage the day-to-day household finances.

Leonie wondered what 'Family' covered. She knew about Hugh's parents and brothers but nothing about Amanda's background. She opened the folder. It contained two emails from Gold Star Private Investigators. The first was a brief acknowledgment of instructions and confirmation of estimated cost of research. The second, also laconic, indicated that the firm had completed its investigation and was attaching its full report, relevant press cuttings and a final invoice.

Leonie opened the first press cutting. *Tragedy strikes idyllic Hampstead family* flashed across the screen. *Loving husband and father hangs himself after bankruptcy.* She gasped. Conscious that time was moving on, she made another instant decision and forwarded the email to herself. Then she deleted the item from the Sent folder, exited the email app and started cleaning. Perhaps Amanda hadn't always had it so easy.

*

Exactly one week after he'd spotted the cover cleaner, Simon arrived at The Lotus Garden earlier than usual. There were no cars in the drive and the side gate and sheds were unlocked; presumably the owners were out and the cleaner not yet here. He'd driven rather than cycled this time. Parking was a problem as the street was reserved for residents and visitors, and he thought he might not be the sort of visitor the council had in mind. He'd booked a two-hour slot in the nearest car park he could find online, advertised as three minutes away. Which probably meant one minute for a brisk walker.

Simon started some very quiet and barely necessary weeding in one of the borders near the house, screened by a flourishing hypericum. Annoying that he couldn't smoke while he waited, but if his suspicions were right he thought the cover cleaner, if it was her, might do a cursory check of the garden to see whether he was here again. He assumed that she hadn't arrived yet given the absence of cars, but even if he had a cigarette now, the smell could linger.

An hour later he heard a small petrol engine come into the drive and scrunch to a gravelly halt. The motor stopped and a car door closed, followed by the sound of a heavier door latching shut. Hoping that the regular cleaner was still away, Simon waited, still and silent. Every ten minutes or so he snuck a quick peek at the rear garage window. He'd brought his binoculars. They were old and heavy, dating from his time as a game warden back in the day, but they had good magnification and focus and still worked fine.

After another hour his patience was rewarded. He heard the muffled scrape of a lock turning and the creak of a door opening. No sound of footsteps on the patio though; perhaps she was just poking her head out to check that the coast was clear. Or so she must have thought, as the door closed and the lock turned again. Probably one of the French windows which gave onto the terrace from what had looked like a living room. Simon had been sitting on a folded sack so his watch hadn't been intolerably uncomfortable, and he'd broken his position with his periodic checks, but he was still glad when he finally saw the light in the home office come on. He edged round the shrub until he was shielded by the neighbouring spiraea, which was conveniently less dense but would hopefully provide enough of a screen to make him near-invisible in his drab gardening gear.

The woman — it was the same one — was undoubtedly sorting through papers and taking photos with her phone.

Simon watched until she turned off the light and moved away from the window. He then slipped out of the side gate and onto the street and jogged the — yes, less than a minute — to his van and drove back. He thought he remembered the Peugeot turning left as it exited the drive the previous week, so waited a couple of hundred yards up the road, his engine idling. A few minutes later the car nosed onto the street and headed off at a less agitated pace than before. Simon followed at a discreet distance until the woman parked on the street outside a Victorian terraced house which looked as though it had been converted into flats and let herself in. A couple of minutes later he saw a glimmer of light in the first-floor bay window as if the door had been opened from a brightly lit stairwell, followed by a glimpse of a woman shrugging off her coat. After a brief wait — a lot of waiting around today — he walked softly to the front door and checked the names on the three-tiered bell panel. The middle one was C. Taylor.

*

Simon went back to The Lotus Garden, did some rather more visible gardening, put away the tools and drove back to Worthy Lane carpark. After further reflection and a couple of pints at the Wykeham Arms, he decided that he needed more evidence of what he suspected C. Taylor was doing before he confronted her. One way or another, someone who could get into a house under false pretences and take photos of what was presumably personal data or inside information could be very useful. He already had an idea about how.

Early the following morning, he drove back to her flat, parked a couple of houses upstream and sat waiting and watching, an old cap he kept in the van pulled down over his forehead. Again, his years as a game warden had prepared him well. Transported back by the thought, he found his African playlist and whiled away a good hour, in both senses, listening to Ladysmith Black Mambazo, Johnny Clegg and Hugh Masekela at an uncharacteristically low volume.

He heard the playlist two or three times before he had to call off his trail and go to that afternoon's gardening job. By then he'd followed C. Taylor to two houses where he assumed she was cleaning, one large and affluent where she spent three hours and the other more modest on both counts. He did the same the next morning and added a couple more of her clients' addresses to his list, both at the large and affluent end of the spectrum this time. A week and two more reconnaissance sessions later there were seven on the list. It was a pity that none of the houses were on his gardening roster. He'd seen no sign of gardeners coming or going at the five larger ones while he waited up the street, and wondered whether he should drop his flyer through the letterboxes. On the other hand, he didn't really want to take on another big job. Or at least not another big gardening job. He had, though, observed from his slow drive past that the rear of one house was accessible; the others all had high gates which he assumed were locked. But how to intercept C. Taylor at her 'work', catch her red-handed without risk to himself?

The solution came to him as he sat, exactly a week after he'd hatched step one of what was then an unfinished plan, reflecting over a couple of pints at the Wykeham Arms. Simon knew most of the bar staff by sight and some by name. Susan was serving that evening. She was — what did the French so chivalrously call it? — a woman of a certain age. She was pulling a pint for a guy in his twenties. After he'd paid and was out of earshot, she said to one of the others behind the bar — Jamie, Simon thought — 'You know, he had no idea that I'd served him his first pint. I knew what he wanted but he clearly had no recollection of me, even though it was only half an hour ago. Women of my age are invisible half the time.'

'You're probably right,' said Jamie. 'You should turn it to your advantage. You could get away with murder if you played your cards right.'

Women of a certain age. Cleaners. Gardeners. Moving below most people's radar. It was risky, even daring, but Simon wasn't afraid of risk. And in any event the risk could be minimised. He had a cover story.

*

L eonie opened Gold Star Private Investigators' report.

Date: 23 January 2022
Client: Mrs Amanda Standing
Subject of investigation: Client's father Arthur Ernest Sedgwick 4 April 1932 - 2 July 1986, in particular his business activities and death.

Mrs Standing instructed us on 30 September 2021 and provided the following agreed statement as the basis for our investigation:

"My mother died of lung cancer on 16 September 1991. I always wondered about my father's background and death but when I asked she would never tell me more than that his business had crashed, he'd hanged himself and she'd found the body. I was thirteen at the time and of course remember those events. Shortly before my mother died, when she was in hospital on morphine, she said some things that have always troubled me. Things like 'He meant well but got in too deep', 'We always wanted the best for you and Jen', 'He couldn't resist', 'They killed him.' I've lived with the uncertainty but decided on the thirtieth anniversary of her death that I wanted to learn more about my father's business and the circumstances of his death. I understand that your investigation may turn up information I would prefer not to know and instruct you to proceed on that basis."

Sources

We have collected information from two primary sources. First, the attached newspaper articles were discovered in the British Newspaper Archive. Second, we have spoken to a number of persons with direct or second-hand knowledge or recollections of Arthur Sedgwick. You will appreciate that, given the delicacy of the subject matter, our investigators needed considerable time not only to track down these persons but also to build sufficient trust for them to divulge sensitive information. Most spoke only on condition of anonymity, hence we are unable to provide further details of identity.

Report

Arthur Ernest Sedgwick ("Arthur") was born on 4 April 1932 in Leyton, East London. His father, Albert, ran a small pawnbroking business, also in Leyton, which Arthur took over in 1961 when his father died. Previously, Arthur had worked as a van driver for a furniture outlet.

Sedgwick Pawnbrokers ("SP") had struggled to turn a profit under Albert but began to prosper under Arthur. By 1970 SP specialised in watches and jewellery and Arthur had built up a good reputation for his knowledge of diamonds in particular. In 1977 SP acquired and moved into more secure premises on the Holloway Road and Arthur bought a large house on Church Row, Hampstead where he lived with his wife Gladys and two daughters Jennifer (7) and Amanda (4). There was reportedly some surprise among those who knew Arthur that he could afford both moves, and speculation about the source of his sudden wealth. Rumours circulated about a connection with the notorious unsolved so-called 'Diamonds are Forever' heist in 1972, when millions of pounds worth of jewellery, including a number of exceptionally high-value diamonds, were stolen in a daring raid on a high-end Bond Street jewellers. Suggestions have been made that Arthur had been quietly providing 'diamond-laundering' services through SP, including to the Leyton-based Stone Dead gang who were suspected of involvement in the 1972 raid.

Arthur's extravagant lifestyle, apparently funded by the increasingly profitable SP, continued until the senior partner of Lewis & Mint, the firm that audited SP's accounts, died and the partner who had taken over the audit alerted the authorities to alleged fraud. Criminal charges were laid against Arthur and his fellow director John Claymore, who is thought to have fled the country and was never found. SP filed for insolvency and Arthur, who like many directors of private companies had given personal guarantees and mortgaged the family home to secure ever more injections of cash, declared himself bankrupt. Two weeks later, on 2 July 1986, Gladys discovered his body in one of the garages of the Church Row house.

We were unable to obtain copies of the police report into Arthur's death. You will be aware that the verdict at the coroner's inquest was death by suicide. However, our investigators have picked up rumours and speculation that this was not the case. The word on the street at the time was that Arthur had tried to double-cross the Stone Dead gang. There were various theories about how he did this, most involved Arthur undervaluing one or more of the 'Diamonds are Forever' diamonds and/or recording them in SP's books as pawned and redeemed. It is probable that he had been doing this on a smaller scale for many years.

There were further rumours that his death was not suicide but that he had died at the hands of the Stone Dead gang, probably by strangulation by their so-called executioner 'The Candle', who would then have rigged the hanging scenario with assistance from another gang member.

Jesus. Leonie let out a long breath before turning to the press articles. Most offered essentially the same tale as Gold Star, embellished with numerous adjectives, adverbs, superlatives and exclamation marks. The latest one however, presumably included as additional interest since it was not strictly within the terms of Gold Star's instructions, provided some information on what had happened to the family after Arthur's death:

Hampstead News 19 September 1991
We have learned with sadness of the death from lung cancer on 16 September of Gladys Sedgwick, who formerly lived on Church Row, Hampstead.
Attentive readers may recall the terrible tragedy that befell the Sedgwick family five years ago when Arthur Sedgwick's pawn-broking company went bust after auditors reportedly found evidence of accounting fraud. Arthur was bankrupted and died by his own hand shortly after. He left a widow, Gladys, and two daughters, Jennifer (16) and Amanda (13).
Gladys moved with the girls to a two-bedroom rental in Clapton, a dramatic fall from residential grace — a fairy-tale castle to a slum tenement.

Leonie snorted. How London postcodes change.

Gladys, who had never worked since she married Arthur in 1969, although there are rumours that she may have worked as a char or cleaner before then, found employment at a travel agent in neighbouring Stoke Newington. Jennifer has taken over her job, while Amanda is studying for a BA in Interior Design at Kingston Polytechnic. We offer them our sincere condolences and wish them all the best.

Leonie poured herself a glass of wine and sat in her living room in Clapton, looking out over the gentrified and expensive Victorian terrace opposite. Amanda was not, then, all she seemed. Her childhood and education torn in two by that over-used word 'tragedy'. Amanda always seemed so serene, so controlled, so socially at ease, but perhaps that was a veneer. Her past must have left deep scars. She'd been rich, then penniless and was now rich again, thanks to Hugh. But she must have had to relearn, or more likely learn from scratch if she'd only been thirteen when it happened, how to be wealthy and glamorous. A challenge that most people would relish, but nonetheless it must have its stresses.

And it couldn't be easy being married to a serial philanderer, however charming, rich and generous. Whether or not she knew about the philandering. In all fairness Amanda had earned her bit on the side. Though Leonie would still very much like to know who he was.

Eleven

September

'Ah, Whiteacre,' said Cathy. 'Yes, we've cleaned that house for years. Since it was refurbed enough to clean. Frances did it for a while I think, then Judy. And now Jane's taken over; I think she asked Judy if she could cover for her holiday and they kept her on. Why are you interested?'

Brenda mentally slapped herself. She hadn't thought of a cover — ha — story and could hardly tell Cathy that she wanted to find out the name of the wife so she could try and blackmail her. She remembered a character in a film saying it was best to stick as much as possible to the truth if you were lying about something. 'I saw it one day from the top of the Castle — I mean Brambles — and thought the garden looked lovely. I just wondered.'

Brenda poured herself a coffee and took a croissant from the Monday morning offerings. She vaguely remembered Jane from a few months back, when Brenda had been in the office to pick up the keys for one of her cover jobs and Jane had come in to finalise her paperwork. Dark hair, older than her, well spoken. She hadn't seen her since. Maybe she came in on Friday afternoons for tea and cake. In fact now she thought about it, their first meeting might have been over cake. That was harder for Brenda as it was around the time she picked the kids up from school but she could try asking one of the other mums to do it this Friday. She worked out who owed her and sent a text.

*

Leonie hadn't got to know many of the other cleaners, though she'd chatted to a few over a Friday afternoon cup of tea. She was trying to disguise her discomfiture as Tina, who she remembered meeting when she'd come into the New Brooms office to sign her contract, asked friendly question after friendly question about her background. Leonie was worried she might sink too deep into the rabbit hole of her semi-fictional past and forget what she'd said, and was making a mental note to remember to jot down today's version when they were interrupted by the woman Tina had introduced her to on the same occasion. Belinda? Barbara?

'Hi Jane, Tina. I'm Brenda,' the woman said helpfully. 'We met just when you were starting here, didn't we, Jane?'

The three chatted idly. Tina glanced at her watch and said she had to go. Once she'd left, Brenda said, 'That's a shame, I was going to suggest we could all go for a coffee or maybe a drink. Not now, I have to go soon also, but maybe one day next week? It would be nice to get to know each other better, compare notes, you know.'

'Good idea,' said Leonie. 'It can be a bit solitary, cleaning, can't it? But coffee's difficult for me — I live in London and don't normally get to Winchester till late morning so I can get the cheapest ticket. Let's meet for a drink early evening one day next week.'

Brenda sounded relieved to discover that Leonie's — mustn't forget I'm Jane though — 'early evening' could be stretched to include five o'clock and they agreed to meet at a pub Brenda knew, the William Walker, on Tuesday.

*

Brenda picked the kids up from school, gave them some milk and biscuits and promised pizza later. It was easier now Tommy was twelve; he was a sensible boy — well, as sensible as boys ever were — and she felt OK leaving him with ten-year-old Lily. Thank goodness for mobile phones and eBay, and she wouldn't be far. She wasn't a big drinker these days — couldn't spare the cash apart from anything else — so she took the car. Easier for the return journey with the pizzas. And if she had to dash back for an emergency.

She found Jane waiting at one of the tables, a large glass of white wine in front of her.

'Hi,' said Jane. 'I just got here. What would you like?'

Jane fetched Brenda a small glass of house white and a packet of cheese and onion crisps and they sipped their drinks in an expectant silence.

Brenda thought she'd better start the ball rolling as it had been her idea to meet. 'How are you finding the job?' she asked.

'Actually,' said Jane, 'I'm enjoying it. It's new for me. Before, I was —' She stopped mid-sentence and frowned. 'Er, before, I was working as a secretary. In a law firm in London. But they got rid of a load of us. All the firms are, probably other professions also. Everyone does their own typing now and sets up their own meetings and so on.'

'Yes, that happened to Tina also,' said Brenda. 'But why cleaning, and why Winchester?'

'My parents used to live here,' said Jane. She reddened

slightly. 'I don't know the city well because we moved when I was still a child but I always wanted to come back. So I thought I'd check it out and maybe move here. And the cleaning? I was trying to think of something I could do that would be a change. Flexible hours, no office, no sitting at a desk. Thought I'd give it a try.' She shrugged and drank some more wine.

'I clean one of those huge houses in Nightjars Holt,' said Brenda. 'It's an amazing area, the houses are all like castles or mansions. Do you know it?'

'Yes, I clean a couple of the houses there. They're like something out of a fairy tale aren't they?'

'I call one of mine The Castle House. Its real name is Brambles but that sounds like a bungalow or something.'

'One of mine's called Whiteacre. I've just started as their regular cleaner actually.'

'That's a weird name,' said Brenda. 'I've never come across it before.'

'It's a bit of a legal joke. When you study land law, when an exam question or example uses one house it's always called Blackacre. Like, "A is purchasing Blackacre from B but wants to know whether his neighbour has a right of way across his lawn". If there are two houses, the second is always called Whiteacre.'

Brenda narrowed her eyes, her head tilted. 'Are they lawyers then, the owners?'

Jane flushed again for some reason. 'Er, I think the husband might be.'

'It makes for a good story. We could check. What's his name?'

Jane looked down at the table. 'I don't know his first name, or hers. But the surname's Standing.'

Waiting in Domino's for three pizzas, Brenda wondered about Jane. It was almost as though she'd been hiding something.

Why was she cleaning in Winchester? Her explanation hadn't been entirely convincing. And why was she reluctant to talk about the owners of Whiteacre? She'd trotted out the meaning of the name readily enough but then dried up.

Brenda took the pizzas. She'd glanced at the menu at the pub while Jane was at the bar. Too pricey by far for her. How the other half lived. She'd seen the contents of the fridges in some of the houses she cleaned and the remnants of what were clearly extravagant dinner and lunch parties. And the stuff that was thrown out … Some owners didn't even bother to use the food recycling caddy, just put it in the normal bin. Once Brenda had taken half a loaf that looked fine even though the 'best before' date had passed; another time she'd retrieved a box of six eggs that had apparently been chucked — though not actually chucked, luckily for her — for the same reason. She didn't like to do it too often in case it was noticed, but in some houses her duties included putting the household rubbish in the dustbin and if the owners were out she felt safe going through it first.

She mentally shook herself; the pizzas would be getting cold. And they weren't brilliant at the best of times. She sighed and headed home.

Later, after she'd cleared away, Brenda tracked down the mysterious Mr Standing via Google. She'd trawled fruitlessly through a page of hits about 'good standing', 'standing counsel' and 'academic standing' before deciding to click instead on 'Images for solicitor standing', where she found him; at least she assumed it must be him. Hugh Standing, partner and head of private clients at Mainwaring & Cox, a London firm. Commuter then. Good-looking guy, around the fifty mark she reckoned. She wondered what private clients were — weren't all clients private? Google helpfully led her to an explanation: 'Private clients are usually very rich and high net worth individuals or landowners who hold massive amounts of properties and other assets.' Brenda imagined their solicitors might also be very rich and hold massive amounts of assets. Which their wives would presumably have access to. Time to get her thinking cap on, as her mum used to say.

*

Tina finished her clean, put the kit away and shrugged on her coat and bag. She waved the fob over the burglar alarm, let herself out and turned towards her car. As she did so, a man came through the gate from the garden. He looked vaguely familiar, and she realised he was the same person she'd seen the previous week at The Lotus Garden.

'You're not the gardener here,' she said. 'I've seen him. He's older.' And less hot.

'I'm just covering for the regular gardener,' said the man smoothly. 'He's on holiday. And we need to talk, Ms Taylor.'

'What ab—' Tina broke off. 'How do you know my name?'

'Because I followed you to your flat. I know your name and where you live.'

'You're a fucking stalker is what you are.' Tina fumbled in her bag and pulled out her phone. 'Just you wait till the police hear about this.'

'I don't think it would be wise to involve the police. I also know what you do.'

Tina's stomach lurched. 'What do you mean?'

'I think you know what I mean. As you've got your phone out, let's see what you photographed today.'

Tina rammed the phone back in the bag. 'You've got a fucking nerve. You want to see photos of my kid? Is that it, you're a perve, or a paedo?'

'Neither,' said the man. 'I'm interested in your photos for quite another reason.'

Tina felt a tide of panic rise to her throat. She gulped. 'Look,' she said. 'Whoever you are. I don't know what you're talking about. And I can't talk here anyway, the owners will be back any moment.'

'OK, let's go and have a drink. And remember, I know where you live so there's no point shooting off. I'll meet you at the Wykeham Arms in ten, I'm on my bike.'

*

Simon didn't see the point of being in a pub and not having a beer. He sat with his pint, an eye on the main entrance. He wasn't worried that C. Taylor wouldn't show; she probably just wanted to make him wait.

He'd seen no signs of a gardener earlier when he turned up at the house where, if she was on a regular weekly schedule, she should be cleaning that morning. He'd had his cover story ready just in case though. A cover for the cover. He'd brought his old binoculars with him again and if challenged would apologise sincerely — well, apparently sincerely — and respectfully explain that he thought he'd seen a lesser spotted woodpecker fly into the garden and couldn't resist rushing after it. There hadn't even been time to ring on the doorbell in case he lost it. Which sadly he had done.

He'd staked out a spot in a shrubby border, similar to his observation post at The Lotus Garden. He hadn't actually seen much; the home office must be upstairs or at the front. But he had spied the woman take a pile of papers out of the recycling bin at the side of the house and sift through them. She took a couple of photos but didn't look very happy with her haul.

She walked into the pub, glared at Simon and said that as he'd dragged her here he could buy her an orange juice but she didn't know why she was wasting her time. Simon came back with the drink, picked up his pint and gestured beyond the central chimneypiece to the rear of the bar, which was empty.

'I've seen you take photographs of your clients' personal documents,' he opened without preamble. 'And I want to know why.'

The woman bit her lip then sat up straight and said, 'Are you a private detective or something?'

'I'm Steven.' He'd decided not to use his real name; he wasn't sure how this was going to play out but it was best to stay incognito, at least until he did. 'And we're not discussing what I do, but what you do. You're obviously stealing confidential information. Contrary to data privacy legislation. And a criminal offence.'

A blush swept over the woman's face like a tide, then her skin paled as suddenly and completely. Her fingers were trembling even though she tightened her grip on the glass. Her hands were rough and chapped with no jewellery. The cuff of her shirt was worn through at the edge. Her hair was badly cut.

'Shouldn't you caution me or whatever they call it? And what if I want a solicitor?' Her voice quavered.

Simon smothered a laugh. Never before had he been mistaken for a policeman. Or indeed a private detective. Might as well go with the flow. She didn't look as though she made much herself from whatever it was that she was doing. He was counting on her not knowing any solicitors well enough to pick their brains for free and not being able to afford to pay for one; he hoped he was right.

'This is just an informal chat at this stage. We can go down to the station and talk there if you want to be cautioned. I'm not necessarily interested in you, though that would depend.

My information is that there are others involved. I want to know who, and how they recruited you and what, exactly, for.'

Ms Taylor pulled out a tired tissue and blew her nose. She opened her mouth but didn't get beyond a croaked 'I—'. Tears rose in her eyes and she blinked furiously and blew her nose again.

'Finn will kill me,' she said.

*

Tina was trembling violently as she settled herself back in her car and had to stab a couple of times before she could slot the key in the ignition. She saw Steven unchain his bike, swing his leg over the saddle and cycle off. She sat thinking for a few minutes. Was he a policeman? He didn't seem like it somehow, though she'd never actually met a policeman so didn't really know. And hadn't he also said there was no need to involve the police? A private detective seemed more likely, but who would he be working for? She didn't see any way of shaking him off: he knew where she lived and he'd pressured her into giving him her mobile number. She heaved a deep sigh, started the engine and drove home.

Over a mug of strong tea, Tina tried to make a plan. Finn was the problem. If it hadn't been for him she wouldn't be in so deep. Or at all. Tina never asked what he did with the information she fed him and tried not to think too much about it, but it was obvious he must have been selling the bank details and so on. She didn't think he was smart enough to use them himself. He paid her with irregular handfuls of notes, which she felt grubby taking but it was hard to turn down any financial help when things were so tight. She was doing it for Peter, she told herself again. It meant she could give him an allowance, buy him the occasional treat. Not to mention feed his teenage appetite. Sometimes Finn was pleased with what she'd caught on her phone camera, other times he swore.

And now she'd been rumbled. Finn would go ballistic if he knew. And this man — Steven — obviously wanted to shop her, or worse. Perhaps she should talk to a solicitor. But she didn't know any and hadn't got the money to pay for one. Maybe she'd ask Brenda. Not tell her the background of course, she'd have to make up some cover story for why she needed a solicitor. Brenda was good at solving problems, she might have an idea. It had been Brenda after all who'd shown her the New Brooms advert after Tina had been made redundant. And if she hadn't been working for New Brooms she wouldn't have got into this mess in the first place. She texted Brenda and suggested they meet for a coffee the next day.

'There was something I wanted to ask you,' said Tina after they'd sat down with their lattes and caught up with their latest news. 'My brother-in-law — you know, Finn — he's in a spot of trouble with the police. He says it's all a misunderstanding and won't see a solicitor but I think he should at least have a chat with someone. They don't know any lawyers and nor do I. I just wondered whether you might, or have an idea at least? I think if you go and see one without a … connection or whatever, the meter starts running as soon as you open the door.'

Brenda stirred her coffee, her eyes narrowed. 'Probably starts running then even if you do have a connection. But as it happens I do know someone. You know that girl — well, woman, I'd say she had a good few years on us, though she looks good on it. Jane. I think she had her interview the same day as you. I had a chat with her in the office last week, in fact you were talking to her when I arrived now I think about it.

Anyway, we had a quick drink the other day and she said she used to be a secretary for a firm of solicitors.' Brenda paused and frowned, then continued, 'Maybe she knows someone.'

Tina brightened. 'Thanks Brenda, I'll ask her. She sounds quite posh, doesn't she?'

Brenda shrugged. 'I've known a few cleaners who sounded like that. There was one who left before you started. Cathy said once that I'd be surprised how many professional women give it a go if they want something local, with flexible hours. Not that this job's very local for Jane.' She frowned again.

Twelve

September

Simon shoved the garden door shut behind him with unnecessary and uncharacteristic force, which added to his irritation. He was normally careful with mechanical constructs like locks, hinges, handles. But he felt out of sorts this afternoon.

Amanda was away. On holiday in Sicily. With Hugh, of course. Hadn't they only recently come back from the Riviera? Though thinking about it, that had been June. Secret iPhones, steamer chairs, *50 Ways to Leave Your Lover*. Seemed a lifetime ago. Since then, Simon had continued to play the role of gallant lover. Not that that was difficult. He enjoyed their evenings. And, he realised, not just for the sex. Although of course also for the sex. Simon had been solitary for a long time, albeit a solitude peppered with brief encounters. He was in the nearest thing to a relationship that he'd had for many years. He was starting to miss Amanda's company at the weekends. And when she was on holiday with her husband.

He'd decided to work in the orchard that afternoon, picking the apples that were ripe for the plucking, and fetched a couple of trugs. He'd already noticed a few windfalls. He could do with a windfall himself. And he'd thought that Amanda was ripe for the plucking, which would have given him the windfall.

She'd changed the subject when he said he thought he was falling in love with her. Even though the context had been perfect: balmy evening, heady music, just the right amount of good wine. That was something else he enjoyed about their evenings. Courtesy of Hugh, he admitted grudgingly.

And then she'd shied away like a startled horse when, on subsequent occasions, he turned the conversation to leaving Hugh. Again, a perfect context. Both times. But Amanda was adamant.

So was she having second thoughts about her relationship with him? Was she using the holiday to get closer to Hugh? To try and mend their relationship, which clearly needed some attention? Was she having sex with Hugh? He couldn't stomach the thought. Or the thought of losing his opportunity for a comfortable future. An opportunity that he'd worked so hard to foster.

He bit into the apple he'd just picked, but it was sour and hard. His fault for having tugged it from the tree before it was ready. Perhaps he'd done the same with Amanda.

*

On her way home from the Castle House on the Thursday after her informative chat with Jane, Brenda had tried to take a detour through the narrow alley that ran behind the garden of the soap-opera house. Or Whiteacre, as she supposed she should start calling it. The name made her think of lawyers and from there to her conversation with Tina. Tina had seemed edgy and Brenda didn't altogether buy the story about her brother-in-law being the one in a spot of bother. Asking for a friend, more like. Though Tina, unlike Finn, was straight as a die and Brenda couldn't imagine what trouble she could be in, and surely she'd have confided in her? A puzzle.

The alley turned out not to be a through road and Brenda cursed. There was a sort of scrubby lay-by gouged out of the copse, presumably by other drivers who'd made the same mistake; it was just big enough to allow her to do a three — or maybe five — point turn. As she eased out of the lay-by for the last time and headed back the way she'd come, she noticed a door set into the wall which she assumed bounded the various gardens. She stopped the car and tried to think through the view from the Castle House, over the copse and diagonally across, and her walk past Whiteacre. There'd been a huge house on the corner and then Whiteacre. So the door in the wall ahead of her must lead into the corner house's garden. She twisted round and saw a similar door behind her. Bingo. At least if she'd worked it out right.

She reversed back into the lay-by and tried the door. It was locked, but looked as though it was regularly used. The handle turned smoothly and the ivy that flowed over the top of the wall was neatly trimmed to frame the brickwork lintel.

Brenda had repeated her visit to the door several times since she'd first tried it. It was always locked and she'd almost decided to give up on the Whiteacre plan, which she'd been nurturing for months now, and try and find another source of extra income, particularly after today's clean at the Castle House when she'd seen no sign of Mrs Standing and the gardener from the turret. The weather was warm and it was very unusual for Mrs Standing not to come out with a beer for her lover, usually followed by a bit of what her mother would have called canoodling. Sometimes quite a bit, and sometimes of what her mother would have called something else. Seeing the garden apparently empty in the sun, she assumed they weren't there for whatever reason. But she did her usual detour and tried the door anyway. It opened. Caught by surprise, she nearly stumbled through it; the hinges must have been oiled and the door swung without effort or sound. She found her footing and pulled the door back towards her until there was just a narrow slice of opening around which she peered cautiously. Some rough ground with a couple of what looked like cages with flourishing raspberry plants. A bed with some herbs — she glimpsed parsley, rosemary and mint in a pot. Sheds on one side, with the tops of small trees visible behind them, apples maybe. Compost heaps ahead. Beyond them a tall, neat hedge, over which she could see the first and second storeys of Whiteacre.

Brenda stepped back quietly and closed the door. Then stopped mid-turn and eased it open again. Slid her hand round the edge. And found a key in the lock.

*

Simon put the apples in the shadiest shed to give to Amanda next week. He was still fretting about her. Had he been neglecting her? Not giving her enough attention recently? He tried to think back. It must have been shortly after he'd made his carefully rehearsed declaration of love and they'd had their abortive discussions about divorce that he'd first seen Tina at work and followed that thread. Perhaps he'd been too distracted by it and Amanda had misinterpreted his distraction as waning interest in her. He hadn't been giving her enough attention and needed to get his act together pronto. The shadowy idea that had displaced his two Whiteacre burglary scenarios had gradually been taking shape since that inspirational spliff, been given a boost by Amanda's revelation about Hugh's pension and crystallised while he worked in the orchard today. As he'd picked apples his thoughts had drifted to Eve, immortalised in countless paintings, naked as she plucked the forbidden fruit. And then to Amanda, naked and beautiful in her big brass bed in that beautiful house with everything she wanted. And a husband who she shouldn't want. But husbands could be got rid of. An accident could happen. Or even be arranged. It would be a long game — a Long game, ha — and he'd need to get it right. All or nothing, double or quits. He'd keep an eye out, perhaps for many months, for an opportunity, but in the meantime carry on courting Amanda, which had its own pleasures, ever more assiduously.

Simon closed up the sheds and headed to the garden door, fumbling in his pocket for the key. He frowned as his fingers failed to find it. Ah, of course, he'd been grumpy and, again, distracted when he'd arrived; he must have left it in the inside lock, which he often did precisely so he wouldn't lose it. But it wasn't there. The door was still unlocked so at least he hadn't locked himself in, though the key couldn't be far away. He scoured the rough plot, the sheds he'd been into, the long grass in the orchard, but there was no sign of it. He shrugged. Careless of him, but it would probably turn up. Just as well he'd made a copy when Amanda had given it to him. He'd have to run back in the van later and lock up properly.

*

Hugh wasn't much given to reflection or analysis, unless it concerned the intricacies of inheritance-tax planning or the quality of the tannins in an adolescent St Estèphe. But he was beginning to wonder about his wife during their week in Sicily.

Amanda was always calm and contained, sometimes to the point of inscrutable. But for the first time in their marriage he sensed a turbulent undercurrent. She was distracted, distant, even irritable on occasion.

He tried to raise it one evening over dinner. It was surprising how hard it was, and he realised they'd been living parallel lives for so long that he'd almost forgotten how to discuss emotions, relationships, marriage.

'Are you — are you all right, Amanda?' He topped up both wine glasses, put the bottle back on the table and rested his hand on hers. She stiffened slightly.

'I'm fine,' she said, her voice expressionless. 'Why?'

'You just seem — I don't know, a bit withdrawn, perhaps? As if you're — yes, as if you're trying to solve a problem. Is there something I can help with? That we could discuss?'

Amanda gave a brief flutter of mirthless laughter. 'I'm fine,' she repeated. 'I think — maybe I'm just tired. That's why we come on holiday isn't it, to have a chance to relax and re-energise.'

Hugh squeezed her hand. He didn't really understand why she should be tired. She should have more time on her hands now that the garden, the last stage of the Whiteacre makeover, was finished. And she had that new — well, not so new now — gardener, who she said was very good, and didn't she also have a wonderful new cleaner? Perhaps she'd been worrying about him. Their marriage. Was she brooding about what he might get up to in London? He'd occasionally wondered whether she knew about his minor indiscretions but couldn't see how; he was very careful to keep his two lives surgically separate, always paying cash at bars and restaurants when he was with his lover du jour, never pocketing the receipt. But maybe she'd become suspicious anyway. Something could have planted the seed, set her wondering — a book, a film, a television programme. Hugh resolved to pay more attention to his wife, to buy her presents, almost to court or woo her again. He mentally caressed the old-fashioned words. His marriage may be passionless but he didn't want to fracture it.

*

A manda, in contrast, was given to reflection and analysis, and had been doing a lot of it during her holiday. And although she also was very careful to keep her two lives surgically apart, she was finding it increasingly difficult in Sicily to stop her other life from breaking out of the locked box where it normally stayed when she was with Hugh.

Even the wonders of Taormina at sunset couldn't distract her from fretting about Simon. He'd said he thought he was falling in love with her and she hadn't replied. Something had held her back, something more than her customary emotional reserve. But now she wondered how he'd interpreted her silence. He hadn't pursued that conversation, but then a couple of weeks later they'd talked about divorce. Admittedly it had come up almost accidentally, but they'd touched on the question of her leaving Hugh. And she'd said she couldn't. She must have sounded very definite, but although mostly she did feel very definite about it, there were times when she wondered. The distance between her and Hugh, while a warm and comfortable and familiar distance, was so different from her closeness to Simon. How would she feel if Simon left her? Was he thinking of doing that, given her coolness about love and divorce? She felt a sliver of ice in her heart at the thought of never seeing him again, the prospect of lonely evenings and solitary nights once more, the image of him with another woman. She knew she'd be able to keep on living her two separate lives once she was home, at least until she came to a decision about whether to dive into the freezing waters of divorce, but she needed more time to reflect. During that time she must pay more attention to Simon, act more warmly towards him, not give him cause to doubt her.

*

Leonie was pleasantly surprised by how friendly some of the other cleaners were. First Brenda had suggested a drink, now Tina had invited her for a coffee. After her intense two-year affair with Hugh had come to its inglorious end, Leonie had reverted to her natural, somewhat solitary self. An only child of older parents who had died, months apart, a few years earlier, she'd always been comfortable in her own company, and though she'd never been short of friends through school, university, work and neighbourhood, she'd formed few close attachments. And, she admitted to herself, she'd let most of those wither during her affair and her previous much longer, though no less disastrous, relationship. Her social life in her new cleaning milieu was turning out to be more convivial than she'd expected. Though when Leonie arrived at Pret, Tina seemed apprehensive and uncomfortable rather than enthusiastic, her legs tightly twisted and frown lines etched on her forehead.

'How have you found your first few months here?' asked Leonie, in an attempt to put her at ease.

Tina shifted in her chair and stirred her coffee with some vigour. 'It's OK,' she said. 'Certainly different from office work but at least it's a job.'

'Yes,' agreed Leonie. 'I worked in an office before also. But I like the independence and seeing different houses and getting to know somewhere new.'

The conversation fizzled out, Tina looking no more at ease. Then she said suddenly, 'Actually, I wanted to ask you something. Brenda said you used to work for a firm of solicitors. I —'

She stopped as abruptly as she'd started, took a swallow of coffee and tried again.

'I, er, well, it's my brother-in-law really, might need some legal advice. It's slightly awkward. He's a bit of a dodgy character — stuff that fell off a lorry sort of thing, nothing major, just little things — but he says now he's being threatened ...' Tina trailed off again.

'Well,' said Leonie briskly. 'I doubt I'd be able to help. My area is — was — EU law, so I don't really know much about —' She also stopped abruptly, closed her eyes for a moment and exhaled a long breath. Shit. Some cover agent she was. All that effort to disguise her past, lost through a moment's inattention. She suddenly remembered that she'd told Brenda how the name Whiteacre came from studying land law, which would have been an odd thing for a secretary to know. Though maybe Brenda hadn't registered what she'd said: in retrospect the conversation seemed to be more of a ploy to talk about the house. Brenda had even asked who the owners were. It was something of a puzzle.

Tina straightened in her seat and looked at Leonie with interest. 'You're a solicitor yourself?' she asked. 'I was sure Brenda said you'd been a secretary. In fact I think you mentioned it when we were all chatting the other day.'

Leonie bit her lip. Probably no point trying to backtrack; for whatever reason, Tina seemed to be excited by the news. Leonie uncrossed and recrossed her legs, drained the rest of her latte and said, 'Yes. It's complicated. I ... to be honest I felt a bit embarrassed when I applied for the job.'

'Did you answer that advert then? We started at the same time, didn't we?'

'We did, but no I didn't answer the advert. It was just a

coincidence. Anyway, I wanted to, er, do something completely different for a few months or whatever. I'd been made redundant. For various reasons it would have been difficult to find a new legal job. I thought Cathy might think I was overqualified.'

'I think they were so keen to find new cleaners she wouldn't have thought twice. Anyway, your secret's safe with me. I won't even tell Brenda if you don't want me to.'

'Thanks. I suppose it doesn't matter really, but OK, let's keep it between the two of us. For the moment anyway.' And while the translation procedure inches forward.

'So,' Tina resumed, 'have you got any advice? About what I — my brother-in-law can do?'

Leonie sighed. 'As I said, I'm not — I wasn't — that sort of solicitor. Never did any criminal law, which is what I guess we're talking about.'

'You must know something,' Tina persisted. 'Didn't you have to study it?'

Leonie snorted. 'Back in the day, yes. But it's been a long day. Even if I could remember anything, it would be out of date.' Curiosity got the better of her, however, and she continued, 'Do tell me if you like, though I doubt I can help. But there's no point if you're not going to give me the full story.'

Tina looked around but there were few others in the café, and none nearby. 'So Finn — that's my brother-in-law — he's a bit of a wide boy as I said. Freelances, he calls it. Among other things. Small scale. Used to "re-home"' — she made quote marks with her hands — 'stolen white goods and so on. But ...' Tina paused, her face reddening briefly. 'Well, he came across somebody's bank details. Nobody he knows, just, well, someone he, er, met in passing who was careless. And he thought he might try and sell the info. But someone else found out.'

Leonie was struggling to keep track. 'And did what?'

'Nothing, yet.'

'So what's the problem?'

'I think he wants to shop Finn.'

Leonie went over to the counter and came back with two more coffees and a couple of biscuits.

'Who is he?' she said, putting one of the beakers and a shortbread in front of Tina.

'I don't know. Well, I don't know his full name, just Steven. I — Finn thought he was a policeman at first, but he said he wasn't. Apparently, I mean. Then he said he was a private detective. He was undercover, posing as a gardener.'

Leonie bit into her biscuit, trying to disentangle what Tina had said. 'Er, well, it does seem a bit odd. I can see why a private detective might want to shop Finn, depending on who he's working for of course, but why would he tell him first? Why not just do it? That's presumably what his client would want. Is he working for the person whose data were stolen do you think?'

Tina was looking puzzled. 'But Finn hasn't met him. Oh shit —' She broke off and rubbed her eyes. 'I'm not very good at this, am I?' she continued with a watery, mirthless laugh. 'Look, I might as well tell you now I've got this far. But don't tell anyone. Otherwise,' she added, 'I'll tell everyone you're a solicitor.'

Leonie shrugged. That didn't seem important really, and she wasn't even sure why she'd hidden it, apart perhaps from a vague thought that it might somehow have compromised her own attempt at going undercover. But again, her curiosity was piqued.

'I won't say a word.'

Tina stared into her beaker for a few minutes. Then she sat up straight, took a mouthful of coffee and said, 'OK. So I was involved. By mistake. I just came across someone's bank details. Stupidly I mentioned it to Finn. He's been pestering me for them, but I … haven't said anything.' Tina flushed rosily. She wasn't a good liar, thought Leonie, reminded of her own tendency to colour at inopportune moments.

'So, this private detective?' Leonie prompted.

Tina blew her nose. 'I don't know for sure,' she said desperately. 'But I think he wants to shop me.'

'But what for?' asked Leonie. 'If you haven't done anything with the bank details?'

Tina fumbled with the paper napkin Leonie had given her with the biscuit, her eyes bright with what looked alarmingly like tears. 'I did give them to Finn,' she choked. 'He probably sold them to someone. He gave me some cash. It was just the once though,' she added, but the rising flush on her face suggested otherwise.

*

Jane, who had so far seemed interested and keen to help, jerked back in her seat. 'For fuck's sake Tina — excuse the language, but you do know that's a criminal offence? A really serious one.'

Tina closed her eyes to hold back the tears that were brimming. 'That's what Steven said. I think he was threatening to go to the police. Data privacy law or something.'

'That's the least of it,' said Jane grimly. 'Like I said, I'm not a criminal lawyer, but you could be talking fraud, theft, God knows what else. Serious stuff. What on earth were you thinking?'

Tina's heart was pounding. 'Finn talked me into it,' she said. Her voice was low and shaky. 'Money's so tight at the moment. I was a secretary at a firm of accountants, I was quite senior and the pay was pretty good then I was made redundant in January. I didn't have much saved — I got divorced a couple of years ago, think I mentioned when we first met, and didn't come out of it well. I've got a teenage son who can eat for England. But now ... I just wish I'd never listened to Finn. And even if Steven doesn't go to the police, I suppose he could tell New Brooms —'

'Jesus, was it a client then? Whose details you saw?'

Tina nodded mutely. She started crying, and rubbed her eyes angrily with the napkin.

Jane leaned back and breathed out a long sigh. 'Tina, do you realise how serious this is? People check their bank accounts you know. If they see a payment they don't recognise they get on to the bank, who I imagine immediately pass it to their fraud department. Leaving aside the risk of Steven going to the police, any bank who sees evidence of fraud will alert them like a shot. In fact, maybe *you* should go to the police.'

'Me?' squawked Tina. 'But —'

'Listen,' said Jane. 'Someone's going to tell the police unless you're incredibly lucky. You could go to prison. At least if you fess up you might get a brownie point. Maybe.'

Tina clenched her fists to stop, or at least hide, the trembling in her hands. 'I can't,' she moaned. 'Finn would kill me. And ... my son, what about him? If I go to prison.' She was sobbing now.

'Tina.' Jane paused. 'Look, I'm sorry to sound so hard. I can understand how Finn might have made it sound trivial and low risk and why you were tempted or persuaded. But you need to face facts. I don't want to know any more details, but if you've done it more than once and the police get alerted by several people all living in high-end houses in Winchester they'll eventually make a link to New Brooms and then to you. And there's another thing. I don't know how clever Finn is but if he, or anyone he's passed the info to, tries to use the bank card or whatever, they'd probably be caught anyway with all the additional steps banks take these days to verify transactions. Either way, the threads would lead back to you, or at least to Finn and from what you say he doesn't sound like the chivalrous type who'd shield you. You need to stop now, before you get a criminal record or worse. That's not going to help your son either.'

Jane stood up and turned to go, then paused. 'And another thing again. If it gets out that it's a cleaner behind it all, New Brooms will never get over it. They'll lose all their clients and probably go bust. And anyone who'd cleaned for them would probably never get another cleaning job.'

She strode out of the café.

Thirteen

September

Tina sat hunched over the dregs of her cold coffee and the soggy remains of her napkin. What on earth had she been thinking? She'd known how dodgy Finn was. And now she could go to prison. It didn't bear thinking about. But she'd have to think about it, about whether and when she should go to the police and how to tell Finn she was stopping. Her usual instinct was to talk to Brenda about problems but she felt so ashamed about this one that there was no way she could talk to anyone. She'd give herself a couple of days to decide what to do and then she'd just have to steel herself and do it. And of course there was still the worry about Steven. She supposed she'd just have to wait and see whether he contacted her again and deal with it then.

Tina squared her shoulders, got up and headed to her next job. As she got into her car her phone pinged. Talk of the devil … It was a WhatsApp message from Steven. Good. Hopefully she could find out what he was planning. And think about the rest of the mess later. One thing at a time.

L eonie walked rapidly towards the station. She felt sorry for Tina and half regretted coming down on her like a ton of bricks. She was also slightly ashamed that she'd been so judgmental. What, after all, was she doing at Whiteacre? Not data theft or fraud, admittedly, but something more than cleaning.

But there was a big difference between her own scheme for petty revenge and what Tina had got herself into. She seemed like a nice woman who'd been talked into doing something uncharacteristic. And criminal. She needed to realise how serious her situation was, and Leonie couldn't risk getting involved herself; it could compromise any chance she had of a future legal job. Still, she'd give Tina a call in a week or so, see whether she'd got herself out of it and if not why not.

*

T he message Simon had sent had been a friendly suggestion that they meet again at the Wykeham Arms on a day and time of Tina's choosing. To his surprise she replied promptly. While he waited for her on the following day, he thought back to their first meeting there, when he'd teased the full story out of her and told her he wanted to reflect further. He didn't think he'd explicitly mentioned consulting his non-existent client, or indeed the police, but hoped he'd left her with the impression that both were options. But of course they weren't, if for different reasons. No, he had a much better idea.

After buying the orange juice and bitter and shepherding Tina again to the empty rear section of the bar, Simon said, 'Look, Tina, I've been thinking. I'll level with you. I deliberately gave you the wrong impression. I'm not a private detective, I don't have a client and I'm certainly not a policeman.' Level so far at least.

Tina put her coffee down, her eyes wide. 'But — why did you say you were? Who are you then? What do you want from me?'

'I was speaking the truth, though, when I said I'd seen you going through papers in the house — two houses actually — where you clean, and taking photos of them. And I think you were also speaking the truth when you told me that your brother-in-law had got you into it and that it would be tricky for you to get out of it. I don't like the sound of that, Tina. I don't think a nice girl — woman — like you should be pushed into something a bit, well, dodgy and only get a fraction of the gain.'

Tina fiddled with her coffee stirrer, chewing her lip.

'He did bully me into a bit,' she agreed eventually. 'He said there'd be no risk if I was careful and he'd pay me well. I — I'm divorced, thank God, then I got made redundant. I've got a teenage son. So money's tight. But now —' She hesitated. 'I wish I hadn't got involved. I didn't realise how serious it was. I don't want to do it anymore.'

'I think I can help you,' said Simon with a smile. 'If you can help me. We'd make a good team. I need to go in a moment, but would you like to meet up one evening for a drink? I'll think some more about my idea and we can discuss it over a glass of wine.'

'OK,' said Tina cautiously. 'Tomorrow?'

'Wednesday would suit me better,' said Simon. He decided it was time to move Tina from his usual watering hole and added, 'And let's go somewhere different. How about the Bishop on the Bridge? It's on the river, at the top of the High Street.'

Steven was standing at the bar when Tina arrived at the Bishop on the Bridge, for which Tina was grateful; she didn't feel comfortable ordering and drinking in a pub on her own.

He waved her to a quiet table in the back, like the first time they'd been at the other pub. Tina felt an involuntary shudder as she recalled how quickly her initial veneer of bravado had crumbled once she realised that Steven knew what she'd done. Though she'd thought he was a policeman, or a private detective. She almost laughed at the idea, then remembered that she still didn't know much about him. He looked good as he came back from the bar with a pint of beer and a glass of wine. It was the first time she'd seen him out of gardening clothes; she supposed they were just a disguise anyway. Now, his navy chinos and blue checked shirt suited him. He smiled as he sat down beside her.

'Thanks,' she said, taking a cautious sip of her wine. It was nice, chilled and crisp. 'I've been meaning to ask you — I was just wondering and realised I don't know where you live.'

Steven lifted his pint and dipped it slightly towards her. 'Cheers.' He took a long draught and rubbed a faint moustache of foam from his lip. 'I'm between houses at the moment, actually. I came back recently from a long trip abroad.'

'That must have been fun,' said Tina.

'Anyway, I'm looking around for somewhere to buy. In the meantime I'm staying with friends or occasionally sleeping in my camper van.'

'A camper van!' echoed Tina. 'That sounds exciting. Is it one of those ones with a little kitchen and a shower and so on?'

'No shower sadly. I swim every morning. Sometimes wild swimming, otherwise at the pool.'

Tina shuddered. 'I always hated swimming at school. Never got the hang.'

Steven took a long draught of beer and let out a long breath. 'Long day. How about you?'

'It was busy also,' said Tina. 'Three cleans. And nothing much for —' She broke off, mentally kicking herself. She was going to stop this, remember. Very soon.

Steven chuckled. 'Don't worry, Tina. I know what you do and, as I said, I think I know why you do it. But I'm not going to shop you. Far from it in fact. I think you deserve better. Someone who could look out for you more than Finn does.'

Tina bit her lip. It was all rather confusing. Steven was obviously not planning to get her into trouble but still, he knew what she did and she wasn't sure whether she should trust him.

As if he'd read her mind, Steven continued. 'As I said, don't worry. You can trust me. I like you, Tina.'

Tina took a long gulp of her wine, then remembered that she was driving home so mustn't have too much more. Perhaps she should walk next time, it wasn't so far and would be good exercise. If there was a next time, of course.

'Thanks,' she said. 'For the wine I mean. And for not — for not … getting me into trouble.' Tina realised with horror that her voice was quavering and her eyes watering. It had indeed been a long day, a long year in fact. And her conversation with Jane had been the final straw. She ran a finger furtively under her lower lashes. She'd put on make-up when she came out — not that she had much, not much call for it lately, but she'd found an old mascara that was still OK and some foundation and blusher that weren't too caked. Maybe she should treat herself to a new lipstick; the only one she had was a rock-hard stump.

'I'm sorry if I sounded threatening last time we met,' said Steven, lightly patting her hand. 'I guess I just wasn't sure about you. Whether I could trust you, I mean.'

Tina stared at him. 'What about?'

'My plan.'

Steven insisted on buying her supper and another glass of wine. The pub was filling up inside and he suggested they move to the terrace, where it was quieter though still warm enough to be comfortable. He outlined his idea over fish and chips.

'This is just a thought at the moment, Tina. We need to get to know each other a bit better, see if you think it will work. I'd like to see more of you. But this is what I'm thinking. Between you and me, I know of someone who can afford and deserves to lose a bit of money. Even quite a big bit. Someone very wealthy. He doesn't treat his wife well —'

Tina stiffened. She hadn't been treated well when she'd been a wife and immediately felt solidarity with this woman and animosity towards her husband.

Steven resumed. 'I know his wife — just as friends,' he added hastily. 'Her husband's away in London all week earning loads of money and only gives her a small allowance. Really, it's medieval. So I thought — well, it would be sort of like Robin Hood. I thought I'd try and get his bank details or bank cards, work out a way to take a load of money out without it being traced to me, and somehow give her the money. But I confess, I'm stymied.'

Steven was looking at her expectantly and Tina obliged.

'How?'

'This is a bit … delicate,' he said. 'Can I really trust you, Tina?'

Tina took a deep breath. What choice did she have, really? After all, Steven knew exactly what she'd done. And he seemed nice now. Wanted to help her. It was a long time since anyone had helped her. Finn didn't really count.

'Yes,' she said, breathless.

Steven beamed and clinked his glass to hers. 'Here's the thing. I'm in their house quite often, for my gardening —'

'You're their gardener?' interrupted Tina, confused. 'I thought you said they were friends?'

'Not the husband,' said Steven grimly. 'I'm more than a gardener though.' She glimpsed the shadow of a smile, almost a smirk, pass across his face, or perhaps she'd been mistaken. 'I run a landscape gardening business.'

'Oh,' said Tina. She thought for a few moments. 'But —' would he think this was nosy? '— wasn't it difficult managing your business when you were abroad?'

'I have a trusted team,' said Steven smoothly. 'And thanks to smartphones no-one's ever out of contact anymore. More's the pity, sometimes,' he added with a trace of a wink.

'I thought you were a gardener,' said Tina, feeling no less confused. 'When I first saw you. I mean, the kind of gardener who gets his hands dirty.'

'I used to be,' said Steven. 'But then I built up the business. Now I spend most of my time on management, but if need be I cover for my team of workers if one of them is sick or away. I like to keep my hand in. Anyway, for these people, the Standings, I've been working on their garden for years. It's huge, and it was a wilderness when they bought the house. Throughout, I've done the design and planning with Mrs Standing, often in her home office. We do it all on her computer, you see.'

'So what's the —'

'The problem,' completed Steven. 'The problem is that in Mr Standing's home office, right next to hers, is a filing cabinet. And I can't — I mean, I need someone to find the key. I can do the rest so there'd be no risk to you at all. And if it works as I hope, I could give you a handsome payment. I must admit, Tina, when I saw you, I thought that you were the answer to my prayers.' He beamed again, and laid his hand on hers, this time letting it rest there for a moment.

Tina felt flattered, almost glowing, but also still confused.

'I don't understand,' she said. 'How would I get in?'

'Do you work for an agency, Tina?'

'I do, yes. New Brooms.'

'That's what I was hoping. The house I'm talking about is called Whiteacre. It's in Nightjars Holt, the same area where I saw you in sev— in the two houses. I wondered whether your agency also cleaned for the Standings, and if so, whether there was any way you could get to clean it? I don't know how it works, of course. I'd need to rely on you for that, it's your area of expertise. As, naturally, would be the next stage, if we get there.' Steven smiled disarmingly.

Tina sat up straighter. This was definitely her area of expertise. It could be the answer to her prayers also: one last little 'job', no connection to Finn, no risk to her and a handsome payment. From a handsome man. And then she'd put an end to her life of crime. In fact, maybe Steven could help her extricate herself. Even protect her from Finn, if it came to that, though she didn't really see Finn as violent. But she wouldn't think about the next steps until she'd helped Steven with his Robin Hood plan.

*

'Yes?' barked Cathy at Tina's timid knock on the open door of her office. She was staring at a page of figures, her brow knotted. She glanced up and said, 'Hello Tina. I can't spare more than a couple of minutes, I'm being chased for the monthly stats.'

'Sorry,' said Tina. 'Just a quick question. About one of the houses we clean in Nightjars Holt. Whiteacre. I know Jane cleans there, and wondered whether I could cover for her when she's next —'

'What is it about that house?' Cathy sounded uncharacteristically irritated. 'Why are you all so keen to clean it?'

'What?' asked Tina, confused. 'How do you mean?'

Cathy scratched her head. 'Jane said something about her mother having lived at the house next door or similar, I can't remember exactly. That's how she came to clean it; she asked to cover for Judy, I think, and they kept her on. And then Brenda was asking about it, said she'd seen the garden from Brambles. Anyway, as it happens I was looking at staff holidays yesterday and Jane hasn't taken any yet. I need to remind her about not being able to roll over more than one week. I'll do that, and if the slots work then yes, of course you can cover. I'll let you know. Sorry to be snappy, can't stand figures!' She ran her hand through her hair and looked back down to the papers on her desk.

*

Simon rose early on Thursday and took the M3 and M27 to the end of the westbound motorway at Cadnam. Between there and Lyndhurst, the A337 bisected areas of Ancient and Ornamental Woodland. Unlike the New Forest in general, he thought, which was neither new nor, for the most part, a forest, the unenclosed wooded pastures lived up to their name. Beech and oak trees, some several hundred years old, straddled the landscape like giant sculptures. Those that died, or branches that fell, were left to rot undisturbed. Birds, bats and insects flourished. As did fungi.

Simon parked his van at Brockishill Green and walked away from the road and deeper into the woods, enjoying the rich perfume of decaying leaves and damp turf. He was aware that mushrooms were increasingly hard to find as a result of excessive amateur and professional foraging, but he'd learnt to spot well-hidden plants and animal tracks when he trained as a ranger. As his eyes adjusted to the filtered light and the subtle autumn tapestry of bronze, terracotta, copper and sepia, stippled with patches of faded grass, he began to distinguish the fungi. The delicately gilled apricot funnels of chanterelles. The shining red and gold of *Russula aurata*. The puffy, blue-green caps of *Russula virescens*. The classic mushroom shape of the coffee-coloured cep. The spreading, gleaming white clusters of wood mushroom. Simon stooped, careful not to stand too close and disturb the surrounding soil.

He handled his harvest gently, savouring the dry, silky texture. Like snakes; the urban English tended to think both were cold and clammy, even slimy to the touch. Simon examined each fungus minutely before putting it in the basket he carried. He had seen and given a wide berth to a few of the deadly *Amanita phalloides* or Death Cap, although not, this time, the less common but equally deadly *Amanita virosa* or Destroying Angel, but wanted to be sure he hadn't collected any in error. Easy to do since they were so similar to the wood mushroom, but he knew how to identify them: the creamy skirt-like ring on the stem, the cup of tissue at the base, the white gills, sometimes telltale patches on the cap. Can't be too careful though. He'd read only the other day that the Death Cap was responsible for 90 per cent of deaths from fungus poisoning in Europe. A couple of mouthfuls could — and, without prompt medical treatment, would — kill a healthy adult. There was no antidote. Pity he couldn't somehow get Amanda to feed some to Hugh by accident. But far too risky if they'd come from him. And anyway she'd hardly be likely to cook a dish just for Hugh.

Simon frowned in concentration, thinking back to the photos he'd scrutinised when he was prowling through Whiteacre. Hugh was tall, though if he recollected correctly from their brief meeting at Easter only a shade taller than him. But he was slight, almost scrawny. Didn't look as though he had much muscle on him. Simon thought of the soft hand that had shaken his, the clean trim nails. And looked at his own, holding the bag of fungi. Strong, calloused, weathered by real work. Another opportunity for putting his plan into action would arise, he was sure. Even if it meant a long wait.

Simon presented his haul to Amanda that evening.

Sunlight seemed to wash over her face, beautiful as ever. 'I'll make risotto,' she said. 'I love cooking that. It's so peaceful.' But then she hesitated. 'Did you pick them?' she asked.

'Of course. In the Forest. Ancient woodland near Brockishill Green.'

Amanda bit her lip. 'I read in the paper a year or two ago about someone who died from eating mushrooms they'd picked. It warned people never to try. I've never dared.'

Simon laughed, and kissed her forehead. 'Angel, you're quite right not to dare if you're not sure you can identify them. But I am sure. The two really poisonous ones do look similar to the commonest edible ones and grow in the same environment — in fact I saw a couple — but they're easy to tell apart if you know what you're doing. You can trust me.'

*

Leonie had bought a lipstick similar to the shade she remembered Margot wearing when she'd briefly met her at the Mainwaring & Cox meeting to introduce new legal staff, and had also invested in a sample size Chanel No 5 spray which she'd found on eBay. But when it came to it she couldn't bring herself to mark one of Hugh's shirts with the lipstick or squirt scent on to a jacket. Somehow it didn't seem important anymore. And if Amanda noticed, she might somehow blame Leonie for ruining the shirt by not using stain remover or something. Although — would Amanda even notice, or be perturbed if she did? She seemed contained, satisfied, reflecting on some inner happiness. Like a cat which knew there was cream to be had. And perhaps, in light of what Leonie now knew about her fractured childhood, she deserved some cream.

Handling Hugh's laundry was strangely disorienting. Sometimes on a Monday she would hold Friday's shirt to her face and inhale the faint vestiges of his vetiver aftershave and the lemony soap in the Mainwaring & Cox loos. The shirt smelt of London Hugh. Winchester Hugh was different. His polo tops from the weekend smelt of Amanda's almond hand soap and the mint shower gel and tea-tree oil shampoo in his shower room. No aftershave — that must be reserved for weekday lovers. Was Amanda the same, wearing scent only on whichever days she saw her lover? But sniffing and comparing Amanda's weekday and weekend laundry was a step too far. Leonie was repelled by the thought. And ashamed.

*

Brenda was pleased to see Tina looking happier than she had done for a while. Or at least less on edge. She'd been worried about her. Brenda knew only too well how hard life could be for a single mother on a low income. But now Tina seemed to have got a bit of her old bounce back.

They were having a quick coffee after bumping into each other in the New Brooms office.

'We must do this more often,' said Brenda. 'The time just flies away, doesn't it?'

'It does,' agreed Tina. 'Between work and children. Even one child, though he's big enough for two now!' She frowned suddenly.

'Is Peter OK?' asked Brenda, concerned.

'I think so. Hard to tell with a teenage boy. He doesn't say much. But he's got plenty of friends and seems to be doing all right at school and there's no evidence he's into drugs. Probably the best I can hope for till he starts speaking again. I've talked to some of the other mums, it's apparently quite a normal phase.' She sighed, then her face brightened. She drank some coffee, then said, 'Brenda, listen, I think I might have met someone.'

'Who's he then?' Brenda would have been delighted to see Tina in a good relationship after her violent marriage and bitter divorce, but worried that her friend could easily be taken advantage of. She was too kind and trusting. Needed a streak of Brenda's cynicism.

'He's called Steven and he's a businessman. Got his own company, landscape gardening. He's nice, treats me well. Happy to put his hand in his pocket. Early days though, it might not lead to anything.' But Tina's small, secret smile told Brenda that she thought that it would, and Brenda hoped fervently that she was right about her new man and wouldn't get hurt again.

Fourteen

October

A couple of weeks later, Cathy called Tina to say that Jane was taking a week's holiday shortly and, with a slight reorganisation of her schedule, Tina could cover for her Monday and Friday afternoon slots at Whiteacre. 'Have a quick word with her in case there's anything you should know,' she added. 'Mrs Standing is very particular.'

Tina was about to text Jane and suggest they meet, then paused, finger hovering over her phone as she thought about their last meeting. Jane knew about Finn and Steven and that Tina had provided Finn with a client's personal information, and had taken a very dim view. A lawyer's view maybe, but it had rattled Tina. And Tina still hadn't spoken to Finn or the police, telling herself she was waiting to do her one good turn via Steven for Mrs Standing. If Jane was going to ask any awkward questions about why she wanted to clean Whiteacre, or more generally, Tina didn't want her telltale tendency to blush to be visible.

Hi Jane, I'm covering Whiteacre for you next week, can we speak some time if you've any handover info? Phone better than meeting, I need to be at home for my son when I'm not working. Thx Tina x

She touched the send icon.

Jane called her the following evening.

'It's a beautiful house,' she said. 'There's not usually a lot to do. Her husband —' Jane stumbled on the words for some reason '— works in London, he's not there in the week. She likes the bedding —' Tina thought she heard a stifled giggle '— changed and washed on Fridays. And there's usually stuff to clear in the kitchen on both days. I think she must have a friend over on Thursdays.' Again, the ghost of a giggle.

'Erm, thanks,' said Tina. 'Anything I should look out for particularly?'

'Not really.' There was a silence, then Jane's voice again, colder now. 'Hey, wait a minute though Tina. You're not planning —'

Tina cut across her. 'No, no, nothing like that. That was just a mistake, a misunderstanding. Please don't tell anyone.'

'But you were still committing a crime. Have you told Finn you're done with it? Or gone to the police?'

'I —' Tina stopped. 'I'm going to tell Finn. Soon. I promise. I just need to find the right moment. Then I … I might go to the police.'

'You do that. And Tina, I'm sorry to sound harsh again, but if I hear that anything dodgy's happened at Whiteacre I'll go to the police myself.'

Tina swallowed. She needed to be very sure of Steven.

Jane's voice again, as if she'd read Tina's thoughts. 'And what about that guy, Steven was it?'

'It was a misunderstanding,' repeated Tina. 'My misunderstanding. It was all fine. He's actually really nice, in fact we're quite friendly now.'

'That's good to hear,' said Jane. 'As long as you're sure. And stick to the rules now.' Jane cleared her throat as if about to end the call, then said, 'Oh by the way, Am — Mrs Standing always puts out really good biscuits if you want to make a cup of tea. Probably good tea also, though I'm not much a tea drinker so not one to judge.'

'Really?' said Tina, surprised, and also relieved at the opportunity to move the conversation onto safer ground. 'I think she used to be famous for never offering anything. I met Frances once, through Brenda — she cleaned there before Judy. Said she was the meanest of her owners.'

'Must have had a change of heart,' said Jane. 'Though come to think of it, I don't think she did offer when I was covering for Judy. Only once I'd started as her regular cleaner. Anyway, enjoy Whiteacre. Feel free to text if you've got any queries.'

'Are you going away?'

'I'm going to Brussels for the week. Catching up with friends from when I worked there ages ago.'

'Have fun,' said Tina. 'We should go for a coffee or a drink again when you're back.'

'Let's do that. See you then, bye.'

'I'm covering two cleans at Whiteacre next week, on Monday and Friday,' Tina told Steven. She'd seen him a few times since he told her about his plan — a couple of coffees and three evenings in different pubs and now they were back in the Bishop on the Bridge on the Friday before her first cover clean. He was good company, good looking, generous and... she searched for the word. Chivalrous, she thought to herself, that was it. Kind and not putting any pressure on her, but obviously interested.

'Well done you! That was quick work. I knew you were the answer to my prayers as soon as I saw you.'

Tina beamed.

'It's a big house,' Steven continued. 'If I were you I'd concentrate on —'

'You telling me how to do my job, Mr …?' Tina realised she still didn't know his surname.

'Long,' said Steven. 'No of course not, I know you're an expert.'

Tina glowed. She'd definitely earned his approval with this.

'It's just that I know the house,' he continued. 'A little,' he added hastily. 'As I mentioned, the filing cabinet's in the husband's home office at the top of the house, at the back. There's a drawer full of keys in the utility room but no key to the cabinet. If you can think of anywhere else to look … Even if you find it, you may not have the time or opportunity to look inside —'

Tina felt a flare of panic. 'I don't want to,' she interrupted. 'I'll look for the key for you. I just … don't want to know anything more about what you're going to do. And … I need to be sure I won't be found out.'

Steven looked shocked, even slightly wounded. 'Tina love, relax. You've been dealing with an amateur so far, and I quite agree that you should stop that connection. I'm much cleverer. I just need you to bring me the key. I'll make a copy as soon as you give it to me and put the original back where you found it. It'll never be missed. And I'll check the filing cabinet when I get an opportunity that I'm sure is 100% safe, and be very careful to leave no trace. Remember, this is for Mrs Standing, whose husband gives her hardly any money. Of which he has masses. And of course some of that masses will find its way safely to you.'

Tina struggled with her newfound determination to stop breaking the law on the one hand and the temptation to get one last, very low risk, much needed payment from a man who she was finding increasingly attractive. And who seemed to be reciprocating. And who didn't do this sort of thing all the time, like Finn. He was a businessman trying to help out a friend. Robin Hood, as he'd said. She'd put the money aside for Peter then go to Finn. And hope Jane didn't keep on at her about the police. 'OK,' she concluded.

Simon tipped his glass to her. 'I'll take you out for a special meal afterwards.'

Later, he walked her back to her flat and kissed her properly for the first time. He squeezed her hand and murmured, 'Good luck! Text if you've any questions, or anything to report. But remember to use WhatsApp. It's more secure; I don't want any trace that you've been involved, for your sake. Good night, love.'

Tina felt a stab of disappointment that he hadn't suggested meeting over the weekend. All the more reason to find that key. He's said he'd take her out for a special meal. And that could lead to more meals, more kisses, more ... Tina felt her heart race, her cheeks warm. She hadn't had a boyfriend since Peter's father left. Steven was older than her, mature and experienced, well off, a businessman no less. And fit. Maybe her luck was about to change. She sighed happily and opened the front door.

*

By now Tina was used to going straight into a new job and focusing on her hidden agenda. She rarely stopped to admire the house, preferring to use the limited time either side of an at least competent clean to look for hiding places. But Whiteacre was different and she gasped when Mrs Standing let her into the elegant balconied hallway. Everything so beautiful, so tasteful.

'I'll just show you where the cleaning stuff is, and also the tea and biscuits — do help yourself — then I have to go out,' said Mrs Standing. 'I'm sure you'll find your way around, it's not a complicated house. And I know Jane's briefed you.'

Tina started at the top. Nothing in the drawers of Mrs Standing's desk — well, lots of stuff, stationery and catalogues mostly, but nothing of interest to her. Keys, she reminded herself. That's all she was interested in now. She whipped the hoover and duster round and moved next door to Mr Standing's office.

As Steven had said, a big fat tempting filing cabinet squatted in the corner but it was cocooned in one of those commercial-grade bar locks. She'd have a look through the drawers on the ground floor in case the keys were there, but in her experience — and Steven was right, she was quite an expert now — people who went to the trouble and expense of buying that kind of kit didn't tend to leave the keys hanging around, more's the pity.

She glanced through the husband's desk but there were no nuggets in the neatly organised drawer. Nothing left in the printer either; she'd occasionally been lucky there. She mentally shook herself — she was on autopilot. Even if she found anything apart from the key she couldn't take it. Not after what Jane had said. And her own resolution to stop; it just wasn't worth the risk.

Again she ran the hoover and duster round and headed down to the first floor. How one couple could have so many wardrobes and bedrooms between them she couldn't imagine. How the other half lived, eh. So many men's suits. Still on autopilot, she ran her hands automatically and efficiently over the fine wool and linen, dipping into the jacket and trouser pockets. She'd often found cash and once a wallet; she hadn't felt it would be safe to take the whole wallet but she'd taken one of the several bank cards and photos of the rest. But this Mr Standing was so tidy, and his wife obviously very efficient at running the house, that she didn't expect —

Tina's fingers brushed a couple of crumpled papers in a jacket pocket. She took them over to the window and smoothed them out. Receipts. Slightly faded but still legible. The first was from Agent Provocateur, a London postcode too blurred to read but starting with EC she thought. Silk ouvert, red, whatever that was. Lace-trimmed suspenders, black. She knew what they were. The second was from Boots, Cheapside, but it wasn't for a packet of aspirin and a bar of soap. YSL Opium perfume. A cool £50. She went back to the first receipt, having not noticed the price in her shock and excitement. £80 for the suspenders. £65 for the mysterious ouvert. Jesus. Obviously of no interest to either Finn or Steven but she slipped them into her handbag anyway.

Downstairs she did a thorough inventory of all the drawers she could find. As Steven had said, there was one in the utility room full of keys, all helpfully labelled, but as expected none was obviously for the filing cabinet. She finished her clean and WhatsApped Steven, feeling that she'd let him down.

> *Nothing so far, sorry, looked everywhere I could think of. Fingers crossed for better luck on Friday. Hope to see you before then? T*

She agonised for a few moments, added an x and sent it.

*

Tina was conscious that this was her last chance. She'd had a meal with Steven on Wednesday; he tried to cheer her up and told her not to worry, maybe she'd strike gold on her second clean. She crossed her fingers as she rang the bell, not sure whether Mrs Standing was home or not.

The door opened and Mrs Standing, as beautiful and elegantly turned out as her house, let her in.

'I've just got a couple of things to do in the kitchen then I'll be out of your way,' she said.

Tina followed her into the breakfast-room-cum-kitchen, en route to the utility room beyond. Mrs Standing paused at a panel of some sort above one of the counters and pressed a button. 'Careful where you step,' she called back to Tina as she swivelled round. A panel in the floor, cleverly camouflaged to match the varnished wood around it, swung slowly open. Tina stared, then, realising she was staring, went through to the utility room and got her kit together. As she headed back through the breakfast room, Mrs Standing rose head first through the hole clutching two bottles of wine, tapped the control panel again and put the wine in the fridge.

Tina was stripping the bed in the master bedroom when she heard the front door close. She glanced out of the window and saw Mrs Standing get into her little red car and drive off. She waited for a few minutes then scooted down the stairs and into the breakfast room. A cellar! Steven hadn't mentioned that. Perhaps he didn't know about it! Even if she couldn't find the key, at least she'd have something interesting to report.

The panel had a simple on/off button, as well as one showing a padlock symbol. Perhaps Mrs Standing locked it if they went away, but for now the hatch slowly rose, lights coming on in the depths below as it did so. Tina looked down and saw a spiral staircase surrounded by shelves holding dozens, no hundreds, of bottles.

Conscious that she didn't have much time and that she still had the laundry to do and the clutter in the kitchen — Jane had been right, Mrs Standing had obviously enjoyed a lavish meal with her mystery guest the previous evening — Tina went down to the bottom of the spiral staircase, looking for gaps between the bottles where there could be a key safe or similar. Even if she didn't know the code, she could at least tell Steven where it was. She was sure he'd be pleased.

By the bottom layer she'd drawn a blank. She sighed and looked around enviously. Not that she was much of a drinker, though she'd enjoyed her recent wines with Steven; he certainly knew how to choose nice ones. He probably earned quite a lot with his landscaping company. All the bottle tops facing her were covered in crinkly gold foil. Champagne. Lots of it.

But something wasn't right... there was one bottle the wrong way round, bigger than most of the others. Curious, she eased it out. She saw the label first — Bollinger. She'd been watching reruns of *Absolutely Fabulous* recently, and even though she knew she'd never be able to afford a bottle of Bolly, at least she could enjoy holding one. But it felt light in her hands. Disappointed, she saw that it had no foil and no cork. It was empty. Why had the Standings kept it, she wondered? Was it a memento of a special evening? But Steven had said the husband was mean to his wife.

She was about to slot the bottle back in the rack when she heard something rattle. There were two small keys inside.

Tina shot out of the cellar, clutching the keys. Her finger trembling, she stabbed the control panel and closed the hatch. She ran upstairs and checked that the keys fit; they did. She sent a quick text to Steven. He'd be so pleased. Maybe he'd want to see more of her now she'd been so helpful.

Found the keys!!! You'll never guess where. Lots to report!
Lots to clean also - Mrs S had a good meal last night judging

by the mess in the kitchen! Let me know when you're free and
I'll fill you in. Tx

*

Brenda wasn't entirely sure how you set about blackmail, and it wasn't really something you could ask about. Or even google comfortably.

She'd seen enough films and read enough Agatha Christies — and had enough common sense — to know that you needed to disguise your handwriting. Cutting characters out of newspapers seemed over the top though — and so last century, who bought newspapers anymore? Often the only one she could find for cleaning windows the way her mother had taught her was that tacky freebie, *Winchester Today* or something — well they'd hardly call it *Winchester Yesterday*, or even *Winchester Tomorrow*, would they?

Brenda tore a few pages out of one of Lily's exercise books and practised writing in a bland, anonymous hand. Then crafted the message I SAW YOU WITH YOUR LOVER IN THE GARDEN. I HAVE PHOTOS. She'd bought a packet of cheap envelopes, printed MRS STANDING, WHITEACRE, WINCHESTER on one, added the note, sealed it and wondered how best to deliver it. Then she realised that she should have been wearing gloves and repeated the process, tearing the original paper and envelope into tiny fragments and putting them into the food-waste caddy. Wouldn't do for the children to find them. She wondered whether she was overdramatising, worrying about fingerprints, but no harm in being careful.

She'd done the easy part then. Well, not entirely easy, all that crouching behind the hedge like something out of *Midsomer Murders*, not to mention all the earlier spying and planning and working out which house it was. And, Brenda admitted, a stroke of luck in finding the key. She'd let herself into the garden several times since, but on her first few heart-in-mouth visits either she'd seen nothing worth photographing or it had been too risky to try. Then, finally, another stroke of luck when she caught Mrs Standing and the gardener in such a passionate clinch that there was no chance either could see her, Mrs Standing with her eyes shut and the lover with his back to Brenda. She'd slunk out — amazing how fast you can slink — crouched low, thinking it would be plain sailing from then on, but she was wrong.

How was she going to deliver the note? She didn't want to put it in the post; she had an uneasy suspicion, though she didn't know why, that it might be traceable. But delivering it by hand was even trickier. After much agonising, she decided to hand deliver the first note so she would at least be sure it had arrived. She fished a few junk mail flyers out of the recycling — she'd brazen it out if she was caught going up the drive.

It was funny seeing Mrs Standing up close. Well, not really close of course; Brenda was sitting in her car a couple of vast houses up the street from Whiteacre, her silent phone pressed to her ear as though she were mid-conversation. She'd say she'd had a warning light come on her dashboard if anyone asked, and was trying to get through to her garage. People round here could be really snooty about parking.

It was a Monday morning and she assumed the husband would have left early to commute up to London. There was a little red sporty number in the drive which she hoped meant that Mrs Standing was about to go out. After an impatient ten minutes the front door opened and Mrs Standing emerged, locked up behind her, flashed her keys at the car and got in. She was slim and elegant and blonde, and Brenda felt frumpy and dishevelled and mousy in contrast. And poor.

The red car headed off. Brenda waited another few minutes in case she came back for something — Brenda was always doing that — then gathered her flyers in one hand, checked that the letter was in her jacket pocket and strode purposefully up the drive. She thrust the junk mail and the envelope through the letterbox, letting the flap sink back against her hand to muffle the sound in case there was anyone else at home; perhaps it was the cleaner's day — Fuck. For all her careful planning she'd forgotten that Jane was the cleaner. If Jane saw her it would be a disaster. She scuttled back to her car, heart pounding. Then, with a deep puff of relief, she remembered Jane saying that she came down from London and didn't arrive in Winchester till late morning. She'd thought at the time that Jane's decision to find a cleaning job in Winchester was odd and hadn't really bought her explanation, but it was none of her business after all, and right now her commuting schedule was very fortunate.

Fifteen

October

Leonie nearly stepped on the letters fanned out on the mat as she let herself into Whiteacre the day after she'd got back from Brussels. She scooped them up and glanced at them idly as she put them on the hall table for Amanda. A brown envelope from HMRC, a handful of flyers for local pizza shops and handymen, a postcard from Dover signed 'Jen' and a small white envelope with Amanda's name and address written in capitals. Leonie was reminded of the note she wrote at the end of her first trial clean at Whiteacre, disguising her writing in case Hugh saw it. Although Leonie hadn't used capitals, the writing on the envelope had a similar air of being deliberately impersonal and unremarkable. There was something else about the envelope though … With a start, she realised that it had no stamp or frank. And no street name or postcode. It must have been hand delivered.

Intrigued, Leonie turned the envelope over and was irritated, if not surprised, to see that it was gummed shut, with no return name or address on the back. With a shrug, she laid it on top of the others then paused as she started to take her jacket off, found her phone and took a photo. Another little mystery.

*

Amanda was also puzzled by the unstamped envelope when she came back to Whiteacre mid-afternoon. She took the mail through to the breakfast room, glanced at the postcard, binned the flyers, put the HMRC letter aside for Hugh to deal with, opened the envelope and pulled out the folded sheet. It was cheap, thin paper, and looked as though it had been torn out of an exercise book. Perhaps a school notebook — though did schoolchildren have notebooks anymore? Apart from electronic ones of course.

Amanda unfolded the paper, skimmed the brief text and sat down, hard, on the nearest chair. The hand-written capitals shouted the message at her:

I SAW YOU WITH YOUR LOVER IN THE
GARDEN. I HAVE PHOTOS.

*

Amanda read the letter again. The print seemed to blur and she wondered for a moment whether she had tears in her eyes, then noticed that her hand had a faint tremor. A sour taste rose to her mouth. She stood up, walked unsteadily to the kitchen area and filled and turned on the kettle. Back on her chair and nursing a mug of strong tea, she stared at the letter as if it was an unpleasant insect that had landed on the table.

But the more she looked at it, the calmer she felt. It must be a mistake. Intended for someone else, though it was addressed to 'Mrs Standing'. A try on at least. First, the garden was not overlooked. One of the things you paid an exaggerated Nightjars Holt price for was exaggerated privacy. The photos, if they existed, must be of them in the garden, as the note said; it was preposterous to think someone could have been roaming around the house when she and Simon were there. So the only way someone could have seen them was by coming into the garden and spying on them. But who would do that? They'd hardly come and hide behind the hedge or in the shrubbery on the off-chance; again the idea was preposterous. And, second, how would they even get into the garden? The gates to the coach-house drive were locked when there was no one at home. She and Hugh each had two copies of the key, one on their house key-ring and one with their car key. The only keys to the door in the wall were Simon's and the two sets she kept in the utility room. She'd ask Simon when she saw him tomorrow but he'd surely have told her if he'd mislaid his. She went through to the utility room and checked the drawer; both sets were there, as was the spare key for the drive gates.

Thinking of the drive reminded her that occasionally, if Simon was in his van rather than on his bike, he texted before he arrived and asked if he could leave his van in the entrance. He'd only done this a few times, since getting an unwelcome ticket once when he'd parked in the road, and anyway it was hardly compromising. No, if there were photos, they must be of the garden. Her thoughts circled back to the impossibility of it.

Amanda swallowed the rest of her tea. Feeling somewhat restored, she stood up, reached for the offending letter and crushed it viciously in her fist, intending to drop it into the recycling bin in the utility room. It seemed noxious, almost toxic, and she wanted it out of the main part of the house. But then she paused, and with a shudder smoothed out the paper and took it, plus the envelope, upstairs. It was unlikely that there'd be any useful fingerprints after she'd handled them — not that she knew, really; her only knowledge of police procedure came from detective fiction and TV series. But still. Maybe she should hold on to them for the moment. Just in case.

She was startled to hear the sound of hoovering in Hugh's office as she approached hers. In the shock of the letter she'd forgotten that it was the cleaner's day. The hoover stopped and Jane reversed out of the room and gave a start as Amanda coughed.

'Sorry, Mrs Standing. I didn't hear you come in or come up. I'm almost finished now.'

'Thanks,' said Amanda absently. She went into her office, which looked very clean and neat, and over to her desk. She pulled open one of the drawers then paused. There were no locks on her desk, or indeed in the room. Anything confidential that needed to be kept was stored in the filing cabinet in Hugh's office. She couldn't put the letter and envelope in there. But Hugh rarely came into her office and she couldn't envisage him rootling through her desk; in any event today was Monday and he wouldn't be back till late on Friday so she could give it further thought. Amanda put the note and envelope into one of the drawers and headed back down, wondering whether it was too early for a glass of wine. She felt that she needed one.

*

Brilliant T, I said u were the answer to my prayers! Let's celebrate on Monday. 6 at Bishop? S

Tina's cheeks were still glowing; her fingers could even feel the warmth as she carefully applied her new eyeliner. But for once her colour was not down to embarrassment or shame. Steven had again called her the answer to his prayers and asked her out to celebrate! Could she dare to think of it as a proper date, now they'd got the business out of the way? Or at least her contribution to the business. She wondered when he'd pay her and how much. She was sure it would be on a very different scale from Finn's few grubby notes. And in a better cause. Tina liked the idea of Steven as Robin Hood. And maybe she'd be Maid Marian …

Her thoughts flowed on to the romantic side of their relationship. They'd had several evenings out now, and he had kissed her properly. Even if only once. He only ever suggested meeting on a Monday or Wednesday, she realised. Weekends were difficult for her as she liked to be at home with her son, though it would be nice to be asked, but she wondered what he did on Tuesday and Thursday evenings.

She looked in on Peter, who hastily flicked out of a screen that looked suspiciously like a chatline and into one showing a list headed 'French vocabulary'.

'I was going to go out to meet a few friends,' she said, and now she was blushing for the usual reason. Not that Peter appeared to notice as he grunted, ''kay. Enjoy,' and spun his chair all the way round, jamming his foot on the floor when he completed the circuit so he was facing the screen again.

'Are you doing your homework? Shall I stay in and help? I don't mind.' Tina sighed. Another lie.

'Nah, yorright.' Was that French, she wondered? It certainly didn't sound like English.

She puffed out a long breath and turned to go with an 'I've got my mobile if you need to contact me.' No reply.

Steven had offered to give Tina a lift but she'd said she'd make her own way. She regretted that as she got into her car, but she hadn't wanted Peter to ask who was picking her up.

Now she wondered why she'd bothered, given his usual lack of interest in where she was going.

Again, Steven was waiting for her at the bar, nursing a pint, and again he suggested she find a table in the quiet rear of the bar while he ordered for her; it was getting too cool for the terrace. But he hugged and kissed her first! She must be right. Things were looking up.

*

Tina had come up trumps. Simon could hardly believe his luck. She certainly had her uses. And now he could back off. She was becoming a little — not exactly demanding, she didn't seem to be a strong enough character for that, but expectant, almost needy, constantly suggesting the next meet. And she always assumed he'd pay — in fairness, he supposed he'd started in that vein, keen to woo her. But not in the usual sense of wooing.

Tina was easy company but somehow a little irritating; too anxious to please, too pink and dewy eyed. He hadn't minded kissing her and wouldn't particularly object to the next stage, but he'd rather concentrate on Amanda. Focus on his plan. Woo her in the usual sense of wooing while waiting for an opportunity to do something about her wretched husband. And in the meantime, once he had the keys, or at least copies of the keys — he must remember to put the originals back wherever Tina had found them — he could look through the filing cabinet whenever Amanda and Hugh were next away. Skiing, hadn't she said? Or maybe she'd go up to London for the day before then. Whatever. He wasn't in a hurry. It was just a possibility for making a bit on the side while he waited. Or even something to keep in reserve in case his plan didn't work out. Though of course it would in the fullness of time, but still. Never a bad idea to have an insurance policy. Especially when there was no premium to pay.

He dragged his thoughts back to the present as Tina came into the pub. She was beaming, almost radiant, and he hastily arranged his features into a rapturous smile.

'Tina!' He stood up and gave her a hug, which he hoped seemed warmer than it was, and a quick kiss on the forehead. She was irritatingly short.

'Hi Steven,' said Tina breathlessly. 'Lovely to see you! I'm so excited. Can't wait to tell you how I found them.'

Simon suppressed a slight shudder. 'I think this calls for a glass of fizz,' he said. 'I'll bring it over if you find a table in the back.'

Tina giggled. Giggled! 'That's very appropriate!' she fizzed.

'Cheers!' he said, raising his pint. 'You're a godsend. Well done!' He flicked a whisper of foam from his top lip.

Tina leaned forward, her eyes bright with excitement. 'They were in the wine cellar.'

Simon frowned. 'Wine cellar?'

'Yes, it's amazing. Like a spiral staircase. But it's really well hidden. Under the breakfast room, kitchen, whatever you call it. There's a sort of hatch but it looks the same as the floor. And there's a control panel above one of the counters. Looks just like a light switch or something unless you look closely.'

Tina took a swig of her fizz. 'I was lucky though. Don't think I'd have found it on my own but Mrs Standing went into it while I was getting my kit. There's a locking switch but she was in a rush to go out somewhere, or maybe she doesn't usually bother. Anyway it was all because of *AbFab*. There was a big bottle — what are they called, a magus or something? — of Bolly and I couldn't resist holding it, then I saw it was empty, then I saw it wasn't empty.' She beamed at him again and handed over the keys.

*

'So what did you think of the house?' asked Jane, almost before she'd put the two wine glasses on the table and sat down opposite Tina. It was the day after Tina had given the keys to Steven and she was feeling almost giddy with happiness, trying not to check her phone too often for an invitation to their next date. She'd texted Jane on Sunday to say that all had gone well at Whiteacre and suggested that they meet for a drink in the Bishop on the Bridge, where she now felt at home. It reminded her of her evenings with Steven. She hoped there'd be many more, and stole another covert glance at the blank screen of her phone.

'Amazing,' said Tina. 'I've cleaned several in Nightjars Holt but though it's not as huge as some, it's definitely the most beautiful inside. And the garden's lovely also,' she added loyally.

'And did you meet Mrs Standing?'

'Yes, but only briefly. She was there when I arrived but then went out both times.'

'She doesn't mingle much even when she is there,' said Jane.

'She's very beautiful too,' said Tina. 'How was your holiday?'

'It was lovely. Nothing beats catching up with old friends. Having fun in Brussels bars. And eating great food. Talking of which, did you see any signs of Am— Mrs Standing's Thursday evening visitor?'

'I suppose it could have been earlier in the week,' said Tina. 'But yes, definitely someone had been to supper before I cleaned on Friday. There were some pans soaking which I imagine she wouldn't have left for several days in her perfect, spotless kitchen. Looks as though they had a good evening!'

'It always does,' said Jane. 'And the bottles in the recycling bin are always good wines.'

Tina started in momentary surprise. She always checked the recycling bins of course, but hadn't thought of other cleaners doing so. Though obviously you'd see what was in the bin if you put other stuff in it, perhaps that was all it was in Jane's case. But you'd have to be quite curious to pull out bottles and read the label. And know something about wine.

'Did you find anything interesting?' asked Jane.

Tina started again, having suddenly remembered the receipts. They'd been somewhat eclipsed by the excitement of her discovery of the keys for Steven. Surely Jane couldn't know that she'd stumbled across them while on autopilot, or indeed that she'd been specifically looking for, and had found, the keys? 'Erm … well I wasn't …'

Jane's smile faded. 'I sincerely hope you weren't. You have to stop, Tina. You do know that, don't you?'

'It was just the once.' The lie came out in a panicked squawk and Tina felt the giveaway colour flare on her cheeks. 'But yes, I do know. Thanks — I don't think I ever said. For making me see how stupid I was being. I'm going to tell Finn when I see him next week.' Tina hoped fervently that Jane wasn't going to mention the police again, and threw out a distraction. 'What did you mean, then, about finding anything interesting?'

Jane shrugged. 'You know what it's like, prowling round these amazing houses, seeing how the other half lives. I've spotted all sorts of fascinating things. Just stumbled across surprises. It helps make cleaning more interesting as well.'

Tina hesitated. Now that she'd remembered about the receipts she was curious. She took a gulp of wine.

'Actually, I did come across something very unexpected. I think it must be about an affair!'

Jane sat up straight and leaned forward a fraction, her eyes bright. 'In Mrs Standing's bedroom? The main bedroom?'

'No,' said Tina, confused. 'Why?'

'Oh … no reason really. I suppose I often think women are more interesting, more likely to have secrets, and better at hiding them.'

'It wasn't in her bedroom,' repeated Tina. 'But on Monday I was, er, running the hoover into one of the walk-in wardrobes and I, I … knocked some hangers off the rail. And when I was rehanging one of the suit jackets, guess what I found in the pockets?'

Jane's eyes suddenly widened. 'What?'

Tina found the receipts in her bag and handed them to Jane with a flourish.

Jane stared at the faded scraps of paper, her face colouring in an echo of Tina's earlier.

'So Mr Standing must be having an affair, don't you think?' pressed Tina.

*

Whatever Leonie had expected, it wasn't this. She stared at the receipts, conscious of her rising blush. Something she and Tina had in common, it seemed, and something that Tina was unlikely to have missed. She had to take a decision in the next few seconds. It was possible that Tina had given copies to her dodgy brother-in-law, though unlikely: after all, this wasn't personal data. At least not in the legal sense. The only way they could be monetised was by blackmail. It was a long shot — they'd have to find out Hugh's address in London, she supposed, as they couldn't send them to Whiteacre, but they knew the surname and maybe knew he was a solicitor — would that be on the New Brooms Whiteacre file? And of course Leonie had told Brenda that he was a solicitor, and Brenda and Tina were friends so she might know anyway. Or have seen the cards he kept in his desk drawer, which also had his office address. She didn't think Tina would have the appetite for blackmail, but she needed to be sure.

When she'd slipped the receipts into the suit pocket in … July, it must have been, she'd expected that Amanda would find them quickly and it would cause a major row. Hugh would have to confess to his affair with Margot and dump her. It had all seemed so simple. But as with other matters, the simple had become complex. Did she really want to damage the marriage? Amanda was having her own shot at that. And did she want to cause the inevitable collateral damage to Amanda, now that she knew what she'd suffered as a child? And would Hugh have given up Margot anyway? And if he did, wouldn't he just find someone else to take her place? Leonie had assumed that Amanda had long since come across the receipts and thrown them out, either not having read them or, having read them, not caring. But if Tina had discovered them so recently, Amanda couldn't have checked the pockets of that suit. Perhaps she didn't go through Hugh's pockets; he was so tidy he probably never left anything to be found. Presumably he hadn't worn the suit since then, he had plenty to choose from after all. Or he had worn it and not noticed.

Whatever, her original purpose in planting the receipts was long since exhausted. If Hugh received photos of them with a blackmail demand, the first question he'd ask himself was where they'd come from. Of course he had no idea that she was cleaning Whiteacre, but he'd have a very strong idea that she must have planted them, because who else could it be? He'd be livid and he knew how to contact her. He would never physically harm her, she was sure, but it would be unpleasant and embarrassing and he could ensure that she lost her job, which at least for the moment was her only source of income.

Leonie heaved a deep sigh and said, 'I put those receipts in the pockets.'

Sixteen

October

Tina stared at Jane, who held her gaze for a moment then looked away, her face burning. Tina could hardly speak, but managed to croak, 'You? Why? What …'

Jane stood up.

'No, don't go, you can't —'

'I'm going to the bar,' said Jane grimly. She did so and came back with two more glasses and a couple of bags of peanuts. She took a deep draught of her wine, put her glass down and let out a deep breath.

'It's a long story and it'll sound very silly. It is very silly. Childish. But I need to be absolutely sure you won't tell anyone.'

Tina gave a mirthless laugh. 'Let's face it, you know something bad about me too. I won't.'

'But first, I need to know whether anyone else has seen the receipts. Did you give them to Finn?'

'No!' squawked Tina. 'Of course not. Why would I?'

'I just thought …' Jane trailed off. She gazed out of the

window, her eyes not moving, and chewed her lip. 'OK. You know I was a solicitor. I worked at the same firm as Hugh. Mr Standing. We had an affair. He dumped me in favour of someone else. I was made redundant on the same day.'

'God,' said Tina. 'Talk about a bad hair day.'

'No kidding,' agreed Jane. 'It was a while ago. I feel a bit more … mature, maybe, about it now. I definitely didn't feel mature about it at the time. We'd had a very intense relationship for over two years. Saw each other nearly every night during the week.'

Jane stopped, rubbed a hand over her eyes and took another long gulp of wine.

'It sounds awful I know. It was just meant to be a bit of fun really. I knew he only went home at weekends and he told me that they led separate lives and he'd had affairs before, ever since they moved to Winchester and he started commuting. He said Amanda — his wife — was emotionally dependent on him and he could never leave. I didn't get the impression they had a particularly interesting or satisfying marriage.'

'I'm not sure many people do,' said Tina.

Jane shot her a grateful look. 'The thing is, it was pretty obvious that if it wasn't me he'd have found someone else to hop into bed with. So I thought I wasn't doing any harm. I'd just come out of a long relationship which had ended badly —'

'Don't they all,' Tina chimed in. She was feeling sorry for Jane, which she hadn't expected. And also for Mrs Standing; Jane seemed to be confirming what Steven had said about Mr Standing. She was pleased that she'd been able to help him in his Robin Hood role.

'Anyway, a brief fling with someone who was good-looking, good company, good in bed …' Jane flushed again and Tina flashed her a complicit grin. '… seemed too good to be true. To tide me over a few weeks while I got myself together. And it was too good to be true. I fell in a big way. I suppose to Hugh it must have seemed that I got more demanding. I suppose I did. Classic affair scenario.'

Tina, having successfully opened her peanuts after a struggle — why did the manufacturers make it so difficult, you'd think they'd want people to be able to get at the contents easily — did the same with Jane's packet and thrust it at her. 'Put something in your stomach,' she advised.

Jane tipped a handful of peanuts into her mouth, crunched for a few seconds and washed them down with another slurp of wine. 'Thanks,' she said absently, then resumed, 'So the day when they told me I was being laid off I wasn't seeing Hugh in the evening. He had to stay late in the office for a video partners' meeting. It was a US firm with offices all over the world and they had meetings at really inconvenient times. I suppose they had to be inconvenient for somewhere. That afternoon, after I was told about the redundancy, I went home and tried to decide what to do.' Jane drained her glass.

'Are you driving?' asked Tina.

Jane shook her head. 'Train.'

Tina went to the bar and bought another round, thankful that she'd decided to drop her car home and walk to the pub for some exercise. She sent a quick text to Peter saying she'd be back later than planned and would pick up some fish and chips on her way.

'Thanks,' said Jane. 'Where was I? Oh yes. I did some solitary venting about the redundancy over some wine. Then I decided to head back to the office and catch Hugh when he left the building after his meeting. I knew the approximate time and wanted to tell him about it. So I did. Go to the office I mean. I waited outside and saw him come down to the entrance — it's a big modern building with lots of glass, you can see people on the escalators — with a corporate partner. Margot. She'd have been at the meeting too so I didn't think anything of it, but I definitely didn't want to talk to anyone from Mainwaring & Cox apart from Hugh. So I followed them.'

She paused to blow her nose and have some more wine. 'I followed them to London Bridge station.'

More wine.

'And they just — sort of fell on each other in this huge passionate clinch. Then she headed into the station and he turned round and more or less walked into me.'

'God,' said Tina again. 'What did you do?'

Jane glanced at her watch. 'I need to head to the station myself shortly.'

'You can't go now and leave me hanging!'

Jane sighed. 'OK, I can get the next train I guess. So Hugh dragged me into a pub. We had a blazing row. He said he'd been planning to tell me the following evening. He felt I was starting to want more — which I was — than he could give me and it wasn't fair to me to carry on. Just a coincidence no doubt that he'd dumped me for a woman who's younger than me and very attractive and very bright and successful, and very rich come to that. Not that Hugh needs more money. But still, we'd had so much fun in each other's company for two years, for fuck's sake, and he just — sort of threw me out. So that was it. In a text the next day he said it was complicated, whatever that meant. Some male doublespeak I guess. Seemed fucking simple to me. Anyway, once I'd recovered from a few monstrous hangovers I decided I wanted to get even.'

Jane paused to have some more wine and peanuts, then resumed. 'So I used my new found free time to hatch a plan. The Cleaning Plan. Partly it was fun, coming up with the idea and working out how to carry it off. I phoned round the Winchester cleaning agencies —'

'But Mrs Standing might have paid cash in hand,' objected Tina. 'Plenty of people do.'

'It was very unlikely. Hugh was a tax lawyer. Well, wills and probate also but mostly inheritance-tax planning. He was involved in lots of legal cases against the Revenue and was paranoid about being whiter than white with his own tax affairs in case they found out if he wasn't and used it against him. So I phoned a few agencies. I … I pretended to be Amanda. Mrs Standing. Said I'd lost my diary and wanted to check the cleaning schedule for Whiteacre. It was a bit lame but it worked. The first three said Mrs Standing wasn't a client and I apologised and said I'd recently changed agency and must have remembered the name wrong. A bit lame also, but I felt quite chuffed to think that they thought she was a dippy airhead. As I said, it was all very immature.'

Jane grimaced and had a swig of her wine, then continued.

'I found out that she used New Brooms then a few days later I emailed to apply for a job. Had an interview — well, you know the rest.'

'But couldn't you just have got another legal job?'

Jane gave a snort of cold laughter. 'You'd think so, wouldn't you? That's what I thought too. Had a series of humiliating interviews with teenage recruitment consultants. I'd just turned fifty, and that's apparently too old — well, they couldn't say it in terms but the subtext was clear enough. Or I had the wrong specialisation, or firms weren't recruiting. It became clear after three interviews that my legal career was going nowhere fast.'

'But still,' prompted Tina after Jane had been silent for a few minutes, 'did you really want to be a cleaner for ever more?'

Jane shook her head vigorously. 'No, definitely not. I don't mind cleaning actually — I don't think I could have carried it off otherwise. But after the recruitment-consultant disaster, I applied for a job as a legal translator. I was — am — fairly confident that I'll get it, but it's a long, slow process. I'm still waiting to hear. So that made the cleaning all the more palatable.'

'Translator,' said Tina, impressed. 'As well as a lawyer. You must speak other languages then.'

'Mostly French,' said Jane. 'It's written translation, which is much easier than simultaneous interpretation. And I'll — I hope — be freelance, working from home, time to consult dictionaries and so on.'

'French,' said Tina thoughtfully. 'That receipt — one of the items was called an "ouvert". Is that French?'

'Yes, it means open,' said Jane absently, then shut her eyes briefly as her face turned a deep and impressive red. 'Oh God,' she said. 'It all sounds so petty. I was a bit obsessed. I thought the Cleaning Plan would be a way of getting Hugh out of my system. I went to an Agent Provocateur that wasn't too far from his office and flat, and had great fun choosing two very sexy items. I thought there might be a problem returning them without the receipt so I chose the cheapest —'

'The cheapest?' echoed Tina.

'You wouldn't believe how much that high-end stuff costs. Even open knickers which are mostly — well, open.'

'Did you get your money back?'

'Yes, I had to argue a bit but I'd paid with ApplePay and my Amex card and I had detailed receipts on both apps and they took pity on me. I said I'd bought them the day before I'd been dumped. Almost the truth.'

'So you planted them in the suit pocket, but Mrs Standing didn't find them evidently. Did you do anything else?'

'I was planning to mark one of Hugh's shirts with lipstick before putting it in the wash, but in the end I didn't. I thought Amanda — Mrs Standing — might think it was my lipstick. Well of course it would have been, but I mean in the sense that

I'd been careless when I was doing the laundry and ruined one of Hugh's doubtless very expensive shirts. And I was beginning to feel a bit more … mature by then.'

'What about the scent?' asked Tina.

'I kept that, I bought the one I usually use. But I also bought a sample size bottle of Chanel No 5 — that's Margot's scent, at least she was wearing it when I met her —'

'You've *met* her?'

'Only in passing, at work,' said Jane. 'She worked at the same firm, remember. Different department but I met her at some drinks do for welcoming new joiners.' She lapsed into silence, her gaze fixed vacantly on her glass.

'So what else did you do?' pressed Tina.

Jane started and blinked. 'Where was I? Oh yes, I bought a sample on eBay and thought I'd spritz it on to some of Hugh's suits or shirts. But in the end I didn't. I was beginning to move on. It seemed silly and trivial, as it was. Not to mention a waste of expensive scent. And also I'd got sidetracked very early — on my second clean at Whiteacre — by discovering that Amanda — sorry, I'm going to give up trying to remember to say Mrs Standing, I've always thought of her as Amanda, have to be really careful when I'm talking to her — was having an affair, which was far more interesting. I figured she was paying back Hugh in the best possible way. I was curious though, so I was trying to work out who her lover was.'

'An affair?' Tina was hooked. 'How did you find out?'

'I saw … signs,' said Jane, reddening again and shifting in her seat. 'When I changed the bedding one Friday. The second time I cleaned there. I was covering —'

'Of course!' said Tina. 'Your affair with Mr Standing. That's why you wanted to clean Whiteacre. We were wondering.'

Jane frowned. 'We?'

'Oh, just Brenda and me. Well maybe Cathy also I suppose.

When I asked to cover for you she said you'd originally asked to clean it because of some family connection and then Brenda had asked about it, said she could see into the garden from one of her houses.' Tina shrugged. 'Anyway, carry on. About the affair, I mean.'

'I saw the sheets. And I knew Hugh was in London all week. It was a bit … voyeurish. But at least it distracted me from my silly plan. I can't work out who the lover is though. So that's the end of my story! I'll let you know if I find out more.'

Jane finished her wine and stood up. 'Sorry Tina but I must go.'

'It's been nice, having a drink,' said Tina. 'I don't have many friends. I lost touch with most of them when I was married. My husband was — well, let's just say he had a bit a temper. There's Brenda, of course — I've known her since we were at school — but we don't get together often. She's got two kids, younger than mine, and neither of us has much money or time to spare.'

'It has been nice,' agreed Jane. 'Let's have another chat soon. Discuss something more humdrum maybe! And please, Tina, tell Finn ASAP you're not doing any more for him.' She headed for the door.

*

Simon was conscious that he was somewhat distracted when he was at Whiteacre the evening after Tina had given him the keys. He prided himself on giving Amanda his full attention when he was with her — there was a limit to what he could offer her so he focused on what he could. Company, foraged and poached food and flowers, cooking and clearing up, and of course sex. Fortunately he enjoyed doing all of them for or with Amanda. She was always a pleasure to be with, and had been warmer than ever since she returned from Sicily, as had he. He hadn't needed to worry.

Tina, in contrast, was not a pleasure to be with. Now that she'd outlived her usefulness, she was becoming a source of intense irritation which was only going to get worse. Outlived. Time to do something about that. He had a plan, of course, which he'd spent time and care perfecting over the last few weeks. All that tracking in the bush had been the best preparation. You needed patience and cunning. And sometimes you needed to take drastic measures to protect yourself. Not just from predators. There was the poacher, and the time he'd disastrously tried to break out into burglary and been interrupted. By the gardener, ironically. Now a late gardener.

Tina knew too much. She was guileless, chatty and not very bright. She was also clingy and fluffy and clearly falling in love with him. He needed to act fast before she started telling her friends about him and what she'd done for him. She'd said she hardly saw any friends, didn't have enough money to go out much and liked to be at home for her son. But still. And he couldn't keep up the pretence of a relationship with her for much longer; quite apart from the near revulsion he now felt in her presence, he needed all his time and energy for wooing Amanda. If he finished with Tina in a lesser sense than he had in mind, she might turn on him, tell Amanda what he'd asked her to do, or even tell the police. Perhaps unlikely given what he knew about her, but he couldn't take the risk to his carefully planned future, which was now finally, gradually, edging into glorious technicolour focus.

Simon parked his thoughts of Tina, comfortable in the knowledge that he'd sort her out tomorrow. For now, he needed to turn his full attention to Amanda. Though as it happened she also seemed uncharacteristically distracted, as if she were focused on a difficult problem of her own.

Simon left Whiteacre unusually early the following morning, foregoing his favourite breakfast in bed. He told Amanda he had to take his van to the garage first thing for its MOT. But instead the van was now parked behind Tina's car and Simon was leaning against it, watching the entrance to her flat.

Tina let herself out of the building and went to get into her car.

'Psst,' hissed Simon. Tina whipped round. He put a finger to his lips and beckoned her over. Her expression a mixture of pleasure and surprise, she edged closer to him.

'Tina,' he said, his voice low. 'Listen, things have hotted up. That's why I didn't suggest a date yesterday. I need to keep you out of it if the police get involved. After all the good work you did, I don't want you to have any trouble. Can we meet this evening? We can go somewhere quiet for a moonlit walk and I'll fill you in. I'll bring a bottle of champagne and we can have another celebratory drink, just the two of us. I'd like to give you a treat as I may have to lie low for a couple of weeks. It'll be hard not to see you but it'll just be till things calm down again. And I'll give you a down payment tonight in case anything happens to me.'

Tina chewed her lip. 'OK. The walk sounds lovely, though it'll be hard not to see you also. But of course if you think it's important. Will you pick me up later?'

Simon shook his head. 'Too risky, love. Can't take the chance of being seen together. I need to get away from you now too. There's a walk along the River Itchen, by Compton Lock. Can you meet me at the lock at 7, say? It'll be dark but there's a path and a full moon and I know the way. Shouldn't be anyone there, I can give you the money and explain what's happened without any risk to you. And don't tell anyone, anyone at all — no one knows about us and it needs to stay that way for the moment. For your safety. If your son asks, just say you're going for a walk to clear your head or something. He could be in danger too if the police find out about us. Delete all our messages also, just to be safe.'

Tina nodded, her eyes huge. 'See you then,' she whispered, and got into her car.

*

Tina had squeezed in a haircut between two of her cleans, thinking she could probably afford the treat now. It looked good, a shiny swinging bob. She'd also splashed out on some upmarket lingerie. Well, not too upmarket — not like that eye-wateringly expensive stuff Jane had bought! — but a nice silky bra and knickers, trimmed with lace, from Marks. She put on a short skirt and a clingy, fluffy sweater, then remembered that they'd be walking by the river and it would be cold, so changed into jeans. She shivered slightly, at the thought of the river rather than the cold — she didn't like water, but she knew she'd be safe with Steven. And she'd better wear boots, it may well be muddy. She didn't want to be teetering round on heels, she'd look silly. Her wellies weren't exactly glamorous but Steven would probably be impressed by how practical she was. Not one of those foolish women who wear unsuitable shoes. She'd put on trainers for driving and change when she got there.

Tina took extra care with her make-up and, sniffing her wrist, checked that she could still smell the scent she'd doused herself with in Boots earlier. Peter as usual expressed little interest in where she was going so at least she didn't have to lie to him — well, not much — just said she needed a walk to clear her head and told him there were some sausages in the fridge for him to reheat. He grunted a goodbye and she headed out to her car, humming happily as the moon cast her shadow.

Tina parked as near to the lock as she could and checked her reflection in the sun-visor mirror. She flicked away a stray speck of mascara, ran her fingers through her hair and refreshed her lipstick. Then she changed into her boots, popped a Tic Tac mint into her mouth and set off towards the lock. The moon was still shining like a huge round lamp and she saw a figure on the path, waiting for her. Her heart raced and she quickened her step. It was Steven! Looking so handsome, his hair silvered by the moonlight, the shiny gold neck of a bottle poking out of one of his pockets at a jaunty angle. Champagne! Maybe even a Bolly. That would be a lovely thank you for her work. She almost ran the last few yards and into his welcoming embrace.

Seventeen

October

Brenda was just finishing her morning clean when the text came in.

Can you come into office ASAP? Need to talk. Cathy

Brenda frowned. It was unusual for Cathy to call cleaners in. Had she, Brenda, done something — Jesus, had Cathy somehow found out about the blackmail? How could she have done? There was no way that Mrs Standing could know her name, let alone where she worked. Brenda had been very careful. Still …

Brenda put away her cleaning kit, rapidly emptied the dishwasher which thankfully was her last chore and set off to New Brooms, her fingers notionally crossed.

Cathy was pale, almost white.

'Sit down, Brenda. I — I have some really awful news for you.' She closed her eyes and took a deep breath. 'I know you're — you were — good friends with Tina.'

Brenda stared. 'What do you mean, "were"?'

'Brenda, I'm so sorry to tell you this. Tina died last night. Drowned.'

Brenda started back in her chair as if she'd had an electric shock.

'No,' she said stupidly. 'Tina would never drown. She can't swim.'

Cathy looked puzzled.

'I mean, she hated water. She wouldn't be in it.' Brenda shook her head and tried to focus. 'What ... what happened?'

'I had a call from Tina's sister. Daisy, is it?'

Brenda nodded.

'She'd just had a visit from the police. Tina's son —'

'Peter,' supplied Brenda.

'— phoned her at 11 o'clock last night. Tina had left their flat around seven, saying she was going for a walk to clear her head, but didn't tell Peter where. He didn't think she was meeting anyone. So Daisy reported her missing. They said it was too early to worry but then, early this morning, a local man who was fishing spotted her — her hand ...' Cathy broke off, took a tissue from a box on her desk and rubbed her eyes savagely. She nudged the box towards Brenda.

'She — her body — was trapped in some weeds. By Compton lock. They think she was mugged as she walked along the path in the dark and slipped or fell into the water. Maybe she struggled with the muggers as she tried to hold on to her bag, or maybe she just — missed her footing in the dark. Her bag was found shoved into some bushes nearby, but her wallet and phone weren't in it.' Cathy blew her nose and blotted her eyes again.

Brenda also grabbed a much-needed tissue. 'Peter,' she moaned. 'What will happen to him? I must call Daisy, see if I can help. But —' She shook her head again. 'I just don't understand. Tina wouldn't go for a walk by the river. Not on her own. She must have been with someone.'

'I don't know. That's not what Peter thought. And no one saw her as far as the police know. Well, apart from the mugger or muggers of course. Daisy said they're appealing for any witnesses to come forward so maybe someone will.' Cathy sighed. 'Take the afternoon off, Brenda. I'll let Mrs Rook know you've had some very bad news. I'll text you if she wants to try and slot in an extra session tomorrow, though I know it would need to be shorter than usual so you can get to the school gate.'

'Oh God,' said Brenda. 'Tommy and Lily. They loved Tina. They've known her all their lives. She's — was — Lily's godmother. Fuck. Sorry Cathy. And sorry you had to break the news.'

Back home, Brenda sat at the kitchen table and tried to gear herself up to call Daisy. She remembered there was a miniature of brandy at the back of one of the cupboards and poured it into a glass. She'd bought it last Christmas for the pudding but Tommy and Lily, who'd wanted to help, had decided that as a surprise they'd reheat the pudding by steaming it; they'd let the steamer burn dry and both pudding and steamer had been ruined. Anyway, she was glad of it now.

She'd known Tina since secondary school. She thought of Peter, going through all the difficulties of adolescence after losing his father to a bitter divorce, now losing his mother in a terrible accident. And Tina in the water — she'd always hated swimming. She was famous at school for having her period whenever it was a swimming day, even if it was only a week or two since the last one. She supposed Tina's sister would take in Peter unless his useless, violent father turned up, but that didn't seem very likely which was just as well.

Whatever Peter said, whatever the police thought, Brenda couldn't imagine Tina walking on her own by a river, or was it a canal? Maybe she'd been with that man she'd mentioned. Steven, was it? Perhaps he'd been the mugger. Or run off when she'd slipped, not wanting to be mixed up in anything. Or, more charitably, perhaps he'd chased the muggers and Tina had slipped while he was doing so. Or maybe Tina hadn't been with him, maybe she hadn't even still been seeing him. When was it that they'd had that coffee? Must have been a month or so ago. And even then Tina hadn't sounded very definite. What had she said? 'I think I might have met someone' or something similar. It might be nothing, but still, she should let the police know. She owed that to Tina. And Peter and Daisy. Daisy. Her heart heavy, Brenda picked up her phone.

Brenda went to the Tower Street police station the following morning after dropping a tearful Tommy and Lily at school. She told the desk sergeant that she had information about Christina Taylor's death. He found the case on his computer and looked expectantly at her.

'It's just that she couldn't swim,' started Brenda.

'Well that's why she drowned, love.'

'No, you don't understand. She was scared of the water. There's no way she'd have walked by the river.'

'But she did.'

'She wouldn't have done it on her own,' Brenda persisted. 'She must have been with someone and it was their suggestion.'

'Who would that be then?' He squinted at the screen 'It says here that she didn't tell her son that she was meeting anyone, in fact he got the impression she was just going for a walk on her own. To clear her head, she said.'

'But she wouldn't have,' repeated Brenda desperately.

The sergeant shrugged. 'What can I say? She was there. No

one's come forward to say they were with her or to say they saw her with anyone.'

'Has anyone said they saw her walking there alone?' countered Brenda.

'No,' the sergeant conceded. 'Who do you think she might have been with? If you give us a name I can enter it on the system and one of my colleagues will follow up.'

Brenda took a deep breath. She knew how this was going to play out. 'She told me she'd met someone. Called Steven.'

'Surname?'

Brenda sighed. 'I don't know.'

The sergeant echoed her sigh. 'Any other information? Where he lived?'

'No,' admitted Brenda. 'Oh, except that he was a businessman.' The sergeant rolled his eyes. 'Er — something to do with gardening. Had his own company.'

'And when did she tell you this?'

'Erm … recently.' The sergeant looked at her, his eyes narrowed. 'Well, a few weeks ago I suppose.'

The sergeant pecked at his keyboard. 'I'll pass it on. But it may not lead to anything. It's a bit … vague. But thanks for coming in.' He turned away from his desk in an obvious gesture of dismissal.

*

Leonie was back at Whiteacre on the following Friday. She liked to vary the order in which she cleaned when it wasn't dictated by the need to work around Amanda's movements, and decided to start at the top. No need to give Hugh's office more than a wave of the duster as he wouldn't have been home since Monday, but she always gave Amanda's office a thorough clean twice a week.

As she pulled the hoover into the room she remembered how on Monday, as she backed out of Hugh's office, she'd almost bumped into Amanda. Leonie paused, thinking back. Amanda had looked — well, different somehow. Normally so cool and poised, she'd seemed slightly flustered, her hair ruffled as if she'd run a hand through it and those arresting green eyes unfocused. And while she was always pale, she'd been almost white.

Leonie dragged her thoughts back to the present, to Amanda's office where dust hovered in the sunlight streaming through the high window. The desk was, as ever, neat and ordered; any papers left out were corner to corner in a pile, subjugated by an elegant shell paperweight. Leonie glanced automatically at the water bill and house insurance policy that were there today. There'd been an HMRC envelope on Monday, she remembered; Hugh probably dealt with revenue communications. And, she suddenly remembered, the anomalous hand-written envelope. And then again she recalled Amanda appearing behind her, ashen and unsettled, and almost scuttling into her office. Holding some paper in her hand.

Leonie knew the desk drawers weren't normally locked — in fact she'd never even seen a key in them. She glanced inside every time she cleaned, curious and feeling the usual frisson of voyeurism, increasingly tinged which something approaching shame, but nothing had changed since she'd looked on her first clean: all but one were devoted to interior design catalogues and samples, and while the wider, central drawer held a few items of stationery and correspondence, she'd only ever noticed odd personal letters or postcards, none of which had been of interest. Now she checked that drawer and saw the postcard from Monday's post. And a hand-printed envelope on top of a thin sheet of paper, which had clearly been crumpled up and then flattened again, inscribed with more printed capital letters.

Leonie picked up the note and smoothed it out a little more so that all the letters were visible. She gasped as she read:

I SAW YOU WITH YOUR LOVER IN THE
GARDEN. I HAVE PHOTOS.

She sat down on Amanda's office chair and read the message again. Not that it took more than a split second. She took a photo and put the paper back in the drawer, then reluctantly started a less efficient clean than usual.

Someone other than her — and Amanda and the mystery lover — clearly knew that Amanda was having an affair. But how? And who? Leonie wasn't familiar with the garden at Whiteacre; she'd always been too conscious of the need to impress with her cleaning to take time out to explore it with the risk of being discovered doing so. Now she put her duster down, went into Hugh's office and looked out of the window. She'd had a quick peek from here on her first clean but hadn't really taken in the detail when there was so much more to be clocked, and since then she'd only seen the garden from the lower floors. She hadn't realised how extensive it was, surveyed from what seemed a great height. It was also well screened on either side with trees and tall shrubs, and she doubted that the immediate neighbours would have much of a view, if any.

The garden seemed to go on for ever — the terrace, the big lawn, a broad stretch of mixed flowers — was that what they called a herbaceous border? — a smaller lawn beyond with a summerhouse, rose beds to the right, an arch of something — ivy maybe? — and a tiny patch of green like a doll's house lawn. Beyond, there were what looked like fruit trees, garden sheds and what might be compost heaps, all set behind a hedge which she thought would screen the more workaday rear of the garden from the terrace, lawns and beds nearer the house, but which from her current vantage point was just a darker line across the green.

Leonie's musings were interrupted by her phone signalling an incoming email. She glanced at it and sat down hard again, this time on Hugh's chair. It was from Cathy.

Dear all, please forgive this round robin but I know I won't be able to see you all in person before the weekend.

I have the very sad news that Tina died in an accident on Wednesday night. Her body was found in the River Itchen yesterday.

I'll let you know as and when I have more news and also details of the funeral.

Eighteen

November

The nights were drawing in even earlier now the clocks had gone back and it was already dusk as Simon worked his way round Whiteacre's front garden, raking up leaves before he prepared the ground for some new bulbs. He'd been lucky last week with the full moon. As he'd expected, there'd been no one else around when he and Tina walked along the river bank. He had his arm round her and made sure she was walking on the outside of the path. The champagne was in one of the poachers' pockets in his tatty old jacket but he didn't expect to have to open it. He'd even offered to carry her handbag for her so she didn't need to worry about it slipping off.

He'd killed a couple of times before — sometimes, as he'd mused a few days ago, it was unavoidable — but spontaneously, as a way out of a sudden tight spot, never as part of a carefully crafted plan. Getting rid of Tina had been surprisingly easy — or perhaps not surprisingly: he'd put a lot of thought into it and she was totally trusting. Like a lamb to the slaughter.

He'd chosen the precise spot earlier in the evening when he'd cycled the route. The path was narrow, the drop steep if not far, the river running deep and swift. He'd done a recce of the patches of scrubby woodland nearby and unburdened a tree of a semi-broken forked branch, which he'd left by the side of the path. So easy to stumble against Tina and flip her into the water. It was immediately apparent that she couldn't swim, as she'd helpfully mentioned over their first evening drink, and she'd probably have gone under quickly without further help, but there was still the risk that she would cry out briefly before being overcome. Simon was a perfectionist who didn't take chances, and it was simple enough to push her head under with the branch and wait for a few minutes. He'd noticed that Tina had thoughtfully worn jeans and wellingtons which would have hampered even a good swimmer.

Simon gathered the pile of leaves into a sack and carried it through to the frame in the compost area reserved for leaf mould. He must remember to fetch the champagne from the fridge in his van and give it to Amanda as a surprise present.

*

Leonie finished a clean at another house in Nightjars Holt and set off towards the station in the early dusk. The tinder smell of bonfires floated in the crisp autumn air and she realised that it was almost Guy Fawkes' Day. She was still reeling from the news of Tina's death. She'd only met Tina a few times but had liked what she'd seen: friendly, perhaps somewhat naive, struggling to make ends meet. And Leonie's grief was sharpened by the worry she could barely articulate to herself that Tina might have killed herself and that she, Leonie, might have contributed by her fierce reaction to the data theft.

Lost in recriminations, she hadn't registered that her route was taking her past Whiteacre until she saw it, illuminated like a birthday cake with several uncurtained windows glowing. The security light outside the porch flooded the front garden where a man was raking up leaves from the small circular lawn and the sweep of gravelled drive. A wheelbarrow held a tumble of bulbs and some tools. As she passed, the man turned to gather the pile of leaves into a sack. Good-looking, she clocked automatically. There was a ghost of familiarity about his face but she couldn't place him. Maybe he looked like someone she'd met in passing.

Leonie was back at Whiteacre a few days later. She was changing the sheets in the master bedroom when she noticed the top book on the bedside table: *Big Little Lies*, which she'd just read. She picked it up, curious to see where Amanda had got to, but was distracted by a book called *An African Odyssey* which was beneath it. The title, in an attractive font, was set against a photo of a tree — a tangle of dry branches in sere shades of brown and cream, with fragments of blue sky visible behind the lattice work. The picture was surprisingly unarresting for a cover, but as she stared at it, the foreground seemed to rearrange itself like an Escher sketch and she could make out a leopard draped languidly on a branch, its limbs and tail dangling, its colours and markings a perfect camouflage. The photo flowed onto the back cover and Leonie followed it over the spine. Inset over a short blurb was a photograph of the author, Simon Long. Who she recognised as the gardener she'd seen the previous week. And — an image of the Wykeham Arms flashed into her head. She'd been sitting at one of the pockmarked school desks a few months earlier. A good-looking man at the next table glanced at her then back at his phone with a wolfish grin. It was the day she was asked to clean at Whiteacre for the first time. In fact, it was at that precise moment — she'd read the New Brooms email as it snaked across the screen of her phone, looked up, triumphant, and seen him.

But why would Amanda have a copy of her gardener's — self-published, she noted — book by her bed? She gasped, clapped her hand to her open mouth and sat down hard on the unsheeted mattress. Would Amanda have an affair with her gardener? It didn't seem in character. Not that she knew Amanda's character. On the other hand, he was very easy on the eye. It could fit.

She wondered how come she'd never seen him before — not that that would have helped, she'd have needed to see the cover photo to, well, blow his cover. He must work different days from her. Probably a deliberate arrangement. She'd seen him last week, on the Thursday. She screwed up her eyes, a memory flickering. Hadn't New Brooms told her when they first offered her the job at Whiteacre that Tuesdays and Thursdays weren't convenient? That must be why. So he must be the mystery Thursday evening supper companion. Leonie's first thought was that she must tell Tina. She swallowed a rising sob and mechanically finished making the bed.

Leonie downloaded *An African Odyssey* onto her Kindle app the following morning. She sat down with a strong coffee, intending to read it from cover to cover in search of clues about Simon Long. If nothing else it would distract her from her constant fretting about Tina.

The opening words were 'I was born on the seventh anniversary of UDI. A true child of Rhodesia.' Curious, she checked on Google, and realised that Simon would be fifty tomorrow. She wondered how he would celebrate it.

*

Amanda had also worked out that Simon would shortly be turning fifty. She didn't tell him she knew, simply said she would buy and cook everything on the Monday immediately after, the eleventh being a Friday.

But what to cook? Autumn food, for cold weather. She would have chosen game but Simon prided himself on catching his own where possible and on using his contacts where it wasn't — for New Forest venison, for example. Lamb was good at the moment though, contrary to the popular misconception that it was best in the spring. She'd do her seven-hour agneau à la cuillère; the darker, more mature meat would hold its flavour well as it slowly melted into a rich sauce. Serve it with coarsely mashed celeriac and parsnip to soak up the juices, with roasted Jerusalem artichokes and salsify on the side. Lots of roots, but Simon had a hearty appetite.

Something light to start, then. Amanda didn't know whether he liked them but took a risk and bought a dozen oysters. Poached quinces to follow — if not poached in Simon's sense. And then cheese. She'd learned a lot about cheese — French ones of course — on her cookery course in Paris, although Hugh had refused to relinquish the English pattern of cheese after dessert. Amanda loved the lyrical names which spun like silk in her mouth as she said them or even thought them. Chaource. St Nectaire. Epoisses. Abondance. Neufchâtel. Reblochon. She'd see what was in season.

A knottier problem was what to give him. She looked at several sites which claimed to sell gifts for camper van owners, but these proved to be either VW-themed trinkets or gadgets designed to make living in the van more comfortable. Amanda didn't want Simon spending more time in the van. She wanted him to spend more time with her. Eventually she bought him a new Barbour jacket from Chaplins in Southgate Street. Perhaps he'd rather have a new gun, she wondered idly, eyeing their extensive range. But she wouldn't have known where to start. Not that she did with the jackets, really. She chose the most expensive, the Longhurst.

On the Monday morning, after dropping Hugh at the station, Amanda went down to the wine-cellar. As she flicked the wall switch to raise the concealed hatch, it occurred to her that the cellar had been Hugh's only real contribution to the reconstruction of Whiteacre. Apart from his money of course. He'd been excited and enthused at the idea, and though he was shaken by the cost he said it was the one thing he really wanted. He called it his liquid assets portfolio.

She loved the clean and elegant design, and as she inched down the spiral stairs she felt an unexpected rush of affection for her husband. Whose treasured wine she was about to share with her lover.

Amanda paused and sat down on one of the wedge-shaped steps. What was she doing? Was her marriage so bad that it was worth risking everything? Didn't all marriages become boring after a time? She looked around at the neat arrangements of bottle necks: a prism of green, brown and clear glass topped with black, red, green and white capsules. Hugh kept a record of what was where and marked shelves with a star sticker to show that the stacked wine was ready to drink. Amanda sighed, rubbed her eyes and stood up. Too late for such thoughts before this evening. She would bat them aside as she always did.

She continued down to the lowest level, where the crinkly gold foil of champagne bottles reminded her of Christmas. Which wasn't so far away, come to think of it. She chose a Perrier-Jouët and picked out a bottle of starred claret on her way back up.

While the lamb simmered, Amanda shucked the oysters.

Another skill she'd learned in Paris, where she'd also bought her professional chef's oyster knife. A strong steel blade with a gleaming rosewood handle, it had come with a soft leather cloth for holding the rough oyster. Hundreds — maybe thousands? — of oysters later, the leather had worn as soft and thin as a handkerchief. A dozen were the work of a moment: the tip of the blade flicked to prise open the hinge joining the craggy shells followed by a second's twist of the sharp edge as it severed the muscle. The briny, seashore smell mingled with the fragrance of wine and rich meat juices from the oven. Amanda arranged the half shells, cradling the black-fringed, pearly flesh, on a plate and put them in the fridge.

It turned out that Simon did like oysters. And the champagne in bed before. And everything else, including the Barbour jacket. He rummaged in the pockets of his old coat and showed her a worn tarnished coin with a hole in it which he transferred to a pocket of the new jacket.

'It's an old Rhodesian penny,' he explained. 'We all used to use them to dismantle our guns for cleaning — they're the perfect size. I keep it as a memento of Zim. And thank you again. It's a fine birthday present.'

'Are you doing anything else to celebrate?

'Not really. And what could be better than this anyway?'

Amanda glowed. 'It's a big birthday though. What about friends and family? Wouldn't they want to see you?'

'I don't have many friends in England. I've travelled too much. They're scattered through Africa and Spain, along my routes. And my family as well. We're classic scatterlings of Africa. I must play you that song. Johnny Clegg and Savuka.'

*

Brenda turned on the TV and sat down with a mug of tea late on Friday evening. Tommy and Lily were finally in bed, even if not necessarily asleep, and Brenda was exhausted after a long day. A long week, come to that. Month. Year. She seemed to be running all the time just to keep in the same place. Like that chess piece in *Alice*. She'd read the book when she was her kids' age, but they preferred the film. Films. Anyway, Brenda didn't mean it literally — she was still a good runner. She'd run for Hampshire when she was in her teens and had tried to keep up her fitness even though she couldn't afford the time to go jogging or the money to join a gym. She always ran up and down the stairs of her houses, though, and given the size of most of them she reckoned that did the trick. But she seemed to stay in the same place financially however hard she worked. She hoped she'd get some help from Mrs Standing. Even though the money wouldn't be given voluntarily, Brenda was sure the woman wouldn't miss it. And it would make all the difference to Brenda. It was more Robin Hood than blackmail really.

She was still wondering what the blackmail protocol was, between tides of grief about Tina. She'd been in touch again with Tina's sister Daisy who'd confirmed that she and Finn would look after Peter and asked Brenda to give a tribute at the funeral. Brenda was almost glad to have the blackmail to take her mind off it. She realised that she hadn't made any specific request or threat in her first letter. She wasn't sure whether that was a deliberate and clever policy to buy herself time or an oversight. Either way, she was stuck with it. And needed to decide what to do next. She couldn't keep putting it off.

She supposed she could get a print of the photo and send it with a follow up-letter. And she could ask for some money. Maybe a lot of money. But in exchange for what? The days of original prints had long since gone. Even if she let Mrs S, as she was beginning to think of her, see her deleting the photo from her phone, so what? For all Mrs S knew, Brenda had a copy on a USB stick or had emailed it to herself or saved it on the laptop she didn't have. And obviously she couldn't let Mrs S see her so that was a non-starter anyway. And even if she somehow came up with a believable threat and the removal of that threat in exchange for a nice pile of used fifties, how could she arrange to get the nice pile of used fifties? She could hardly ask Mrs S to post it to her. At one point she had the brilliant idea — admittedly pinched from some old film or TV series, she couldn't recall — of agreeing that she'd leave the photo in some hiding place and Mrs S would collect it and leave a nice pile of used fifties in its place. But when she thought it through, that idea turned out to be not so brilliant after all.

Brenda heaved a sigh before heaving herself off her chair and finishing the clearing and washing up. Maybe if she slept on it … Not that she'd been sleeping much recently.

She did, however, have a further thought the next morning. She remembered a reference to burner phones in something she'd read recently. Or seen, more like. She couldn't afford to buy a new phone, even a basic one, but wondered whether she could buy a new SIM card and use it in her phone just for texting Mrs S. It might be tricky to work out when to use it but it would be much cheaper. She'd noticed a small corner shop advertising 'best price' mobile phone services near one of her houses on the other side of Winchester. Time to pay them a visit.

She came away with a new SIM card, which she paid for and immediately topped up using cash. She'd told the guy behind the counter that she needed to change her number so that her violent partner, whom she'd just left, had no way of tracing her, and was assured that this would do the trick. And he'd shown her how to change the card, which looked surprisingly easy.

Brenda agonised over where to print her prized photo. As far as she could see online, neither Boots nor Tesco in Winchester had a photo printing machine. She eventually found a branch of Copyman on Jewry Street who did it for her. She felt the heat rise to her face as three copies of the photo were handed to her — three for luck, she'd thought — but the spotty youth doing the handing gave no indication of having even clocked what was in the picture, let alone any interest in it. She posted her second letter, plus photo, having decided that it would be riskier to lurk outside Whiteacre waiting for an opportunity to slip it through the letter box without being certain that the house was empty.

*

After receiving the anonymous threatening letter in October, Amanda rescheduled several appointments so she could be at home when the postman came. Not logical, given that the mystery letter had been hand delivered, but still. She jumped every day when she heard the ricochet of the letter-box flap clanging back down, and wondered how she hadn't previously found the noise intrusive, even menacing. She seized the post almost as it fell to the mat, and when nothing had arrived nearly a month on she was beginning to dare to hope that for whatever reason the matter was finished. Until, part fearful, part almost relieved, she scooped from the mat another hand-printed envelope, identical to the first except that it was stamped and postmarked.

Amanda had tried not to worry too much about the first letter. She told herself time and again that the garden wasn't overlooked so nobody could have seen her and Simon. Except from the house, she supposed, but again she reminded herself that for obvious reasons there had never been anyone else in the house when she and Simon spent time together. It must be a try on. But the fact remained that, in addition to knowing her name and address, the writer apparently knew she was married and either knew or suspected that she had a lover. And also — for if there was any follow up it would surely be a demand for money — knew she had a lot of money and a lot to lose. Though she supposed that the former, and by extension the latter, could be assumed from the house.

She hadn't mentioned the letter to Simon, reasoning that she might as well wait and see whether there were any more. She had, however, asked him whether his key to the door in the garden wall had gone missing. They were in the kitchen and he'd gone through to the utility room where he always hung his — now new — waxed jacket, fished in one of the numerous pockets and dangled the key in front of her.

'Why do you ask?'

Amanda murmured something about doing an annual inventory of all keys for the insurance company and didn't mention it again.

Now, she took the post through to the breakfast room, put it on the table and made a strong cup of coffee while she steeled herself to open what she already thought of as the blackmail letter.

Nineteen

November

Although the second letter had come in the post, it was obvious from the handwriting, even disguised as it was, that it was from, or at least written by, the same person as the first. Amanda was about to open it then paused, put it down, went into the utility room and rootled around in the cleaning cupboard until she found the box of disposable latex gloves that her previous cleaner had asked her to provide. The envelope would have been handled by the postman and maybe others at the sorting office, as well as briefly by her, but the letter that she imagined was inside it would presumably have been touched by only one set of fingers. And hence only one set of fingerprints. She didn't know whether this would become relevant — how do you deal with blackmail, assuming this is what it was? You could hardly google to find out — but she might as well play safe with this letter and any subsequent ones in case she had to get the police involved. She pulled on the gloves, paused for a moment at the thought that the blackmailer had probably done the same, shrugged and carefully opened the envelope and withdrew another sheet torn out of an exercise book:

TEXT 06721 963455 9 - 10 AM THIS WEEK IF U WANT THIS DELETED FROM MY PHONE. OR THE NEXT COPY GOES TO HUGH. IN LONDON.

Amanda let out a sound which could only be described as a squawk. Seeing the word 'Hugh' in the bald, anonymous capitals was like a punch to the stomach, leaving her winded, her heart racing. It somehow made it more real. Even more real.

How did this person know Hugh's name? Or hers come to that? Or that he worked in London, maybe even the address of his office? Surely it couldn't be friends or family? Hugh's octogenarian parents (hardly likely) and brothers (ditto) all lived in London. She and Hugh didn't have many joint friends in Winchester and rarely socialised at weekends. Nor could Amanda imagine any of her local women friends wanting to blackmail her. Or, again, having the opportunity.

There was, of course, one person who knew Hugh's name. And hers. And that Hugh worked in London and that Amanda was having an affair. For a wild moment she wondered whether the notes had come from Simon. But then she slid out the other item in the envelope.

*

Simon wasn't really identifiable in the photo, except perhaps to someone who knew him well. He was turned away from the photographer and was wearing the faded, frayed old cap he usually kept for gardening. Amanda remembered now: it had been an unseasonably hot, sunny day in … maybe October, shortly after she'd got back from Sicily. Simon had been even warmer and more, well, loving than usual. As had she, after her holiday musings. She'd just come out of the breakfast room and put a tray of cold drinks on the table. He'd showered and changed but had put his faded old cap back on, having forgotten the less tattered one he normally had. She'd teased him about it, and he'd said that in Africa they took the sun seriously and everyone wore a hat, however tatty, when it was hot.

She, in contrast, was not wearing a hat and was really identifiable, even though the photo was not sharp or close up. Her face was partly shielded by Simon's half-profile but you could see her hair, her cheek, her clothes. And her arm curved around Simon's neck. And his arm draped under hers, his hand resting on her hip. It was obvious that they were in the midst of a passionate kiss. *In flagrante delicto.* Fragrant delight. It didn't smell so good right now.

Amanda put the photo down, went up to her office and came back with a clear plastic folder. She slid the note and photo delicately into it, positioned so that both were visible, and added the envelope above them. A Southampton post mark, she noticed, but most Winchester post came through the Southampton sorting office so that didn't prove anything. Then she peeled off the gloves and made another strong coffee, her first cup having gone cold after the first sip.

There weren't many options, which normally made decision-making simpler. But that was on the basis that some options were palatable. Here, Amanda reasoned, she had three, none of which was palatable.

First, do nothing — impossible; she couldn't risk the photo being sent to Hugh. It would destroy him. Double standards of course, but she knew he wouldn't be able to cope with evidence of her infidelity. Maybe divorce. Definitely a wrecked marriage.

Second, go to the police. Her skin crawled at the thought of an officer — well, anyone really — seeing that photo. And it could only go one of two ways: either they'd not be able, or maybe willing, to try and find the blackmailer, in which case nothing would have been gained and the blackmail would presumably continue, or they would find him or her and maybe prosecute. Amanda was hazy about criminal law and again didn't feel inclined to google, but she assumed that if there was a trial she'd have to give evidence. There's be publicity. Everyone, including Hugh, would see the photo and know about her affair. Same result as first option.

Third, text the blackmailer. Find out what they wanted. Which meant how much. And indeed how. She'd do it tomorrow morning and maybe take herself out for lunch and a walk today to think things through.

Amanda wondered why the blackmailer had set a time slot for her to text. Didn't people have burner phones for this sort of thing? Perhaps she only had it on her for an hour a day. Perhaps there was a whole gang of blackmailers sharing a burner phone, passing it round like a party game. In the course of her rambling thoughts Amanda suddenly realised that she herself had what was almost a burner phone, if a rather upmarket version. She would text from her secret iPhone. She set a reminder, finished her coffee, which had again cooled in the cup, and took the folder up to her office. She hesitated after putting it in the drawer with the first note, realising that she had forgotten to conceal that letter. She looked through another drawer, pulled out a hefty catalogue of wallpaper samples and placed it on top of the blackmail notes. In the extremely unlikely event that Hugh came into her office and opened the drawer, she couldn't see him going further.

*

Amanda was out when Leonie arrived at Whiteacre that afternoon. In the four weeks since she'd noticed the handwritten, unmailed envelope on the mat and subsequently seen the note itself in Amanda's desk drawer, she'd managed to check the drawer a few times but there'd been nothing new. It was an easy decision to start cleaning at the top, and the first thing Leonie did after setting the hoover down in Amanda's office was to open the drawer. There was a shiny catalogue of wallpaper samples in it, which was odd because all the numerous interior design brochures and magazines were normally neatly stacked in the deeper drawers. Leonie picked up the catalogue and felt a surge of excitement. There was a clear plastic folder containing an envelope, a piece of paper and what looked like a photo, all blank side up.

She whipped the folder out of the drawer, scattering the contents. She picked them up one by one, hoping she could remember how they'd been arranged, and turned them face up on the desk. And gasped, first at the new note — TEXT 06721 963455 9 - 10 AM THIS WEEK IF U WANT THIS DELETED FROM MY PHONE. OR THE NEXT COPY GOES TO HUGH. IN LONDON — and then at the photo.

It was definitely blackmail. And it was definitely Amanda in the photo. Leonie felt a momentary flicker of irritation — someone else had clearly succeeded where she'd failed in identifying the lover. Or at least in seeing him. Not that Leonie had really tried, just some idle wondering until she'd stumbled serendipitously on the information ten days earlier. Whereas whoever was writing these notes must have been stalking Amanda. And knew Hugh's name and that he worked in London. And had somehow got into the house, or at least the garden, to take the photo.

Leonie took a photo of the new note and the print and another of the original letter, which had been underneath the folder, so they'd all be together on her phone, then took the print into Hugh's office and held it up as she peered down into the garden. It looked as though it must have been taken from behind the hedge that separated the terrace, lawns and flower beds from the working area. She couldn't see enough of the man to be sure that he was the gardener, which was disappointing. But whoever he was he was very obviously the lover. And Amanda didn't seem to be discouraging him.

The front door slammed shut and Leonie shot back into Amanda's office, reassembled the montage in the folder in what she hoped was the right order, shoved it back under the catalogue and started hoovering noisily.

*

The next morning, Amanda stared at her secret iPhone for what seemed an age. Eventually she took a deep breath and pecked out a text, her finger trembling: *What do you want?* It was a bit bald, though less so than 'How much?' which was what she really meant. She swallowed and pressed send.

She had texted in the specified time frame and the reply pinged back promptly. *£1000. Cash. Every month.*

Amanda frowned. Had the blackmailer upped his or her game, or had they just forgotten that they'd previously dangled the unverifiable deletion of the photo in return for what she'd assumed was intended as a one-off payment? Of course she knew — from screen and page at least — that blackmailers never give up. She'd decided to go along with it for the moment provided the amount was … well, reasonable was hardly the right term, but at least doable. Maybe the contact with the blackmailer, who she was beginning to refer to in her mind as B, or the mechanics of payment would reveal something about their identity and she could put a stop to it then. How, she didn't know. Perhaps Simon could pay them a visit; she imagined he could come across as threatening if he put his mind to it, though she didn't think he'd have it in him to do anyone any actual harm.

She composed a text in reply, flicking a mental apology to Hugh who, whatever his other failings, was generous to a fault. Whatever that meant. And he might be less generous, let's face it, if he knew the money was going to someone who was blackmailing his wife after taking a compromising photo of her with her lover. Amanda gave a rapid shake of her head. Keep the two lives separate. Think about it later. And Hugh left the management of the bank accounts to her anyway so there was no risk that he'd ask her about the money.

> *Too much for me. My husband gives me an allowance and will notice. If he finds out he'll go straight to police, where he knows someone senior. I can manage £500 but no more.*

*

Brenda had thought long and hard about how much to ask for — no, not ask, demand, she told herself. I'm in charge here. But she didn't altogether feel in charge. It was one thing being handed a fistful of notes in return for silence, but quite another, she was finding out, to be dictating the terms. And the mechanics.

She'd decided on £500 a month, which she assumed would be small change to the wife of a 'usually very rich and high net worth individual' while it would be far from small change to her. And after all, Mrs S didn't have to work for her money. Her wealthy husband and lavish lifestyle were surely the result of a simple twist of fate. Both could have been Brenda's if things had turned out differently. And Mrs S had presumably always had a rich and pampered life. She'd doubled the amount on principle and sent her first text, her finger trembling as it jabbed the phone, within seconds of receiving Mrs S's. The reply had been as prompt.

Brenda wasn't really surprised that Mrs S was bargaining her down. That was life, after all. But she felt almost indignant on Mrs S's behalf that her husband was so mean and controlling.

He should give you more, she texted, *but I don't want trouble so OK.* She wasn't sure whether she believed the bit about the policeman friend, it was all a bit too convenient, but then didn't very rich and high net worth individuals play golf and things with senior members of the council and police force? She was sure she'd seen a film on the telly recently where the plot hinged on something like that. To do with corruption, she thought. So it was possible, and she'd definitely take £500 a month rather than nothing. Brenda added *I'll text in next few days about arrangements* and sent the message.

Twenty

December

The week after she'd seen the blackmail photo, Leonie explored the garden at Whiteacre. She'd ventured onto the terrace in warmer months to clear the odd abandoned wine glass and ash-tray, but other than that she hadn't investigated the grounds at all. She'd brought a change of shoes and prayed that Amanda would be out when she arrived.

Amanda was in but was about to go out. 'I won't be back until after you've gone,' she said. 'Have a nice weekend.'

Leonie waited ten minutes in case Amanda had forgotten something. Then she put her spare shoes on and went for a quick tour outside. She'd viewed the garden many times from the upstairs windows but it seemed different — bigger, more complex — from ground level. Obviously not the time to see it at its best — she must repeat her exploration in the spring and summer, if she was still cleaning — but she could appreciate the planning and structure.

As she'd seen from Hugh's office window, there was a hedge

screening the working area from the lawns, beds and terrace. Leonie crouched behind it. It was taller than it looked from above, and denser — some sort of evergreen — and at first she could see nothing through it so assumed she in turn wouldn't be visible from the house, at least the ground floor, or terrace. But then she noticed a couple of spots where the foliage was lighter and she could just make out the terrace. The blackmailer must have waited until the kiss then taken a rapid and daring photo, or more likely series of photos, over the hedge. Or maybe he or she had made a hole in it which had now grown over, or the surrounding branches had sprung back. Leonie had tried to ring the blackmailer's mobile number a few times out of curiosity, but the calls were either unanswered or went straight to an impersonal 'temporarily not available' message.

Turning round, Leonie saw a door set into the wall behind the rough ground. So that's how the blackmailer got into the garden, though it didn't solve the problem of how he or she knew about Amanda's affair in the first place. Leonie tried the handle but the door was locked — another puzzle, the blackmailer must somehow have a key. As she headed back towards the house she brushed against a leafless plant whose flame-coloured spidery flowers cast a spicy scent reminiscent of Hugh's aftershave. The memory reminded her of the laundry and London Hugh, and that she hadn't yet tried to get into his laptop. She felt in the interests of thoroughness that she should at least try to do so, but there were practical difficulties which she needed to think through. With a sigh, Leonie went in and started to clean.

After she'd finished, she worked her way round a minor maze of quiet streets until she was at the back of Whiteacre, in a narrow alley which fed into the side road in one direction and petered out into a pedestrian-only path in the other, running between a copse and what must be the back walls of Whiteacre and its neighbours. She found the door into the garden without difficulty, but it was of course still locked.

*

Brenda had given a lot of thought to how the money would change hands. She needed somewhere busy enough that she could be near the drop-off and pick-up point without being too obvious, but not so crowded that she risked being jostled away from it. It was essential that she could see Mrs S arrive and leave the money, be near enough to grab it promptly but not be too noticeable. She assumed that Mrs S would be watching and maybe hoping to catch and identify her or try and follow her.

A car park seemed a good possibility. She thought the one at the station must be busy and it was easy enough for her to get to. She passed by a few times but the earliest she could get there was after getting the children off to school, by which time the car park was chock full of cars but almost empty of people. London commuters, she supposed, who'd doubtless be a perfect seething crowd but too early for what she planned.

Brenda brought up a map of Winchester car parks on her phone and drove home one afternoon via the ones that were most accessible. Worthy Lane seemed the best. There were spaces for coaches, and both times she checked there were what looked like tour groups milling aimlessly around; there was also a rubbish bin next to the Ladies which would be easy to describe.

*

Amanda's secret iPhone pinged. The text was from B. *Worthy Lane car park. Leave £ in envelope in old plastic bag under rubbish bin by Ladies then go away. 12 noon tomorrow.*

Worthy Lane car park. That was where Simon kept his camper van. Which could be useful, she mused, if she involved him later in trying to identify or at least discourage B. She imagined him sitting in his van, his cap pulled down over his forehead, probably listening to one of his African playlists while he watched like a leopard. But Amanda wanted to have a go first.

*

Amanda felt foolish as she tried to — not exactly disguise herself, that was too strong a word, but blur the edges of her appearance a little. It would be awkward if she bumped into one of her friends or former clients as she stooped to leave an old plastic bag on the ground under a rubbish bin by a public lavatory. She tied a square scarf under her chin, feeling like 1970s minor royalty or — more attractively — a blonde Audrey Hepburn. *Charade* maybe. She never wore the scarf, but it had been a present from her sister so she hadn't liked to get rid of it. She sighed as she shrugged on a dingy jacket she used to wear when she prowled round the garden to see what the landscaping firm had done, or sometimes not done. She never felt she needed to check up on Simon in the same way.

She drove into the car park feeling faintly ridiculous, parked and paid for two hours just in case she caught a glimpse of B and was able to follow on foot.

Amanda headed towards the rubbish bin by the Ladies holding the plastic bag. She looked rapidly around her as she approached but there were a lot of people coming and going, particularly around the bays where coaches were parked, and it was a hopeless task to pick out someone you wouldn't recognise. She had a hunch that B was a woman but perhaps that was because she associated blackmail with women. Too much Agatha Christie maybe.

She set the bag down under the bin and backed away, trying to keep her eye on it. There was a knot of people behind her and she stood on the edge, watching the bag. She felt her secret iPhone vibrate in her pocket; it was a text from B. *Go now.* Obviously B must be watching her; her disguise wouldn't have confused someone who was waiting for a woman to put a plastic bag under that bin at that precise time. Amanda turned and headed towards the car. She looked back after a few steps; the bag had gone.

*

Brenda also felt slightly foolish as she tied a headscarf over her hair, but it was important that Mrs S couldn't see any distinguishing features. Not that she had any really. She was taller than some but otherwise so average that no one really noticed her. Mousy hair. Brown eyes. Medium build. For once she was glad to be unremarkable. She wished she had some sunglasses, then remembered that Lily had a cheap off-the-shelf pair from the market. They'd be tight on her but they were always slipping off Lily so they'd probably do. She found them in the tiny box room that her daughter had to squeeze into now that Tommy was too old to share with her.

Mrs S looked positively dowdy. She too was wearing a headscarf, and some tatty jacket. Brenda might not have recognised her if she'd passed her in the street, but it was hardly likely that another woman would be putting a plastic bag under that bin at noon today.

Brenda watched her from what she hoped was a safe distance. Mrs S backed away and then stood there, staring at the bag like a hawk. Did she think that she, Brenda, was stupid or something? Brenda sent a curt text. She wasn't near enough to hear whether Mrs S's phone chimed — shit, what if Mrs S called her and identified her by the ring tone? Brenda hastily put her phone on silent. She saw Mrs S pull hers out of her pocket, glance at it and walk away. Keeping one eye on her retreating back view, Brenda strolled briskly towards the bin, let the disposable lighter she was carrying slip from her fingers, and bent down to pick it up. Together with the bag.

*

The envelope was so slight and light that Brenda had a flash of panic that she'd been conned. But no, ten fifty-pound notes slid into her hand.

She didn't feel the elation she'd expected. Oh, it was wonderful to have all that cash suddenly, and £500 would be a big help, though of course £1000 would have been better … maybe she should have stuck to her guns. But maybe Mr S did have a pal in the police force. She needed to come up with a better handover plan for the next drop. This one was just too risky. Mrs S could have had a friend watching. Except how would she explain that to her friend? Unless the friend was the lover.

Brenda felt the beginnings of a headache. Who would have thought blackmail would be so complicated? It always looked so easy on the telly. And who would have thought Mrs S would have such a penny-pinching husband?

*

Amanda drove straight back to Whiteacre. She whipped off the headscarf and jacket as soon as she was over the threshold; they made her feel grubby and soiled. The frisson of excitement that had unexpectedly buoyed her as she acted out her spy thriller role had as quickly evaporated. She needed a shower ASAP.

She couldn't keep on doing this. The money wasn't itself a problem but the whole context was degrading. Next time she'd put more thought into how she might be able to identify B. And the third time would have to be the last, whether she'd done so or not and whatever next step she decided to take.

Twenty-One

January

In the end, Brenda stuck with Worthy Lane car park for the second drop. She'd racked her brains but despite a month of thinking about it she failed to come up with anywhere better, and even if she found somewhere else for the handover, the risk of being spotted and followed would be no less. Maybe more: at least Worthy Lane was busy with all the coach traffic. She texted Mrs S and dug out her scarf and Lily's sunglasses again. One o'clock on Thursday.

*

Amanda put on her headscarf and old jacket, checked that she had the plastic bag containing the envelope and headed off to Worthy Lane car park. Despite a month of thinking about it, she'd failed to come up with a better way to spot B. She'd have to talk it over with Simon if she didn't strike any gold today. Though it was B rather than her who was striking gold.

She didn't know why she hadn't mentioned it to Simon already. She'd intended to a couple of times but had changed her mind at the last minute; the words she'd planned to utter had morphed into variations on the theme of 'Another glass?' or 'Shall we eat earlier or later?' Partly she felt that same grubbiness; an affair that had originally been exciting, exhilarating, almost liberating was now tarnished. And she had the uncomfortable feeling of being spied upon. The affair had been hers and Simon's alone, an adventure in her unadventurous life. Sure, there'd been an element of risk — which doubtless added to the spice — but it was small and in her control. And now it was bigger, potentially much bigger, and out of her control.

Amanda went through the same pantomime as previously. She tried to spot someone watching her, but it was hopeless in the shifting crowds of shoppers and tourists. She'd had the idea of phoning B and hoping to hear the ringtone, but abandoned it; there were so many people and so much ambient noise — engines, slamming doors, crying children, chatter. And of course mobile phones ringing and being shouted into in all directions. She dropped the plastic bag and slunk back to her car, not even bothering to check her mobile when it vibrated with the message which she correctly assumed was *Go now.*

*

Simon was eating a lunchtime sandwich in his camper van when he saw a familiar scarlet Audi drive into the car park and reverse neatly into a space. Amanda got out — at least he assumed it was Amanda, she was the right height and shape and moved like Amanda but her golden hair was hidden beneath a hideous scarf with snaffle bits and saddles on it and most of the rest of her was hidden beneath a somewhat dirty jacket which looked more like something he'd wear for gardening.

She was carrying a scruffy plastic bag. Curious, Simon followed her with his eyes as she headed towards the Ladies. He lost her for a second in the jostling throng, remembered he'd left his binoculars in the glove compartment after their recent productive outings and found her again, the scarf a helpful marker.

He watched as she walked, head down and shoulders hunched, past the Ladies, paused, and dropped the plastic bag on the ground beneath an overflowing rubbish bin. She glanced around and then, her face — definitely Amanda's — set, turned and trudged towards her car. Her eyes were downcast and she showed no sign of having seen Simon.

Simon swung his binoculars back to the bin and saw a woman edge out of the crowd, walk to the bin, drop something, dip down to retrieve it and in the same movement scoop up the bag.

He kept her in his sights. She'd turned and was moving away from the pedestrian exit and towards the parking area. She stopped by a small green car, rummaged briefly in her handbag and reached for the door.

Simon started the van, pulled smoothly out of the bay, turned against the one-way arrow painted on the tarmac, spotted the green car nosing out of its slot and towards the busy exit and slipped into the queue a few cars behind it.

*

Brenda had sat in her car for a moment, her heart hammering. Something else they didn't make clear on the telly. Fucking stressful this blackmail business. She wasn't sure she was cut out for it to be honest. Still, not a time for loitering here and she had a job to get to. She straightened up, took a deep breath and started the engine.

It had seemed such a good idea. Not just for the money, though of course mainly for the money. But also exciting, different, almost glamorous. An exit from her dreary round of breakfast, school run, cleaning, school run, supper, bedtime. Rinse and repeat. And something that was under her control. Nobody telling her what to do, where to go, when to be there. She was setting the terms. But she hadn't thought through the risks and how to deal with them. Blackmail was a crime. She'd tried to resist the temptation to find out more but had eventually given in and asked Google. It had sternly informed her that blackmail was a serious criminal offence with a maximum fourteen-year prison sentence. 'Technically,' the site of a firm of solicitors told her snippily, 'it is an offence under section 21 of the Theft Act 1968.'

And looking further back, all that spying with her binoculars seemed silly and childish now. Like one of those Alex Rider books that Tommy liked. She was almost beginning to wish that she hadn't walked in on that couple in bed. The easy gain of a few hundred pounds had been seductive.

Thinking about the binoculars reminded her that she was due at the Castle House shortly and she did a hasty left turn.

*

Simon was also due at his next job shortly but wanted to see where the woman went and had no idea how long that would take. She might be going out of Winchester for all he knew. He sent a quick text at a convenient red light.

Babe think I'm coming down w sth, feverish and achy. Taking today off if that's OK, don't want to risk giving it to u. Will text tomorrow Sxxx

He suddenly noticed where he was heading. Was he on autopilot towards Whiteacre, having lost his quarry? No, the green car was still ahead of him. Could the woman also live in Nightjars Holt? Neither she, from the admittedly little he'd seen, nor her old, rust-scarred car seemed right for the affluent suburb.

Simon followed the car past the turnoff for Whiteacre, climbing slightly beyond the copse then left into a wide road of massive houses. The woman turned left again into a driveway, a wooden sign proclaiming that the house was called Brambles. He preferred Whiteacre as a name. Amanda had explained the derivation. Whatever else, Hugh must have a sense of humour.

Simon coasted to a quiet stop on the right-hand side of the road just before the drive. The green car — a Ford Fiesta he saw — was tucked beside a gleaming Range Rover, a Mini Countryman and a Smartcar with an open soft top. The woman got out, walked up to the front door and rang the bell.

*

Amanda's secret iPhone pinged. It was on the table in front of her. She'd been staring at it mindlessly, wondering whether she'd hear from B — but there was no reason to think she would — or whether she should text B — but what would she say? But the text was not from B. Amanda had forgotten for a moment why she'd bought the phone in the first place and who normally had the monopoly on using it.

> *Babe think I'm coming down w sth, feverish and achy. Taking today off if that's OK, don't want to risk giving it to u. Will text tomorrow Sxxx*

Amanda felt a flicker of surprise. Simon, like Hugh, seemed to be blessed with rude health. She'd never known him — either of them in fact — to be ill, except once years ago when Hugh had had a bad bout of the flu. She hoped that Simon was being over cautious, though he didn't seem the type for caution. She replied *Look after yourself, hope to c u Tues Axxx.*

She put the phone back on the table and continued to stare sightlessly at it. She normally looked forward to Simon's afternoons, and even more so to his evenings and sometimes, increasingly, nights. But today she couldn't shake off that feeling of grubbiness and was almost glad he wasn't coming. And she was still no nearer to identifying B or deciding what to do.

*

Brenda knew the envelope was tucked safely in her backpack handbag but felt compelled to look or feel in the bag every few minutes. She was annoyed to see so many cars in Brambles' drive; probably one of their family reunions. Mrs Castle, as she called her (must remember she's really called Mrs Rook), had appeared flustered when she let Brenda in, but said it would be fine for her to clean everywhere except for the 'children's' bedrooms and the kitchen. Brenda hadn't been able to check her bag until she'd got to the top storey. The envelope was, of course, still there, folded in the tired plastic carrier. Her knuckles grazed her binoculars and she decided to risk a quick sneak recce of Whiteacre's garden. Mrs Castle would probably be busy in the kitchen making petits fours, whatever they were.

Brenda focused the binoculars. No sign of the gardener. And Mrs S was sitting on the terrace on her own. Slumped in her chair, giving off an air of dejection. Brenda felt a flicker of guilt, then a flash of concern. Had Mrs S finished with the gardener? Is that why he wasn't there? Brenda supposed he could be in a shed, but he was normally very visible even when he was working. And if Mrs S was outside she'd go and chat to him now and again, take him a cup of tea or a glass of water, give him a quick kiss. Brenda frowned and bit her lip. If they'd split up, would that be the end of her short-lived career as a blackmailer? Had she even caused the split?

*

The woman obviously didn't live at Brambles then. No surprises there. Simon reversed the van a few yards so that it was less visible from the house while giving him a view of the drive entrance. Or exit. And settled down to wait. He seemed to be doing a lot of that lately.

As an hour passed, then two, he began to regret the whole idea. Whiteacre was tantalisingly close. By now he'd be over halfway through his gardening and looking forward to a cold beer with Amanda on the terrace followed by wine, food and sex in one order or another. As the time inched forward another hour he wondered whether to give up. He also regretted the excuse he'd chosen. He should have invented something more temporary. A sprained wrist which he wanted checked at A&E maybe. Oh well, he'd had to come up with a story in a few seconds at the traffic light, no point fretting now.

He stiffened, like a dog that's caught a scent. The Fiesta was nosing out of the drive. Simon put the van into gear. He was in luck: the car turned away from him so he didn't need to do a three-point turn. He was a good driver but it was a decent sized vehicle and a narrow street and he would have lost valuable seconds. As it was, he set off behind the car and followed it until it pulled up on a narrow street of small houses and cramped maisonettes. In an echo of his shadowing of Tina a couple of months earlier, he waited until he saw the woman let herself in and a light come on in what he assumed was the entrance hall. A few minutes later he walked softly to the door, but there was no name. Still, he made a note of the number and the road.

Thinking longingly of Amanda's cooking and other skills, he parked back at Worthy Lane and walked to the Wykeham Arms for a pint. Worthy Lane reminded him of the scene he'd witnessed that had started him on what now seemed like a wild goose chase. What an earth could Amanda have been doing? Was she returning something of the woman's? But it was a very odd way of giving it back. And why was Amanda dressed like a bag lady? Well, relatively speaking anyway. Maybe he'd ask her about it, but she'd looked furtive and as if she didn't want to be recognised. Perhaps she'd be annoyed that he'd seen her. And wouldn't it seem odd that he'd ignored her? He could say that he knew she wanted to keep their relationship secret. But how would he explain that he'd rushed to follow the woman and sent the lying text? He took a long swallow of beer. Best leave it for the moment, see whether she mentioned it. He thought she would if it was anything dodgy and she needed his help. And at least he knew where the woman lived.

*

Amanda was out when Leonie arrived on Friday. Leonie had a quick glance round the kitchen on her way to pick up her cleaning kit and was surprised to see no signs of the usual lavish meal on the previous night. And Amanda and Simon can't have gone out to eat — not that she imagined they ever did, for obvious reasons — because there was what was clearly the residue of a meal for one. Cheese omelette, boiled potatoes and salad by the look of it. Frugal and solitary. Almost forlorn. Had Amanda split up with her lover?

Leonie started cleaning at the top. She was flicking her duster over Hugh's laptop when she remembered, again, that she still hadn't tried to get into it. In her first few months of cleaning at Whiteacre she'd thought about it constantly but had always been brought up short by two apparently unresolvable difficulties. Apart from not knowing the password, there was the problem of opportunity. If she logged on from the laptop while Hugh was on his desktop in the office, he'd get an immediate alert. Leonie had briefly thought she could try on Monday morning or Friday evening when Hugh would be commuting, but of course she wouldn't be at Whiteacre then. And at that point she'd given up each time she wrestled with the puzzle. Now she decided to make a conscious effort to think of possible passwords while she cleaned the rest of the house. One problem at a time.

She was polishing the silver photo frames on the piano when the problem resolved itself, though not in the sense she'd expected. She'd picked up a studio portrait of Hugh. It was a good photo, catching his easy charm, his boyish humour, the hint of fun and games behind his glasses. And she realised that getting into his laptop didn't matter to her. She already knew who'd supplanted her and didn't want or need to know any more. She had memories of good times with Hugh and now that she had more distance, and knew more about Amanda, she had no desire to stir up trouble for either of them. The Cleaning Plan was well and truly dead.

Amanda arrived just as Leonie was finishing. She seemed distant, almost dull. Was she still being blackmailed and was that the reason? Or was there trouble brewing between her and Simon? Or indeed between her and Hugh? Again, Leonie was reminded that Hugh's wife, who she'd always assumed sailed serenely through an effortless life funded by her husband, didn't have it easy.

Twenty-Two

February

Simon knew that Amanda would be out all afternoon on a Thursday three weeks later. She'd explained that she was going up to London for the day; she was having her hair done and then she and Hugh were taking Hugh's parents out for lunch, which they tried to do every couple of months. She said she should be back between five and six and would text if that changed.

They'd agreed that Simon would arrive an hour later than usual for his gardening slot, but he decided that he'd keep to his usual time and put the extra hour to more fruitful use. Inside rather than out. He'd driven to Whiteacre and, by agreement with Amanda, parked his van in the drive, blocking the view from the road to the front door. He'd taken the keys and burglar alarm fob from the key safe in the garage on Tuesday, assuming it was unlikely they'd be missed, so was able to let himself in in the shadow of the van.

Simon checked whether the wine cellar was locked — it was — and then had a quick look in the key drawer in the utility room. He recognised the key to the door in the garden wall, tagged as 'spare', and made a mental note of it in case he ended up changing the lock, though he imagined there might be another whose whereabouts he didn't know. Otherwise he found nothing of interest.

Then he went straight up to Hugh's office, where he knew he'd find something of interest. Simon had had the keys to the filing cabinet for three months now. He'd had copies made but hadn't been able to return the originals as the wine cellar had been locked on the rare occasions he'd tried the controls when Amanda was having a shower. Unfortunately she hadn't used the same code as for the key safe and burglar alarm. He'd thought about sneaking downstairs in the middle of the night when she was asleep, but even if she'd left the cellar unlocked he didn't know how much noise the hatch made when it opened and decided not to risk it. He'd also reasoned that it was best to wait until he'd returned the keys before taking any further steps in case he succeeded in siphoning some money out of Hugh's account and their absence was discovered. Again, a risk not worth taking. But now he was in the house on his own and even though he couldn't get into the wine cellar, he could at least take a look at Hugh's financial information, assuming there were relevant documents in the filing cabinet.

There were. Up-to-date statements from several banks and from his investment and pension fund managers. Simon sat down at Hugh's desk under the high window, feeling suddenly light-headed. So much money. More than he'd ever imagined. Not to mention the house and contents, including Hugh's wife. Except she'd be his widow by then.

He pondered for a while then put everything back where he'd found it. Again, it was a question of weighing the risk. Simon's plans regarding Hugh had clarified over the last few months and even if he had to continue to wait for the opportunity to put them into practice — execute them, he thought with a black laugh — that opportunity would come eventually and he'd be one significant step nearer a share of all that money. Better not to run the risk of being discovered to have helped himself in advance.

He might as well check Amanda's office as he was here with time to spare, though he knew from his earlier scouting visit that her desk contained nothing much other than routine stationery and books of wallpaper and curtain fabric samples. And indeed the first six drawers, three on either side, contained exactly that, with the two deep ones entirely devoted to fat, glossy catalogues. Feeling he might as well be thorough, he opened the centre drawer and was surprised to see a fat, glossy catalogue. He moved it, momentarily startled by the weight, and revealed a clear plastic sleeve containing what appeared to be an envelope and two pieces of blank paper.

Simon took the folder out of the drawer and turned it over on the desk. And froze in a tableau of shocked stillness, his fingers holding the plastic, his eyes fixed on the contents.

*

Simon's first thought was how beautiful Amanda looked in the photo, amateur and long range as it was — eyes half closed, her arm draped over his shoulder. She looked like a film star and the pair of them looked like an erotic sculpture.

His second thought was that it had been taken from within the garden.

He turned to the note. TEXT 06721 963455 9 - 10 AM THIS WEEK IF U WANT THIS DELETED FROM MY PHONE. OR THE NEXT COPY GOES TO HUGH. IN LONDON. Simon glanced at the postmark on the envelope. The letter had been posted on 16 November 2022.

He was about to put the folder back in the drawer when he saw there was another envelope and a note, which had obviously been crumpled up then smoothed out, under it. The first move. No postmark or date.

He took photos of the two envelopes, two letters and the print, arranged everything, including the catalogue, carefully back in the drawer and went into Hugh's office again. Of course he knew the garden inside out but nothing beat an aerial view. He'd forgotten how high Whiteacre was and how steeply pitched the roof. But it had its advantages, and the perspective confirmed his initial suspicion that the photo must have been taken from behind the screening hedge.

Simon left the house the way he'd come in, re-setting the burglar alarm as he did so. Then he walked round to the alley and let himself into the garden. After replacing the keys and fob in the key safe, he collected a pair of secateurs and a bag for the trimmings and worked slowly round some of the more vigorous shrubs doing some judicious snipping and tidying while he thought.

So the missing key to the garden door was explained. Whoever took the photo must somehow have taken it and let him or herself in. Herself, of course; it must be the woman he'd seen pick up Amanda's dropped plastic bag in the car park. When had she come in, he wondered? How many times? How much had she seen? How many other photos were there? He had a sudden memory of sex on what Amanda called the tea lawn one unseasonably warm and heady day.

But he had the advantage. He may not know who she was — though he knew where she lived — but he did have an idea of where and when he might be able to find out. Or at least, with luck, get hold of the phone.

He thought about calling the number, but decided against

it, at least for the moment. The blackmailer was hardly likely to identify herself on request, especially to a man, and if she suspected that someone other than Amanda knew her number she might be extra cautious, even abandon the blackmail. Which would of course be a good outcome, but he had a better idea for achieving that, if he could pull it off.

*

'Yes, Sandra?' Hugh glanced up from his trainee's summary of a recent Supreme Court judgment as his secretary put her head round the door.

'Just a reminder — today's the eleventh. Shall I order the usual bouquet for Mrs Standing?'

'Thanks, yes,' said Hugh absently, looking back down at the document. Then he paused, marked where he'd got to and rubbed his forehead pensively. He tried to think back over the last few months. Amanda in Sicily, unusually closed and distracted. The dinner in Taormina, when she'd shaken off his tentative concern. Once they were back she'd slid effortlessly back into her usual easy, unruffled self for — a few weeks maybe? But then she'd seemed to become distant again, giving that same impression of worrying away beneath the surface at some undisclosed problem. He'd thought she was just busy with the arrangements for Christmas, which this year for the first time they were spending in a hotel near his parents who were now too frail to make the journey to Winchester, for New Year's Day when they hosted her sister and his brothers' families, and for their week's skiing in early January. But now he thought about it Amanda had continued to have that preoccupied, almost troubled air in Verbier and on their return. When he'd been swallowed straight back into the accelerating stress at work as the end of the tax year drew nearer.

Hugh remembered how he'd resolved in Taormina to

become a more attentive, more loving husband. Which he'd failed to do. He'd be frantic for the next few weeks but could at least give her a more lavish than usual Valentine's Day bouquet. He scribbled a few lines on the notebook on his desk, tore off the page and went through to the secretaries' area. Sandra was holding the phone and keying in a number. He signalled at her to stop and handed her the paper. 'Could you order extra special flowers this year? And ask them to put this message on the card instead of the standard one. Thanks.'

He paused at the door to his office and turned. 'Oh and Sandra, could you make a booking for two at the Hotel du Vin in Winchester for Saturday evening? Eight o'clock say?'

Feeling lighter, almost virtuous, Hugh resumed his edit.

*

This has to be the last time, thought Amanda, wearily knotting the scarf under her chin. But she didn't know what would happen after. Probably she'd be saying the same thing in a month, and then another month, and another … She couldn't risk Hugh seeing that photo. She could afford the money. She still didn't want to tell Simon, and she still didn't know why. Except that she'd always felt in control of their relationship, and this was one thing she couldn't control

She went through the motions as if she were playing a part that she'd rehearsed to perfection. Which she supposed she was. The car park was as busy as usual, despite the grey day. She did her drop, lingered while she scanned the crowds, and felt her secret iPhone vibrate with the usual injunction to leave. She turned and, heavy-hearted and eyes on the ground, set off towards her car. She was vaguely conscious of a woman shouting behind her but the sound was instantly lost in the usual swirl of noise and she didn't even bother to look back.

*

Simon was standing at the edge of the milling knot of people on the other side of the Ladies from the rubbish bin. Who were all these people and where on earth were they going? Shoppers, of course, and day trippers who'd come up by coach, he assumed. But there was at least one who was neither shopping — or at least not yet — nor tripping. Or at least not yet.

He had been working on the assumption that the money — it had to be money — changed hands regularly and in the same place. The handover that Simon had witnessed had been on 17th January, a Thursday, at around one o'clock. Handy that he'd texted Amanda as he was following the woman who picked up the bag she'd dropped. He'd checked and his message had been sent at 1331 on that date.

He'd arrived at the car park at half past twelve today, Thursday 14th February. If nothing happened, he'd try again on the 17th. If it wasn't a regular weekly or monthly occurrence he'd change tack and try phoning the number once he'd come up with a plausible cover story that might elicit some information about the blackmailer's identity.

Simon had found a spot with a clear view of the bin, which of course meant that Amanda would have a clear view of him. She'd probably be so focused on what she was doing that she wouldn't notice him — the previous time, he recalled, she was looking down, hunched over, but she had briefly scanned the crowd after putting the bag on the ground. He'd found a broad-brimmed hat and an old grey fleece that she'd never seen and hoped she'd be sufficiently distracted not to clock him.

His eyes raked the throng around him. At five to one he found her. A woman, wearing a headscarf and, despite the dull light, sunglasses. Staring fixedly at — he followed her gaze and saw Amanda, also wearing a scarf, the hideous horsey one she'd worn before, and the same dowdy old jacket. He hastily moved his gaze back to the other woman and edged himself quietly through the shifting crowd until he was beside her.

Amanda moved forward and put the carrier bag down. She glanced round and Simon saw the woman next to him pull out her phone and stab a finger at it. Amanda turned away. The woman started to move forward, still clutching her phone. Simon lurched to the side and half fell against her, his leg in front of the right leg she'd just raised. She tripped and swore loudly as she pitched forward. Simon grabbed her hand. 'Careful, love,' he said. 'Let me help you up.' He dropped her hand and melted back into the crowd, slipping her phone into the pocket of his fleece.

*

Simon shrugged off the fleece and hat as he passed behind the coaches, going the long way back to his van. Once in the driver's seat he had a quick sweep round with his binoculars. The bag was no longer on the ground and he assumed that the blackmailer had picked it up. He'd thought for a nanosecond about grabbing it before disappearing, but instantly dismissed it as too risky. Pity, he could always do with extra cash. He wondered how much the blackmailer was squeezing out of Amanda. Maybe enough to replace her phone.

As he cycled to Whiteacre, having waited for Amanda to leave the car park first, he decided that he'd offer to return the phone. Not out of any moral sense, though he had no use for it, it wasn't as good as his. And in any event he didn't know the passcode. But he'd thought of a way of finding out, and thereby perhaps finding out who the blackmailer was and whether she was blackmailing others. And hopefully getting her to stop blackmailing Amanda.

Simon mulled over what, if anything, to say to Amanda about what had just happened. He couldn't admit to knowing about the blackmail without also admitting to having seen the letters. Which would involve admitting that he'd let himself into the house when she was out and gone through her desk. And while it was plausible that he'd been in that car park earlier, he could see no plausible explanation for his having tripped a random woman in the crowd and then stolen her phone. No, he would say nothing.

He'd have to think about changing the lock on the garden door though, to make sure that the blackmailer didn't try again. That would also be tricky as he'd have to tell Amanda either that he'd lost the original key, which would mean telling her he'd had a spare made as soon as she'd given it to him, which would also be an implicit admission that he'd lied to her when she'd asked him whether his key had gone missing, or that he'd lost his key since that conversation, which would be galling. He'd have to do it without her knowledge, which would involve finding and replacing the spares she had so they'd all fit the new lock. He sighed. Why was life so complicated?

*

Amanda took off the scarf and jacket as soon as she got home but couldn't shed so easily the feeling of being somehow sullied, tarnished. And Simon was due any moment. She didn't really want to see anyone. Perhaps a leisurely shower would help. Which it did, she had to admit. She dried her hair and smothered herself in frangipani lotion, put on clean, crisp — the new cleaner was a dab hand at ironing, as with so much else, she thought in passing — jeans and a sage green linen blouse, and checked herself in the mirror. Looking a bit peaky … She stroked on a light foundation, a warm blusher and a coat of mascara. Better.

She went downstairs, saw Simon crouched in one of the rose beds, weeding, and took a cold beer out to him.

'You're a sight for sore eyes,' he said, standing. 'And bearing beer too! Not that I'm complaining' — he took an appreciative swallow — 'but are we celebrating something by drinking so early? Or at least I am, what about you?'

Amanda shrugged. 'I'll have one later, with your next beer. I just thought maybe you'd like one. I've had a stressful morning … Shopping, you know. The crowds in the centre. I came back feeling a bit frayed and thought we'd have a drink together, but after showering and changing I feel fine. I'll wait.' The doorbell rang and she went back into the house.

The delivery man was almost hidden behind the flowers. Red roses of course, but this year leavened by pink peonies, lilies and feathery emerald foliage. Amanda was sure the bouquet was more luxurious than usual and wondered whether that was Sandra's doing. But neither Sandra nor the florist would have written the words on the card.

For my very special, very beautiful wife. Thank you for everything. Your loving husband.

Amanda frowned. Hugh wasn't usually so effusive, so romantic. She often wished he was, or used to. Was he feeling guilty about something? Though it was Amanda who was feeling guilty now. On top of the blackmail stress, the turmoil of emotions was almost too much to bear. She shook her head as if to shake her two lives back into their separate boxes. She'd leave the flowers in the utility room sink for the moment, arrange them tomorrow once Simon had gone.

*

Simon went round to the side door and let himself into the utility room to wash his hands. But the sink was occupied by the biggest bunch of flowers he'd ever seen. No, not a bunch of flowers, he thought sourly. That was what he gave Amanda, small sad posies of stolen blooms. This was a veritable bouquet, shrouded in shiny clear plastic, tied with a silky red ribbon. Red … mostly red roses. Shit, was it Valentine's Day? He'd missed a trick there. Worse, he'd been outshone. Outclassed. He saw a small envelope on the counter with a gilt-edged card half tucked into it.

> *For my very special, very beautiful wife. Thank you for everything. Your loving husband.*

Simon swore under his breath. He felt like seizing the flowers, putting them through the garden shredder and onto the compost heap. Why was Hugh getting all lovey-dovey? Did he suspect that Amanda was in love with him, Simon, and was he trying to make a move to stop it? Simon needed to focus on his plan now he'd heroically foiled the blackmailer, at least for the moment. Too late for him to get hold of Valentine's Day flowers; not that any he could afford could compete with Hugh's. And the irony — he'd given Amanda a better present today than her prissy, cosseted husband ever could, the best present she could have at the moment, and he couldn't even tell her about it.

Twenty-Three

February

'Mum, you're not listening,' complained Lily. 'Again.'

Brenda shook her head. 'Sorry love. Tell me again.'

She couldn't go on like this. It wasn't fair on the children and it was driving her mad. The events of yesterday went round and round her head, leaving no room for anything else. How could she have been so stupid, holding her phone in her hand while all her attention was on Mrs S? Asking for trouble in a crowd. And she was usually so careful.

Still, at least she'd got the money. But she'd have to spend some of it on a new phone. And a new burner SIM card, though that was the least of it.

She heard the slap of the letterbox, though it was a bit early for the postman.

'I'll get it!' sang Lily, wriggling off her chair and running into the hall. She handed Brenda one letter.

'Thanks love,' said Brenda absently. Then looked at the envelope and froze.

'Why's there no stamp?' asked Lily. She liked to collect them and take them into school for some charity. 'And it's not even grown-up writing. And look, your name's not on it. What's an occupier? It might be for me! Mum?'

Brenda picked up her backpack handbag and shoved the letter into it, her hand trembling slightly. 'Look at the time,' she snapped. 'Come on, get your stuff. Tommy,' she bellowed up the stairs. 'Come down, now. I'm leaving in two minutes, with or without the two of you.'

Once she'd dropped them off she headed to the nearest car park — not Worthy Lane, thank God — and pulled the envelope out of her bag. She had some time in hand having bundled a confused Tommy and Lily off to school earlier than usual.

There was indeed no stamp and her address was written in careful capitals. And, as Lily had noticed, there was no name, just 'The occupier.'

She swallowed, wishing she'd thought to stop in a café instead. She hadn't finished her breakfast and could do with a shot of caffeine and sugar. She opened the envelope and took out the letter.

GET SOMEONE TO TEXT YOUR PASSCODE
TO 04218 784393 AND I'LL DELETE THE
PHOTO AND RETURN THE PHONE. NO
MORE BLACKMAIL. I KNOW WHO YOU ARE.

*

Leonie had noticed that Amanda's Thursday dinners had resumed after the solitary omelette evening, but she found herself less and less inclined to spend time trying to reverse engineer the meal from the residue. Somehow, now that she knew who Amanda's lover was, there didn't seem to be much point. In fact, she realised, much of her original rationale for inveigling her way into Whiteacre had gone.

She'd met Amanda, who'd turned out to be far from the shallow Stepford wife she'd imagined. Childhood torn in two, father possibly murdered by a gangland executioner after laundering stolen diamonds, deep in a torrid affair with her gardener, blackmailed by someone unknown who'd apparently sneaked into the garden to take a compromising photo — what would be the next dramatic development in Amanda's life? Hard to see it getting any more eventful.

And — she coloured at the memory — she'd planted a clue to Hugh's latest affair, and look how well that had gone. Amanda hadn't found the receipts; instead Tina had discovered them and —Tina! Leonie's eyes watered in an unexpected rush of grief. And guilt. She pushed the worry away.

The Cleaning Plan had helped her get over Hugh, she supposed, if by somewhat unorthodox means. But for whatever reason, Hugh was out of her system. She'd carry on cleaning for the moment, she needed the income, but as soon as she heard, as she hoped she would, that she was through the translation selection procedure, she'd hand in her notice. In the meantime, she'd try and be a more conventional cleaner. Keep her head down, just dust and hoover, wash and polish. Which she'd better get on with. Maybe she'd drop into New Brooms for a slice of cake when she'd finished.

*

Just as well she hadn't had anything to eat; she would certainly have thrown it up.

Brenda sat staring at the letter but the message stayed the same. She frantically tried to remember what other photos she had on the phone. Loads of the kids, that's for sure. Lily looking blonde and angelic. Even Tommy was fine-boned and elfin. Both fodder for a pervert. Is that what this was really about?

But if he — she was pretty sure it was a man who'd jostled her and grabbed her phone, though it had happened in such a blur she wouldn't swear to it — really did know who she was and what she was doing, he must have mugged her deliberately. He must have followed her. He knew her address, that was clear. But she hadn't gone to Worthy Lane car park from her house yesterday, she'd gone from a cleaning job. Brenda rubbed her clenched fist over her eyes, turned the key in the ignition and headed slowly towards her morning clean.

She worked at nothing like her normal pace, frequently pausing, duster or hoover or mop in hand, while she fretted away at the problem. Perhaps he really was only concerned about the blackmail. Which now seemed a mad and reckless folly. She might have put Tommy and Lily in danger. No amount of money was worth that.

She needed her phone back though. Could it make things worse to send him the passcode? He could probably crack it anyway. It was her birthday, which she'd always known was risky, but then she'd never expected to lose her phone to someone who, apparently, knew who she was. Or at least where she lived. And there were probably dodgy shops which would crack a code for money. It was a very basic smartphone, and a model that must be outdated by now, so the security was likely weak.

Brenda sighed and gave the kitchen counters a distracted wipe. She would text him. But how? She recoiled at the thought of using Tommy's phone. He'd pester her with questions if he knew she'd had hers stolen, he was like a dog with a bone sometimes. And somehow she felt her foolishness, which could even be dangerous now, would pollute him. The man would have his phone number. Or maybe Tommy would know how to hide it, but what reason could she give for asking him to do so? It was all too horrible.

She could call the mugger's mobile from her landline, but the thought of hearing his voice made her gag. And then he'd know her home number. She could call him, she supposed, from the landline here. But what if the owners were funny about their phone, worried about the cleaner running up bills? Maybe they monitored calls and would see that someone, which could only have been her as there was no one home, had called that number. Maybe they'd complain to New Brooms. Or call the number and speak to the mugger and complain a lot more to New Brooms. No, she couldn't risk it. She'd need to ask a friend if she could send one text from their mobile. She could make up a credible story. But who? Brenda didn't have many close friends; being a single mother of two small children and trying to make ends meet kept her too busy to socialise, and even if there was money left over at the end of the week, she didn't like to spend it on herself. There was always a bill to pay or something Tommy or Lily needed more than she needed anything.

If only Tina were still here. Brenda was still regularly ambushed by the piercing loss of her oldest friend. She sighed, and shook her head, trying to shake away the memories. She knew some of the school mums well enough to ask though, and might just have taken the risk of calling one and leaving a pound coin and an apologetic note explaining that she'd lost her phone. It was academic, though, because of course Brenda didn't have anyone's number as all her contacts were in her phone. But it was Friday, tea and cake day at New Brooms. Brenda knew some of the other cleaners and might run into one of them. Or if Cathy was there, she probably wouldn't mind. Brenda wouldn't be able to stay, she'd need to pick up the kids and again had no means of texting any of the other mums to ask them to do it. But her afternoon clean was — by her request — a short one. She could be at New Brooms before three and would just have to hope she'd see someone she knew before she had to leave. At least she'd have her car.

Brenda was in luck; Jane arrived seconds after she did. About bloody time, she thought sourly; she was due some luck.

'Jane,' she gabbled. 'Sorry, I'm in a real rush so can't even catch up which I'd like to, but I've got to get to the school gate in a minute. But I'm in a bind. I'll explain properly another time, but I've lost my phone and someone found it, I've got his number and just need to text him so we can arrange for him to return it. Could I ask a favour — could I send one short text from your phone?'

'Sure.' Jane dug around in her bag, found her phone, tapped the passcode and handed it to Brenda. Brenda turned slightly away from her, fished the letter from her pocket, hunched over the phone, typed in the mobile number and a short message, and touched the 'send' icon. Then swiftly deleted the message and handed the phone back to Jane.

'Thanks,' she said. 'You're a lifesaver. Let's go for a coffee soon. I'll text you as soon as I've got my phone back. Gotta run now.' She grabbed a brownie and wrapped it in a paper napkin.

'No worries,' said Jane. 'Hope you get it back. And have a good weekend.'

*

Simon had slipped Brenda's phone through her letterbox after opening it with the code she'd texted from an unfamiliar number and deleting the blackmail photo. He'd thought about emailing a copy to himself but it was an unnecessary complication; he had a photo of it on his phone already, and knew where the print was. He also knew the blackmailer's name and number from her phone settings. He parked at Worthy Lane, walked to the Wykeham Arms and settled down with a pint and a headful of thoughts.

When he'd opened Brenda's phone there'd been one text which said *Go now*. It had been sent at 1301 the previous day to 'Mrs S'. There were no earlier messages and he assumed that Brenda had been diligent about deleting the virtual trail. He checked Mrs S's details in Contacts and saw that Amanda had communicated with Brenda using her secret phone. It wasn't surprising but he did feel as though their privacy had been invaded, and wondered whether Amanda had been as conscientious with the delete key as Brenda had.

There'd been lights on in Brenda's house but he'd made a rapid and silent getaway after posting the phone, wrapped in several layers of newspaper he'd retrieved the day before from Amanda's recycling bin. As he'd done this morning when he slipped the note through her door, he'd pulled a beanie over his head and wrapped a scarf round his chin and was brandishing a handful of junk mail flyers from the same source; if challenged, he would claim to be at the end of his delivery round. Even if Brenda saw him, he doubted that she'd recognise him — especially this evening in the dark — and in any event he doubted she'd want to speak to him. And while he did want to speak to her, he wanted to reflect further before doing so.

Simon was sure that she must have the lost key to the garden door, and needed to retrieve it to save the hassle of replacing the lock and Amanda's keys. Of course it was possible that she'd taken a copy, as he had when Amanda had first given it to him, but if he asked her face to face he could probably judge whether she was telling the truth.

But while he now almost certainly knew how she'd come into the garden and taken the photo, that didn't answer the more pressing question of how she'd known that he and Amanda were having an affair in the first place. It seemed unlikely that she'd chanced upon the key and let herself in in the hope of seeing something to her advantage. So she must have had access to the house as well as, and probably before, the garden. The key ... He thought of other keys and how he'd got hold of them. Could Brenda also be a cleaner? That would fit, he now realised, with the three hours or whatever it was that she'd spent at Brambles, having rung the doorbell. She must be Amanda's cleaner.

*

Brenda was also doing some serious thinking.

Tommy had found the phone on the hall mat, wrapped in pink newspaper. She'd carried that off OK, telling the kids she'd left it at the New Brooms office earlier and one of the other cleaners had kindly offered to drop it back. Thankfully Tommy hadn't known enough to ask whether cleaners usually read the *Financial Times*. Brenda had briefly had the same thought about muggers who stole phones before she flicked through her photos and saw that the one of Mrs S and her lover had gone. Was that an end to it, she wondered? Then she scrolled further back and saw all the snaps of Tommy and Lily, which retriggered her fear that whoever had stolen her phone might have sent himself copies of those as well. She looked at the sent emails folder but there were no mails other than her own; similarly for text messages. But he would surely have kept a copy of the blackmail photo, so he must have deleted the cover email or text, if that's how he'd done it. Obviously a careful person. Or at least good at covering his tracks.

Brenda suddenly remembered that the phone still had the burner SIM card in it. She retrieved the other SIM card from her handbag, the wristband that Lily had made for her getting tangled with something in the process. As she disengaged the threads, she saw that it was the key to the door to Whiteacre's garden.

She paused, frowning. The phone thief must be the lover: how else would he know about the blackmail? So he must be the gardener. Would he want to have the key back? Hard to believe it would be important to him; it didn't look like a special security key — she'd seen enough of those on her clients' New Brooms key-rings — but perhaps he'd be, or been, in trouble for having mislaid it? It was a weak bargaining chip, but it was the only one she had. And she had to know — or be as sure as possible — that the children's photos hadn't left her phone.

She rooted around in her bag some more, being careful not to get the wristband tangled again, and found the letter from him, folded into a tiny square in her make-up case. She left the burner SIM card in the phone as she pecked out a short text.

*

Simon's phone pinged with an incoming text from Brenda as he was about to go to the bar for another pint.

Thx 4 phone. I have sth 4 u. Can we meet Mon in Pret in High Street bet 12.30-1?

*

Brenda arrived early at Pret on the basis that she should be able to recognise the lover/gardener easily while he'd only seen her in her blackmailer's disguise. She felt that this would give her an advantage, though she wasn't sure how. And it assumed that it was the lover/gardener who had stolen her phone, which, however likely, wasn't definite.

It was confirmed, however, when he came through the door a few minutes later and paused, looking around. She gave a small finger wave as his gaze swivelled towards her. He nodded and raised his eyebrows in a question as he raised an imaginary cup to his lips. Brenda shook her head, indicating the non-imaginary cup on the table in front of her.

The lover/gardener returned from the counter, complete with coffee, and sat down.

'You said you had something for me?'

Brenda pulled the key from her bag and dangled it in front of him. He reached for it. She snatched her hand back and their fingers briefly touched.

'I don't really need it you know,' he said. 'Though out of interest, how did you get hold of it?'

'I imagine you know. I tried the door in the wall a few times. One day it opened and I found the key in it, on the inside.'

'Yes, careless of me,' said the lover/gardener with an easy smile. 'It was out of character. Anyway, I'm happy to take it off your hands now you've got no further use for it. I've got another copy of course.'

Brenda shrugged. 'Up to you. I need to know whether you sent yourself any other photos from my phone.'

He frowned. 'No. Why would I have?'

Brenda clenched her hands on the table. 'I know nothing about you, except that you're a gardener and you're having an affair with a rich married woman and you mugged me for my phone —'

'While you were in the middle of a blackmail pick-up.'

'I'm talking about you now,' snapped Brenda. She felt

fierce, almost tiger-like, defending her cubs. 'For all I know you're a paedophile, or sell photos of children to paedophiles. And you know my address.' She swallowed to quell her rising nausea at the mere thought.

The lover/gardener paled. 'I'm no angel, any more than you are. But no. I'd never do that. I just skimmed through the photos till I found the one you'd sent Am — Mrs Standing. And talking of that photo, you must have kept a hard copy.'

Brenda fished an envelope from her bag and handed it to him.

'Thanks,' he said, taking it and checking the contents. Or content. Good call, thought Brenda, to have taken three prints for luck all those weeks ago.

He leaned back in his chair and gave her a level look. 'So you're Mrs Standing's cleaner, obviously.'

Brenda blinked in surprise, though now she thought about it it was a reasonable assumption.

'No.'

The lover/gardener frowned again. 'So how did you know? Do you know the cleaner? Did she tell you?'

'No. I mean yes I do know her as it happens. But no, she didn't tell me.'

'So how?'

Brenda drained her lukewarm coffee and stood up. 'Magic powers,' she said briskly. 'All women have them. Only way we can survive.'

Twenty-Four

March

'**D**o you see your sister often?' asked Simon, picking up a photo of Jennifer from the piano and turning it to the light. 'She looks like you, but not like you. Not as beautiful.'

Amanda fiddled with an earring — which Simon thought might be emerald — as if embarrassed. 'I'm seeing her in a couple of weeks. The last weekend of the tax year. It's the only time Hugh works at home. He comes back late on the Friday and works solidly all day Saturday and Sunday. He won't even go out for lunch. Just locks himself in his office and gets grumpy if I interrupt. So I leave a load of food for him and take Jennifer to a spa.'

A cog shifted delicately in Simon's head.

The following day, Simon had a one-off gardening job for someone who wanted his beds kick-started before growth began in earnest. Simon found gardening, like walking and smoking a joint, conducive to creative thinking. He did a lot of that as he planted, pruned, divided, hoed and mulched. Particularly when he noticed a slate that had been blown off the garage in the recent equinoctial high winds.

It would be risky, but a less risky way may not fall into his hands again, or at least not for a long time. And it wasn't as though he was particularly risk averse. What did they say, faint heart never won fair lady? Or something similar. And he'd waited long enough.

'Time for the plan, man,' ran through his head to the rhythm of his spade. A weekend when Hugh would be alone in the house was a gift. He needed to arrange a holiday abroad. Somewhere a day or two's drive away. He had a half- — or was she a step- ? — sister who lived near Montpellier. She would do.

But before taking any other steps he would prune the vigorous rose, a Madame Alfred Carrière that climbed up the rear wall of Whiteacre to cast its dreamy scent in drifts over the terrace in early summer. Not now, of course; now it was a latticework of bare, black branches.

When Simon was working at Whiteacre later that week, he took the long ladder from the coach house and went up to gutter height with secateurs and his lightest gardening gloves.

'I've pruned the climbing rose,' he told Amanda, indicating the neater framework he had created. 'Not that it needed much, but it'll benefit from tidying up. And cutting back — I had to go up onto the roof. I've kept the trimmings — they'll be good on the braai once they've dried out.'

*

Amanda inched nearer to Simon, who ran his hand over her hip and down her thigh. They were lying in bed, drowsy and relaxed. She hadn't had a blackmail text or letter since the mid-February drop and was gradually daring to hope again that, for whatever reason, the nightmare was over. A weekend at the spa while Hugh locked himself in the house for his fraught end-of-tax-year marathon was just what she needed.

'I'm sorry you won't get the benefit of my post-spa skin,' she said. 'Soft and silky. Fragrant.'

'You're already soft and silky and fragrant,' said Simon, and planted a kiss on her forehead. 'Anyway, I will get the benefit. Just deferred. I'll be back in ten days or so.'

Amanda pouted, then smiled and kissed him back. 'I'm looking forward to the reunion already.'

They went downstairs and ate. Amanda had spent the day preparing meals for Hugh's weekend. She'd done a slow-cooked beef casserole for his Saturday evening meal and made enough for Simon and herself that night. When her book club had read *To the Lighthouse*, everyone had a view about Mrs Ramsay's boeuf en daube. They argued about which cut of meat, how long to marinade (there was a consensus that the three days signalled by Woolf was excessive), what (apart from the olives, bay leaves and wine that were mentioned) to add. Over the next few meetings — which fortunately spanned a cold and damp winter — they each in turn cooked their recipe. Amanda's was voted the clear winner, though she suspected no one wanted to eat daube de boeuf for many months after.

'This is wonderful,' said Simon. Amanda warmed with the glow of the compliment as she savoured the melting ox cheek, the glistening sauce dimpled with olives, the subtle undertow of red wine, thyme and orange peel.

'So what else does your lucky husband have to look forward to?'

Amanda shrugged, avoiding eye contact as she mentally flinched at the collision of the two strands of her life.

'Cold meats and cheese and salad for lunch. Chicken pie for Sunday evening. It has to be either cold or easy to reheat. Hugh has his head down all weekend and won't bother to eat if he has to make an effort. Not that he's a cook at the best of times.'

Simon smirked. He sat up a little taller and squared his shoulders, and Amanda again buried the troubling thoughts about her future.

'So when are you back, exactly?' Amanda asked.

'Not sure, exactly.' Simon scooped a spoonful of creamy, near liquid Vacherin Mont d'Or out of its spruce hoop and ate it with slow relish. 'It depends on my sister. It'll take me a couple of days to drive down to Montpellier. I'll get the shuttle on Friday, set off early, before the rush hour. She's got stuff she needs me to help her with and she's asked me to stay a few days. I'll text you anyway.'

'I'll have a lot of lonely evenings then,' said Amanda, with a catch in her voice. She hadn't spent many evenings on her own since Simon came into her life.

Simon looked up. She was rubbing her eyes. 'Sorry,' she mumbled. 'The onions were really strong and the trimmings are still in the compost bin.'

Simon got up and put his arms round her. 'I don't think it's the onions. Don't worry. I'll be back soon. I'll keep texting.'

Amanda sniffed. 'I told you, I won't see them when I'm at the spa unless I'm in my room — phones are banned everywhere else. And I've got wall-to-wall treatments booked. So don't worry if I don't reply until the evening.'

*

249

eonie read the note Amanda had left for her. *I am away for the weekend and my husband won't be home till late so please leave the porch and hall lights on as well as the ones on automatic timers.*

Of course. The final weekend of the tax year. Her first dinner with Hugh had been prefaced with champagne to celebrate its passing. She knew he'd be arriving late and exhausted tonight and would work flat out all weekend. She'd seen how stressed the period made him. What would he do for food with Amanda away, she wondered? He didn't cook and she couldn't see him spending precious time going to a restaurant. And she definitely couldn't see Hugh ordering a takeaway. Curious, she looked in the fridge and saw charcuterie, cheeses, a neat stack of Tupperware boxes. 'Daube de boeuf and pots: MW for 5 mins, stirring once; serve with frozen peas.' 'Chicken pie. Eat hot or cold.' 'Potato salad.' 'Mixed salad; add dressing (in jar in door) just before eating.' 'Scotch eggs.'

Leonie bit her lip. Amanda was something else. She obviously did care for Hugh, despite her own extracurricular activities. Or was it just guilt? Maybe she, Leonie, could also do something to ease the weekend for Hugh.

She'd done her usual clean of the house but had, unusually, cut a few small corners; with Hugh here on his own all weekend she imagined the kitchen, breakfast room and his bedroom — or would he sleep in the master bedroom? — wouldn't be pristine by the time Amanda returned, so she wouldn't know. But she'd laboured over his office, where she knew he'd like everything to be neat and ordered.

Sitting at Hugh's desk, Leonie surveyed the room, pleased with her work. She admired the polish she'd put on the fine, sleek wood; she'd cleaned the window, glancing out over the steep roof and the garden; she'd dusted the laptop, the printer, the fearsome filing cabinet; she'd given the carpet a thorough hoovering. Satisfied, she headed back down, put away her cleaning kit, left on the lights as instructed by Amanda and let herself out. She decided to treat herself to a quick one at the Wykeham Arms before heading to the station, pulled out her phone to check for train delays, and cursed as she tripped. She'd stumbled on a cable snaking across the pavement between a van parked by the kerb and the house next — in a relative sense — to Whiteacre, from where she could hear faint strains of music.

A couple of not-so-quick ones later, Leonie was tugging on her gloves and zipping up her jacket before she ventured outside. The door to the street opened abruptly and a man came barrelling in out of the cold. Leonie half-registered that it was Amanda's gardener-cum-lover but thought nothing further of it as she quickened her pace to be sure of her train.

*

Thank God the cleaner had finally left.

Simon had been waiting at the corner of the road, shielded from view by a convenient hedge while still able to keep a weather eye on the entrance to Whiteacre. Amanda had said she was good; she must have overstayed. Not the ideal afternoon for it from his perspective.

Amanda had also said Hugh got home very late on the Friday of his end-of-tax-year weekend, but Simon didn't want to take any risks by postponing his visit any further. He walked round to the alley behind Whiteacre and slipped in through the rear door. Wearing his lightest gardening gloves, he carried the long, sectioned ladder from the garage, opened it to its fullest extent and leaned it against the back wall of the house. Unseen, at least now that he'd dealt with the blackmailer, since the garden wasn't overlooked at all. Like all the houses round here, in huge plots with lots of high walls and hedges and trees. He supposed that people who paid Nightjars Holt prices wanted their privacy. Which suited him perfectly right now.

From his backpack he took an angled tool and a plastic bottle of water drawn from the butt, tucked them into the capacious pockets of his jacket and shinned up the ladder and onto the steep pitch of the roof that he'd worked out was above Hugh's office. How thoughtful of the roofers — he assumed — to have fixed handholds above the flashing. It was easy to slip the blade of the ripper under a slate, pull out the two nails which secured the one beneath and gently prise off the lower slate. Simon put it and the damaged nails in a pocket, slid the blade into the crack between the two slates he'd uncovered, nicked the underfelt and trickled water into the narrow gap. He scrambled down the ladder and put it back where it belonged. From another pocket he pulled out a handful of old, rusty or bent nails he had recently selected from his gardening customers' workshops and garages. He picked out a couple that were much the same size as the ones he'd removed from the roof and laid them with the slate on an appropriately positioned patch of soft ground. Then he slipped away like a shadow through the garden door.

He texted Amanda over a quiet pint at the Wykeham Arms:

Drove straight thru, got to Montluçon, tired but enjoying warm eve. Hope ur having great time at spa. Sxxx

*

Unable to muster the energy to walk, Hugh took a taxi from the station. It was almost eleven when he let himself in; he'd worked in the office until after eight, had a steak at the

Argentine chain on Watling Street and just made it to Waterloo for the nine thirty-five.

He checked the fridge and saw that Amanda had, as usual, left him a neat pyramid of boxed and labelled meals for the weekend. He poured himself a whisky and slumped onto a chair at the breakfast table. His private life, which he normally found so easy to pigeon-hole — to seal in a leak-proof container, like the 'Daube de boeuf' and 'Chicken pie' — seemed to be unravelling. Amanda looked after him so well, and was so dependent on him, and how was he repaying her? He'd treated Leonie badly also, letting her find out like she did, though that hadn't been his intention. Conscious of the conflict between these strands of regret, Hugh took a swig of the drink, hoping it would make him feel better. It didn't.

He couldn't go on. He needed to change. He thought back to Sicily, six months ago, when Amanda had seemed unaccountably distant. As she had been since they got back. In Sicily and then again before Valentine's Day he'd resolved to start wooing her again, but had got sucked straight back into his old life — fun in the week, increased workload in the New Year, a tired commute home on Friday and the weekend in recovery mode. Perhaps he was getting too old for all this juggling. Time to stop the philandering; he'd had a good run at it. Maybe even cut back on the work, spend more time down here with Amanda. He could try and rekindle something of his marriage, fall in love again with his beautiful wife who adored him, who relied on him, who went to such lengths to look after him. He felt a wash of unaccustomed guilt. At least he had other matters to focus on over the weekend. His thoughts turned to work and the looming deadline of the end of the tax year.

Hugh took his glass up to his dressing room, dropped his briefcase and draped his jacket crookedly over a chair before shedding the rest of his clothes, leaving a muddled tangle of trousers, shirt, boxers and socks on the carpet. After a cursory wave of the toothbrush he collapsed into the double bed, relishing the crispness of new sheets. He preferred to savour the taste of peat and smoke rather than mint as he drifted off so he finished his whisky and turned out the light.

Not that he did drift off immediately. Alone, he usually slept better in the king size bed, where he could stretch out his long frame slantwise with a comfortable margin all round. But tonight his head was full of figures and flickering worries that he might have missed a critical error. Even though he had the whole weekend as additional time to check and re-check, it was impossible to ignore the jostling numbers and the tapestry of ever-changing tax avoidance schemes and reliefs. But he knew that if his brain wasn't invaded by fiscal problems he would just come back to his guilt about how he'd treated Amanda, so he let them spool on.

He didn't wholly succeed, however, in displacing the guilt. His last thought before he was finally embraced by sleep was about his wife. The words from their marriage service floated into his head. *Wilt thou love her, comfort her, honour, and keep her, in sickness and in health; and, forsaking all others, keep thee only unto her, so long as ye both shall live?* He'd somehow forsaken her, he fretted, instead of all others. Leaving her down here, alone in her huge empty house. Once I'm through this week, he promised himself, I really will change. I'll make it up to her. New tax year's resolution.

*

A t about nine the following morning, Simon cycled up the alley behind Whiteacre and chained his bicycle to a tree in the copse. He unlocked the door in the wall then walked round via the road to the front entrance.

Amanda had said Hugh got up early on his tax marathon weekend; she always left him decent bread for his breakfast as he wouldn't cook anything more substantial, even a boiled egg. Simon rang the bell. The door was opened by Mr Standing — Hugh, as Simon now thought of him — his good looks marred by a scowl. 'Yes?' he barked.

'Sorry to disturb you,' said Simon. 'I'm your gardener. We met a few months ago if you remember. I was working here yesterday and saw that a couple of slates had come off the roof — must have been the recent high winds. I had a quick look and there's a bad leak. I thought I could fix the slates back on if you like — it wouldn't be perfect but it would keep the rain out until you can get a roofer.' Given what Amanda had said about the virtual ban on mobiles at the spa, Hugh was unlikely to be able to contact her to check who he was. Or, more relevantly, where he was. Or even, judging by Hugh's evident impatience, to want to take the time to try.

Hugh rubbed the back of his neck. 'I'm incredibly busy this weekend,' he snapped. 'I really don't care —' He paused. 'I'm sorry, that's very rude of me. It's good of you to offer. Yes, please, thanks so much. There should be a ladder in the garage.'

'I'll set it up. I just need you to spare me a few seconds so I can show you, otherwise I won't be covered by my professional liability insurance. I can pop back later with the paperwork if you're busy. Or next week even.'

Hugh ran his hand through his hair and grimaced. 'I suppose so. If it's necessary. I really can't think about anything else now.' He looked distracted, almost tormented. Who'd be a tax lawyer? Though perhaps there were other reasons for his stress. Apart from an unfaithful wife and her covetous lover, of which he presumably had no suspicion.

Simon slipped on his gloves and set the ladder up. He went to knock on the kitchen door but Hugh was already there.

Surely he wouldn't even notice Simon's gloves, let alone wonder about them, in his current state. Or be too interested in where the water had come from — a man who couldn't even start a braai without lighter fluid or mend the hinge on a steamer chair.

'I've just been in my office and you're right, there's a leak right there,' said Hugh, his voice taut. 'I can't risk any damage to my computer or waste time getting out a roofing specialist, especially on a Saturday. So thanks again. Can we get it over with quickly so I can get on?'

Simon got it over with quickly. He went up first and grabbed one of the roofers' rails, then extended a hand to Hugh, pulled him up, showed him the gap where he'd removed the slate and pointed at the damp marks. Hugh peered closely and Simon gave him a hard shove. He didn't even have time to scream.

Twenty-Five

March/April

Amanda turned into the drive on Sunday evening, surprised
that there were no lights in or outside Whiteacre. Hugh
must have gone to bed and turned them all off without
thinking, though he was normally good about that sort of
thing. The security light came on as she stepped out of the Audi
and picked her way across the gravel and round the circular
lawn to the front door. She let herself in and turned on the
porch and hall lights, then returned to the car for her overnight
case and spa purchases.

'Hugh?' she called up the stairs, but not too loudly as she
didn't want to wake him if he was sleeping. It was only just past
nine but he'd be exhausted after his heavy weekend; he must
have turned in early. She shrugged off her shearling jacket and
hooked it over the newel post before running lightly upstairs.

Amanda eased open the door to the second spare room
where Hugh usually slept, but the bed was empty and still neatly
made up. Of course, when he was home alone he preferred the

king-size bed in the master bedroom; he must have used it for a third night without thinking. But there was no sign of him there either, though it had been slept in. She carried on upstairs in case he was in his office, but again drew a blank. He wasn't in hers either.

Puzzled, Amanda went back down, checking the bathrooms, dressing rooms and main spare bedroom then the sitting room, dining room, TV room, breakfast-room-cum-kitchen and utility room. All were empty. Could he be outside? She supposed he might be sitting in the dark nursing a whisky — she'd noticed a bottle of malt on the kitchen counter. But the door to the terrace was locked. She flicked on the patio lights and gave an involuntary yelp when she saw a crumpled body on the paving at the foot of a long ladder.

Fingers trembling, Amanda unlocked the door and ran onto the terrace. Her legs gave way — she'd thought that was just an expression, but it was exactly how it felt. She sank into a sort of extended curtsy, ending up kneeling on the flags as if in prayer. The light was harsh and merciless and with clinical detachment she noticed the crimson stain slowly blossoming on her cream jeans. The iconic image of Jackie Kennedy cradling her dying husband in her blood-spattered lap came into her head. But Hugh was not in a state to cradle. She turned and vomited up the remains of the indifferent meal she'd eaten with Jennifer before dropping her at her flat and heading wearily towards home.

Amanda felt a cry of anguish rise in her, a primitive, unvarnished urge to keen or howl. She swallowed it down, forced herself to stand on shaking legs, and went in to phone 999.

She couldn't leave him out there on his own. She grabbed a mug from the sink, sloshed a hefty slug of whisky into it and took it out onto the terrace to keep a lonely vigil until she heard the sirens approaching. Although by then she knew that there was no need to rush. No need for the ambulance at all in fact.

*

Seeing Amanda's car in the drive on Monday, Leonie rang the doorbell. There was a long wait and she was fumbling for her keys when the door opened. A ghost of Amanda stood in the doorway. No make-up — no, even worse, what could only be the partial remnants of yesterday's — hair unbrushed, wearing grubby jeans and a wrinkled linen shirt that looked as though it had been slept in. The ghost stared blankly at Leonie for a few seconds then said, without expression, 'Oh. Jane.'

Who? Leonie glanced round, then remembered that she was Jane. Hard to keep track sometimes, especially after a weekend. 'Er — Mrs Standing. What's happened? Is something wrong?'

Amanda shook her head like a dog and said, 'Yes. Come in for a moment. But then you'll have to go.'

Bewildered, Leonie followed her into the hall. Even that looked different. A scatter of shiny stiffened paper carrier bags threaded with dinky twisted rope handles littered the floor. A small suitcase was on its side with one of Amanda's handbags spilling its contents beside it. A shearling jacket hung crumpled over the newel post.

Amanda turned to face Leonie. 'I don't know what to do,' she said, her voice cracking. 'You'd better go home today. My husband died over the weekend.'

Leonie's knees started to buckle. She lunged for the bannister and grabbed a handful of soft suede. Thankfully the rib of wood beneath supported her. She thought she would throw up, but swallowed down the acid bile.

'Come and sit down for a moment,' said Amanda, going into the breakfast room.

Leonie made it to the table and sat down. 'I'm sorry,' she managed. 'I mean for your loss.' She hoped that in her own grief and confusion Amanda would not have registered — or at least wouldn't recollect — the intensity of her cleaner's reaction.

'What happened?' she croaked.

'I came home late last night from a weekend away. After dropping my sister. The house was pitch black. I knew Hugh wouldn't have gone out, it's the end of the tax year.'

Amanda didn't seem to notice her cleaner's lack of obvious puzzlement at this apparent non sequitur.

'So I looked all over. Eventually outside. I found him on the patio. He must have gone up on the roof and slipped.'

Leonie felt — eviscerated, yes that was it. And at the same time frozen; she mustn't forget who Amanda thought she was.

'Can I do anything to help, Mrs Standing?' she forced out in a voice that she hoped passed for normal in the context. 'Make you a cup of tea?' Leonie was not a tea person apart from her life-giving mug first thing, otherwise preferring it with ice and lemon and another letter earlier in the alphabet, but wasn't a cup of sweet tea what you should give someone in shock?

Amanda shook her head.

Leonie tried again, willing herself to focus. 'Should you have someone with you?'

Amanda rubbed her forehead and opened then closed her mouth as if forgetting where she was and who she was with. Leonie caught an unexpected breath of whisky. 'My sister's coming for a few days. She had a problem with her car but she'll be here this evening I think. You'd better go. No, wait. I can't bear to go into his dressing room or his office and see his clothes all lying around. Could you ... um ... maybe just bundle them into a bin bag? I don't want to see them. I'll sort it all out later. If you leave his wallet and things on his desk. And then perhaps you could come another time to clean?'

Leonie fetched a bin bag from under the sink in the utility room and, holding the bannister to keep steady, made her way upstairs. She went up to Hugh's office first. His laptop was open, his work phone beside it. There was a small puddle of clear liquid on the desk; she wondered whether he'd knocked over a glass of water. She headed down to his dressing room where she picked up his jacket, draped at a rakish angle over the chair, checked the pockets, took out his wallet, keys, a handful of change and his non-work phone and put them on the small table. Trying not to inhale the lingering scent of his aftershave, she scooped up the clothes he'd left on the floor, stuffed them, with the jacket, into the bin bag and went back downstairs. Amanda was still sitting, spectre-like, at the table.

Leonie hesitated. 'I've left the bag in the dressing room, is that all right?'

'Thank you,' said Amanda in a mechanical voice. 'I don't — you can't clean now. We can leave it till Friday. Will you let the agency know? Obviously you'll be paid.' She scrubbed at her eyes with a crumpled hankie.

'I'll let New Brooms know, of course. Have you let Ma — er, your husband's work know?'

'No. I've done nothing except all the horrible stuff last night, the ambulance and police and funeral directors. I'll call his office in a minute.'

Leonie wasn't sure whether she should leave Amanda on her own. But Amanda insisted she'd be all right and would phone a local friend once she'd called Hugh's firm so Leonie headed off towards the station, stopping for a much needed and much earlier than usual drink at the Wykeham Arms.

*

After the cleaner left, Amanda sat slumped at the breakfast-room table, staring into the garden. Someone had put a blue tent over the part of the terrace where she found Hugh's body. She couldn't remember who — the police maybe? There'd been so many people milling about. Noise, movement, questions. Photos, the flash cleaving the darkness like sheet lightning, then fierce arc lights illuminating the scene in hideous graphic detail. Then the funeral directors took Hugh away and the others drifted off in dribs and drabs. She'd asked them to leave the tent up for a few days. She couldn't face the thought of seeing the marks on the paving. Amanda rarely drank whisky but had felt she needed another drink. She'd found a more suitable receptacle, a cut-glass tumbler, poured herself an inch, her hand trembling, and swallowed it in one long gulp, barely registering the burn as it went down. Unable to face going upstairs, she'd passed a fitful night on the sofa in the TV room.

Now, she forced herself to get up from the table and phone Mainwaring & Cox. Hugh's secretary started crying and transferred her to HR. Amanda gave the bare details and the HR person offered condolences, asked if she had a friend or relation with her and said someone from the firm would be in touch in a few days to discuss practical matters. Amanda wondered what those would be, but didn't really care.

Everyone she'd spoken to since dialling 999 said she should have a friend or relation with her. But who? Amanda realised that she had no close friends in her local circles, just people to socialise with. Jennifer wouldn't arrive till later and she had no other family. Oh God, she would have to let Hugh's family know. Or would the police have done that? Her vision blurred as tears dribbled down her cheeks. She would phone Tristan, he was kinder than Peregrine. But not just yet. There were only two people she wanted to see right now and one of them was dead. She texted the other:

Terrible news. Hugh fell off roof and is dead. Please come back soon. Axxx

*

Simon's phone pinged and displayed a message from Amanda's secret iPhone. She must have used it out of habit, though it was no longer necessary. He replied:

Babe that's terrible. How did it happen? Are the police there? I'll be back as soon as I can but can't leave my sister for a few days, she has no one else to help her. Can't call now, very dodgy reception. Let me know if you're alone later and I'll try and find a good spot. Love you Sxxx

Amanda responded promptly:

Roof leaked above his office. He must have gone up to see and slipped. Ladder was up. Police called funeral director, something to do with coroner. They took him away. It was horrible. J coming later so I won't be alone. Axxx

Fell off the roof, goof. Though he felt bad about Hugh. Sorry for you, Hugh. But at least it had been instant. Immediately afterwards, Simon had melted away through the garden door, locking it behind him, then cycled at a leisurely pace to the station carpark where he chained his bike up among a shamble of others, some of which looked as though their owners had long since abandoned them. His chain wasn't strong and the bike would no doubt soon be stolen. If not, it would be well camouflaged. And he avoided the station CCTV cameras, which he'd previously checked and mapped in his head. He picked up his van from a nearby street, headed for the motorway and made his way to Folkestone and the shuttle.

He hoped Amanda would text again to say they'd released the body, or whatever they did when there were no suspicious circumstances. Or when they thought there weren't.

She did text again later in the day:

Fun dir called. Coroner will certify accidental death after speaking to police tho will take a while to get formal clearance but at least I can plan funeral. Will keep me busy I suppose. Xxx

Simon lit a joint as he sat outside his camper enjoying the early evening sky. *Honey I shrunk the risk.* He was up on the Causses above Montpellier, parked on a narrow side road with the van well hidden by a cluster of mimosa trees, their winter flowers over and their foliage browning. He'd head to his sister's in the morning. He'd told her he was coming for a few days' break in the south after an English winter.

Twenty-Six

April

Brenda had continued to keep a beady eye on Whiteacre's garden, feeling at times almost nostalgic for the heady excitement of the pre-blackmail days, but hadn't seen much soap-opera activity for a while. Of course it wasn't the time of year for anything too interesting on that front — even a warm April had a sting in its tail — but still, she hardly saw any signs of affection between the gardener and Mrs S. Were they drifting apart? Or, she suddenly thought, had they, or at least he, worked out that the garden was overlooked? And that therefore she could still be spying on them, as she was? Even if they hadn't worked it out, Brenda could imagine that knowing they'd been spied on in the garden might drive them into the house.

She'd just arrived at the Castle House and decided she'd clean first, from the ground floor up, and take a look before she left. It made her rush things a bit though. She was drying one of the Rooks' super sharp knives — Global, according to the blade, and really easy to clean as it all seemed to be made out of one piece of metal, no fiddly bits where the handle joined — when she cut herself. Cursing, she found a plaster in her bag and put the knife away. Funny thing, they looked really expensive those knives, there were a whole load of them and they were just jumbled together in a drawer. Most of her houses had huge knife blocks.

Finally Brenda was in the turret room, which got a very quick shake of the duster. She raised the binoculars and zoomed in on the garden. There was a sort of tent on the terrace. Almost like a mini-marquee but blue, which was odd. And very mini. On the previous Thursday she'd seen marquees being erected in the garden next door to Whiteacre and assumed there was some grand celebration planned. Could this tent be connected? But it was a week on, and the tent was very small. It reminded her of something she'd seen recently … With a gasp she realised that it was the forensic tent in an old *Line of Duty* episode.

Brenda googled 'Standing Winchester death' on her phone and gasped again when she saw the first hit, an article from the online version of *Winchester Today*.

Tragedy in Nightjars Holt, screamed the headline. *Nightjars Holt householder Hugh Standing tragically fell to his death on Saturday. The circumstances are not known; his wife Amanda was away all weekend at a spa retreat and there were no witnesses. There was a ladder leaning against the wall and it is thought Mr Standing, a solicitor, must have climbed on to the roof to investigate a possible leak and lost his footing. Your trusty local paper will report more as we know more about this tragic event.*

Blimey. Brenda let out a long breath. Poor Mrs S. Better get on with the clean. She put the binoculars back in her bag and switched on the hoover. Then she remembered that Jane cleaned Whiteacre. Would she know already? If not, maybe she should, and if so, maybe she'd have some more info. Brenda turned off the hoover and sent a short text.

> *What's going on at Whiteacre? Saw the forensic tent and googled the news. Brenda*

The reply was prompt, if brief.

> *Horrible isn't it. Is the tent still there now? Don't know much, am back there tomorrow. Leonie*

Who on earth was Leonie? The number was Jane's and the message was obviously in response to Brenda's. She texted back:

> *Hi is that Jane? Only you signed off as Leonie! Brenda*

A reply flashed up after a short pause:

> *Oh sorry, yes it is me, Jane x*

Brenda thought for a few minutes and sent another message.

> *I've got another nearly 3 hours but if you're up for a drink I could have a quick one later? W Walker again? Bx*

Jane sent a thumbs up emoji and Brenda texted one of the other mums asking if she could pick up the kids and keep them for an hour or so. She was in luck — Sandra would pick them up and give them supper.

*

'So how's Mrs S taking it?' asked Brenda once they'd agreed on a wine and sat down with a bottle and two glasses.

Leonie felt a start of surprise. She cast her mind back to her drink with Brenda the previous summer. Hadn't Brenda been almost interrogating her about Whiteacre? She'd found it odd at the time. And Brenda hadn't known anything about the owners until Leonie told her.

'Do you know her?' she asked.

'No,' said Brenda. 'But you told me their name, remember? I can see into their garden from one of the houses I clean so I see her sometimes. She's very beautiful.'

'Really? I'd always assumed it wasn't overlooked,' said Leonie, then trailed off and stared at Brenda, cogs turning.

'What?'

Leonie leaned back in her seat. 'The thing is,' she started, then trailed off again. She raised her glass and said 'Cheers' in an effort to reset the conversation. The problem was that she couldn't remember who knew what. Best to play safe.

'Am — Mrs Standing is looking terrible at the moment to be honest. Which isn't surprising.'

'Do you know what happened?' asked Brenda. 'I mean apart from what they said in the paper, which wasn't much?'

Leonie shook her head. 'Not really. Mrs Standing was away all weekend though. It was the last weekend of the financial year. Hugh —'

'*Hugh*?' echoed Brenda. 'Didn't know you knew them so well. How come? I don't know anyone in Nightjars Holt who gets friendly with their cleaner.'

'Erm … I don't know them that well, I just find it easier to think of people by their first names.' Including herself. Maybe it was time to officially revert to hers before she screwed up again. 'Anyway,' she continued, 'I do know that he's a tax lawyer and Mrs Standing — Amanda — went away to a spa for the weekend while he worked at home. So there was no one else in the house. I don't know why he'd have gone onto the roof though.'

'That's how I saw that police tent thing,' said Brenda with a shudder. 'I mean, from Brambles. I thought it might be some sort of marquee at first. On the Thursday — that's my cleaning day there — before, I saw lots of marquees being set up in the garden next door to Whiteacre. Must have been for a wedding or something. Then I realised what the Whiteacre tent must be and checked the local paper.' She shuddered again and drank some wine. Then frowned, and added, 'About him being a lawyer. Reminds me, when we met that time and you told me where the name Whiteacre came from — how d'you know that then if you were just a secretary?'

Leonie took a deep breath. 'Because I wasn't just a secretary. Sorry, I don't really know why I didn't want people to know I was a solicitor. I was embarrassed I think at having been made redundant, and thought Cathy might think I was overqualified.'

'I can't imagine she'd have cared,' said Brenda. 'So why was Mr S — Hugh — on his own all weekend?'

'He was a tax lawyer. Inheritance tax. It was the last weekend of the tax year. He always worked flat out, making sure everything was up to date.'

Brenda narrowed her eyes. 'You sure you didn't know him?'

'I — sorry,' mumbled Leonie, and tried to bat away the memory of Hugh inviting her to dinner for the first time. He'd suggested a date a couple of weeks ahead. 'Can't do earlier I'm afraid — it's the end of the financial year, when I'm guaranteed to be frantic. Downside of being a tax practitioner. Good excuse for champagne when it's over.' Appalled, she realised that she was starting to cry. She rubbed the tears away fiercely.

Brenda topped up Leonie's glass. 'I don't know what happened there, girl, but my guess is you were reminded of some good times with someone you cared about. Someone who's just died.'

Leonie took a long draught and Brenda obligingly made up the level again.

'I did know Hugh, yes,' said Leonie. What did it matter now if Brenda knew the truth? Or some of it anyway. Hugh was dead, the Cleaning Plan a petty scheme which had run its course. She took another deep breath. 'It's a long story.'

Brenda snorted, then said, 'Sorry Jane, but let me guess the short version. He seduced you then he ditched you?'

Leonie gave a watery laugh. 'Something along those lines. And I was made redundant on the day he ditched me. So here I am.'

'Well, there's a gap there but you're all upset now. You can fill in the blanks another time. So here you are, but who are you? And who's Leonie?'

'I am. I don't know why I — well I suppose I do. I wanted to get inside Whiteacre. Cause trouble. And Leonie's an unusual name. So I told Cathy I went by my middle name. And my mother's maiden name, come to that. But now … With Hugh dead it all seems so childish and trivial. To be honest, it started to seem childish and trivial a while ago. I got … diverted. Because I found out that Amanda was having an affair. And I think you found that out also.'

Brenda was silent for a few minutes, turning her wine glass round and round. 'I could see them in the garden,' she admitted. 'It was obvious that he wasn't her husband. He's the gardener.'

'I know,' said Leonie.

Brenda raised her eyebrows in a question.

'I recognised him. It's another long story, for another time.'

'Here's the thing,' said Brenda. 'Why I suggested a drink. At least you already know about the affair, means I don't have to explain. I was wondering … do you think he, or Mrs S, might be involved in Mr S's —Hugh's death in some way?'

Leonie almost dropped her glass. Then took a large gulp of the contents. 'God. I've no idea. It hadn't even occurred to me. I've barely been able to think straight about anything these last few days.'

'Well it wouldn't be the first time,' said Brenda drily. 'Wife and lover murder husband. Or the lover on his own. Probably doesn't only happen on the telly.'

'I guess not.' Leonie bit her lip, thinking fast. 'But I don't know how we'd find out. Except …'

'What?'

'Er … I know that she — Amanda, Mrs S — has a secret iPhone she uses to contact the lover. At least I assume that's what it's for. It's not her usual one and she keeps it hidden away in a zipped pocket in her handbag.'

Brenda leaned back and gave Leonie a level, admiring look. 'Well, well. Not just a lawyer but a detective then! Full of surprises you are, Leonie-Jane!'

Leonie felt a flush rising. 'It was silly. Just part of the childish stuff. I was curious.'

'Don't knock it,' said Brenda. 'Curiosity might have killed the cat but it might help us find out who killed Mr S. Or if he was killed. I only had the thought because I knew about the affair. It's been going on for a while.'

'Yes,' said Leonie thoughtfully. 'Since before my first — no, second — clean there, which was in July last year.'

'I first saw them around then too. June I think. But getting back to what happened to Mr S — could you try and get Mrs S's secret phone? There'll surely be texts between her and the gardener.'

'Yes,' agreed Leonie. 'I can't think what else she'd use it for.'

'The texts might show where they both were over the weekend. I know she's supposed to have been at the spa but you never know. Could be a cover story.'

'Yes,' repeated Leonie after a pause. 'Getting the phone would be a start. I'll keep an eye out for an opportunity. It's funny though, I feel sort of shabby, poking into her life like I've been doing. It started as a bit of fun, trying to cause trouble for Hugh and then to work out who the lover was, but I — we — know that now, and what she does isn't really my business.' And Leonie remembered again about Amanda's awful childhood.

'But what if she — or they — were involved in murder? Especially Hugh's murder. So look at it that way. Get the phone, and if there's nothing dodgy on it you — we — will know and you can put it back and move on. But you need it for more than a few minutes. And it's bound to be pass-coded. This isn't going to be as simple as it first sounded.' Brenda gave a brittle laugh.

Leonie's shoulders sagged. 'God knows how we could crack the code, even if I could get the phone. I could have a couple of stabs, her birthday, Hugh's birthday —'

Brenda snorted. 'For a secret lover's phone? Dream on. Could be the secret lover's birthday though.'

'Yes, that's an idea. But even if — wait, listen, Brenda I've got his birthdate! It's in his book —'

'His what?'

'He wrote a book and Amanda has a copy by her bed. That's how I blew his cover — I saw his photo. On the cover as it happened. He's called Simon Long. Anyway, once I suspected he was the lover — I wasn't 100% sure, but now from what you've said it seems definite —'

'It is definite,' said Brenda grimly.

Leonie was about to ask Brenda whether she'd taken the

blackmail photo but decided to focus on one crime at a time. And she didn't want to alienate Brenda now that it seemed they might be able to work together to find out whether Hugh had been murdered. That, surely, was more important.

'I read his book. With everything that's happened since, I'd forgotten the birth date reference. Later on he insinuates a few unsavoury situations but nothing that couldn't have another explanation. I think he's clever.' Leonie pulled her iPad from her bag. A few stabs with her finger took her via the Kindle app to the opening words of *An African Odyssey* and then to Google. 'He was born on 11 November 1972.'

Brenda raised her glass in a mock toast. 'Well done Leonie-Jane!'

'Thanks,' said Leonie absently, taking a mouthful of wine. 'But even if that's the code, I've still got to get the phone in the first place without her noticing. And have it for long enough to read what's on it. I need to be able to "borrow" it for a few days between cleans.'

'Buy a toy phone and put it in her bag instead,' suggested Brenda. 'I bought a couple for the kids when they were little. I just got cheap ones but there was a big range of models, and I'm sure they'll have got better since. And Mrs S probably isn't even using the secret phone now and she'll never know. And if she did notice it wasn't working she'd probably assume it had died. Sorry, bad choice of words. But she's got two phones.'

'And a lot on her mind at the moment. OK. As it happens, I know the model.'

Brenda rolled her eyes.

'I know, it was a while ago,' said Leonie ruefully. 'I don't like the idea but I guess I owe it to Hugh.'

Ten seconds on Google on the train that evening brought up a number of sellers of dummy phones. Another ten seconds on eBay and she'd ordered a superficially identical 'Non-Working Dummy Display Toy Fake Model' iPhone for the grand total of £9.99. Leonie hoped again that Brenda was right and Amanda wouldn't take her secret phone to be repaired — a phone shop would surely spot a fake a mile off, and then she really would wonder. Leonie had to fork out rather more for the case, which she bought from Apple so as to be sure that it was the genuine article, or at least indistinguishable from the genuine article. A pity it wasn't a slide-in case rather than the more expensive — and trickier to substitute rapidly — clip-on one, but Leonie was prepared to suffer for the cause.

The cause — could Amanda or Simon really have been involved in Hugh's murder? But the secret phone might well be the key to that knowledge, so either way it was worth a try. Leonie rubbed her eyes and realised from the wet smear of mascara on the back of her hand that she'd been crying slow, seeping tears. She'd tried to keep thoughts of Hugh at bay but there were too many triggers.

*

When Leonie went back to Whiteacre on the following day she was still numb and hollowed out, but Amanda looked even worse than Leonie felt. Charcoal-dark smudges under those striking green eyes. The normally lustrous golden hair dull, stringy and unbrushed. And while today's blouse didn't look as though it had been slept in, Amanda had buttoned it unevenly so that one lop-sided corner of the collar seemed to hover over her throat like a poised blade.

Amanda ran her hand through her hair, dishevelling it further. 'Oh, Jane. I'd forgotten you were coming. Sorry, it's just been …' She trailed off and blew her nose on a disintegrating tissue. 'Sorry. Come in. Thank you for letting New Brooms know, they sent me a card which was kind. If you could do the usual. Don't worry if you finish early. I have to go out shortly. To see the funeral director. My sister's here but she's coming with me so you'll have the house to yourself.' She rubbed her mascaraless eyes.

Leonie followed Amanda into the breakfast room where a jumble of papers and several cups of half-drunk coffee littered the table. She mumbled more words of condolence then took herself up to the top to be out of the way. When she heard Amanda and her sister leave, she went down to clean the ground floor. Amanda had cleared the papers; maybe she'd taken them with her. Leonie put the dirty cups in the dishwasher and steeled herself to look out onto the terrace. As Brenda had said, the forensic tent was still there. Presumably it would be removed at some point; she felt sick at the thought. Weren't there specialist firms who cleaned up after bloody accidents? She hoped there would be no trace when the paving was revealed.

Did the grass look a little shaggier, less perfect than usual? There were a few weeds in the nearest border. And something even more out of place — a mug, lying on its side. Steeling herself further, Leonie went out. She had to go closer to the tent than she'd have liked but at least she avoided brushing against it as she edged past. She bent down to retrieve the mug. There were a couple of rusty nails on the soil next to it, plus a small disc with a hole in it. She picked it up, intrigued. It was so faded she couldn't read what felt like raised lettering, like a coin. She slipped it in her jeans pocket and took the dirty mug in. It smelt faintly of whisky.

Twenty-Seven

April

Leonie dropped into the Wykeham Arms for a quick glass of wine on her way to the station after she'd finished at Whiteacre. As she settled into her seat ßshe felt something hard dig into her buttock, reached back and found the mystery coin in her pocket. She put it on the table and pulled her phone out of her bag intending to try and find out more about it, though she wasn't sure what to google given that she couldn't read the writing. But as she opened the app, her thoughts turned instead to Amanda's phone and the question of Amanda's whereabouts the previous weekend. And the gardener's — Simon Long's — whereabouts. Leonie had been able to put off the increasingly unsavoury task of 'borrowing' Amanda's secret phone as she was still waiting for the dummy and the case to be delivered. But they may well have arrived today, or would surely have done so by Monday, in which case she needed to look harder for an opportunity. Or make one.

The previous weekend … Her mind drifted, inevitably, back to Hugh. Her brief period in Whiteacre on Monday was a blur, or rather a collage of unconnected fragments — the bags in the hall, the jacket on the newel post, Amanda looking like a dishevelled ghost, the ominous tent on the terrace. But there was something else, something that didn't seem right. Leonie frowned in concentration. Hugh fell off the roof. Why was he on the roof? Wouldn't he call an emergency roofer? She didn't have the impression that he was very practical; certainly she couldn't see him shinning up a ladder to fix a leak. Especially not in his busiest week of the year. She sniffed back a sob as the end-of-tax-year reference triggered more memories of their first dinner.

He'd taken her to Rucoletta, a small, family-run Italian restaurant in a narrow street off Cheapside. 'Do you know who you remind me of?' she'd asked. It was the glasses, and by association the owl they somehow conjured. And the black — or mostly black — hair flopping over his forehead. 'Yes,' said Hugh, with an appropriately boyish smile that was briefly eclipsed by the glass of wine he was raising. 'Older, probably taller, certainly none the wiser — I never did master spells or potions.'

After the meal he'd insisted on walking her to Liverpool Street. In Ironmonger Lane, narrow and dimly lit, he turned to her, caught her in his arms and gave her a full, lingering kiss. 'Can I see you again?' he asked. Leonie giggled. 'It would be hard not to, seeing as we work in the same building.' 'You know what I mean. I mean can I see you properly. Like tonight. I may be no good at spells or potions but I think you've bewitched me.'

'Eye of newt,' mumbled Leonie, 'or something. Pissed as, more like. Yes, it was fun, let's do it again.' She felt heady and reckless, and thought she was due some fun. After all, it wasn't as though anyone was going to get hurt.

And now Hugh was not only hurt but dead. As Brenda said, if there was any chance that Amanda and/or her lover were implicated, she owed it to Hugh to try and find out, however uncomfortable she felt about getting hold of and getting into Amanda's secret phone.

Leonie pictured Hugh's jacket, hanging crooked on the back of the dressing-room chair. He'd have been exhausted when he got home on Friday evening. Probably long after she'd left. Tears caught her throat as she saw herself polishing his desk on Friday, and his trousers and boxers puddled on the carpet on Monday. Puddled. She remembered the liquid on his desk on the Monday when she'd gone up to check whether he'd left any clothes in his office. But she'd sat at that desk on the Friday afternoon and there had definitely been no puddle. Did it rain that weekend? She couldn't remember, but Google could. It didn't. Another puzzle. A puddle puzzle. She sighed. Too many puzzles. One of the prints in the dining room at Whiteacre floated into her mind — Don Quixote tilting at windmills. Maybe that's what she was doing.

She drained her glass and headed out of the bar onto the street. As she did so, a man came barrelling in. Leonie stopped dead; the man barged into her and swore. But she barely noticed. She was thinking back to the Friday before Hugh died. It seemed an age ago but was only a week. As so often, she'd dropped in to the pub for a quick one. Or possibly a couple. And as she left, a man came barrelling in. Amanda's gardener. Amanda's lover. Simon Long.

*

The Amanda who opened the door on the following Monday looked marginally less dishevelled than the previous week, but strained and distant. Her face was bare of make-up so that she still had a ghostly air, lines were etched on her forehead and she was so taut that Leonie could see the sinews ribbing her neck. She mumbled an indecipherable few words of what might have been a greeting and turned away in silence. Leonie slid past with a mixture of relief that she didn't have to engage and mortification at what she hoped to do. The dummy iPhone in its bright green case seemed to be burning a hole in her jeans pocket. It was hidden by a long sweater; she must remember not to pull it out, thinking it was hers, in front of Amanda.

Amanda returned to the landscape of paperwork on the breakfast table. Had she abandoned her office? Leonie started at the top of the house. Far from abandoning her office, Amanda had obligingly left a bundle of death certificates and copies of the police and coroner's reports on her desk. Leonie took a rapid photo of each document then headed down to the first floor. She worked her way round to the master bedroom where she changed the bed linen, forgetting that it was Monday. No dirty sheets. Was Simon away — that would explain the unkempt lawn — or were he and Amanda refraining from sex in the circumstances?

On the ground floor she hoovered and dusted in the sitting room, dining room and TV room, then hesitated. Amanda was still in the breakfast room. Leonie knocked lightly at the open door. 'Excuse me Mrs Standing, but would you like me to do in here and the utility room? And the downstairs loo? I don't want to disturb you.'

Amanda looked at her as though unsure who she was. As well you might, thought Leonie, and again pushed aside the nibble of guilt. Enough is enough — I need to stop. I'll just do this one last thing. And not think about it in the meantime. I'm a past master at putting my head in the sand and deferring difficult decisions. Or rather past mistress.

'I'm going out in a minute,' said Amanda. 'I'll be back after you've left. So you'll have the ground floor to yourself. I may see you on Friday.' She tidied up her papers and went into the loo.

Once Leonie had heard the bolt drawn across, she slunk over to the handbag on the hall table, a knot of tension in her stomach. The green iPhone was no longer hidden in the zipped pocket. Confirmation that it was a lovers' phone, if confirmation were needed. Again conscious of a sharp scratch of shame, she plucked the phone out of the bag and slipped the identical dummy model in its place.

*

Leonie got back to her flat, poured herself a glass of wine, found an old envelope in the recycling bin and sat down with Amanda's phone. The passcode was indeed 111172. Maybe I can have a new career as a phone-hacker, she thought. Or a spy. Or a private detective. She and Brenda — The No. 2 Ladies' Detective Agency. Bound to be more interesting than law or legal translation. Or maybe even than cleaning.

To her surprise there were two strings, one on WhatsApp with Simon Long and the other as text messages with a number which hadn't been given a name. Curious, she opened that string first. It started out of the blue with a text from Amanda in November:

What do you want?

There was an almost immediate reply:

£1000. Cash. Every month.

Lord, it was Amanda's response to the second blackmail letter. Followed by another prompt text:

Too much for me. My husband gives me an allowance and will notice. If he finds out he'll go straight to police, where he knows someone senior. I can manage £500 but no more.

Leonie thought for a few seconds, then gave an admiring snort of laughter. No way had Hugh given his wife an allowance, and Leonie would have been surprised if he even noticed how much cash Amanda drew out. She remembered the email folder called 'Banks and finance' on Amanda's Mac and suspected that Amanda had dealt with all non-tax financial matters. Amanda was smarter than Leonie had given her credit for.

She snorted again at the blackmailer's response:

He should give you more but I don't want trouble so OK. I'll text in next few days about arrangements.

Then in December:

Worthy Lane car park. Leave £ in envelope in old plastic bag under rubbish bin by Ladies then go away. 12 noon tomorrow.

There was a curt *Go now* on the following day, then no further texts to or from the blackmailer until mid-January:

Same place, 1 pm Thursday
Go now

Then back to the blackmailer in February:

Same place, 1 pm Thursday
Go now

There were no more blackmail texts after that. Had the

blackmailer given up? Or been persuaded to give up? And was it Brenda? There was only one message that had any colour to it, but even though Leonie didn't know Brenda well, she could well imagine her saying that Hugh should give Amanda more. She checked the blackmailer's number against Brenda's contact details in her phone but it was different.

Leonie turned to the WhatsApp messages. She scrolled to the beginning of what proved to be a long string. How on earth had Anna Karenina and Emma Bovary managed? Not to mention Mrs Jones. Or even Mrs Robinson, her generation's model of the sexually active and attractive older — though now younger, she realised — woman.

As she'd expected, the texts were all between Amanda and Simon. Mostly assignations. Lots of variations on a few themes:

> *Can I come over tomorrow eve? I'll bring sth to braai 4 u Sxxx*
> *Can u stay the night? Axxx*
> *Missing u Axxx*
> *U 2 babe Sxxx*
> *C u soon Axxx*
> *U r the hottest woman I know Sxxx*
> *Can't wait to c u, weekends such a drag now Axxx*

She scrolled down, glancing at the texts but not reading every word of the standard variety. And glancing also at the dates — the string had started in early July last year. They continued in similar vein until mid-January, when Simon sent a more prosaic message:

> *Babe think I'm coming down w sth, feverish and achy. Taking today off if that's OK, don't want to risk giving it to u. Will text tomorrow Sxxx*
> *Look after yourself, hope to c u Thurs Axxx.*

After that, the lovers' banter resumed until the Friday of the weekend when Hugh died:

> *Drove straight thru, got to Montluçon, tired but enjoying warm eve. Hope ur having great time at spa. Sxxx*
> *Fab thx, scrubbed smooth and soft for ur return! Can't wait. Axxx*

A few more suggestive and playful exchanges. One from Amanda late on Sunday saying she had dropped J in Folkestone and was heading home. Then nothing till Monday afternoon:

> *Terrible news. Hugh fell off roof and is dead. Please come back soon. Axxx*

> *Babe that's terrible. How did it happen? Are the police there? I'll be back as soon as I can but can't leave my sister for a few days, she has no one else to help her. Can't call now, very dodgy reception. Let me know if you're alone later and I'll try and find a good spot. Love you Sxxx*

> *Roof leaked above his office. He must have gone up and slipped. Ladder was up. Police called funeral director, something to do with coroner. They took him away. It was horrible. J coming later so I won't be alone. Axxx*

> *Fun dir called. Coroner will certify accidental death after speaking to police tho will take a while to get formal clearance but at least I can plan funeral. Will keep me busy I suppose. Axxx*

Leonie started writing a list of dates and times on the envelope:

Fri 29 March 1812 S in Montluçon, drove down that
day so must have left early; Google says c 9 hours 20
Sun 31 March 2103 A sets off from Folkestone to Winchester

She opened the photo of the death certificate on her phone.
Hugh had died on the Saturday. No time was mentioned but
the police report and the coroner's report gave an estimate of
between eight and eleven o'clock in the morning. She included
the information in the timeline.

She remembered about the puddle puzzle and added a
reference to water on Hugh's desk on Monday shortly after
noon. Then she wrote:

Fri 29 March c 1620 no water on H's desk.

Leonie stared at the two entries for Friday. She had gone from
Whiteacre to the Wykeham Arms. And Simon Long had come
into the pub as she left. She'd caught her usual Friday train,
the 1818.

*

Leonie settled into her seat on the train the following morning
and turned on her iPad. She couldn't, however, settle into
reading. Was it significant that Simon Long had been in
Winchester when he'd told Amanda he was in France? Or was
it unconnected with Hugh's death? And how could she find
out? She could do with talking it through with someone, and
Brenda was the obvious choice. She decided not to mention
the blackmail messages for the moment — if she was the
blackmailer, Brenda may well assume that Amanda had deleted
them, and again, one crime at a time — composed a text and
sent it as her train pulled in to Winchester.

Hi Brenda, fancy another drink? Got into A's phone last night. Lots of lovey-dovey texts bet S & A inc 1 v suspicious one, will explain later. L-Jx

Brenda's reply pinged back while Leonie was walking to her first clean.

Def! Could do this eve, kids on sleepovers. W Walker? Bx

*

'So,' said Brenda as they sat down and Leonie poured them each a glass of wine. 'What did you find out? I bet it was a cover story, her being at the spa and all.'

'I don't think so,' said Leonie. 'There's no suggestion of it; on the contrary, there's a text about how silky and fragrant she's going to be for him, or words to that effect.'

Brenda mimed retching into her hand. 'So what does the suspicious text say then?'

Leonie reached into her bag and pulled out Amanda's phone. She opened it, put it face up on the table and said, 'A few minutes before this was sent, I saw the gardener — Simon — come into the Wykeham Arms.'

Brenda stared at the glowing message:

Drove straight thru, got to Montluçon, tired but enjoying warm eve. Hope ur having great time at spa. Sxxx

'You're saying that text was a lie to make Amanda think he wasn't here?'

'Yes,' said Leonie. 'Montluçon's in the middle of France. Over nine hours' drive from here according to Google.'

'And you think it means he murdered Mr S?'

'I don't know. But he must have had a reason for the lie.'

'Are you sure it was him?' asked Brenda. 'Coming into the pub, I mean?'

'Yes.'

'So we could go to the police?'

Leonie sighed. 'I've been thinking about that. I never practised criminal law. But I know enough to know that even if the police believed me, which they wouldn't, and prosecuted him — Simon — for murder on the basis of one piece of circumstantial evidence, which they wouldn't, I'd be torn to pieces in court. I'd be cross-examined by his barrister, who'd know that I was the victim's ex-mistress and had knowingly and intentionally been deceiving his wife for months. Including after he died. Stealing phones, spying, lying about who I was. And even if I handed the phone in to the police, you can imagine the chain-of-evidence issues. I stole it. I could have tampered with it. Not that I'd know how, but I could have asked some passing five-year-old.'

'I think that's a no, then,' said Brenda. 'But there might be CCTV showing Simon going in or out of the pub. Or the barman might remember him. And what if he did go to France, after pushing Mr S off the roof? He'd surely have driven, so there'd be a record of the crossing.'

'But all that would only show he'd lied about where he was,' said Leonie. 'I'm sure he'd be able to come up with an explanation. He could say he was two-timing Amanda.'

'Perhaps he was,' said Brenda.

They fell silent for a few minutes then they both spoke at once.

'Do you think —' said Brenda.

'I think it's time —' said Leonie. She took a long swig of wine. 'It'll be difficult. I'll feel a real prat. Well, I suppose I have been.'

'Here's the thing, Leonie-Jane,' said Brenda. 'If we're right, and Simon did somehow push Mr S off the roof, then Mrs S might be in danger from him. Although,' she paused, her eyes narrowed, 'maybe not, at least for now. Won't he want to move in with her? Marry her?'

'In fact,' said Leonie, 'she might be in more danger if he thinks she suspects him.'

They fell silent again.

'But,' said Leonie, 'I still think she ought to know. Everything.'

'I think you're right.'

Leonie sighed and took a swig of wine. 'I suppose the worst that can happen is that I get the sack. And I've almost got a Plan B —'

'Have you got a new job lined up then?' interrupted Brenda.

'Sorry, I'm losing track of who knows what. I thought I'd told you, but no, it was Tina I mentioned it to. God, poor Tina. You must miss her, Brenda, I know you'd been friends since you were at school.' Again Leonie felt the tug of guilt — had she helped drive Tina to her death? But she couldn't bring herself to ask Brenda whether Tina had committed suicide. She pushed the thought away.

'I do,' said Brenda, 'and we were. It's horrible. Still wake up in the night thinking about it. And I still forget and think I'll send her a text, suggest a coffee. I must call Daisy again. Anyway. Your new job?'

'I've applied to be a freelance legal translator but it's taking ages to go through. But I think I've got a good chance.'

Brenda snorted. 'You're wasted on the law, Leonie-Jane. And on cleaning.'

'I didn't expect cleaning to be so exciting,' said Leonie with a brief grin, then felt the prick of sudden tears. 'Sorry, that sounds awful. I meant working out about Amanda and Simon was a diversion. Not what happened to Hugh.'

'Well, that's why we're here,' said Brenda kindly. 'And you may have found out something very important. But if you give Mrs S her phone back, take a photo of that text first.'

And then, thought Leonie, the cleaner can come clean.

*

Simon let himself in through the door in the garden wall. Not for much longer, fingers crossed. Don't do this wrong, Long. Remember the plan, man.

He'd texted Amanda and she was waiting for him on the terrace. She leaned against him, and he felt her breathe in deeply and relax. He held her for a few quiet minutes. They went inside. She poured them each a glass of wine and they sat down in the breakfast room.

'What a thing to happen,' said Simon. 'I'm so sorry. I came back as soon as I could. Are you bearing up?'

'Just about.' Amanda looked strained, thinner in the face, but as though she'd made an effort to find decent clothes and put on some make-up.

'So what's the problem with your secret phone?' She'd been texting him from her normal phone since Monday; apparently her other one wouldn't even turn on.

'I don't know. It's dead. I thought it must be out of juice but it won't even charge. I suppose it doesn't matter now.' There was a catch in her voice.

'I'll take a look at it,' said Simon. 'But it's probably not worth the expense of trying to fix.' He pocketed the phone that Amanda handed him.

Simon had been relieved to hear that the secret phone wasn't working. He had a nagging doubt about the text he'd sent from the Wykeham Arms saying he was in Montluçon. Not that there was any reason to think anyone suspected him. But still, if anyone ever did, that text was demonstrably false. The following morning Simon wrapped the phone in a plastic bag and posted it into a dog poo bin next to a small park where he'd observed a high concentration of public-spirited dog walkers.

Later that day Simon went back to Whiteacre. Amanda had told him that she'd be in London in the afternoon seeing the probate lawyers and that he didn't need to worry about the garden. He'd replied that it was looking a bit untidy after ten days of neglect and he'd be happy to do a stint. But what he was hoping was to tie up another loose end which he couldn't do with Amanda's knowledge without prompting potentially awkward questions. He'd discovered when he was having a coffee as he waited to board the Shuttle to France that his Rhodesian penny was no longer in his jacket pocket. It could have slipped out anywhere and was probably now invisibly lodged in one of the flower beds but he wanted to check that it wasn't in the gutter, which would be harder to explain. Though not impossible, he thought, and congratulated himself on his foresight in pruning Madame Alfred Carrière.

The forensic tent had gone. The whole terrace had clearly been pressure hosed while he was away. He imagined Amanda must have got a specialist firm in. He'd been hoping that she wouldn't ask him, and that he wouldn't have to see the stains on the paving. Best to move on.

Going up to the roof was OK though, he just fixed his thoughts on his lost talisman and his eyes on the gutter. It was empty and gleaming. He remembered Amanda saying she had a firm come and clean them twice a year — autumn for the leaves and spring to get rid all the stuff that washes off the roof in which weeds would otherwise take root. Simon tried to recall whether the gutter had been clear the last two times he'd been on the roof. But he'd had other matters on his mind both times and hadn't noticed. Oh well, if the cleaning firm had come since then, at least his coin would have been removed. If indeed it had fallen into the gutter in the first place. He felt round some of the slates, also without result, shinned back down the ladder, moved it along and went up once more, then gave up on the roof and gutter and poked around the nearest flower bed. He found a couple of old nails, probably the ones he'd put there, but there was no sign of his penny.

*

So Mrs S had finally got rid of the tent, thought Brenda. No sign of her or Simon — wait, there was movement by the garage. It was Simon, carrying a long ladder. She watched him angle it against the wall that had the big rose climbing up it. Just as well he'd pruned it recently. She'd seen him do it, and even through the double vertigo of her own and Simon's height above ground she'd admired how agile he was on the ladder, leaning over and up and cutting off lots of growth.

Simon extended the ladder to its full length and climbed carefully up. He didn't go all the way onto the roof but seemed to be checking the gutter, looking left and right and feeling with his free hand. He reached up among the lower slates also, then went down and moved the ladder along to repeat the process. He seemed to give up after a few minutes, went back down to the terrace and resumed his apparent search at ground level, poking around in one of the flower beds. Then he stood up with a shrug and returned the telescoped ladder to the garage. When she next looked out, he was mowing the lawns. Brenda paused before she started cleaning again to send a text.

Hey L-J, nice to c u Tues. Am at Brambles, S is at W and has been up ladder, seemed to be trying to find something in gutter and then in flower bed. Any ideas? Bx

Twenty-Eight

April

On the following Monday Amanda's car was in the drive when Leonie arrived at Whiteacre. Amanda had been out all afternoon on Friday and Leonie half hoped she'd be out again so the discussion would have to be deferred. Not that that would make it any easier. Better to get it over with, especially as it was Easter next weekend so she wouldn't be cleaning. She gritted her teeth and rang the doorbell.

Amanda opened the door.

'Hello Mrs Standing,' said Leonie, feeling a little faint.

'Hello Jane. Please call me Amanda. It's been long enough.'

Leonie took a deep breath. 'Please call me Leonie. It's been long enough.'

Amanda looked puzzled. 'Who's Leonie?'

'Mrs Standing — Amanda — we need to talk.'

Leonie followed Amanda into the breakfast room. 'Do you mind if I sit down?' she asked. 'In fact, would you have any wine open by chance?'

Amanda raised her eyebrows but poured Leonie a glass of Villa Maria Sauvignon Blanc from a bottle in the fridge, and after a moment's hesitation poured herself one too. She sat down and said, 'Jane — Leonie — whoever you are, what is this all about?'

Leonie sat down, clutching her jacket around her and her bag in her lap. She took another deep breath followed by a deep swig.

'I knew your husband,' she said, forgetting the coherent and articulate speech she had planned, with everything set out in orderly fashion. 'Before I started cleaning here, I mean.'

'You knew Hugh? How? Were you cleaning for Mainwaring & Cox?'

'Er, not exactly. I worked there. As a solicitor. Amanda, you must have known that Hugh had affairs in London. Nothing meaningful, just little flings.' Her voice caught. She wasn't sure whether it would be worse or better if that were true. Or even whether it had been true.

Amanda put her glass down slowly and looked hard at Leonie. 'How dare you say such a thing? Who are you?'

'I'm very sorry to say,' Leonie stumbled on, 'that he had an affair with me.' Her face felt as though it was on fire. She stared down into her glass then risked a sideways glance at Amanda, who in contrast looked frozen. Leonie swallowed and turned her eyes back to her glass. Just get it over with.

'And ended it. On the day I was made redundant. Out of the blue, the redundancy I mean. Well, both — but I was reeling from the redundancy first. And I was very pissed off with him. Sorry for the language, but I was. So I wanted to get some sort of petty revenge. And I needed a temporary job while I decided what to do. So I started working for New Brooms. And eventually started cleaning here. I was going to plant a few clues around the house so you'd know — er, think — that he was having an affair and he'd get into trouble with you. It was very petty and childish. But in the end I didn't.' The words were cascading out of her. Definitely not the coherent and articulate speech she'd planned. She drained her wine.

Amanda picked her glass up and took a long, slow sip. Her face looked as though it was carved in marble. 'I think you'd better go. Now. Don't come back.'

Leonie's cheeks were still warm, her throat dry. 'I'm sorry. It sounds mean and petty. It was mean and petty. But I was very upset. And needed something to occupy me. But I didn't plant any clues in the end.' No way was she going to mention the receipts.

'Go now,' repeated Amanda, echoing the last text in the blackmail string on her secret phone. Leonie seized the straw.

'I know about the blackmail,' she gabbled.

Amanda stood up violently, her chair falling backwards as she did so and knocking against the wall. 'Get out,' she spat. She grabbed Leonie's arm and pulled her roughly up. 'How dare you lie your way into my house then sit here telling more lies to my face.' She dragged Leonie into the hall and towards the door.

'Amanda,' croaked Leonie. 'Mrs Standing. I'll go, but hear me out. There's something you need to know. About Hugh's death.'

'I've heard quite enough.' Amanda was shouting now. She opened the door, propelled Leonie out of it and slammed it behind her with a last, 'And don't come back.'

*

Amanda stumbled back into the breakfast room. She righted the fallen chair and then stood, raking one hand through her hair and biting down on the other. She realised she was physically shaking. She looked wildly around and seized a tumbler on the sideboard holding a small posy that Simon had picked for her. She hurled it to the floor and felt a searing satisfaction as it smashed. The wave of tension that had been building in her broke and suddenly she could barely stand. She sank into a chair and stared vacantly at the shards of glass, the scattered flowers and the cloudy water spreading over the tiles. Then she let out an anguished cry. It wasn't any old tumbler that she'd broken. It was her father's whisky glass, the last of his set from the Whisky Society engraved with his name. She'd treasured it as one of her few mementoes of life Before.

Biting back a sob, Amanda reached for her phone. It was all that fucking cleaner's fault. Lying her way into Amanda's house, spying on her, trying to stir up trouble. Not to mention what she'd said about Hugh. What she'd done with Hugh. The … the whore didn't deserve to keep her job. Amanda wished she'd pushed her out of the door more forcefully, pushed her over, spat at her, thrown something after her. Her fingers trembling, she found New Brooms in her contacts but paused before stabbing the call icon. Most of her adult life had been lived in the shadow of her father's death and the mystery around it. And now her husband had died, and hadn't the cleaner — Jane, Leonie, whoever she was — said she had some information that Amanda needed to know? Perhaps that bit was true. If there was anything dodgy about Hugh's death, Amanda needed to know; that was more important than getting Jane fired. She closed her eyes and tried to think. She'd been on the point of telling New Brooms that Jane was an imposter and an intruder and should immediately be sacked, if not reported to the police. But she should maybe hear Jane out first. And Jane would hardly want to come back and tell her whatever it was she knew if Amanda had caused her instant dismissal. She needed to squeeze out some sort of apology, however unpalatable. She composed a reluctant text.

Jane/Leonie, I don't know who you are but I'm sure you'll understand I was very upset by what you said. But I shouldn't have pushed you out like that. I would like to hear what you wanted to say. Is there a time when you could come and tell me? Amanda S.

She sighed and pressed send, then bent to clear up the mess from the broken glass.

*

L eonie had started to walk back into the centre but was so shaken that she'd stopped at the nearest café, which wasn't very near given the relentlessly residential nature of Nightjars Holt. She sat down with an espresso and a chocolate brownie, hoping the caffeine and sugar combination would shake her back to something approaching normal. Though a glass of wine would have been better.

What a fuck up. She should have realised Amanda was unlikely to take her revelations lying down. And now she'd almost certainly lose her job and her only income.

Leonie pulled out her phone, though she wasn't sure who she could usefully call. And was surprised to see an incoming text from Amanda. She felt marginally calmer after reading it; perhaps something could be salvaged. At least she'd have another chance to try. She wasn't sure whether it would be better to go back to Whiteacre later in the week, when Amanda had had a chance to calm down, or to seize the olive branch now in case Amanda thought better of it. She opted for the latter.

I'm still in the area and could come back any time this afternoon. I'm sorry again, I can understand how it must have sounded. Leonie (Jane)

There was a short pause, then Amanda replied.

*Come back now if it fits. Or later, I'm home all afternoon.
Amanda*

Amanda opened the front door, her face white and her hands clenched. She said nothing and Leonie followed her into the breakfast room again, where she sat down and gestured to Leonie to do the same. Their two glasses were still on the table, empty. After a pause, Amanda spoke.

'I shouldn't have shouted at you or pushed you. I apologise for that. But I think you have a lot of apologising to do. And explaining.'

Leonie bit her lip. 'I know. I'm sorry. But please hear me out this time. As I said, there's something you need to know. Something important.'

She paused, wondering where to start. She really needed to tell her everything, otherwise the main piece of information wouldn't make sense. 'There's … er, quite a lot,' she said tentatively. 'It gets worse. I mean what I did gets worse. A lot worse. I realised you were having an affair —'

Amanda looked up sharply.

Leonie ploughed on. 'And worked out who with. I was curious. I'm sorry, it's unforgivable, it's nothing to do with me. I think I admired you really, getting your own back, and of course Hugh had no idea. He thought you were totally dependent on him. Still in love with him. Would be destroyed if he left you.'

'Don't talk to me about my husband like that. Just say what you want to say.'

Leonie's face was burning. She gasped, 'I — I took your secret iPhone.'

Amanda sat up straight. Then she stood up, went to the

fridge and topped up her glass. She hesitated, then slopped some wine into Leonie's also. 'So it's you who broke it?'

'Thanks,' said Leonie, and took a grateful sip. 'No, I didn't break it. I replaced it with a dummy. It was only the other day. I just meant to take a quick look and then return it. The thing is —'

She stopped. 'I'm sorry. I'm telling you lots of different things. It's all a muddle. I'll come back to the phone. But on the Friday of the weekend when Hugh — when he died, I st— er, worked here later than usual, and I sa— er, dusted his desk. And there was no water on it. So I started wondering. Since he d — I mean, when did he die? Did you find out?'

For the first time since Leonie had started her confession, Amanda looked as though she was interested as well as hostile. 'They say it was on the Saturday morning. Between eight and eleven o'clock if I remember correctly.'

She had remembered correctly, thought Leonie, and continued.

'I assume that he noticed water on his desk first thing Saturday. But would he go up to the roof on his own? Wouldn't he call an emergency roofer? You obviously know him — knew him — much better than me, but —'

Amanda heaved a long sigh. 'I know — knew — the Winchester Hugh. I'm sure you knew the London one much better than me.' Her voice was cold as steel.

Citrus and vetiver. Almond and mint and tea-tree oil. Did Amanda distinguish by smell also? Or by geography? Or did she have her own criterion?

Amanda continued, 'But you're right. He wasn't practical. He didn't have a problem with heights but he'd have had no idea how to fix a leak in the roof. And that weekend — the last weekend in the tax year — he planned to work non-stop. He always did. The last thing he'd have wanted to do was waste time clambering round the roof looking for a leak he couldn't fix.'

'Did he call an emergency roofer?'

'I assumed not. I just assumed he was so stressed he acted out of character.' Amanda got up, fetched the nearest landline handset and pressed a couple of buttons. 'No, there are no calls out on Saturday. And he'd have used the landline.'

'Wouldn't he have called or texted you? Asked whether you had a number for a roofer or handyman or someone?'

'Normally, yes. I keep a list on my phone — I used so many workmen when we were doing up the house. But I was at the spa and he wouldn't expect me to pick up. Mobile phones are prohibited except in your bedroom. And I always swim first thing, then it's breakfast, then treatments all day. As many as I can pack in. So no, he probably wouldn't even have tried. But what's this all got to do with what you said I needed to know? I'm very tired. And really don't want to hear any more than I have to. Or see you for any longer than I have to.' Her voice, now icy again, trembled.

Leonie tried to remember where she'd got to. Perhaps the wine had been a bad idea, but she wasn't sure she'd have had the courage to come clean at all without it. And maybe it was helping Amanda; there was a lot to take in, none of it good news.

'When I left here on the Friday before … the Friday before Hugh died, I went to the station and stopped at the Wykeham Arms for a drink. I sometimes do that. Clears my head for the train journey. Anyway, I left the pub just before six I guess — I walk fast and went straight to the station and got the 1818. But as I was leaving the pub, Simon' — Amanda jerked back, perhaps she shouldn't act so familiarly — 'the gardener — came into it.'

Amanda looked puzzled. 'So what? He often drinks there. He likes it. It's a nice pub.' She made a small choking sound.

Leonie fumbled in her bag and found Amanda's phone. She opened it —

'How did you know the code?' asked Amanda sharply.

Leonie sighed. 'I saw Simon's — I'd seen him in the front garden a few days before when I was walking past from another clean — I saw his book on your bedside table. I noticed the cover. It's very striking. I wanted to take a closer look at it, then I noticed his photo on the back. And I was curious —'

'You don't say,' said Amanda sardonically.

'I downloaded his book and as you know it starts with a reference to his date of birth so I tried that.'

'More fool me. It just seemed an obvious passcode that no-one except me would think of. And, as you've no doubt discovered, I didn't delete the texts. Oh —'

Amanda broke off and pinched the top of her nose, her eyes closed. She looked exhausted.

'We can stop,' offered Leonie. 'I'm sorry. Truly. On top of everything else this must be horrible for you. But I'm nearly at the one thing I wanted to tell you.' Though Leonie was surprised by how Amanda was bearing up. After seeing how she'd cracked earlier, Leonie had expected her to fall apart again, but she was holding herself together in the face of yet more distressing and intrusive revelations. And the worst was still to come. She hoped the new, steelier Amanda would be able to cope with it.

Amanda pulled an already sodden handkerchief from her pocket and blew her nose, then sat up straighter. 'That's how you know about the blackmail. From the phone.'

'Thanks. Yes. But that's none of my business —'

Amanda gave a derisive snort. 'That doesn't seem to have been a problem so far.'

Leonie felt her face burn again. But no point stopping now. Cut to the chase. She opened the Simon-and-Amanda string, scrolled briefly and handed the phone to Amanda. 'That text,' she said, 'was sent minutes after I saw Simon go into the Wykeham Arms.'

*

Jane — or rather Leonie, as Amanda must now remember to call her — had finally stopped spouting her horrible revelations and left. In fairness she'd offered to clean, pointing out that she wouldn't be back till after Easter. Then she'd stopped mid-sentence and said, 'Sorry, I forgot. I won't be back at all. I'm sorry again about everything. I'll give my notice to New Brooms, they'll want to sack me anyway when you tell them.' Her voice shook but she'd squared her shoulders as she buttoned up her jacket.

Amanda had relented. 'I won't tell New Brooms. Let's leave it for the moment. As you say there's a break now until you're due back. And I don't really want the hassle of a new cleaner at the moment, on top of everything else. I found everything you said very hard, obviously, but I have to say that you're a very good cleaner.' And with that Amanda had ushered Leonie out of the house — somewhat more gently than earlier — shut the front door forcefully behind her and poured herself another glass of wine. Deciding that she didn't have the energy to cope with anything more today, she texted Simon, remembering to use her regular iPhone as he had what he thought was her broken secret one:

> *Am exhausted. May be coming down w sth. Going to sleep, c u tomorrow assuming I'm on the mend? Will text. Axxx*

She then sat for a long time at the breakfast table, her now-not-so-secret iPhone in front of her.

In a strange way the whole extraordinary saga had taken her mind off Hugh's death. She supposed she must still be in shock to have accepted Leonie's confessed shenanigans so calmly. Well, the second instalment anyway. Even though she'd always suspected that Hugh had his affairs, she would have expected to feel more hurt and anger at being confronted with one of his lovers. Even an ex-lover. But an ex-lover who had come into her home under false pretences and snooped on her. Somehow in the context none of that seemed important now: partly because nothing seemed capable of breaking through her numbed and frozen state, but perhaps also because other things Leonie had said raised more pressing questions that Amanda needed to address.

Maybe Leonie was wrong about seeing Simon on the Friday evening? She said she wasn't planning to go to the police as she couldn't swear to it. But she sounded very sure. And if she was right, then one of the possible interpretations was too bleak to contemplate.

And the water. Amanda had checked back over the weather that weekend and it hadn't rained in Winchester on the Friday night. She knew from a problem they'd had shortly after buying Whiteacre that water could pool on a rafter and slowly accumulate until it overflowed, even in the absence of rain. But still.

Even before Leonie's confession Amanda had realised that her feelings about Simon were changing. True, she had been starting to shift from her view that leaving Hugh was, largely on financial grounds, unthinkable. But now Hugh had left her. What was that song on one of his playlists? *I can see clearly now.* And something about rain? Except there was no rain. She was beginning to see that Simon had been a diversion from her marriage rather than a real threat or alternative to it.

She'd have to think about it some more tomorrow. Before Simon came round. In the meantime, a minor bit of insurance.

Amanda turned on her once-secret iPhone, intending to take a screenshot of the text from Simon purporting to be from Montluçon. When she opened the messages app she saw, as well as Simon's latest message, the last one on the blackmail string. The short string gave little away, though it was obvious enough that it was blackmail, and she wondered whether Jane — Leonie — knew more. Maybe she knew who it was? She certainly seemed to know a surprising amount about a number of matters. Amanda might ask her about it when she next saw her, if she could bring herself to be civil. She was pleased, though, that she'd relented on her initial never-darken-my-doors-again stance; breaking in a new cleaner would have been one chore too many. Especially as there'd be a lot more than usual to do what with two cleaning days being bank holidays and Jennifer staying for the Easter weekend.

Amanda took the screenshot and emailed it to herself, then went up to her dressing room, turned the once-secret iPhone off and tucked it under a pair of shoes in one of the stacked shoeboxes.

The following morning she texted Simon again:

> *Headache and hot and cold, think it's flu. Jennifer insisting on coming for weekend to look after me. Axxx*

The reply pinged back promptly:

> *Keep warm babe. Let me know when I can take over looking after u. Sxxx*

Twenty-Nine

April

Leonie was literally dragging her feet as she approached Whiteacre. A few long-buried words of Shakespeare drifted into her mind — something about creeping like a snail unwillingly to school. She rang the bell — please let Amanda be out.

She wasn't. She opened the door and, to Leonie's surprise, looked almost pleased to see her.

'Leonie, come in. How was your Easter weekend?'

'Er, fine thanks. I hope yours was OK. In the circumstances.'

'It was, thanks. In the circumstances.'

Leonie took off her coat and headed into the breakfast room to collect the cleaning kit from the utility room beyond. Amanda followed her as far as the kitchen end. 'Coffee?' she asked.

'Thanks, I'd love one.'

'Nobody else knows about Simon,' said Amanda. 'Except the blackmailer, of course, but that fizzled out.' Amanda paused, then shook her head. 'I wanted to ask you about that, but it can wait.'

Leonie had also been tempted to ask about the blackmail but Amanda forged on.

'Nobody else even knows that I have a lover. Had, maybe. So the thing is, I can't talk to anyone else. About anything really, because it's all bound up with Simon. Or may be.' Her voice caught.

Leonie had taken a paper in diplomatic relations as part of her Masters. It hadn't prepared her for this. She tried to focus. Hugh was dead and she was drinking coffee at Whiteacre with his widow. Discussing the widow's lover.

Amanda rubbed her eyes and drained her cup. 'Sorry,' she said. 'I'm all right. It's just all so strange. Surreal. My sister came to stay over Easter and obviously I couldn't talk to her about it which made it a very long weekend.'

After they'd each had a second coffee, Amanda opened a bottle of New Zealand Sauvignon Blanc and poured two generous glasses. 'I don't usually drink in the day,' she said. 'But I think normal rules are suspended. Let's sit on the terrace, it's warm enough. And I have to — I have to get used to going out there.' Her voice shook and she blew her nose.

Me too, thought Leonie, but felt that it was the least she could do. Outside, Amanda sat for a while staring into her glass while Leonie tried not to stare at her. She was paler than before. Thinner. Hair less perfectly coiffed. Still that arresting beauty though.

Amanda sighed. 'I've spent the weekend thinking. About Simon. If I'm honest, he insinuated himself into my life. But gently, politely. He made me realise that I was very lonely. He was kind, always bringing stuff to cook and then cooking and clearing up.' She took a long mouthful of wine and added, 'He was good in bed too.'

Beyond surreal. Dear Abby, my ex-, and now late, lover's widow gives her possibly ex-, possibly murderous, lover a gold star for his sexual performance. Should I tell her how I rated her late husband — as it happens, also a gold star?

Amanda exhaled something between another sigh and the ghost of a giggle. Was the wine going to her head? She probably wasn't eating much.

'Don't worry,' said Amanda. 'I wasn't going to ask you about Hugh. But getting back to Simon, I realise now that I became emotionally dependent on him. He was good company. Interesting. Undemanding. Helpful.'

'Do you think he was hoping for more?' ventured Leonie.

'Yes. That's what I was obsessing about all weekend. That's why I need to talk to someone. And as I said, there's no one else. But I'll go mad if I can't talk it through.'

Amanda must be very lonely, thought Leonie. But as she knew herself, an affair brought its own loneliness.

'We did talk once about my leaving Hugh,' Amanda resumed. 'Ages ago, last summer I think. I said I couldn't, because I couldn't bear to be poor again. He didn't push —' Amanda's voice wavered and her face crumpled. 'But it's a big step from hoping to — '

'Do you think he knows you suspect him?'

Amanda shook her head. 'No. I've barely seen him since it happened. He only got back a few days ago. He'd been in France for ten days, at least so he said. He came round once, when I gave him the phone. I've put him off since then. Said I had flu and Jennifer — my sister — was here, and then of course she was here for Easter. And now there's the funeral on Thursday so I can put him off till after that at least.'

Leonie had assumed that the funeral had already taken place and must have looked surprised, as Amanda added, 'There was ... more paperwork than usual. With the coroner and so on. And we had to wait ages for a slot — Hugh's parents are too frail to go far so there was only one possible church, crematorium and venue for the wake.' She paused and said, colouring, 'Umm, did you want …?'

Leonie shook her head. It would be both painful and awkward. Seeking a diversion, she forced herself to look round the terrace, her eyes skirting the wall with the climbing rose and the bed underneath. Which reminded her about the coin. 'I wanted to ask you something,' she said to Amanda, and fetched it from her bag. 'I found this in the garden. On the Friday after I noticed a mug had been left out here, it was in that flower bed by the — the wall with the rose — and when I picked it up I saw this.' She held out the bronze disc, worn wafer thin and smooth, with a hole in the middle.

Amanda turned it over. 'It's an old Rhodesian penny. Something to do with cleaning guns. Simon always kept it in his jacket pocket as a sort of talisman.' She looked at Leonie, her face more drawn than ever.

'It doesn't prove anything,' said Leonie. 'He could have dropped it at any time, when he was gardening.'

*

Leonie heard the chime of a text after she'd left Whiteacre. She was debating whether to drop into New Brooms for tea and cake or head straight to the station.

> *Hi L-J, saw u earlier having a chatty drink w Mrs S! Fancy catching up over a coffee? Brenda x*

Hadn't Brenda said she worked at Brambles on Thursdays? Which was of course how she'd been able to spy on Simon and Amanda. Still, Leonie was in no particular rush to get the train.

OK but would prefer alcohol! When do u have to be home?
L-J x

Kids at sleepovers again hooray! WW at 5? Bx

'How come you've got to be so pally with Mrs S then? Looked like a right cosy chat you were having,' said Brenda. 'Not to mention the drink. Frances used to bitch something rotten about how Mrs S never offered so much as a sugar lump, let alone a coffee or biscuit.'

Leonie poured them each a glass of white and took a sip of hers while she thought about her answer.

'It is a bit odd,' she agreed. 'The cosy chat I mean. She started inviting me to help myself to coffee and biscuits ages ago. But now — I feel sorry for her, I guess.' And not just because of Hugh, she thought, remembering again the brutal events of Amanda's childhood.

Brenda leaned back and gave her a level look. 'She know about you and Mr S?'

Leonie started. 'Er ...' She paused. She'd been about to deny it but was beginning to feel overwhelmed, not just with the lies but with remembering what she'd said to whom. She took a larger gulp of wine.

'Yes, actually.'

Brenda gave a snort of laughter. 'You're a right one, Leonie-Jane. How's that then? Did you just come out with it while you were dusting?'

Leonie smiled in spite of herself. It was hard not to like Brenda, with her street-smart, sassy way of going straight in. She reflected further as she struggled with a bag of peanuts.

'I told her about Simon's text, as we'd discussed. I tried to think of a way of doing it without all the rest, but gave up. It wasn't a pleasant conversation. She pushed me out of the house and told me not to come back but then relented, and then there was Easter so today was the first time I've seen her since. She was quite chatty, it was weird. Said no-one else knows about her and Simon. Except, er, the blackmailer. She said that had fizzled out.' Leonie took a sudden decision. She picked up her phone, opened it, scrolled through the photos until she found the one of Simon and Amanda and put it on the table between them.

'Brenda, did you take this?'

Brenda had just had a gulp of wine. She choked and spluttered most of it into her hand, which she'd clapped to her mouth. 'What the fuck? Where did you —'

'I guess that's a yes,' said Leonie.

Brenda rubbed her face and hand dry with a paper napkin and bit her lip. 'I suppose you found it in Whiteacre. Mrs S must have put it somewhere and you came across it.'

'More or less. So — were you the blackmailer?'

Brenda paled. 'What are you talking about?' she managed, but it was unconvincing.

Leonie heaved a long breath. 'I think we might need another couple of glasses,' she said, and stood up to go to the bar.

'Make it a bottle,' said Brenda.

'Look, Leonie-Jane,' said Brenda when the bottle had been procured, opened and poured. 'I know about your getting to clean Whiteacre as a cover for mischief. I think it was clever, quite cool actually, but I won't hesitate to shop you if any of this gets out.'

Leonie shrugged. 'Understood. Though Amanda knows about my cover story now anyway. And I don't think I'll be cleaning for much longer.' And blackmail was a serious crime. But Leonie didn't have the stomach for another conversation about that. Again, she thrust the nagging guilt about Tina away.

'It was only three times,' said Brenda. 'I thought he — Mr S — must be so rich he could spare a bit. I was really struggling. My partner had buggered off. No child support, no nothing. I'd walked in on one of my owners in bed with her lover, and she gave me a load of cash to keep quiet. Which gave me the idea. And just after that I found some binocs going for a song at Lily's school fair. Really good ones too, probably some rich twitcher had just upgraded to the latest model. Anyway, so I started checking what I could see from the houses I cleaned. Had to wait a long time, but eventually I struck gold with Whiteacre.'

She took a long draught. 'It's good to get it out actually. It turned out not be as easy as it looks on the telly. Organising the drop — fucking nightmare. And then I — I stopped.' Brenda blushed, and fiddled with an empty peanut packet.

'Think of it as whitemail,' said Leonie. 'I won't say anything. I wanted to ask you something else,' she added. 'Two things, actually. You said you saw me at Whiteacre today but I thought you normally cleaned Brambles on Thursdays?'

Brenda shrugged. 'They asked if I could change my day this week. Must have wanted it extra spick and span for the weekend — probably had their preppy grown-up kids coming home. Why?'

'I just wondered whether you might have seen anything on the Friday before Hugh died. Did you see anyone tampering with the roof for example?'

'I wish. I wasn't there that Friday, no. Saw the marquees being set up next door on the Thursday as I mentioned, but nothing else. I'd have said if I had. What was the other thing?'

'I realise I never replied to your text about seeing Simon on the ladder. Sorry about that. It was just before I ... came clean to Amanda and it got a bit lost in everything else whirling round my head. It must have been shortly after he got back from France. When you saw him, I mean.'

'If he ever went there,' said Brenda darkly.

'Yes. Though Amanda said he did go, at least as far as she knew. For ten days. Anyway, a few days before you saw him — I think it was the Friday after Hugh died — I found an old coin in one of the flower beds. Under … under that part of the roof. Amanda said it was Simon's. Something to do with guns and Zimbabwe. And he kept it in his jacket pocket like a — a charm or something.'

*

Back home, Brenda sat at the kitchen table reflecting over a cup of tea. Bit late in the day for tea really but she needed something to counteract the wine and settle her before she went to bed. It was so quiet at home without the kids. She missed the constant noise and activity. She shuddered as she remembered her fears that Simon had sold their photos to a paedo or similar. Stupid to have done something which might lead to such a risk. She'd kept the £1500, hidden in an envelope in her underwear drawer which she knew wouldn't fool a burglar but would certainly keep Tommy and Lily at bay. She'd taken one £50 note to buy treats for Easter — chocolates for the kids, a half leg of lamb for a roast, a simnel cake for dessert. And then popped into a charity shop and found two pairs of curtains which had brightened the kitchen and Lily's room. The rest was still in the envelope; somehow it didn't seem right to spend it.

She half wondered whether she should give the money back to Mrs S, who must be going through hell now. She could do it through Leonie-Jane, she was sure; that woman had a lot of tricks up her sleeve. But there again it would be bound to lead to awkward questions, and anyway surely Mrs S would have even more money now that her penny-pinching husband wasn't controlling her spending? Though she might have someone else looking over her shoulder, checking how much cash she had, if Simon moved in.

The funny-sounding coin that L-J had found did seem like another clue, but L-J, while agreeing, had said that as evidence it was even more circumstantial than the text, which apparently in lawyer-speak meant it wasn't much use. Not without a lot more at least. Brenda wondered what Mrs S had thought when L-J told her where she'd found the coin. Was Mrs S scared of Simon, or did she think the idea that he'd had anything to do with Mr S's death was ridiculous? Again, Brenda thought that everything must be horrible for her right now. And she didn't even have children to comfort her. Though it would be very hard for children, even grown-up ones, to lose their father like that, even if it was just an accident. Like poor Peter losing Tina; she must call Daisy again and see how they were all doing. Brenda couldn't risk anything happening to herself; what would Tommy and Lily do? She shuddered again at the thought.

Brenda took her mug to the sink. Time to stop the rambling thoughts and go to bed. But she'd continue to keep an eye on Whiteacre and Mrs S every Thursday from Brambles. And L-J would be there on Mondays and Fridays. And maybe she'd let Simon know they were keeping tabs on him. She'd wait until she was sure he and Mrs S were still an item though.

Thirty

May

Amanda sat rigid, as still as a statue, her legs like iron. She stood and kneeled mechanically at the appropriate moments, mouthed prayers, responses and hymns, and remembered very little afterwards other than snatches of words. *My heart was hot within me, and while I was thus musing the fire kindled … Deliver me from all mine offences: and make me not a rebuke unto the foolish … It is sown in corruption … it is sown in dishonour … the secrets of our hearts … there is a time for every affair under the heavens … forgive us our trespasses … lead us not into temptation … the burden of the flesh … perfect consummation and bliss … to earth come down … must tumble down.*

She remembered almost nothing of the brief cremation at Mortlake Crematorium after the church service. And not much more of the short wake that followed in the Putney Town Rowing Club, chosen for its proximity to the crematorium.

Peregrine was muttering about organising a memorial service in Winchester College's Chantry, but Amanda couldn't see that there'd be many more in attendance. Some of their — although in reality more her — Winchester friends and neighbours, she supposed. Possibly a few of the Old Wykehamists with whom Hugh — although again in reality more her once the communication had drifted down to Christmas card level — had maintained desultory contact. Amanda was beginning to think that her house, which had been a constant and rewarding companion over the last few years, was turning out not to be a friend in need. Nor the garden. Nor, indeed, the gardener.

*

Leonie was on her usual half-empty train to Winchester, flicking through a crumpled copy of a magazine that someone had left on a seat. *Hampshire Society.* A window into another world. She glanced idly at the photos of expensive restaurant interiors and smart guests at parties and weddings. There was a whole double spread devoted to a lavish reception held in what was described as 'the most select residential area in Winchester'. She looked more closely, assuming that the reference was to Nightjars Holt. Several shots in what must be a huge garden with marquees in the background and patio heaters in the foreground — glamorous women, men in morning suits or kilts, doll-like children with angelic smiles, waiters wielding magnums of champagne, a rococo wedding cake of startling proportions. And a stunning aerial view, presumably from a drone.

The magazine did not, of course, reveal the address, but it did give the date of the wedding — Friday 29th March. The last weekend of the tax year. The day when she had tripped on a cable going from a van into the house next door to Whiteacre.

And, she suddenly remembered, the day after Brenda had seen marquees in that garden.

Leonie scrutinised the detail of the aerial shot but it had been carefully trimmed of even a sliver of any neighbouring property.

Underneath each photo was the tag '(F)airy Fotos©'. She googled on her iPhone and found what looked like a prestigious studio in Kensington.

That evening Leonie did some legal research for the first time in over a year, reacquainting herself with data protection law. And tracked down a small box of her business cards from her days as a solicitor with Mainwaring & Cox.

*

Leonie arrived at the studio of (F)airy Fotos a few minutes after they'd opened, armed with a crisp new copy of *Hampshire Society.*

'Good morning,' she said to the young woman on the reception desk in the small entrance hall. 'I'd like to speak to the owner or manager please. About a photo that this magazine has recently published.'

The receptionist showed her through to another room and introduced her to one of the two partners, John Defoe. Leonie handed him her card and, brandishing the magazine, said, 'I represent one of the immediate neighbours of the house in Nightjars Holt that features in this edition. My client is concerned that you might have breached her data privacy rights.'

Defoe frowned. 'Please sit down, Ms' — he glanced at the card — 'Holden. I assure you that we take data privacy law very seriously indeed. What seems to be the problem?'

Do people really say that? Leonie stifled a smirk. She gave Defoe her most severe lawyer's look over her reading glasses and said, 'It is clear from the aerial photo, which I assume was taken from a drone, that the original would have included edges of my client's property immediately to the east of the subject. Including in particular the roof. Those details are my client's personal data. Processing the data without her consent was unlawful.'

Defoe leaned back in his seat and smiled. 'Ms Holden, you misunderstand. You're correct, the original shots did include segments of neighbouring properties which may have included your client's. But we trimmed the shots we used and deleted the untrimmed photos.'

'With respect,' said Leonie, using the words in the lawyer's sense of the precise opposite, 'I fear that it is you who misunderstand. The Data Protection Act is unambiguous. Section 3(4)(f) defines "processing" to include erasing or destroying the data.'

Defoe frowned again. 'But — if we deleted it, it can't have damaged your client, can it? Although in fact' — his face cleared — 'I believe it's not permanently deleted. So I don't see the problem.'

'Whether you've deleted it or not, you've processed it by recording and holding it. Either way, you needed my client's consent. However, if you haven't permanently deleted the photo, we may be able to resolve the issue. If you can let me have a soft copy of the original photos, my client is prepared to overlook the breach. If not, I will advise her to lodge a complaint with the Information Commissioner's Office. Which, as I'm sure you know, has power under section 157 of the Act to impose monetary penalties of up to twenty million euros.'

Defoe blanched. He stared down at Leonie's card for a few moments then heaved his shoulders and said, with an irritable sigh, 'This seems to me to be a storm in a teacup. But I'm a busy man. I'll ask Deborah to email you a soft copy of the original drone shots including the relevant edge.'

'And all trial shots and unused shots please. Including before the reception and when you were setting up earlier in the day. I understand from my client that there were some encumbrances on the pavement. My client's cleaner tripped on what might have been one of your cables. It's fortunate for you that she didn't sustain a serious injury.'

Leonie had brought her laptop with her. She waited until the receptionist Deborah confirmed that she'd sent the soft copies then found a nearby Caffè Nero with free WiFi.

As she'd expected, some of the photos did show part of the Whiteacre roof above the second floor. None showed Simon on the roof; that would have been too much to ask for. But there were a couple of shots early on Friday afternoon which, on maximum zoom, showed that there were no missing slates. And another floodlit shot later that evening which showed that one slate had gone.

*

Leonie texted Amanda from the train:

> Sorry, was held up in London so running late, there in c 1 hour, will you be home? L

> Yes, see you then. A

As soon as Amanda had let her in, Leonie said, 'Amanda, I need to talk to you again. I found something out. Shall I clean first or after?'

Amanda looked around at the parquet floor shadowed with footprints, the cherry table smeared with dust, the misted mirror above it. 'You know, right now I'm not bothered whether the house is clean or not. It doesn't really matter, does it?'

'Um, well that's up to you of course. But I can work extra time and do it later.'

'I've lost interest in the house. Turns out there are more important things.'

'You shouldn't be paying me not to clean though.'

Amanda shrugged. 'I suppose I won't have to worry about money now.'

They went into the breakfast room again. 'Coffee?' asked Amanda, spooning espresso grounds into the machine's basket and tamping it down. It smelt — it smelt like Macchiato, the Italian café near Hugh's flat. The place where he'd invited her to dinner for the first time. Leaning forward to brush some crumbs off the table, he'd knocked over his cup. Coffee flowed onto Leonie's newspaper. 'Oh God how clumsy, I'm so sorry Leonie. Unfortunately the *Guardian* seems to be rather more absorbent than this paper napkin … I don't normally throw coffee all over people. Can I take you out to dinner to make amends?'

She hadn't hesitated for long. Better than a lonely trek home to an empty flat, and Hugh was good company and good looking. Afterwards, at her desk, Leonie wondered about the spill. Hugh didn't seem clumsy. On the contrary, he gave the impression of being neat and circumspect in his movements. He had attractive hands: smooth, long-fingered.

She batted away the ambushing memory and sat down at the table with Amanda. Fortified by her first mouthful of the strong, dark roast leavened by perfectly frothed creamy milk, Leonie pulled the *Hampshire Society* from her bag and opened it at the photo spread.

'I picked this up in the train yesterday. I assumed it was a house in Nightjars Holt, then remembered that there'd been cables and music next door to you on the Friday before — the Friday before Hugh died.' She gulped, and drank some more coffee.

'Yes,' said Amanda. 'It was Alice's daughter's wedding. They keep themselves to themselves. We weren't invited.'

'So — I hope you don't mind, but when I saw that aerial photo of the garden, I thought that if it had been cropped, the original might have shown your roof. I visited the photographer earlier. That's why I'm late. He's emailed me the full versions of several aerial shots.'

Amanda raised her eyebrows. 'I'm surprised he handed them over without argument.'

Leonie shifted in her seat and spooned foam into her mouth. 'Um — well, he didn't, entirely. But I said he'd breached your data privacy rights but that you wouldn't lodge a complaint if he gave me the originals.'

Amanda looked hard at Leonie. 'You pretended that I was your client?'

'Um,' said Leonie again, not sure whether Amanda was disapproving or disbelieving. 'Well, sort of. Well, yes, really. I just thought —'

Amanda shook her head with a glimmer of a smile. 'What did you tell him?'

Leonie relayed her conversation with Defoe.

'Is that true?' asked Amanda. 'That recording or even deleting required my consent?'

'Technically, yes. If the photos could identify you or your address.'

'Hmm. And could it …' Amanda trailed off. 'Are you saying what I think you're saying?'

Leonie put her laptop on the table, opened it and typed

in her password, then turned the screen towards Amanda and showed her the photos.

Amanda was immobile, her eyes fixed on the images. She looked older, tireder and paler than she had a few minutes before. Leonie wondered whether her hair had turned white under the gold. Impossible to tell.

'Whoever did it,' Leonie began carefully, 'must have used a long ladder. That's a high roof and a steep pitch. I know — do you have one here?'

Slowly, Amanda turned her stricken gaze to Leonie.

'Yes. He had it out — I'm not sure, a few weeks ago? Before … He said Madame Alfred Carrière needed a trim.'

Leonie felt as though Amanda had broken into another, unknown, language. Perhaps it had all been too much for her. Hairdressing?

'It's a rose,' explained Amanda. 'A very vigorous climber. Or a rambler, I can never remember which. Anyway, it's on one of the house walls, over the terrace.' She gestured through the window, towards the vast tracery of knobbly black branches that Leonie had noticed when she'd explored the garden a few months before, now frilled with emerald furled buds and unfurling leaves.

So there'd be an explanation for any fingerprints. Leonie had been intending to tell Amanda about Brenda's more recent sighting of Simon up the ladder and apparently searching for something, but wasn't sure Amanda could take much more. And she was beginning to feel out of her depth.

So, it seemed, was Amanda. 'I have no idea what to do,' she said, her voice bleak, empty of all emotion. 'Should we go to the police?'

'I last looked at criminal law a quarter of a century ago. I wasn't very good at it then, but I know a bit about court procedure. Mostly from novels though if I'm honest.' Leonie opened a new tab on her laptop and started googling. She realised too late that her Mac had found and joined the Whiteacre WiFi, which she'd keyed in on one of her previous visits, but Amanda gave no sign of having noticed.

'The police can't arrest someone unless they have reasonable grounds for suspecting that he committed an offence,' she said after a few moments. 'I don't know. It's very circumstantial. Quite apart from your feelings.' And quite apart from the question of the credibility of any evidence that Leonie might give. And she and Amanda would both be torn apart on the witness stand. Where Amanda would have to disclose that she'd had an affair with her gardener.

Amanda sagged, but clenched her fists on the table as if to give herself courage. 'I don't know either. And I'm starting to feel afraid. Through the numbness. Because if he did do it, what might he do to me if he thought that I suspected?'

It didn't seem to be an appropriate time for hot sweet tea, but clearly something was needed. Leonie opened the fridge and scanned the contents. There wasn't much, and what there was looked tired and wilted — a bit like Amanda — but she found some cheese, set it out on a wooden board that was on the work surface and put it in front of Amanda. 'Sorry to poke around your fridge,' she said, 'But maybe you should try and eat something. Do you have any bread or biscuits?'

Amanda pointed at a cupboard where Leonie found a packet of oatcakes. She added it to the board and put out a couple of plates and knives.

'Thanks,' said Amanda. 'You're right. I'm not eating much. Perhaps I need Simon here after all.'

Grim humour, but better than none. 'Have you seen him since we last spoke?'

Amanda shook her head. 'No. I kept up the flu story to give me some time to think, and then my sister came back to stay for Easter but I gave him the impression that she was here for longer. And then there was the funeral. But the thinking just keeps getting worse. And I can't have flu and family and funerals indefinitely.'

She cut a small piece of desiccated Brie and nibbled it without apparent interest. 'I'll have to start seeing him again and give the impression that I don't suspect him. If I finish with him now, he'll wonder. And if we're right, God knows what he'd do.'

'Well, if he was convicted of murder he'd get a life sentence …' Leonie stopped, not liking to repeat that Simon might not even be arrested, let alone charged. And the most dangerous outcome of all must be for him to know they suspected him but had no real evidence. Or no, even more dangerous would be for him to be prosecuted and tried but acquitted on the basis of insufficient or inadmissible evidence. And to know that they had given it.

'I'm sure I'll act strangely,' Amanda continued as if she hadn't heard, 'but I can put it down to everything. While I decide what to do.'

'Doesn't anyone else know about you and him?' asked Leonie. 'You need someone to check in with now and again. Tell them you're OK.'

Amanda snorted mirthlessly. 'In case he bumps me off too, you mean? Anyway, no they don't. Just you. And the blackmailer, whoever they were.' Leonie opened her mouth before deciding that now was not the time.

Amanda ate a corner of cracked cheddar and added, 'I suppose I could say that I think the police suspect something — that they keep sniffing around. Make it clear that in my view it's nonsense, it was obviously an accident, just the sort of thing Hugh would do when he was stressed and overworked. But it might discourage him from spending too much time here.'

Or doing anything worse, thought Leonie, wondering whether Amanda was thinking it too.

*

A fter Leonie had left, Amanda texted Simon:

> *Feeling a bit better, tho still weak. And glad to have funeral out of way. Looking forward to seeing you. Axxx*

The reply was prompt:

> *Good to hear. Shall I come over this eve? Can't wait to c u. Sxxx*

Amanda showered, made an effort with the hairdryer and put on fresh clothes and make-up. She looked at herself critically in the full-length mirror and decided that she passed muster. Her face was still pinched, and pale and tired even under the makeup, but that was surely to be expected.

She saw Simon walk through the ivy arch and over the big lawn, having presumably let himself in through the door in the garden wall. She put out a hand to a chair to steady herself. He looked just the same — handsome, smiling, carrying a small packet of something. Perhaps all her worries were fantasy. Whether or not, she needed to go through with this, at least for the moment.

Amanda met him on the terrace again, and again leaned in to him as he wrapped his arms round her. He followed her into the breakfast room and she poured them each a glass of wine.

'I've brought trout,' said Simon, going to the fridge with the packet. 'It's chilly out today. I'll cook it here, later. You should keep warm.'

Amanda was trembling, and hoped he thought she was shivering. She pulled her cashmere pashmina more closely round her shoulders, comforted by the softness against her neck. They went through to the sitting room.

'So how are you bearing up?' asked Simon.

Amanda shrugged. 'OK I guess. Could have done without the flu. Everything's difficult enough as it is. The funeral was hard. The solicitor dealing with the probate keeps calling me, asking for information and wanting me to go to meetings to discuss it. The police keep coming round.'

Simon looked up. 'Why? That's the last thing you need.'

'They won't say. They climbed up onto the roof and took photos. Asked about ladders. Just double-checking I guess. But — we need to be careful. Not be seen together. If we're seen by some busybody who tells the police … Of course we know it was an accident but they might keep poking around.'

Simon's face was impassive. He squeezed her hand.

'I might need some time,' added Amanda hesitantly. 'Before we go to bed again I mean. It's all a bit difficult.'

Simon kissed her hand. 'Take all the time you need, angel. It's a hard time for you.'

A snatch of Hugh's music floated through her head. What was the song called? *A Hard Rain's a-Gonna Fall.* Except there had been no rain. And it was Hugh who'd fallen. Perhaps with help.

*

Brenda recognised the figure instantly. He was slumped on a bench outside McDonald's, picking disconsolately at a carton of fries.

'Peter,' she called, and ran over to him. He looked up, his eyes red.

'Oh, Peter,' she said, tears rising to her eyes also. She sat down next to him.

Don't hug him, she thought, which was what she wanted to do. He'd probably die of embarrassment. She clenched her hands in her lap. She'd seen him since Tina died of course, at the funeral and again a couple of times when she dropped in on Daisy, who'd called him down from his room. His lair, she called it. He'd appeared briefly each time, blinking as if emerging from the dark, mumbled a greeting and slouched back upstairs.

'Would you like something more to eat?' asked Brenda. 'Or a hot drink, or a coke or something? I'll treat you.'

'Coke,' he muttered, then added, 'Sorry. Please. Thanks.'

Brenda wondered whether Tommy would turn into a monosyllabic teenager. She'd better get used to the idea, he'd be thirteen in a few weeks.

Perhaps primed by the coke, Peter managed to squeeze out a few more words as they sat inside.

'I'm OK. Thanks. Daisy's kind.'

A pause for a swig and a surreptitious rub of the eyes.

'But I really miss Mum. It su— it's so unfair.'

'It is. I can't believe it. I think of her every day. Get my phone out to text her all the time.'

Brenda paused. 'Peter,' she said carefully. 'Do you think she was meeting someone? When she went for the walk, I mean?'

Peter shrugged hopelessly. 'I don't know. She said she wanted to think or something. Clear her head. I told the police. I don't think she was meeting anyone.'

'Was she …' Brenda wondered how far she could reasonably probe. 'Was she dressed up? Smart?'

Peter shrugged again. 'Dunno. She looked nice I suppose.' He screwed up his eyes. 'She was only wearing jeans though.

Not a dress. But —' He frowned. 'She smelled. I mean nice. Like perfume or something. I smelt it in my room after she'd gone.' He choked on a sob and Brenda gave up resisting the urge to put her arm round his shoulder. He leant against her and wept.

Thirty-One

June

Amanda was at home when Leonie arrived at Whiteacre a couple of weeks later. She looked less shell-shocked than she had been: her face was pale rather than spectral and her hair glossy if untidy. She offered coffee but Leonie insisted on at least cleaning the ground floor first.

'Let's sit outside,' said Amanda. 'It should be warm enough in the sun.' She put two large coffees on a tray with a plate of biscuits and they went out onto the terrace. 'We may need to move on to wine,' she added, 'depending on stress levels.'

'And how are the stress levels?' asked Leonie.

Amanda took a mouthful of coffee and said, 'Not too bad I suppose. In the context. I've bought some time out of bed with Simon but I can't keep him at bay forever. But I have to be certain about what happened to Hugh before I can decide what to do about Simon. I really need to get him to admit it. Even if only indirectly. But it won't be easy.'

'No,' agreed Leonie. 'I don't suppose it will. Be careful.'

She nibbled a biscuit, thinking. 'Could you say to him, do you think,' she said slowly, 'that under Hugh's will you can't inherit if there's any evidence you're in a relationship within the next year? Or something similar. I don't even know if a clause like that would be valid, but Simon won't either. It would give you a reason for not wanting him here all the time, in case he's spotted by a nosy neighbour. Not that any neighbour could spot anything that goes on here —'

She broke off. Of course Brenda could spot things and had done so. But Leonie decided again not to mention that to Amanda for the moment; she had enough to worry about.

'And if we're right,' she resumed, 'he'd have a strong incentive to toe the line.'

Amanda stirred her coffee for a few seconds, her eyes on the terrace. 'It's a good thought. If the whole horrible suspicion is justified, I can only assume that he wants to marry me for my money.' She looked bleak and pinched again for a moment, then visibly stiffened her back and shoulders in a mime of strength.

*

Simon came to Whiteacre that evening. Amanda had bought a lamb rack which was marinading in a slick of olive oil, lemon juice, crushed garlic and chilli when he arrived. She hated the thought of cooking for him but forced herself to go through the motions occasionally, while mostly leaving him to barbecue as the evenings got longer and warmer.

'You shouldn't have to cook,' he said, his arms round her, his chin resting on her head. 'I can always cook for you.'

'I know. And I love it when you do. But I mustn't lose the knack. I'll want to cook for you sometimes.'

Amanda hadn't been conscious of tension in Simon's body

against her, but she felt what was almost a bolt of release. He stroked her hair.

'But,' she said, 'we need to talk about something.' She turned the meat over and ground salt and pepper over it, then poured them each a glass of wine. Simon followed her to the terrace. She'd left alpaca blankets on the two steamer chairs and wrapped hers around her, again drawing comfort from the soft wool against her neck.

'I have to see the solicitors doing the probate,' she said. 'On Tuesday. But they called this morning. Hugh's will is complicated. Obviously I inherit most of the estate, with gifts to his brothers and nieces. And to my sister, which was good of him. Anyway, it seems that I won't get it for a year. And only if the executors are sure I'm not in another relationship by then.'

Amanda sensed rather than saw a ripple of stiffness washing over Simon, and continued, 'So. I want to stay with you. And for you to stay with me. But we need to be very careful. For a while.'

*

You'll just have to wait, mate …

Simon drummed his fingers on the countertop over the hob in his camper van. He hadn't expected to sleep in the van the previous night but Amanda was still pleading tiredness and stress, and now the condition in Hugh's will, as grounds for him not to spend much time at Whiteacre, and specifically not to spend much — well, at least for the moment, any — time in her big brass bed. He was worried that his future was slipping away from him. After all his planning and waiting. And action. Execution of the plan, he thought grimly. Which might be stymied by the executors.

But there were good signs also, he reasoned. Amanda had said in so many words that she wanted to stay with him and him to stay with her. And he'd be able to see her some of the time. And presumably she'd be back in bed with him before too long. Maybe he'd nip over to Chandler's Ford and pick up a coil of boerewors to braai for her on Thursday. And carry on down to Sway, ask if he could barter a couple of days' help in the vineyard for a bottle of Charlie Herring's sparkling wine.

He reached to the back of the drawer under the rear seats, looking for his stash, and brought out a pair of small keys which were caught in the tobacco pouch. Shit, the keys to Hugh's filing cabinet. He'd forgotten about them with everything else going on in the last few weeks. He wondered whether Amanda had missed them. Maybe they were spares. From what that girl had said — what was she called, Tricia or something? — their hiding place would have been inconvenient for everyday use. He shrugged, and rolled a joint. He'd doubtless have full access to the wine cellar soon and could slip them back in the bottle.

*

'Champagne?' said Amanda. 'From Sway?'

'Champagne method anyway,' said Simon. 'Someone I know. Tim Phillips. He trained in South Africa, which is where I met him. Planted a vineyard in an old walled garden in Sway.'

Amanda took a cautious sip and raised her eyebrows. 'It's excellent. Clean and dry. Good for a warm summer's evening on the terrace.' Hugh would have been interested. She was skewered by a sudden shaft of sorrow and shame. Just seeing this through, Hugh. Just till I know, though. But then what?

Simon had set up the Weber and was grilling the spicy sausage, also skewered. Amanda had prepared potatoes dauphinoise and a salade tiède of French beans in walnut oil and lemon juice. She topped up their glasses while Simon flipped the boerewors.

He ran his finger down her cheek. 'You're quiet this evening.'

'Sorry. A lot on my mind. All the paperwork. I'll try not to think about it.' Amanda wrapped her arms round Simon, hoping that if he picked up on her tension — she felt rigid, like the painted wooden Dutch doll she'd had as a child which moved only at the joints — he'd put it down to tiredness and stress. She needed to keep him on side, and not let him suspect that she suspected, at least for now.

*

Ah, there they were finally. Brenda adjusted her binoculars, but there was no mistaking it. Simon and Mrs S on the terrace, holding what looked like champagne flutes. A barbecue going. Simon stroked her face and she flung her arms round him. Well, that answered her question — clearly they were still an item.

Later, she dug out her pay-as-you-go SIM card and sent a text.

Hi Simon, good to c u and Mrs S sharing some fizz. Hope ur looking after her. Btw did u find what u were looking for in the gutter last month?

She felt better knowing that Simon knew he was being observed. While she agreed with Leonie-Jane that there was no reason why he'd want to hurt Mrs S at the moment, or even at all, there was no harm in keeping an eye on him.

*

'How's it going?' asked Leonie. She'd managed to get an hour's cleaning done before Amanda came down from her office, where she said she'd been ploughing on with the paperwork, and offered coffee.

'OK, I suppose. I used your idea. He accepts that he can't spend as much time here as he'd like. At least for the moment. That makes things easier but it's only a short-term solution. I still need to know what happened. And I have no idea how to find out.'

Leonie frowned into her cup, stirring the froth. 'Hmm. Does he drink?'

Amanda gave a hollow laugh. 'Don't we all? Talking of which …' She went to the fridge and poured two glasses of white wine. 'But yes, of course he does.' She stood, also frowning. 'I'm not sure — I'm not trying to make excuses for myself, but I'm not sure I'd have done it without alcohol. Had an affair, I mean. With Simon, in particular. I was lonely, and hadn't realised it, and I'd run out of house-and-garden things to distract me from the fact that I had nothing else. With Hugh in London.'

Leonie put her head in her hands.

'I always thought that was just an expression,' said Amanda, not unkindly. 'Putting your head in your hands I mean. I wasn't getting at you. I know you weren't the first. Or indeed the last. And I expect Hugh was the instigator. No — I don't want to hear. I was talking about myself. It was so out of character. A coincidence of loneliness and boredom and a charmer who popped up at the right time and saw his opportunity. And I oiled the wheels with lavish applications of wine. Talking of which …'

She put the glasses on the table and sat down.

'But it must have been incremental,' said Leonie. 'He can't have popped up with the whole game plan in his head.'

'No,' agreed Amanda. 'I think maybe he was planning burglary at the outset. Wanted to get into the house, perhaps, to see what there was? And he was definitely the instigator, prompted me to offer him coffee and started bringing me things.' She coloured at the mention of the coffee.

'What sort of things?'

'Food, mainly. Which he cooked for me a couple of times. He was good company, interested in me. Which Hugh didn't seem to be anymore. And then he must have thought he could get sex as well as burglary. Which he did. I mean the sex, not the burglary.'

They were both quiet for a while, sipping their wine.

'He did say once,' added Amanda, 'that he was falling in love with me. But looking back I suspect it was just part of the plan. He could be very convincing. But I didn't say it to him. And I never gave him any suggestion — well, not explicitly anyway — that we'd get together.' She shivered. 'And thinking about it now, thinking back, I don't recall him ever showing any real emotion. He seemed warm and caring and generous and considerate and so on but it could have been a clever veneer. I was — almost star-struck I suppose. That someone was giving me time and attention.' She shook her head wearily.

'I asked about the drink,' said Leonie, 'because I wondered whether he might be loose-tongued if he had more than usual?'

'I doubt it. He's got a good head for alcohol. And I suspect he's careful what he says.' Amanda sighed. 'I guess I'll just carry on until … But I'm stuck with him for now. What's that song — it's on one of Hugh's playlists? *Stuck in the middle with you.* That's how I feel. Funny how things turn out.'

'No kidding,' said Leonie. 'But yes, I can't see him going quietly now. So until we know —'

'It's normal service resumed,' finished Amanda, with a moue of distaste. 'Well, the wine oiled the wheels before, let's hope it can do so again.'

*

Amanda invited Simon to stay for supper on the following day. She'd bought a good chicken, anointed it with olive oil and lemon juice, tucked garlic, rosemary and the eviscerated lemon in the cavity, and put it on to roast as he came in. Potatoes, carrots and onions were ready to add to the roasting tray after twenty minutes, and washed and torn lettuce was waiting in the fridge. With a white Burgundy.

She'd anointed herself too, slathering on her favourite frangipani cream after a long, also frangipani-scented, bath that she hoped would relax her. She slipped on a silky, jade-green dress and checked the effect. Mirror, signal, manoeuvre, she thought. The manoeuvre will be the difficulty. What I want to do is reverse. But I can't until I know. And if and when I do know, I may need those annoying bleepers to warn me of danger behind.

And there may be danger for others also. Leonie, for instance. Who yesterday had said 'until we know' about Simon's involvement in Hugh's death. Leonie had provided a lot of very useful, if distressing and worrying, information, and bizarrely — but then everything in Amanda's once colourless life was now bizarre — had become something of a friend and confidante, but this was Amanda's problem.

*

Just as Amanda seemed to be warming to him, even inviting him into her bed, other problems were manifesting themselves. Simon had thought that once he'd got rid of Hugh, his life would be on a simple, upward curve. Of course he'd expected a short period of mourning and he felt that he'd acted the supportive, caring partner-in-waiting convincingly. But he hadn't anticipated the clause in Hugh's will and the consequential need to continue to wait, and to creep around while doing so. And now Brenda's not-so-thinly-veiled threat.

She must know something. Something more than his name, and how did she even know that? But that was the least of it. Somehow, she could see into the garden. He'd suspected as much after the whole blackmail saga, though he still had no idea how. But this latest text left no room for doubt. Had she even seen him on the roof the evening before Hugh died? It was clear that, for whatever reason, she suspected him. And he was so near his goal, even with the delay. She would have to go. He'd need another detailed plan carefully carried out. He sighed. Really, would he never be able to relax and enjoy the fruits of his last detailed and carefully carried out plan? Or plans, if you included — Tina, yes that was her name, not Tricia — though she hardly counted. No challenge at all.

Simon's mind drifted back to the previous evening. Amanda looking ravishing again. A delicious meal followed by an even more delicious session in bed. Afterwards, he'd tried to think through what she knew about the blackmailer. Presumably nothing. Of course her number had been in Amanda's phone, but it was obviously a SIM card that she'd used only for those texts, hence the time slot stipulation and the lack of any other messages on Brenda's phone. She'd used the same number when she'd texted him before she handed the key back and then again on Thursday.

But Amanda couldn't even know the blackmailer's burner SIM card number, unless she'd memorised or made a note of it, because he had so cleverly got rid of her secret phone. Nor could she know the blackmailer's name or even her sex; Brenda had been careful. And he assumed that Amanda still believed that the garden wasn't overlooked, though she must have puzzled about how the blackmailer knew about their affair. So nobody knew, or was in a position to know, about his connection — such as it was — to Brenda. And there was no reason why she would have told anyone else about her blackmailing activities.

He, however, knew where she lived.

Thirty-Two

July

Over the next few weeks Leonie saw Amanda become paler and thinner again. She'd told Leonie that she was back on course with Simon.

'Your idea worked,' she said. 'I'm keeping it to two or at most three evenings a week. It's OK up to a point — he's still good company. And still good in bed, but that part's really hard.'

'I can only imagine,' said Leonie. 'But I guess women have been faking pleasure for years. Centuries. Millenia even. Though not usually with the lover.'

Amanda gave one of her ghostly half-laughs. 'The problem is, I can't keep it up forever. I need to move on. I feel as if I'm frozen in aspic. Or do I mean amber? Anyway, you get the drift.'

'I do. Has he given any hint? Have you tried to broach it, even indirectly?'

'As in, "Dear, did you by chance murder my husband?" Not easy. I think I should talk more about how unfair it is to have to wait for the money.'

Leonie reflected. 'Maybe you can start being short of cash?' she suggested. 'Explain that without Hugh's drawings, and with everything else frozen, but the bills coming in regardless, things are getting difficult.'

'I could try that. As long as I don't need to economise on wine. That would make the whole thing impossible. But I could say I'm having to reduce outgoings. Like cash in hand to gardeners.'

The talk of money reminded Leonie that she'd finally heard that she'd made it through the translation competition. 'Amanda,' she started, then paused. She felt uncomfortable about walking away while Amanda was still in potential danger, and rapidly edited what she'd intended to say. 'Amanda, I've been offered another job. A legal job. But it's freelance and I doubt there'll be much work till September — it's doing translation for the European Court of Justice and it'll be the judicial vacation soon, and I can decide when and what work to accept anyway. So I won't give notice to New Brooms for a while, but I wanted to let you know.'

*

Simon flipped over the trout on the Weber. The smoky fragrance and the transition from virgin quicksilver to black-striped gunmetal took Amanda back to the previous summer. *Summer nights*. Fragments of lyrics floated into her head. Even though she wanted nothing more now than never to see Simon again once she knew what had happened, the memory of those evenings on the terrace, and in bed, stirred her. She had been ripe for the picking, she realised. Lonely. Would it have happened with someone else if Simon hadn't been circling? She would never know.

She sighed. Simon looked over to her, his face etched with concern. 'Babe, are you OK? You're still looking tired.'

Amanda gathered her thoughts as she topped up their glasses. 'It's the paperwork. The lawyers. It's endless. And now there's another problem.'

She saw Simon's head almost jerk back. He kept his eyes trained on hers, a double crease between them.

'I told you I can't get any money until a year after … until next April. And of course I don't have any income now, everything's frozen because of the probate. But the bills keep coming. I'm going to hit a problem with cash soon.' She sighed again, more deeply. And watched Simon closely from under lowered lids.

A cloud passed over his face, so swiftly that it was barely perceptible. A lightning flash of — fury? frustration? Too fleeting to read, but it was something dark and savage.

'That's terrible,' he said. 'How could your husband do that to you? Didn't he trust you?'

Amanda felt a piercing barb of guilt. Hugh had trusted her, she was sure. It turned out that he'd been wrong to do so and, possibly — probably — as a result, he was dead. And now she was vilifying him, the most generous of men. Again. She clenched her fists. It's in a good cause; hold on to that.

'I expect it's something inheritance-tax lawyers always advise. But I can't change it.'

Simon shook his head. 'I think it's mean-spirited. Not that I want to speak ill of the dead. Well, I guess we'll just have to manage. For the moment.'

*

Brenda was waiting for a pause in the traffic so she could cross to Tesco when she heard her ringtone. Since Simon had stolen it so easily from her, she'd stopped carrying her phone in her hand or a pocket when she was in crowds. And she was in a crowd right now when several things happened almost simultaneously.

She twisted away from the kerb to shrug her backpack bag off and get her phone. As she turned, she felt a sharp thrust in the small of her back which knocked her forwards. Unbalanced, she stumbled and her left foot slipped off the kerb and folded excruciatingly under her. Her body rotated agonisingly round it as she fell into the road. She heard the violent blast of a horn and the scream of brakes. The last thing she saw before she slammed on her back onto the tarmac was Simon's face, staring back at her from the crowd, as the bus grille loomed above her.

*

Simon elbowed his way triumphantly through the rubberneckers. He'd had a brief but satisfyingly clear view of the blackmailer's shocked, white face as she fell backwards in front of the bus. He'd heard the squeal of brakes and the screams and gasps of the crowd. Job done. He remembered that his phone had rung just as he was about to push her. He checked it. A missed call from Amanda, followed by a text asking whether he'd like her to pick up any meat for later.

Thirty-Three

July

Arms reached out to pull her back onto the pavement. Someone said, 'Just as well you twisted as you fell — I think that's how the bus could stop in time.' Brenda assured those trying to help that she was all right, must have slipped off the kerb. Feeling shaken and bruised, her back sore, her left ankle shooting pain if she tried to put much weight on it, she worked her hobbling way through the shoppers who had at last started to move again, though heads were still straining to see what the noise was about and exchanging excited comments about how some woman had fallen in front of a bus and almost been killed. She stumbled into the nearest café, sat down with a latte with a much needed extra shot and checked her phone. No missed calls. Must have been someone else's phone. Tommy was always trying to get her to change her ringtone to something more interesting but perhaps the boring default one had saved her life. She texted Leonie-Jane, her fingers shaking slightly.

Leonie-Jane met her later at Pret and Brenda filled her in.

L-J thought for a while, frowning. 'Am I being dense?' she asked. 'I can't see why Simon would want to — to hurt you. He doesn't know you can see into the garden does he?'

'Of course he does,' said Brenda, then paused. 'Oh. I never told you why the blackmail fizzled out. We got diverted didn't we, when you told me about the coin. It's another long story, but he found out I was the blackmailer and, er, persuaded me to stop.'

'Did you tell him that you could see into the garden though?'

'Not exactly, no. Not then. But I assumed he figured it out. Though come to think of it, maybe he didn't. At that point he thought I was the cleaner at Whiteacre. Though I told him I wasn't. Has he ever seen you there?'

'No. I clean Mondays and Fridays and I think he gardens Tuesdays and Thursdays. When I started cleaning, Amanda told New Brooms that those days weren't convenient for a cleaner to be in the house.'

Brenda smirked. 'I bet she did.'

'So if he doesn't know you can see into the garden,' persisted Leonie, 'why does he think you're a threat? Which he must do. Unless he thinks you'll blackmail Amanda again. But you can hardly threaten to send the photo to Hugh now.'

Brenda looked down into her mug. 'I fucked up,' she mumbled. 'I thought Simon did know, but you're right, he didn't. At least not from me, though I suppose he might have worked it out. But I sent him a text.' She opened her phone and showed Leonie-Jane the message:

Hi Simon, good to c u and Mrs S sharing some fizz. Hope ur looking after her. Btw did u find what u were looking for in the gutter last month?

*

eonie read the text through twice.

'I think you fucked up,' she agreed. 'Though I imagine with good intentions. Were you sort of looking out for Amanda?'

Brenda sighed. 'I guess so. I just thought — I feel quite guilty about the blackmail to be honest. When I think of what she must be going through now. I mean, I didn't feel that at first, when I thought she might have been involved. But it sounds from what you say as if she can't have been.'

Leonie hesitated, then said, 'You were right when you said that she and I had become quite pally. And it is odd. But I think she feels lonely and — exposed, almost. I found a photo of the roof on the day before Hugh died. A slate had been removed.' She took Brenda through her discovery of the magazine article and her visit to (F)airy Fotos.

Brenda shook her head. 'Leonie-Jane, you've done it again. You do pull out some trump cards.'

'Ha. At least my legal training hasn't entirely gone to waste. Anyway, I showed Amanda the photo. And there's the text and the coin. She's worried. And — I think she's in a sort of limbo. She needs to know one way or another before she can move on. So she's keeping up the pretence of a relationship with Simon. Well, not wholly pretence. She doesn't want him to know she suspects him.'

Leonie thought some more. 'Amanda needs to know that Simon tried to shove you under a bus. It's another piece of the jigsaw. A big piece. Because why would he have done that if he wasn't guilty? And it shows what he's capable of. Which makes it more likely that he killed before. And remember he knows you're capable of blackmail. And that you could put a spanner in his whole planned future, if we're right. You need to watch your back Brenda. Literally.'

Brenda bit her lip. 'It's horrible. I just — I keep thinking of the kids. What would happen to them if anything happened to me?'

'The thing is,' Leonie continued, 'I'd have to tell Amanda — well, quite a lot. So she knows why Simon would think you're a risk to him.'

'I could pay the money back,' said Brenda miserably. 'I've still got most of it.'

'I wouldn't worry. I don't think Amanda's short of money, though she's pretending to be — she's told Simon that she can't inherit under Hugh's will if she's in another relationship a year after his death.'

Brenda gave Leonie a long, level look. 'I wonder who came up with that idea?'

*

'**A**re you sure this will be OK?' asked Brenda anxiously as she and Leonie stood on the doorstep of Whiteacre.

'Yes,' said Leonie, ringing the doorbell. 'I texted Amanda to say I was bringing you. She doesn't know you were the blackmailer but if it comes out, so be it. This is more important.'

Amanda swung the door open. More faint lines cobwebbed her face. Or was it less make-up? She was dressing more casually than she used to, her hair less coiffed, even as her posture radiated more tension every time Leonie saw her.

Leonie plunged in. 'Amanda. This is Brenda. She's — we've — got something to tell you.'

Amanda raised her eyebrows. 'Is it a coffee something or a Sauvignon Blanc something?'

'Definitely the Sauvignon. It's important, something you need to know,' said Leonie. Let's hope we don't get chucked out like the last time I said that, she thought.

They went through to the breakfast room. Amanda had her hand on the door to the terrace when Leonie said. 'Er — is there any chance that Simon could be in the garden?'

Amanda paused with a slight start. Letting her hand drop, she turned to face Leonie and said slowly, 'Well, he shouldn't be here today. But I suppose I can't guarantee it. I seem to have walked through the looking glass and don't feel sure of anything anymore. He does have a key to the door in the back wall so it's possible.'

They sat at the breakfast room table and Amanda poured three glasses of chilled white wine. Leonie took what she fervently hoped would be a strengthening mouthful and began, choosing her words with care.

'Brenda cleans a house that overlooks your garden —'

'It's not overlooked,' Amanda interrupted. 'We were assured when we bought it. It's very private round here, it's part of what you pay for. They even seem to have kept Google Street View at bay for most of the area.'

'It's a house called Brambles,' continued Leonie. 'You can just see a sort of turret, beyond your garden and the copse.' She gestured through the window.

Amanda peered out. 'I can't really see without my glasses, it's too far away. But we were definitely —'

'You can see into your garden from the turret. With binoculars.'

Amanda went white, then red, then white again. She sat in silence for a few seconds, drumming her fingers on the table, then turned to Brenda, who was sitting with her legs tightly entwined and shoulders hunched.

'So you're the blackmailer?'

It was Brenda's turn to pale, flush and pale again. She opened her mouth but nothing came out.

Amanda was clenching and unclenching her hands. She sat up straight, her shoulders stiff, her back like a ramrod. Leonie looked sideways at her. Was she feeling another surge of the rage that had so unexpectedly overflowed before Easter, when Leonie had started her inept confession? She decided to break the moment. Amanda needed to hear this. 'She —'

'It's OK.' Brenda found her voice, though it was a shadow of her usual bantering tone. 'Mrs S — Mrs Standing. I'm sorry. It was a horrible thing to do. I — one of my owners paid me off, lots of cash, when I walked in on her in bed with her lover —'

Amanda seemed to have recovered herself and her usual poise. She raised her eyebrows, though there was the ghost of a smile on her lips. 'Did you say Brambles? The Rooks' house?'

'No. I mean that's not where that happened, but it gave me the idea. I started looking out of windows. And from the Castle House, I mean Brambles, I could see into your garden. I was just — so short of money. I've got two kids. Their father walked out on me. I thought it would be easy money and that you wouldn't even miss it. I'm sorry,' she repeated, then added, 'especially when you said your husband didn't let you have much housekeeping. I even felt a bit sorry for you.'

Amanda flushed again. 'I shouldn't have said that. I was just — bartering. Hugh was a very generous man.'

'Anyway,' Brenda ploughed on, 'you know what happened after I'd seen you with the gardener. Simon. I ... I can give you back most of the money. I just spent a bit on Easter treats for the kids and some curtains from a charity shop. I was going to buy a dishwasher but — it felt dirty, spending it.' She scrabbled in her handbag and took out an envelope which she offered to Amanda.

Amanda shook her head. 'Keep it,' she said, looking round at her state-of-the-art kitchen. 'But you can't have taken the photo from your turret?'

Brenda bit her lip. 'No,' she mumbled. 'I got into the garden.'

Amanda looked a question at her and she stumbled on. 'I worked out that the house I could see was Whiteacre and saw that all the houses in this road had doors from that little street at the back. I used to stop off on my way home from Brambles, and sometimes from other houses I cleaned locally. I tried your door each time but it was always locked. Until one day it wasn't. It opened and the key was still in the lock inside, so I took it. And crept in sometimes, if I'd seen that you were in the garden together.'

Amanda turned a deep shade of red again, then frowned. 'Did you keep the key?'

'Yes,' said Brenda. 'Until — until after Simon had frightened me off. Then I gave it back to him.'

Amanda was staring at Brenda, her colour restored to normal, her brow knotted. After a pause she said, 'One thing at a time. I asked Simon if he'd lost or mislaid his key. I don't think I'd even seen the photo at that point, but I knew there was one. I thought the blackmailer must have come into the garden and I couldn't think of any other way. He told me hadn't. He even showed me his key —'

'Must have had a copy made when you gave it to him,' said Brenda briskly, recovering her usual voice.

'I suppose so.' Amanda's voice, in contrast, sounded strained, almost frail.

'So what was his theory?' asked Brenda. 'When he saw the photo? Did he mention the key then?'

Amanda frowned again. 'But he didn't see the photo. He didn't know about the blackmail.'

It was Brenda's turn to stare. 'But he must have. Like I said, he frightened me off. Mugged me at the last drop and took my phone.'

Amanda shook her head. 'I never told him about it. I don't know why. I think at first I convinced myself it wasn't really happening and then I felt I should try and sort it out myself. And I felt — ashamed, I suppose. A bit grubby.'

Brenda flushed again. Really, thought Leonie, it was a bit like watching a tennis match, but more colourful. Both sight and sound.

'Well,' said Brenda. 'He definitely knew about it one way or another. I don't know how or when but at the third drop he jostled me just as I was texting you' — on cue, Brenda reddened — 'and stole my phone. Put a letter through my door, so he must have followed me home, and said he'd delete the photo and give me back my phone if I stopped the blackmail. Or something similar.'

Amanda was still frowning. 'What I don't understand is how he saw the photo and knew about the blackmail in the first place.'

Leonie now felt her own face warming. 'Amanda, could he have seen it somewhere in the house?'

'I don't see how. It was hidden in a drawer in my office, with the two letters. He's never even been in my office.'

'Let's leave that puzzle for the moment,' said Leonie, 'because the real reason — well, one of the reasons — I brought Brenda here is because of something she saw after Hugh died. It must have been just after Simon got back from France.'

'He put the ladder up,' said Brenda. 'He was looking for something in the gutter, feeling round the slates. Then looking round the flower bed under ... under that part of the roof. Then Leonie-Jane here told me about that coin she found.'

'Actually,' said Leonie, 'we know the date. Brenda texted me. But I didn't think about it, there was so much else going on. It was just before I, er, told you about his text, Amanda. And before I'd seen the aerial shot of the roof. And when I told you about that … well, I thought you had enough to deal with to be honest. Anyway, it was 11th April.'

'It would have been a Thursday,' added Brenda.

Amanda sat silently again, her hands clenched on the table. 'It's more circumstantial evidence, you'll say, especially as he went up on the roof … before … to prune the rose,' she said to Leonie, who nodded.

'It's another tiny piece of the jigsaw, but still nothing that couldn't be explained away. But Brenda's got something else to tell you. Also useless as evidence, but you need to know.'

And Brenda told Amanda how Simon had tried to shove her under a bus after she sent him what he'd have seen as a threatening message.

*

Amanda recoiled as though she'd been punched in the stomach. She pushed herself up from her chair, went to the fridge and took out the wine bottle. Leaving the fridge door open, she moved to the window and stood staring into the garden, the bottle held loosely in one hand. There were ripples in the wine, she noticed absently; she must be shaking, or trembling. Leonie got up, closed the fridge and gently took the bottle. And solved the problem of the ripples by emptying it into the three glasses.

Amanda turned round and shook her head vigorously, as if clearing her ears after swimming. She tore off a sheet of kitchen towel and dabbed her eyes. 'I think that's — almost conclusive,' she said eventually. 'But you'll tell me there's no point going to the police.'

'Like I said before,' said Leonie, 'it's not my area. But no, I doubt it could be used in court as evidence. And even if it could, it would have no weight at all after Brenda had been cross-examined by any half-competent defence counsel. And that would be a really bad scenario. If Simon got off, I mean, but knew that we knew. And that we had some evidence. Even if it wasn't enough for a conviction.'

That 'we' again, thought Amanda after Leonie and Brenda had gone. There was real danger, then. And it was reaching beyond her; her reckless escapade with Simon had put another woman at risk. She'd been right to quell the tide of rage and shame which had risen when she realised that Brenda was the blackmailer. She'd been glad that she backed down and heard what Leonie had to say before, and if the information on offer this time was as significant as on that occasion, she knew she needed to hear it. She'd pressed her teeth into her tongue, focusing on the pain until she felt calmer, and had then listened.

And now she needed to keep a clear head. Cut down on the wine. She started by making a strong coffee and sitting back at the breakfast table. And stopped fighting the knowledge that she was surely now also at risk. It was almost certain that Simon had murdered Hugh and tried to kill Brenda. Would she be next? Was his plan not just to take Hugh's place, to move in and enjoy life with her? Was he thinking longer term, to marriage? To becoming a rich husband? And then … to becoming an even richer widower?

Thirty-Four

July

Amanda sat for a while sipping her coffee and turning things over in her mind. A plan was gradually forming. For the last couple of years she'd borne the knowledge that her father had very probably been murdered, and now it seemed certain that her husband had met the same fate. She felt strength and resolve building in her, perhaps a legacy of her mother who had squared her shoulders after her life with Arthur had collapsed and done what she could for her daughters. She must have had her suspicions, maybe even knowledge, about Arthur's death. But she, unlike Amanda, had never had the opportunity to avenge her husband.

Amanda called her hair salon in London and pleaded with them to squeeze her in for the following day. She explained why she hadn't been for four months and that she had resorted to a local hairdresser at half time. Her stylist eventually agreed to work late. She also booked a manicure and pedicure for earlier in the afternoon.

She texted Simon:

Babe, have to go to London tomorrow to c lawyer, want to try and sort out sth re cash. And am tired of looking like a scarecrow for u so going to get hair and nails done which estate will have to cough up for. So won't be here but can't wait to c u Thurs. Axx

She then went through the fridge. Not that there was much in it; she was still living hand-to-mouth between Simon's frequent barbecues and the occasional meals she forced herself to cook for him. She threw out some very out-of-date milk and juice, a slimy lettuce, olives with a skein of mould on the brine, a soft cheese whose name she couldn't remember and whose grey furry pelt made identification impossible. And a packet of bacon that was best before some weeks ago. 'Sainsbury's Taste the Difference' according to the plastic sleeve, which was straining at the seams. I bet. She had no recollection of buying it, but the last few months had been a foggy blur. From which, perhaps, she was finally beginning to emerge. *I can see clearly now* she hummed. She put on one of Hugh's playlists. And thought some more about the bacon.

Amanda gave the inside of the fridge a wipe with vinegar and water and rummaged through the freezer. To her relief she found a supply of meals she had cooked, labelled and frozen in happier days. She took out a portion of pumpkin risotto that must have been there too long and probably hadn't flourished but would do for now. And decided it was time to give more attention to cooking again.

*

Leonie and Brenda were again slotting in a couple of jigsaw pieces. Or trying to.

They'd gone for a coffee and a bite after leaving Whiteacre.

Brenda chewed her sandwich slowly, her brow furrowed, her eyes unfocused.

'What are you thinking?' Leonie asked eventually.

Brenda stirred her coffee. She glanced around as if to check that there was no one within earshot. The café was half empty — they were too late for most of the lunchtime trade — and she took a deep breath and said, 'I've been wondering about Tina. Do you think Simon could have done it?'

Leonie rubbed her eyes. 'I've been wondering myself, now we know he shoved you. And we're pretty sure he murdered Hugh. But why? It's obvious why he killed Hugh and tried to do the same for you. But Tina? She was so nice, or seemed that way to me. How could he have felt threatened by her? How did he even know her?'

'She told me,' said Brenda, 'and it must have been quite soon before she died — I don't know exactly when, we just bumped into each other by chance and went for a coffee so I don't even have a text I can check. But she said she'd met someone. He was called Steven though. And he ran a landscape gardening business. Does Simon do that?'

'Definitely not,' said Leonie. 'Amanda says a friend of hers recommended him. He'd put flyers through all the big houses in Nightjars Holt. It was only …' She screwed up her eyes. 'I think she said it was February last year. Around the time I started at New Brooms. And Tina too, I guess. Anyway, he's just a jobbing gardener as far as I know. Was a drifter. Lives in his camper van. Likes wild camping in remote parts of the New Forest apparently.'

'When he's not living the high life at Whiteacre,' said Brenda. 'He never told me his name. When I met him, after he'd stolen my phone that time. But if he was up to no good he could easily have given Tina a false name. And Steven's very similar to Simon.'

'But what could he have wanted from her? He was already deep into his affair with Amanda months before Tina died. He had an entry into Whiteacre through that. Amanda said she thought he initially wanted to burgle the place and disappear, but he had the opportunity to get into the house once the affair had started. Though …' Leonie trailed off. 'Tina covered two cleans at Whiteacre for me. I knew exactly when, I went to Brussels for a week. It was the middle of October. Only a couple of weeks before … Wait, Brenda, I'm just remembering something. We had a drink after I was back. It didn't go to plan — oh God, it's like another era now, especially since Tina …'

'Spit it out, girl,' said Brenda, leaning forward intently.

'She'd found some lingerie receipts I'd planted in one of Hugh's jackets.'

Brenda snorted, nearly knocking over her coffee.

Her face hot, Leonie continued. 'I ended up telling her all about our affair and the Cleaning Plan. But she said something which didn't really register at the time. She said when she asked to cover me, Cathy told her you'd said you could see into the Whiteacre garden from Brambles.'

Brenda looked blank. 'Is that it? You know that already. It's the whole basis for the blackmail. How does it change anything?'

'No, not that. Tina said she'd heard it *when she asked to cover me.*'

Brenda sat up straighter. 'Why would she have done that?' she asked slowly.

'Brenda, what do you know about her brother-in-law? Finn, is it?'

Brenda snorted again. 'Total loser. Can't think why Daisy married him. Shotgun wedding, but she'd have been better off going it alone.'

'Tina talked to me about some problem Finn had, but then it turned out it was she who had the problem —'

'I remember,' interrupted Brenda. 'She mentioned it to me, asked whether I knew a lawyer. I said she should ask you as you'd been a legal secretary so might know one.' Brenda rolled her eyes.

'She did talk to me about it.' Leonie bit her lip. 'I wish my memory was better. But I remember she'd been seen photographing a client's personal information —'

'What? Tina? No way would she do that.'

'She said she gave the info to Finn and he sold it.'

'He's a wanker,' said Brenda. 'He could have bullied her into it I guess. She probably didn't want to tell me, knew I wouldn't have approved.'

Leonie raised an eyebrow and Brenda had the grace to blush. 'Fair point. Tina and I were both having a hard time financially and, like me, she couldn't say no to easy money. Or what she thought would be easy. She'd have done it for Peter, and thought the rich people she cleaned for wouldn't miss it.'

Brenda sighed, then suddenly paled. 'You don't think she was killed for it?'

'I don't know,' said Leonie slowly. 'Let me think more about what she said. She'd been caught in the act. By someone called Steven. It was all very confused, especially as it started off being Finn who'd been caught then Tina gave herself away and admitted it was her. She thought this Steven was a policeman or private detective. He was undercover, posing as a gardener. She thought he was going to shop her. And then I —' Leonie broke off and took a swallow of tepid coffee. 'I was really fierce. When she told me it was a client's bank details. I told her she was committing a criminal offence, could go to prison, needed to stop. I rattled her, intended to rattle her because I thought she needed to know what deep water she was in.'

Leonie stopped again and rubbed her eyes. 'Brenda, I've always worried that maybe I pushed her too far. That she … that she might have killed herself. Because of what I said.'

Brenda shook her head vigorously. 'No. Here's the thing — Tina hated water. If she had wanted to commit suicide, which I would swear she didn't — she'd never leave Peter — there's no way she'd have done it by drowning. I even went to the police to say that, so they'd investigate, but they brushed me off.'

'God, that's a relief. Sorry, that sounds awful. I just mean I've been carrying that worry around since she died. Tried not to think about it but talking about … about Tina now, it brought it back.'

'You can shed that load,' said Brenda briskly. 'It's a definite no. But we still don't know for sure how she died. What happened after you'd had a go at her?'

'I'm just … So it was after that, but quite soon after I think, that she suddenly texted me and said she was covering Whiteacre and could we have a chat for any handover info. And she said something like should she be looking out for anything in particular. I thought maybe she meant she was going to be looking for data so I got a bit fierce again.'

Leonie paused and tried to remember exactly what had been said. 'I think,' she resumed slowly, 'I asked her whether she'd told Finn she was stopping. She said she was going to do so soon, was waiting for a good time or something. Anyway she was adamant she wasn't going to be looking for data or whatever at Whiteacre. Kept saying that the stuff she'd told me before was a misunderstanding and the man — Steven — had turned out to be very nice and they were quite friendly now.'

'Sounded like more than that from what she said to me. Two-timing Mrs S, it seems. Assuming it was Simon. Anyway, what about the receipts? How did she find them?'

'Apparently went through Hugh's suit pockets.'

'Must have been looking for something then.'

Brenda sat in silence for a few minutes then finished her

coffee in one long swallow. 'We know, almost for sure, that Simon killed Mr S. And there's — what do you lawyers call it, circumstantial evidence — that he killed Tina. Oh —' Brenda paused, frowning. 'I've just remembered something Peter said. Tina's son. I bumped into him in town a few weeks ago. Poor lamb. Anyway, I asked if he thought she'd been going to meet anyone and he said no. And she was wearing jeans, wasn't dressed up. But he said she smelled nice. As if she was wearing scent.'

Leonie and Brenda looked at each other. Brenda shrugged.

'More of that circumstantial stuff I know. But still. And even if we're not 100% sure about Simon and Tina, we know, definitely for sure, that he tried to kill me. And probably will again. I must go, time to pick up the kids.' She pushed her chair back with some violence, choked back a sob and strode out of the café.

*

Brenda set a brisk pace as she strode towards her car, fuelled by anger and adrenaline. But when she sat down behind the wheel she sagged. The thought of Tommy and Lily waiting at the school gates had brought her up short like a blow to the stomach. She swallowed her tears and headed off.

That evening Brenda felt as though her head was literally spinning, whirling like that merry-go-round Tommy made her go on once. It gave her a headache, made her feel sick. She let the kids slump in front of the telly while she slumped at the kitchen table, trying to think it through. Decide what to do. Simon would try again, she was sure. And she had to stay alive. But how?

She could run away. With the kids of course. Go and

live somewhere else. But moves cost money, took time, and she didn't have much of either. And the kids — losing their friends, new schools. Which she'd have to find, as well as a new job and a new place to live. She couldn't do it, not on her own.

Go to the police? But she had no proof. And she'd gone to them about Tina and a fat lot of good that had done.

She could watch her back, as L-J had said. She'd never go on a roof anyway, even the thought made the room swim, and she never wanted to walk by a river again, she'd just think of Tina. She angrily rubbed away the tears; thank God for the telly, the kids hadn't noticed. But he'd surely try something different next time. What, though? She thought frantically about crime series on the telly. He might mug her again, but take more than her phone. So don't walk in dark streets. Or a hit and run. So don't walk in quiet streets. He might — she gasped, and glanced at the kids, but the sound was on high and they hadn't heard. He might break into her house. At night, murder them all. Or set it on fire. Was she getting carried away? But she knew he was a ruthless killer. And he'd find a way, she was sure.

There was only one other way — to be a ruthless killer herself. Brenda closed her eyes, felt her heart beat faster. Could she bring herself to do something so … Wrong. Wicked. Evil. But then Simon/Steven was himself evil.

She shook her head. She still couldn't even think about it, let alone do such a thing. Wearily she heaved herself up. Time to get Lily into her bath and ask Tommy about his homework. First though she slid the bolts across the front door. Quietly so they wouldn't ask why. She didn't usually bother, but she had to make the house as safe as possible.

*

eonie was still mulling over her conversation with Brenda. She checked the dates and confirmed that she'd been in Brussels from 13th to 21st October, so Tina had cleaned Whiteacre on the 15th and 19th. And had died on the 24th. Less than a week later. How could Leonie not have connected the dots? It was around the time she'd found the blackmail letter and got distracted by it. She sighed. She almost certainly couldn't have prevented Tina's death, even if it was murder, but she could have kept her eye on the ball.

But she could see whether she could tie up that loose end at least. She wasn't due at Whiteacre for another four days, which was too long to wait. She texted Amanda, choosing her words with care in case Simon was there.

Think I must have left something at Whiteacre, any chance I could pop in today or tomorrow? Thanks, Lx.

'Is Simon here?' mouthed Leonie as soon as Amanda opened the door to her.

Amanda shook her head and they went through to the breakfast room.

'I was talking to Brenda after we left here earlier,' Leonie started. 'Do you remember Tina, the cleaner who covered for me when I went to Brussels? In October?'

'That poor girl who drowned? Yes, I do remember, probably because I saw it in the paper shortly afterwards. Terrible accident.'

'I'll explain, but — did you miss anything after she'd cleaned? Notice something wasn't where it should have been? Anything — a bank statement, a utilities bill …'

Amanda was quiet for a couple of minutes, evidently thinking. 'No, nothing,' she said. 'And we keep all that sort of stuff locked away in the —' She stopped, her mouth open in an elegant, lipsticked 'O'. 'In the filing cabinet,' she continued. 'And the spare keys to the cabinet went missing.'

'When?'

'Honestly, I don't recall when I noticed. They were the spares, as I said. Hugh and I each had a set on our key-rings, so I never needed them. And around that time I got caught up in … all that blackmail stuff. I wasn't very focused. And then shortly after the blackmail stopped Hugh died. I forgot about it till just now, to be honest.'

'Where were they kept?'

'In the wine cellar.'

'Wine cellar? How can I have missed a wine cellar?'

Amanda laughed and gestured to the floor. 'You're sitting on it. Move your chair back.' She got up and touched a control panel above one of the counters and the hatch slowly lifted.

Leonie followed Amanda down the spiral staircase, marvelling both at the quantity and quality of the wine they passed and at how she could have failed to notice it. In fairness, both the hatch and the control panel were very well camouflaged.

At the bottom, surrounded by the glittering gold foil of champagne bottles, Amanda eased out a reverse-facing magnum. It was empty, containing neither Bollinger nor keys.

They went back up, Amanda plucking out a bottle of red Burgundy en route. 'Let's have some of this,' she said. 'It'll be change from white and the perfect temperature for a warm evening.' She opened the wine, poured them each a glass and they sat back down.

'Are you saying that that poor girl — Tina — stole the keys?' she asked.

'I think Simon asked her to. It's a long story and I'm only just beginning to put the pieces together. I'll give you the short version for now, or as much as Brenda and I've worked out. Tina sometimes stole personal data from New Brooms clients.'

Amanda gasped. 'That's —'

'I know,' said Leonie grimly. 'That's what I told her. I'll come to that. Anyway, Brenda knew Tina well, they were at school together, and says it was very out of character but thinks her dodgy brother-in-law got her into it. Tina was really struggling financially at the time; she'd been made redundant and had an acrimonious divorce. And a teenage son. She talked to me about the data theft because she found out I was a solicitor. This was before she cleaned here by the way, it was another client. Or clients. She also mentioned the dodgy brother-in-law and said someone had seen her taking photos of papers and threatened to shop her, though she wasn't sure who to. He'd been posing — or she thought it was posing — as a gardener and said he was called Steven. She thought he was a policeman or a private detective.'

Amanda was staring at Leonie, eyes wide, face paler than ever. She managed half a bleak laugh. 'That would be a first, Simon being mistaken for an officer of the law. If it was him.'

'Yes. So when Tina told me all this I read her the riot act, told her she could go to prison, that she had to stop. Then I spoke to her before she cleaned here and asked whether she'd spoken to Finn, the brother-in-law, and stopped all that nonsense and she said she was about to but that she'd been wrong about Steven, he was really nice, he ran a landscape gardening business and they'd got very friendly. Around that time she told Brenda that she'd met someone. And I realised from something she said after she'd cleaned here — but it only clicked this afternoon, when I was talking to Brenda — that she'd asked to cover Whiteacre for me. Usually Cathy just sorts the cover cleans on the basis of who's available, but Tina specifically asked.'

'But why — oh. You mean that Simon, assuming it was him, asked Tina to clean here? And look for … the keys to the filing cabinet?'

Leonie nodded, trying not to think about the receipts.

'And that he was in some sort of relationship with her?'

Leonie shrugged. 'Feigning it, probably.'

'And that ... once he'd got what he wanted ...'

'Yes,' said Leonie grimly. 'That's exactly what I mean. But it's all supposition, of course.' Leonie took a mouthful of the Burgundy and suddenly added, 'But how would Tina have known about the wine cellar? Even I didn't notice it, and I'm a nosy lush!'

Amanda was silent, tapping her fingers gently on the table. 'One of the days she came I was running late for something, I can't remember what. And I wanted to put some wine in the fridge before going out. I went down to the wine cellar and she saw me coming out of it. I was in a rush, I could have forgotten to lock it. I do forget now and again. Hugh used to tell me off about it, said the insurance would be invalidated.' She bit her lip, getting lipstick on her teeth, then rubbed her eyes.

'I'm not sure how much of this I can take,' she said. 'I don't think Simon can have stolen any data though, or whatever he was planning to do. I keep a close eye on the bank statements and use a password manager for all the online stuff. And Hugh was super careful with the investment accounts and so on.'

'Maybe,' ventured Leonie, 'it was around that time that Simon realised he didn't need to steal Hugh's money because there was another way to get it.'

Thirty-Five

August

In an echo of an evening several weeks previously, Amanda emerged from the steamy bathroom in a cloud of frangipani. That evening — of the roast chicken and the silky, jade-green dress — seemed a lifetime ago. It had been Before, while now was After. Since she was thirteen she had severed her past into Before and After her father's bankruptcy and suicide, and that distinction had governed her life. But it turned out that there were other Before and After dividers which, in retrospect, were also life cleavers, some of similar heft. Buying Whiteacre and the London flat. Beginning an affair with Simon. Hugh's death. Knowing about Simon. Even, now she thought about it, getting a new cleaner.

Amanda pulled on cream capri pants — they didn't fit as snugly as they used to, she must start eating properly again — and a leopard-print top, with elegant sandals revealing her blood-red toenails. She had cooked chicken chasseur. Not very exciting, but she liked the name.

She saw Simon walking across the lawn and went out to meet him on the terrace. She'd put a bottle of Sauvignon Blanc in an ice bucket on the table and poured two glasses. One of Hugh's playlists was providing a rhythmic backdrop — *You Ain't Seen Nothing Yet*, she registered with half an ear. The balmy air was infused with an intoxicating cocktail of her frangipani and the sweet rose scent that wafted from Madame Alfred Carrière. The climber towered above them, a jewel-green cascade frothing with ivory flowers. Perhaps it had benefited from Simon's pruning.

'So,' said Simon, 'you sorted something out? In London?'

Amanda leaned back languorously in her chair and stretched her freshly manicured hands above her head. 'I got us a pass. Sorted some cash flow. But there's still a catch.'

Simon froze and Amanda carried on serenely, 'Only the one-year thing you already know about, but the lawyer reminded me about it. It just means we have to be extra careful. So it's essential that there's no evidence of us. Do you still have our WhatsApps on your phone?'

Simon unclenched his fists and his shoulders loosened. 'Sure. But that's easily dealt with. I'll google how to permanently delete them.'

'Great, we'll do it when we go in.'

'How will we keep in touch then?'

'I think it's best we don't have any recorded contact for the moment. So each time you're here, we make a plan for the next. It's only for another few months.'

*

Simon had taken an old copy of *Winchester Today* from the recycling pile in the garage to light the barbecue. He was crumpling a page when he saw the headline.

Woman miraculously survives fall in front of bus

He unballed the paper and scanned the short article:

Brenda Wilkinson, 39, had a narrow escape from death yesterday in the High Street near Tesco. She tripped on the kerb and fell dramatically into the path of a Park & Ride bus. She was fortunate that the driver, Gus Brown, had the experience and quick reactions to slam on the brakes just in time, preventing what would certainly have been a fatal accident. Ms Wilkinson was shaken and bruised and had a badly sprained ankle but was able to get up and walk (with a limp!) away from the scene.

Please be careful on our streets!

Simon felt a wave of rage wash over him. How could that have happened? He'd seen her in front of the bus. He'd been so sure she would die. He started as Amanda put her hand on his arm.

'What are you reading? Oh yes, I saw that. It was a couple of weeks ago. Lucky woman!'

Simon took a deep breath and clenched his teeth. He was so tempted to tell Amanda that the lucky woman was the fucking blackmailer, was obviously intending to blackmail him and deserved to die. Sense and a cool head prevailed though, as they always did with him; no point opening that can of worms. But now he had to get rid of her, and soon. He'd think of something. She wouldn't see it coming and this time he'd make sure there were no miracles.

He crushed the page, tossed it into the Weber and turned to Amanda with what he hoped was a convincing smile.

'She was very lucky. Could have been a horrible death.'

'You're quite pale,' said Amanda. 'You're too soft, that's your problem!'

Her laugh sounded almost ironic. Just as well she knew nothing about his dark side.

*

Amanda had bought a new iPad when she was in London, a mini version which she could tuck into the zipped pocket in her handbag where she used to keep her secret iPhone. She felt ashamed when she thought about that now. As she did when she thought about much that had happened in the past year or so.

She spent some time every day searching and researching on her new toy and some time every afternoon or evening cooking. She was rediscovering the pleasures of her kitchen.

And so, she hoped, was Simon. They settled into a pattern — an echo of earlier times — where he stayed over on Tuesdays and Thursdays after doing the garden. She told him she'd organised a steady trickle of cash from the probate lawyer so she could pay him again and keep the fridge and wine cellar stocked. He also came over on some Saturday evenings for the night. But she said that anything more was too risky. For both of them. For their future. To her relief he seemed to accept it.

*

Simon was feeling more relaxed than he had since Hugh's accident. He was still having to sneak in and out if he stayed over at Whiteacre, and still only allowed to spend three nights a week there at most, but Amanda seemed to have sorted out a solution to her cash-flow problem. And he was still gardening, both for Amanda and for his other clients, but was at last daring to hope that he could soon give that up. Next April at the latest. And then he would start the next phase of his plan, hopefully ending with confetti and an exotic honeymoon. Where a terrible accident could happen.

Amanda also seemed more relaxed. She'd had her hair cut on her trip to London and was once again always beautifully dressed. And sometimes beautifully undressed. And she'd started to cook for him most evenings when they were together.

'I'll cook next time,' he'd often say, but she would reply, with a light kiss, that she enjoyed looking after him and it was good practice for when they got together. 'Remember,' she said, 'that I haven't cooked much except at weekends for years. I need to get back into the habit.'

Thirty-Six

August

As the summer slanted towards autumn, Amanda took to driving to Brockishill Green where she would walk for miles through the beautiful woodland. Ancient and Ornamental, according to Google. Beech and oak. And fungi.

She carried with her a copy of *The Mitchell Beazley Pocket Guide to Mushrooms and Toadstools*, a handy, slim volume with a dark green cover that she had found second-hand in Skoob Books in Bloomsbury, and a paper bag.

On a Wednesday in early September, Amanda cooked mushroom risotto and liver pâté. And on the following day she cooked mushroom risotto again.

*

Simon stayed over as usual that evening. Amanda was heading off the next day, taking Jennifer to France for a week.

She heard him come down the stairs after his post-gardening shower and poured two glasses of chilled white.

Simon glanced at the bottle. 'Angel, you bought a South African wine!' He smiled and kissed her forehead.

'I liked the label,' said Amanda. It showed a coiled, crouching leopard, gazing severely over its shoulder.

'Tierhoek. It's Afrikaans for animal corner.' He turned the bottle round. '"Elegant and refined with a steely core, this wine is expressive with a tension that adds complexity",' he read out.

'I haven't had time to cook today,' said Amanda. 'I had a long call with the lawyer. All going in the right direction, it seems. Anyway, I had to cook yesterday as I was hosting my book club, so I made extra of everything. But the liver pâté was very popular — there's only one portion left which I kept for you. A big portion though. With risotto and salad after.'

Simon ate the pâté with enthusiasm while Amanda reheated two shallow bowls of risotto one after the other as the microwave wouldn't take them both.

'I'm sorry it's not freshly cooked. Especially as it's our last evening together for ten days.'

Simon waved away her apology. 'No worries. It's all delicious. And the most important thing is that the legal stuff is going well. As you say, only a few more months of this creeping around.'

In the early hours Simon stumbled out of bed and just made it to the bathroom. He had violent vomiting and diarrhoea. Amanda pressed water on him to counter the dehydration and supported him in the shower. She helped him back to bed and kept a flannel on ice to wipe his face.

'Oh my God, it must have been the pâté,' she said, her voice shrill, after checking her phone. 'A couple from the book club had the same yesterday. They each had two helpings. The butcher insisted the liver was fresh but it can't have been. I didn't have any. I'm so sorry.'

Simon grunted. 'I'll have got rid of it by now. From both ends. Stomach still cramped but there can't be anything left. I'll be right as rain in the morning.'

And he did seem much better a few hours later. Weak and tired but able to stand, dress and go downstairs, though he couldn't face any breakfast.

'I could drop you near the van,' said Amanda, a tremble in her voice. 'I'm just worried about being seen. Only a few months now.'

Simon shook his head. 'Not worth the risk, babe. I'll be OK. I'll take it easy and cancel my job today.'

'Maybe you shouldn't wild camp over the weekend. You should stay warm.'

'Stop fussing. I'll be fine. It's just a dose of food poisoning and the Forest is as good a place as any to rest. I'll go back to the van now and drive down later. You're heading off soon aren't you?'

Amanda nodded. 'I packed earlier and the cleaner's coming this afternoon so I don't need to clear up. I'll set off once you've gone.'

But she did after all do a little clearing up after Simon left. She scraped the remnants of pâté and risotto into a twist of foil which already contained the trimmings from the mushrooms and the liver and wrapped the package in a plastic bag together with her new iPad, wiped of all history, and the Mitchell Beazley mushroom book. Later she would stop for a coffee at a service station on a French motorway and poke the crumpled bundle deep into one of the overflowing rubbish bins. And she wrote a note for Leonie.

Sorry I haven't seen much of you recently. I'm off to France with my sister, back on Monday week. Ax

Brenda had been fretting constantly, while being very careful whenever she was out on her own, since Simon had pushed her under the bus. The loop in her head was always the same. First option — keep doing just that, stay alert, watch your back. Second option — the unmentionable. So back to first option.

But maybe she should at least think about whether it would even be possible for her to … to do it. Because if not, she could just stop thinking about it. So she went over and over it as she ferried the kids to school and back, as she drove between her jobs, cleaned the vast houses, shopped and cooked and cared.

Simon was tall and no doubt strong from his manual work while she was shorter and weaker. But she kept herself fit. All that running up and down stairs and heaving hoovers and buckets of water around. She'd still have to catch him alone though. And surprise him.

She ran through the awful scenes she'd imagined when she was thinking how he could kill her.

Hit and run? Too risky. Simon could probably pull it off with his big van. But her car was small and anyway Brenda knew she'd instinctively swerve at the last minute, or miss, or injure rather than kill.

Mugging — no chance. Even if she could bring herself to try and stab him he'd almost certainly be able to duck, or grab her arm. And then what? Even worse than chickening out of the hit and run. He'd surely seize her knife and turn it on her.

Arson? But didn't he live in a camper van? When he wasn't at Whiteacre, but she could hardly risk burning down the house with Amanda in it as well.

Back to option one. But gradually the images of her

stabbing Simon and of Simon in his van merged. What if she caught him in the van? Somewhere with no one around? Knocked at the door and lunged as soon as it opened, when he wasn't expecting it?

She'd have to do some research — where to stick the knife, what angle and all that technical stuff that came up in crime series on the telly. But she'd been good at biology at school, and surely it just came down to that? She could google anatomy. In fact she could use her burner SIM card, she still had it somewhere, hook it up to the WiFi in a café or just rely on the 4G, then get rid of it.

And she'd need to follow Simon like he'd followed her, find a time when he was alone in his van without people around. Hadn't Leonie-Jane said he sometimes wild camped in the New Forest? She could use her blackmail money to buy a tracking device to stick under his van — Amanda would surely approve.

She'd need a good knife. She only had a bread knife and her old carver, both too long, and a smaller one she used for chopping and peeling, but that was too short and, to be honest, on the blunt side. What she wanted was something with a really sharp blade. Ideally something she could 'borrow' and then replace after a thorough clean, so it could never be traced to her. So it had to be a knife that wouldn't be missed. Oh ... She bit her lip as something snagged at her memory. A cut, a jumbled drawer ...

Except ultimately she didn't think she could do it. Back to option one again. Or pray for a miracle.

*

Ten days after Amanda had left her a note saying she was going to France, Leonie arrived at Whiteacre, rang the doorbell and waited for a few minutes. Amanda must still be away. Leonie let herself in, picking up the copy of *Winchester Today* which was lying on the mat with a couple of letters. She hung up her coat and bag and headed for the utility room to collect the cleaning kit. On her way through the breakfast room she folded the paper and put it on the table. And saw a photo of Simon on the front page with the headline *Local man dies of mushroom poisoning.*

Leonie sat down, hard. She read on, racing through the dense, smudgy print:

Simon Long (50) was found dead in his camper van at Lord's Oak car park in the New Forest early last week. He was discovered by a volunteer ranger who noticed that the van had been there for several days. The post mortem examination revealed that he had consumed Amanita virosa, commonly known as Destroying Angel.

The highly toxic fungus can be found in many sites in the New Forest. The Destroying Angel is closely related to the Death Cap (Amanita phalloides), which also grows in the New Forest. Both are similar in appearance and habitat to the edible Wood Mushroom (Agaricus silvicola) and over the years a number of foragers have died as a result of mistaken identification.

Long lived in his van which was usually parked at Worthy Lane car park in Winchester. It is thought that he was wild camping in the remote car park in the Nomansland area, where mobile phone signals are weak or non-existent, when he was taken ill. Jim Sullivan, who often overnights in Worthy Lane in his motorhome, told us that Long used to boast about how much of his food he poached or foraged and how he would sometimes wild camp in the Forest and cook over a fire. He was also open about being a frequent user of cannabis, and police sources say that a quantity was found in his van together with a shot gun and hunting rifle, several fishing rods and nets and a (contd on p. 5) selection of knives.

While Long no doubt saw his food sourcing as an economy, his death is a stark warning of the danger of eating wild mushrooms. There is no antidote to Amanita poisoning and as little as half a mushroom cap can be fatal. The early symptoms are similar to those of food poisoning — vomiting, diarrhoea, abdominal pain and cramps — and usually disappear after a few hours, leading the victim to assume that he is over the worst. But the symptoms recur a day or two later by which time it will probably be too late. The victim will likely suffer liver and kidney failure and enter a hepatic coma, ending in death. Only two years ago, Public Health England reported 84 cases of mushroom poisoning just one month into the autumn foraging season. Readers should heed this warning, and should also note that foraging for fungi, lighting fires outside designated barbecue zones and wild camping are all prohibited in the New Forest.

Leonie read the article again. She pulled her phone from her pocket, intending to text Amanda, then suddenly thought of Brenda. She could stop watching her back now, worrying about her children. Leonie stabbed out a quick message:

Wtf, S was murdered last week, poisoned by deadly mushroom. Lx

She was about to compose one for Amanda when a key scraped in the front door followed by the sounds of footsteps and wheels dragging on the parquet. Leonie turned round. Amanda parked a small suitcase at the foot of the stairs, shrugged off her coat and tossed it over the newel post. It was the sensuous ivory shearling, and the sight of it reminded Leonie of learning of another death after arriving at Whiteacre. She flipped the newspaper over and stood up.

'Amanda,' she said, 'Have you heard about Simon?'

'Hi there. No, I haven't heard. I've just got back. What about him?'

'Er — it's in the paper. It says he died last week. Some poisonous mushroom.'

Amanda came into the breakfast room, picked up the paper and stared at the front page. She sat down.

'He brought me wild mushrooms a few times,' she said. 'I was anxious the first time, didn't want to cook them. He told me not to worry, he was an expert, knew how to identify the edible ones.'

'Looks like he didn't,' said Leonie. Her phone chimed.

Omg. Does Mrs S know? Bx

Amanda stood up and moved towards the kitchen end of the room. 'Coffee?' she asked. 'Or something stronger? To be honest — this sounds awful — I feel like champagne. But I think that would be inappropriate. As in it wouldn't be chilled.'

'It sounds like a horrible way to die,' ventured Leonie.

Amanda tucked a stray wisp of hair behind her ear. She'd picked up some colour and looked younger and fresher than when Leonie had last seen her. Must have had a relaxing holiday. 'I suspect falling off a roof isn't much fun either,' she said.

Acknowledgements

*T*he *Grass Widow* and her predecessor *Some Like It Cold* are, like most books, the product of a village rather than a parent. Countless friends and relatives nobly read and commented on countless drafts. Those closest to me endured the roughest ride, having had excruciating-in-hindsight early versions thrust upon them, followed by a raft of revisions. The kindness of non-strangers kept me going through three years of writing *Some Like It Cold* and the additional year of remaking it as *The Grass Widow*.

Thanks first to my late mother Felicity and my son Fred, who gave me unwavering support, encouragement and belief in myself from the start (and in the case of my mother, and indeed my late father, from the real start).

And thanks also to (in alphabetical order to avoid the impossible and invidious task of evaluating and ranking the contributions of so many — the superheroes / heroines know who you are!): Alev, Alison, Andrew A, Andrew T, Barbara,

Caroline, Conrad, Courtenay, Di, Helen, Jeanne, Joan, Judy, Lisa, Loueen, Lucy B, Lucy C, Lynn, Maura, Mike G, Paul, Penny, Phillip, Rhonda, Richard, Sal, Sam, Shelagh, Suzanne.

Finally, a nod to the wonderful Saki (H H Munro), whose words 'The cook was a good cook, as cooks go; and as cooks go, she went' inspired what is now the third sentence of the first chapter. (The quote is from *Reginald on Besetting Sins.*)

About the Author

Vanessa Edwards is a lawyer turned writer who lives in London.

vanessaedwardswriter.com
Facebook and Twitter: Vanessa Edwards, Writer

Milton Keynes UK
Ingram Content Group UK Ltd.
UKHW022238010823
426157UK00014B/116